Bad Boy

Episode I

The Legendary Adventures of Avery "Ace" Craig
An '80s American Teen Epic

Bodaciously True & Totally Awesome

EPISODE I: BAD BOY

An Episodic Novel by

Chris Orcutt

Have Pen Will Travel · New York

Bodaciously True & Totally Awesome
Episode I: Bad Boy
by Chris Orcutt

The author thanks and acknowledges the following patrons whose heroically generous financial support and encouragement made possible the promotion and publication of this 9-book episodic novel: Jeff Atwood, Maia Heymann, Joseph Kubancik, Alexas Orcutt, Alfred and Susan Orcutt, and Jason Scott Sadofsky.

First edition published in 2026 by Chris Orcutt, Have Pen Will Travel, Pleasant Valley, New York. Cover and book jacket design by Victoria Heath Silk.

ISBN 978-1-965999-00-4 (Hardcover - Ingram)
ISBN 978-1-965999-01-1 (Trade Paperback - Ingram)
ISBN 978-1-965999-02-8 (eBook - Amazon Kindle)
ISBN 978-1-965999-36-3 (Trade Paperback - Amazon KDP)

FICTION. Coming of Age; Romance (Historical – 20th Century; New Adult); Literary; Cultural Heritage; Music; Action & Adventure.

Library of Congress Control Number: 2024923966

Printed in the United States of America.

10 9 8 7 6 5 4 3 2 1

For Alexas, the divine Muse who made it all possible.

ace
adjective
The best; awesome; terrific.

—In the 80s – Glossary of Eighties Terms

bodacious |bōdāSHus|
adjective N. Amer. informal
excellent, admirable, or attractive: *the restaurant serves
bodacious grilled lobster.*

• U.S. audacious in a way considered admirable: *those
bodacious dudes have an excellent time playing games
with death.*
ORIGIN mid-19th cent. (in sense **'complete, thorough'**):
perhaps a variant of southwestern English dialect *bolda-
cious*, blend of **bold** and **audacious**.

—New Oxford American Dictionary, electronic resource

Contents

Foreword

Exactly one decade ago, when novelist Chris Orcutt asked to interview me for a novel he was writing about Avery "Ace" Craig, I was beyond stoked. As Ace's classmate at Harrison Hancock High School in West Troutkill, NY, I can personally attest to Ace's charm, charisma, and the epic scale of his adventures.

Today I'm a professor of American Studies specializing in cultural history, and an occasional commentator on documentaries and TV programs about the 1980s. Neither Ace nor I could have imagined I'd one day have a Ph.D. (I routinely relied on his summaries of stories for English class), but as an academic now, an academic who knew Ace in his teen years, I'm uniquely qualified to provide cultural, historical, and literary context for this epic-length narrative.

A contemporary online search for Avery "Ace" Craig returns a paltry list of results—the most prominent being mention of this novel series: *Bodaciously True and Totally Awesome: The Legendary Adventures of Avery "Ace" Craig; An '80s American Teen Epic.* Indeed, were it not for newspaper, magazine, TV archives, and recently declassified CIA files for this period (1986–87), the feats of Avery "Ace" Craig would surely be lost to history.

Using those materials and supplementing his research with extensive interviews of many of the principals, Orcutt has written not only a comprehensive 9-episode novel about Ace, but for the first time he's given our routinely disregarded generation a bold and authoritative voice, and he's painted a clear, intimate portrait of suburban teen life in the 1980s.

An Epic Year

In 1986–87, the United States was, without question, the most powerful and influential nation on Earth—politically, economically, technologically, and culturally. Our nemesis, the U.S.S.R. (Union of Soviet Socialist Republics, or Soviet Union), was crumbling, and the icy relations between our countries had begun to thaw.

Ronald Reagan, our President at the time, was a former B-movie actor, and was tall and a commanding speaker. Democrat or Republican, no one could deny that Reagan had restored our national pride, giving '80s teenagers hope about the country's future. In 1986, Madonna and Whitney Houston were pop music's undisputed queen and princess royal. It was the year of several landmark '80s movies—*Pretty in Pink* and *Platoon*, *9½ Weeks* and *Hoosiers*—and three movies that, for many American teens, became instant classics: *Aliens*, *Top Gun*, and *Ferris Bueller's Day Off*.

Also in 1986, after speeding through our solar system for nearly a decade, the Voyager probe reached Uranus and sent back its first images. A few days later, the event was overshadowed by the horrifying explosion of the Space Shuttle Challenger. Most significantly, the return of Halley's Comet early that winter—a celestial event that happens only once every 76 years—lent an auspicious aspect to the year ahead; its return seemed to herald a year of many other exciting and rare occurrences. If you were a teen in January 1986, somehow you sensed that, for better or worse, it was going to be a year to remember.

A Mega-Hunkalicious Studmuffin

It's fitting that, throughout this series, Orcutt alludes several times to *The Odyssey*. Like Homer's epic hero Odysseus, Ace had some incredible adventures, and many of his problems involved women; apparently, he dated a *lot* of them that year. This is understandable when you consider what a mega-hunkalicious studmuffin Ace was in 1986.[*] Unlike many authors, Orcutt doesn't make readers suffer through clumsy, self-indulgent scenes in which the hero uses his idle

---

[*] While considered a new word for 1986, "studmuffin" (the vegetarian equivalent of "beefcake," used to describe a hunky young man) had actually been in use by teenage girls for a couple of years.

moments to study himself in every reflective surface imaginable: bathroom mirrors, limpid pools like Narcissus, or panes on passing glass company trucks. Since Orcutt doesn't describe Ace's looks in much detail, I am delighted to do so.

Before early 1986, girls seldom gave Ace a second glance. With the return of Halley's Comet, however, something happened; it was as though the gods had transformed him overnight from an average teenage boy into a hunky young man. Indeed, Avery Craig had become the swoon-worthy dreamboat that female rocker Joan Jett croons about in her song "Fantasy." He had sprouted up to 6'0" and added head-turning muscle to his athletic frame. His hair, wavy and boyishly tousled, was the color of rain-dappled straw drying in the sun; his eyes were multifaceted emeralds; his eyelashes were enviably long and lush; his nose was ruler-straight; his cheekbones were pronounced and preternaturally high; and his jawline? That bad boy was sharp enough to slice bread.

Ace was also a remarkable athlete. Having been an All-Star Little League Baseball player and a Pop Warner Football quarterback, Avery had a preposterously strong throwing arm. He held high school records in tennis, swimming, and track, and had won several endurance cross-country skiing races. He was a Life-rank Boy Scout, and he was a freakishly talented dancer—a talent nurtured by his mother, a former Radio City Rockette.

And as if all that weren't enough, Ace was a genius—although if you called him one, he would dispute it. His favorite subject in school was English, and on the Verbal section of the PSAT he scored a remarkable 780 (out of 800). Sundry stories about Ace were flying around back then. According to one story, because of his astoundingly high IQ score, the CIA recruited him while he was still in high school, and he even performed some covert missions for them.

There was another story that Ace hung out with an assortment of celebrities including Senator Ted Kennedy, Eddie Van Halen, Johnny Carson, Robert Palmer, Hugh Hefner, Whitney Houston, and Michael Jackson, as well as a mélange of movie stars. At the time, his peers dismissed the stories as rumors, but when I asked Orcutt about these stories, he said that 90 percent of them were true.

Ace's adventures of that year are all the more noteworthy when you consider his ordinary middle-class background. At the time that this novel begins, he was living in a split-level ranch in a plain vanilla suburban development in Upstate New York, in a community where the parents of every other family worked for one of two employers: Big Blue (a.k.a., IBM) or the state prison.

By February 1986, when *Bodaciously* opens, it was clear that, like Mount St. Helens, which had exploded just six years earlier, Avery Craig was about to erupt.

Introducing the Teen Epic

Before you dive into Mr. Orcutt's ennead of novels, allow me to proffer a few observations about *Bodaciously True & Totally Awesome.*[†] Like other groundbreaking novels, *Bodaciously* transcends existing labels. It's a coming-of-age story, a love story, an adventure story, and an odyssey; it's what you'd get if you put *Fast Times at Ridgemont High*, *The Odyssey*, and *War and Peace* into a supercollider; it's an epic-length tale about an age group that has seldom been taken seriously in literature—teenagers—and it's written for the routinely disregarded generation of adults who lived it. To my knowledge, Orcutt's *teen epic* is the first of its kind, the naissance of a new genre in American literature. While there have been scads of novels about teens and teen angst, some of them considered classics, most have a rather limited scope, and, in my opinion, not one of them dramatizes the world of teens as comprehensively as Orcutt does in this series.

It is clear that Orcutt thoroughly researched not only 1986–87, but the entire 1980s. His lavish references to '80s pop culture (movies, TV shows, commercials, current events, and music) orient the reader in the cultural landscape and *zeitgeist*. This is especially true of the music and music videos of this period. For example, the importance of the original portable music player, the Sony Walkman, cannot be overstated. To young people of the 2020s and beyond, the Walkman might seem quaint, even primitive, but for '80s teens, it

---

[†] As you read the nine books, you will see that, rather than a series of standalone novels, *Bodaciously* is actually one gigantic novel split into 9 episodes. For this and other reasons, I consider Orcutt the American Tolstoy.

was a revelation: it was the first device that allowed them to listen to whatever music they wanted, wherever they wanted.

Another cultural cornerstone of the '80s teen experience was MTV (Music Television). Repeated viewing of music videos prompted the purchase of albums and the creation of "mixtapes"—collections of favorite songs with common themes. Teens penned messages on cassette case liners (artistic, heartfelt arguments for each song's inclusion on a tape), drew cover art for their homemade recordings, and traded them with their friends and sweethearts. Because music and music videos were so important to teens in the 1980s, each episode of the novel has places where Orcutt mentions a song title (e.g., ♫"Material Girl"♫). The reader should view the ensuing scene as a mini music video for the mentioned song. From time to time, the story slips into present tense and scenes are shown as if the characters were in a music video. Having basked in MTV on a daily basis as a teen, when I read these scenes, I imagined them in the style of '80s music videos, where the visuals and music are tightly syncopated with '80s video effects like split-screens, fades, wipes, stop-motion animation, and soft-focus. At the back of each episode of *Bodaciously*, the author provides a "mixtape list" for that episode.

I believe *Bodaciously* is the *avant-garde* of a new form of literature—an "immersive literary experience"—that uses technological innovations to expand and enrich the reading experience. Within a few years, multiple reading devices (including virtual reality headsets, internet glasses, and contact lenses) will enable readers to read anything (including old, printed books) and turn them into hypertextual, interactive experiences, giving readers instant access to places, TV shows, movies, and songs mentioned in the text. I predict that, in time, other novels will follow *Bodaciously* in this approach.

Let's Talk About Sex

Naturally, because it's about a 1980s American teenager and his cohort of friends, *Bodaciously* contains a great deal of sex—some episodes more than others. While some of the scenes are highly erotic, they are never gratuitous or excessively graphic, and instead serve to advance the plot or reveal the characters. These scenes range from a male teen's observations about women's bodies, to flirting with the opposite sex, to kissing, to … well, *all* the bases get reached. Having read many novels about teens' coming of age, I find Orcutt's inclusion of sex scenes in *Bodaciously* to be refreshingly honest and authentic. Myriad novels about teens gloss over "the sex stuff," which, to this scholar, makes those novels fundamentally false. Sexual awakening and experience is undeniably a major part of a teen's development; yet up to now it has seldom been dramatized with such honesty.

Finally, Orcutt's 9-episode novel contains some foul language and crude humor, but since its central characters are teenagers, a certain amount of this is to be expected. There are scenes of violence, drug and alcohol use, peer pressure, bullying, car joyrides, theft, vandalism, and other illegal acts. Regarding other "triggers" (a term that didn't exist in the fend-for-yourself, "go play in traffic"‡ 1980s), *Bodaciously* contains mention of alcoholism, domestic violence, divorce, addiction, unemployment, financial hardship, racism, homophobia, AIDS, STDs, academic pressure, anxiety, moving to new communities and schools—in short, most everything that shaped a suburban American teen's experience in the 1980s.

Stop Calling Us "Generation X"

The generation born between 1964 and 1980 (my generation) was shoddily labeled first by a cultural and literary historian named Paul Fussell in his 1983 book *Class*. Then, in 1991, Canadian author Douglas Coupland published a novel titled *Generation X: Tales of an Accelerated Culture*. Despite some critics calling the novel meandering and pretentious, its title stuck to my generation. The label is terrible because it makes it seem like we're a "Planet X"—an unknown heavenly body too far from Earth to be seen. Well, World, we're right here, and

---

‡ "Go play in traffic" was something the parents of our generation would say when they didn't want us pesky *kids* around. Parents from the "Silent" and "Baby Boomer" generations were generally so thoughtless about their parenting responsibilities that they had to be reminded that they even *had* children who might be getting into trouble. In the '80s, every evening on TV sets across the U.S., a public service message would play: "IT'S TEN P.M. DO YOU KNOW WHERE YOUR CHILDREN ARE?"

have been since 1964. To remedy this insult to my generation, I hereby proffer the following alternatives: "The Trickle-Down Generation,"[§] "The Free-Range and Feral Generation," and (in the vein of "The Greatest Generation"), "The Totally Awesome Generation."

With *Bodaciously*, Orcutt has written over a million words exploring that magical time, possibly the greatest time ever to be a teenager in America: the 1980s. If you were a teenager (or young) in the '80s, this 9-episode novel will be a time machine, taking you back to your youth. If you were a parent in the '80s, this series will give you insight into what your kids might have been doing back then. And if you're the child of parents who grew up in the '80s, this 9-episode novel will help you understand why your parents might be overbearing. They're probably overcompensating for a lack of parenting they received.

To my fellow members of The Trickle-Down Generation, The Free-Range Generation, or The Totally Awesome Generation: ultimately, this epic series is for *us*. Settle in for an exciting and enjoyable trip back to the time when we ruled the world. I loved *Bodaciously* in manuscript format, and I'm now looking forward to reading each episode in book form when it's published. While I'm proud to have written this foreword for novelist Chris Orcutt, I'm most proud to have been friends with this most extraordinary of teens, Avery "Ace" Craig.

Summer Jensen, Ph.D.
Widworth, Mass.
June 5, 2025

[§] We are the "Trickle-Down Generation" because we were largely unparented (we were the first generation of "latchkey kids"—those without a parent home after school) and had to rely on our peers for guidance and support. Economically, we received the "trickle-down" dribs and drabs; we're the first generation in American history to be, on average, less successful than our parents. Finally, our generation, tiny compared to the two that bracket it (the Baby Boomers and the Millennials), has largely been ignored.

Episode I

Bad Boy

1

∿

O Divine Poesy, goddess, daughter of Zeus, sustain for me this tale of a brilliant and bodacious teen, a teen lavishly gifted by the gods, a teen who, having advanced to the hallowed halls of Hancock High, was shedding the clearheaded chrysalis of boyhood and taking flight as a young man. Tasting the sweetness of girls' love and carnal affections, navigating the stormy seas of emotion, exploring the uncharted territories of the female form and romance, the sport of his customs, good and bad, while his heart, through all the wayfaring, ached with an agony to return to his boyhood world. Vain hope for him—the fool! His own hormones cast him aside. To spurn the gifts of mighty Aphrodite, wherefore the Love goddess blotted out the course for his return. Make this tale live for us in all its many bearings, O Muse.

FADE IN. A blizzard rages, shrouding the landscape in a gray haze. Trees, fences and buildings appear as vague, shadowy shapes through the wind-driven snow. Wind howls, tree limbs clack, and an unseen piece of metal clangs. Far in the distance, a lone silhouette approaches and Van Halen's ♫"Eruption"♫ begins to play, the otherworldly guitar solo rising in volume and drowning out the storm. The shape draws closer: it's a strapping teenage guy on cross-country skis, towing a plastic sled. Amber-tinted ski goggles, a parka hood, and a scarf cover his face. Eventually the music fades out and the blizzard's fearsome noises return, but the young man skis on through the storm undaunted.

It's February 1986, and as we zoom in on our hero, he's exulting in the bitter cold and the malevolent wind piercing his layers of winter clothing. He envisions himself fulfilling a boyhood dream—exploring Antarctica or the Yukon—when in actuality he's in the woods of South Wellington, only a mile from his grandparents' house. Although a voice inside him whispers that what he's doing is dangerous, that he could die if he's not careful, Avery "Ace" Craig forges ahead. His young friends, Harold Crawford and Jimmy Flynn, are in trouble.

Nearly an Eagle Scout, Avery has ample training and experience in cold-weather camping, first aid, outdoor survival, and orienteering, and for the past three Christmas breaks he's attended an elite cross-country skiing academy in Lake Placid, where he's won several endurance races. A *MacGyver*, James Bond, and *A-Team* aficionado, Avery Craig is better prepared, trained, and equipped to do this than anyone else in the area. He has dubbed this rescue mission "Operation Barnstorm."

Head down against the driving snow, synchronizing his poling with his strides on the skis, Avery is blissfully unaware that the recent return of Halley's Comet is about to upend his life. A fortnight from now, half a dozen teenage girls and young women—for the first time noticing his intelligence and wit; his charisma and self-confidence; his muscular build; his blonde hair, green eyes, and teen heartthrob jawline—will besiege unsuspecting Avery. Indeed, over the next eighteen months, Avery's life will become unduly stressful, even perilous, because of *girls*.

For the moment, Avery still has the clear head of boyhood, with only three simple things on his mind: rescuing Harold and Jimmy before dark, eating some of his grandmother's homemade donuts, and dreaming of making out with his fantasy girl—stacked stoner classmate Dina Tempestilli.

Avery could imagine Dina in Princess Leia's puffy white snowsuit in *The Empire Strikes Back*. Especially if she braided her hair like Leia's, wore a tight white sweater, and kept her vest unzipped, showcasing her *fantabulous* boobs.

Damn, Ace … would that be awesome or what!?

Echo-Three to Echo-Seven

Avery had been skiing for over an hour. He'd been with Harold and Jimmy when the snowmobile ran out of gas. After they'd taken shelter in the abandoned barn at the foot of Thicket Hill, Avery skied back to Jimmy's for a jerry jug of fuel, then stopped at Pa and Gram's to pick up some food and his backpack of survival gear in case they got stranded overnight. Now he was on his way back to the barn, following the fence line outside the Crawfords' top pasture. Although he'd skied only about three miles today, the near-whiteout conditions and the deep snow made those three miles feel like ten.

Despite his exhaustion, Avery reveled in the adventure of this. He imagined himself as one of the great Polar explorers he'd read about— Amundsen, Peary, Shackleton. The last storm Avery had experienced that was this fierce was the Blizzard of '78. It had snowed for four days straight, and when the skies finally cleared, six feet of snow covered the ground, and the snowdrifts reached the roofs of houses. Today's storm was forecast to end by morning with only two feet of snow.

In an hour, when he made it safely back to his grandparents', there would be a roaring fire in the fireplace, his favorite dinner of baked ham and scalloped potatoes, and his family gathered with birthday gifts for Avery and his grandfather. In the meantime, Avery was enjoying playing Arctic Explorer. Breathing deeply of the sharp and piquant air, relishing the icy sting of the gusting snow against his cheeks, savoring the hiss of the wind through a nearby pine tree, he wanted to remember this moment forever.

The only thing that would make it better was if his Roman goddess Dina were here, and they were snug inside a tent and sleeping bag, holding each other nude while the blizzard raged outside. God, he wanted her. He wanted to smother her with kisses, inhale the pot and perfume aroma in her hair, crush her sculpted breasts against his pecs. This year, he would somehow muster the courage to ask her out.

Avery glanced at his digital Casio, set to military time: 15:07. He had to get to Jimmy and Harold; it would be dark soon. When he reached the end of the fence line, the walkie-talkie in his musette bag squawked. The signal was faint in the storm, but Avery could tell it was Harold calling him.

"Echo-three to echo-seven. Ace, old buddy, do you read me?"

Ah, the opening dialogue from *Empire*. Avery pulled out the walkie-talkie and extended the antenna.

"Loud and clear, kid," he said. "What's up?"

Harold wanted to know how much longer Ace would be. Shortly after Ace had left, the Drew boys showed up with their giant older cousin Bart. Harold and Jimmy had to lock themselves in the barn against a brutal snowball bombardment.

"We opened the door for a second," Harold said, "and they unloaded like a hundred ice balls on us!"

"I'm in the woods above your place, about to cross the road." Avery shuffled ahead on the skis as he talked. "I should be there in ten. I'll be coming in from behind, through that hole in the back of the barn."

"Roger," Harold said.

"Okay, I'm shutting off the walkie-talkie now, so you guys don't blow my cover."

"Good luck, Ace."

"Over and out."

Avery switched off the walkie-talkie and put it away. He steadied himself with the poles and herringbone-stepped up the steep embankment. At the top, he crossed the road and plunged into the woods again.

When a Plan Comes Together

Avery climbed a ridge that rose steadily through the woods. When he reached the peak, he leaned against a big oak, took the binoculars out of his bag, and trained them at the barn.

In the distance through the shroud of snow, the barn was purplish gray. Carrying faintly in the wind were the taunts of Bart and the Drew boys, and the muffled thumps of snowballs. Three small figures darted around while one giant figure stood eerily still.

Bart Drew. A few years ago, Bart had been visiting his pissant cousins, and Avery had gotten in a fight with him. The guy had turned into a raging bull, and the only way Avery could subdue him was with a chunk of firewood. Reputedly, he was a farm kid and had been husky since he could crawl. He was now 18 years old, and a menacing 6'3", which made him three inches taller than Avery.

However, Avery wasn't the same guy he was three years ago. His build had improved dramatically from daily weight training, and he was a lot smarter. Avery would now likely win in a fight against Bart, but why fight if he didn't have to? As Colonel John "Hannibal" Smith once said on *The A-Team*, "Never attempt a frontal assault when a covert insertion is the smarter, less risky option." Avery put away the binoculars and skied along the ridge until it connected with a hillside that sloped down behind the barn. Fallen limbs and stumps stuck out of the snow. He wove around the obstacles to the bottom of the hill.

When he emerged from the underbrush, he went to the hole in the barn, released his ski boots from the bindings and crawled inside, pulling in the sled and his skis after him. There was a gaping hole in the roof, which lit up the inside but allowed the snow to fall in. Harold and Jimmy, wearing snowmobile suits, hustled over. They were about to shout when Avery put a finger to his lips. He removed his hood and goggles. The two boys were shivering.

"You made it," Harold said. "Ace, w-we're starving. Did you bring anything?"

"Y-y-yeah." Jimmy grinned and quoted the old woman in the Wendy's commercial: "'Where's the beef?!'"[1]

"Where's the beef?" Avery pulled out a Thermos of hot cocoa and a bag of his grandmother's homemade donuts. "Here's the beef!"

The boys gasped. After Avery poured cups of hot chocolate and handed out the donuts, he filled the snowmobile gas tank from the jerry jug and quietly re-latched the hood. Then he did what TV's MacGyver always did: he made an inventory of what he had to work with and formed a plan. Avery would go out first to create a diversion—to get Bart and the Drew boys away from the barn doors—and then Jimmy and Harold could blast out on the snowmobile. It would work. It *had* to work.

---

[1] "Where's the beef?" was an advertising slogan for the fast-food chain Wendy's Hamburgers. The TV ads with curmudgeonly actress Clara Weller debuted in 1984. After that, "Where's the beef?" became a mainstream catchphrase used to question the substance of a product or idea.

The barn doors rattled. There was a flurry of thumps against the slats, and Bart shouted, "Are you pussies coming out or what?! We're not leaving until you do!"

Avery ate a donut and took a sip of hot chocolate. He waved Jimmy and Harold over and drew on the snowy ground with a ski pole.

"All right, guys," he said, "here's the barn and this is them." He made four X's. "First, we'll turn the snowmobile around so it's facing the doors. Then, I'll go out back and create a diversion."

"Diversion?!" Jimmy said. "Screw that. Let's just bust out of here!"

Avery glared at him. "Haven't you watched *The A-Team*? *MacGyver*? This is how it's done." He punctuated his reprimand with a crisp nod. "Trust me."

"Sorry, Ace." Jimmy shrugged. "Go ahead."

Avery wolfed another donut and continued. He drew two parallel lines to represent the road and said he would lead Bart and the others there, away from the barn. In the meantime, Jimmy and Harold would hitch the sled to the snowmobile and wait for Avery's signal. When he shouted, they would blast out of the barn and wait for Avery at the road. Avery would jump in the sled, and they would haul ass to Harold's house.

"All right, guys ... we have to go," Avery said. "It's getting dark. Questions?"

"Yeah, I've got one," Jimmy said. "Any more donuts?"

Avery stuffed the last one into his mouth. "Nope. *Wezgoh*."

They turned the snowmobile around and hitched the sled onto the back. Avery grabbed his skis and poles, put up his parka hood, and lowered his goggles. He went to the hole in the back wall.

"Remember ... wait for my signal."

He ducked outside, snapped his boots into the ski bindings, and skied along the backside of the barn. He stopped at the corner to press play on his Walkman. The tense opening of ♫"Bond 77"♫ came over his headphones.

Avery skied along a stand of birches, following the brush line up the hill to open pasture. He was now above and to the side of the barn. Bart and the Drew boys were yanking on the doors in front. The wind and snowfall had slowed, so Avery was able to see them more clearly than when he first got here.

He figured he was about 200 feet away from Bart—like shallow center field to home plate. In Little League, Avery had been an All-Star relief pitcher and an outfielder who always threw straight to the plate, never to the cutoff man. Screw the cutoff man. Avery took his throwing hand out of the pole strap, removed the mitten, and made a snowball—baseball-sized and dense. He only made one, but with *his* arm, one was all he'd need.

He let the snowball melt in his bare hand for a moment. Because Avery would be throwing with the skis on, he couldn't follow-through with his back leg; this throw would have to be all arm. He dug in the skis to brace himself and watched Bart. The second Bart sneered, Avery hurled the snowball.

As the snowball hurtled stealthily through the driving snow, disappearing into the hoary haze perfectly on target, time seemed to stop. The song also stopped—a one-second rest that seemed an eternity—and Avery lost sight of the projectile. The instant the song kicked back in, the snowball rematerialized and exploded against Bart's face. Even from this distance, Avery could see the massive red welt. Visibly stunned, Bart stumbled backwards, trying to wipe the snow away.

"Sweet," Avery muttered. Blasting in Avery's headphones, "Bond 77" went into its scorching, horn-fueled finish, and Avery did a gloating little dance in the skis. He reflected on his throw for a moment. It wasn't a legendary one like "The Egg," but it was pretty friggin' awesome.[2] He put his mitten and pole strap back on.

Bart glowered at Avery, made a half-assed snowball and flung it; Avery leaned faintly to one side as it whizzed by, and his nonchalance only enraged Bart further. The giant gave chase, post-holing through the deep snow. Avery glided across the hillside and glanced over his shoulder. His diversion had worked: Bart and the Drew boys were 100 feet from the barn. "Go, guys, go!" he shouted.

---

[2] The legend of "The Egg" will be recounted in riveting detail in *Episode II: True Blue.*

Beneath the blustering wind were the faint sounds of a sputtering engine. Bart stopped and doubled back toward the barn.

"Hurry up!" Avery shouted. "Bart's coming back!"

The engine coughed and sputtered again, and then it whined to life. The barn doors flew open and slapped against the slats, and not a second later, droning above the howling wind, the snowmobile streaked out of the doorway with Jimmy and Harold tucked behind the windshield and the plastic sled trailing behind. Bart rushed to cut them off, but the snowmobile zoomed past him. Bart threw a snowball at them, but Jimmy ducked and blew past him, cackling like Woody the Woodpecker and flashing Bart a toothy grin.

While the snowmobile raced across the field, Avery hurled a snowball at the oldest Drew kid, Andy (he loathed the sniveling weasel), smacking him in the neck. Andy squealed and flailed like he was on fire. Avery skied down the hill, toward the road, where Jimmy and Harold were waiting. When he got there, he pressed the quick-release buttons on the bindings, put the skis and poles in the sled, and lay down. Bart and the Drew boys stumbled out of the field.

"Jimmy," Avery shouted, "hit it!"

Jimmy floored the engine, but before they could get away, Bart dove and grabbed a rope trailing from the snowmobile hitch, and hauled himself up, hand over hand. Despite being dragged on his stomach, Bart reached the sled and curled his fingers over the lip. Given the similarity of Bart's feat to Indiana Jones' in *Raiders*, Avery couldn't help feeling a twinge of admiration for Bart, but ... that didn't stop him from stomping on the bully's hand.[3] Bart yelped and skidded into a snowbank, he and the Drew boys shrank into the distance, and the gray shroud consumed them.

Avery whistled the iconic seven-note refrain from ♫"Theme from *The A-Team*."♫ He shouted to Harold and Jimmy, quoting Hannibal's famous catchphrase: "'I love it when a plan comes together!'" The boys grinned back at him, but Avery felt hollow inside. Somehow, he knew that this had been his last boyhood adventure, and that his

---

[3] In the movie *Raiders of the Lost Ark*, while recovering the Ark of the Covenant from the Nazis, archaeologist Indiana Jones is dragged behind a truck, but pulls himself back aboard the truck with his trusty bullwhip.

life was about to change. He wasn't sure how it would change, and whether it would be better or worse; all he knew was that it would be very different.

Help Me, Avery Craig

Once Avery and Jimmy dropped off Harold, they took the snowmobile back to Jimmy's house, and then Avery started skiing home. Instead of taking the direct route, he decided to cut through the woods. He passed his grandparents' driveway and continued toward their old driveway, the one they used to share with the Bransons. Mr. Branson had moved his family to a new house on their farm a few miles away, and the driveway, which crossed an old bridge to reach his grandparents', was now grown-over and impassable—especially on skis. Avery planned to ford the brook upstream and ski through the woods. He imagined himself reaching the woods' edge above Pa and Gram's, every part of him chilled to the bone, and seeing the warm lights streaming out the back windows and smelling the reassuring woodsmoke against the prickly, sour cold of the snow.

Everything was so dark, he worried that he'd miss the old driveway, so he took hold of the barbed-wire fence. He skied alongside it to the corner, then turned and followed the fence line to the pasture gate. He was now in the Bransons' front yard. The windows and doors were boarded-up, the shutters were crooked, and the roof sagged. In the darkness of the blizzard, the place looked haunted.

Avery skied past the house and along an embankment above the brook, then brushed through a stand of evergreens into total darkness. It was as though he'd stepped into an enchanted forest. He took a mental inventory of the equipment in his knapsack and realized with a wince that, while he had waterproof matches to build a fire, he didn't have a flashlight. He'd thought he'd be home well before dark, so he hadn't brought one. Dumbass.

His instincts told him to turn around, to go back to Pa and Gram's driveway, but he was only a few hundred yards from his grandparents' house, and he didn't want to backtrack. He was hungry and cold. He forged ahead into the darkness. His mittens were wet, and his hands were ice. Soon, though, he'd be in the warm house with his favorite dinner in front of him, and with a great story to tell—a story that might prompt Dad, Pa, and great-uncle Cal to talk about snowstorms they'd—

The snow collapsed under his skis. Avery slid sideways and tumbled down a steep grade. A branch whipped his cheek, a ski pole ripped off his wrist. As he fell, he fumbled in the darkness for something to grab onto, but a blur of brush slipped through his fingers. Finally, after what seemed like ten straight seconds of falling, he splashed into water, banged his arm against something hard, and stopped. He was disoriented and, because of the darkness and the snow, couldn't see more than a few feet in front of him.

His left ankle was twisted and tender, but he was pretty sure it wasn't broken. He groped around. Miraculously, his skis had stayed on. He had broken through the ice and landed in a shallow part of the brook, but he was now drenched. He was drenched in 10°F with a 20-mph wind. Soon, the windchill would make it feel like twenty-five below zero. In Jack London's "To Build a Fire," this is exactly how the guy dies. A scalding throb of panic surged through his chest.

With his remaining pole, Avery got back to his feet and crossed the brook. Should he build a fire to get warm? But build a fire out of what? Everything was covered by two feet of snow. Besides, his grandparents' place was only a couple hundred yards from here. Now, which way? The Bransons' was southwest of his grandparents', so … northeast. He'd brought a glow-in-the-dark orienteering compass with him. It was attached to a lanyard around his neck. He dug it out of his parka, took a reading, and headed NE in the pitch darkness, keeping his head up to catch any signs of light. Every few steps, he slapped his legs to keep the blood flowing. He could only see a foot or so ahead of him, so he kept bumping into blowdowns and had to feel his way around them.

When he took another reading with the compass and he shivered uncontrollably, he knew he was in trouble. He could friggin' die out here. He'd die without having driven through the Alps, mushed a dogsled in Alaska, or written a book. He'd die a virgin too, having only ever held two girl's breasts—Inge Ibsen's and Shelly Silversmith's. He'd die, only a few hundred yards from home. His predicament reminded him of Luke Skywalker's on the ice planet Hoth in *Empire*, except in Avery's case, Han wasn't going to rescue him. Avery was on his own.

The forest floor pitched gently uphill. This was familiar terrain, and as the ground leveled out, dim light silhouetted the trees ahead. Snow seemed to be swirling around in a clearing up there, but Avery was so cold that he thought he was hallucinating. Shivering, teeth chattering, he staggered forward one labored ski stride at a time. *Was he hallucinating?* If so, hypothermia could be setting in.

Avery thought about Luke's escape from the *bantha* (the snow monster) in *Empire*. After he gets away, Luke struggles to stay on his feet and eventually succumbs to exhaustion and exposure. Could it happen to Avery? Could he die so close to home? The blizzard made him wonder what polar explorer Ernest Shackleton would do in this situation, and then, bizarrely, he pictured Princess Leia in her *Empire* snowsuit, which led to him visualizing the poster of her on his bedroom wall at home: Leia reclining in her slave bikini from *Return of the Jedi*; Leia's creamy bare skin, her pink pouty lips, her long coppery braid, one leg extended and the other bent at the knee, and her defiant brown-eyed stare as glowing steam wafts behind her.

In Avery's delusional imagination, a recumbent Princess Leia sat up and exclaimed, "Help me, Avery Craig—you're my only hope!"[4] Reaching behind her back, she unfastened her bikini top. *This* got his blood pumping. Avery was now liberating Leia from that fat turd Jabba the Hutt. He'd rescue her and receive his reward: losing his virginity to the petite and sexy princess.

When he reached the silhouetted trees, he realized he was on the woods' edge. The snow he'd thought he'd seen earlier was indeed snow, swirling around in the lights from Pa and Gram's greenhouse. Avery staggered out of the trees. *Thank you, God.*

Shuffling in the skis, he passed the bird feeder and the window. Sabrina and her friend Lacy were snug inside watching TV. At the back door, he propped his skis and his one pole against the house.

---

[4] Princess Leia utters these famous words to Obi-Wan Kenobi in the first *Star Wars* movie, *Episode IV: A New Hope*.

Tomorrow, he'd look for the lost pole.

Avery grabbed the doorknob and paused. He took a moment to savor the numbness in his hands, feet, legs, and cheeks, and to look forward to the warmth that awaited him on the other side of this door. After dinner, he and Pa would blow out the candles on their birthday cake, and Avery would wish for one thing: to lose his virginity and get a girlfriend this year, and for the girl to be Dina Tempestilli.

He had come perilously close to death. One more misstep, one more wrong turn, one more minute wandering aimlessly in the blizzard, and he might have died out there—died without knowing a girl's love. He turned the doorknob and staggered inside.

2

Avery's birthday was a few days after his grandfather's, so every year they celebrated together on Pa's birthday, and Pa would say, "God willing, Avery, you'll always make it to the anniversary of my natal day, but my making it to yours is not a certainty."

Apparently, Avery's family considered his turning sixteen a significant rite of passage, because they showered him with presents. From his parents, Jackson and Jillian, he got a pair of high-fidelity headphones, and, to complete his bedroom stereo system, a second pair of Minimus-7 bookshelf speakers. His younger sister Sabrina gave him gift certificates to Record World and Spencer Gifts, while his older sister Julia, living in L.A., sent him an authentic British commando sweater—forest green wool with leather patches on the elbows. From his Uncle Beau and Aunt Lainey—classy, well-to-do Virginians—Avery received a special gift: an expensive Mont Blanc fountain pen. His great-uncle Charles ("Cal") perplexed Avery with his gift: a $100 bill, a jump rope, a pair of boxing gloves, and a book on boxing techniques. It was as though Cal wanted Avery to taunt other young men with the money and then beat them up when they tried to take it.

But it was Pa and Gram who outdid themselves, giving him a top-of-the-line Dunlop Black Max graphite tennis racquet (John McEnroe's racquet). "We want you to get to Wimbledon next summer, Ace," Pa said with a chuckle, "beat that kraut Boris Becker, and support us all in the manner to which we will most happily become accustomed."[5] Avery didn't know about that, but one thing he was sure of: with this racquet, he would finally beat his nemesis, Jeff Leonardo (a.k.a., "Daniel-son"). Pa also gave him a well-traveled but sturdy suitcase with more gifts packed inside: a toiletry kit, travel chess and Scrabble sets, a copy of *The Short Stories of Ernest Hemingway*, a map of Washington, D.C., a dozen monogrammed handkerchiefs with his nickname of "ACE" and a dozen plain ones, and finally a leather billfold ("Classier than a wallet," Pa said) with a $100 bill inside.

The next day, after helping get the property shoveled and plowed out, Avery went home with his plunder. He spent the afternoon helping his father shovel out their driveway in Birch Knolls, so it wasn't until that night, when Jack and Jill went out, that Avery could look over his gifts. He called Mallory, Lee, and E.B. to gush about the spectacular haul.

His Secret Superpower

On Sunday morning, Avery and Sabrina were in the dining room, eating pancakes and bacon he had made, when Jill appeared in the doorway in her dance skirt and leotard.

"I hope you remembered you and Sabrina are helping me with class today," his mother said.

Sabrina huffed. "It's not going to take all day, is it?"

While Jill and Sabrina were talking, all that Avery could think about was the fact that it was February. Who needs dance lessons in the dead of winter? Every other spring weekend, Jill, a former Radio City Rockette, would drag him and Sabrina to her latest dance lesson for bridal couples. Fortunately, because of Jill's day job as a secretary, she only needed their help on the weekends. Avery didn't feel like doing this today, but it was the only time he got his mother's undivided attention—as her dance assistant.

"Sure," Avery said, "but I have to pack for the D.C. trip tomorrow."

"It's only one couple. Two hours, in and out. And … I'll take you guys to McDonald's afterwards."

---

[5] In 1985, 17-year-old West German Boris Becker had won the Men's Singles title at Wimbledon, becoming the youngest man to win the title.

"Sold," Sabrina said. "Mom, you need me to work with the groom?"

"That would be perfect, dear," Jill said. "Avery can work with the bride, and I'll choreograph some steps for their first dance."

"But wedding dance lessons in the middle of *winter*?" Avery said.

"They need a *lot* of practice," Jill said.

When they got to the IBM Country Club and walked into the multipurpose room, Avery was surprised to find the lights on and the reflections of a dozen people in the mirrors on the walls. He whispered to his mother: "You said it was one couple. Who the hell *are* these people?"

"I'm not sure," Jill said. "I'll handle it."

While Jill spoke to the couple, Avery and Sabrina set up his boombox and stretched. The bride was visibly embarrassed, and when Jill returned to Avery and Sabrina, she explained that the whole wedding party had come along to give the bride and groom moral support. The family was either Greek or Italian, and *everyone* seemed to be there: the Best Man, the Maid of Honor, the bridesmaids, and the parents and the grandparents of the bride and the groom. The bride was a doe-eyed 20-something girl, but her mother was an overweight shrew.

"Excuse me, Mrs. Craig," she said, "but I'm paying for lessons by a professional. Who are these two *children* with you?"

Jill explained that Avery and Sabrina were her son and daughter and had been her assistants for three years. The mother of the bride mumbled a comment, but Avery couldn't hear her. Jill, however, apparently did hear her and was livid; she gave the woman a death stare.

"Ma'am," Jill said, "I'll have you know that my children have been dancing since they could walk. My son is one of the finest male dancers I've worked with—a true natural. But if you'd like proof..."

Jill smiled at Avery. He knew what was coming. Once in a while, his mother got a "pain in the caboose" client who needed to be shown what an amazing dancer she was. Avery stood and walked to the center of the room with her. Tall and blonde with unearthly long legs and flawless skin, even in her forties his mother was spellbinding.

Now smiling at the mother of the bride like she was performing in the Radio City Christmas Spectacular, Jill said, "Sabrina … a tango."

Sabrina popped a cassette in the boombox, and Avery put his mother in a slightly offset frame—close but not the intimate embrace of the Argentine Tango. They would be doing the American or Ballroom Tango, where the emphasis was on sharp, staccato movements with quick head turns and precise footwork. Their posture was tall and proud, their heads held high, their shoulders back. The music started, and Jill, who always led with this dance, silently counted off then nodded, and they launched into the tango.

Avery had done this dance with his mother so many times that he didn't have to think about the elements—the corte and recover, the staccato walk, the promenade position, the contra check, the fans and flicks with their feet, and particularly the head snaps—his only thought was of executing perfectly and making his mother look good. When they were lockstep during the promenade position, moving in parallel with synchronous footwork, and when they snapped their heads in unison at changes in direction, Jill glanced at him with a gleam of pride in her eyes and a faint smile on her lips. It was only when he was dancing with his mother like this, and dancing well, that he felt anything akin to love and affection from her. He didn't want their dance to end. But when they did their big finish, and Avery wrapped Jill back into him for the last time, she gave him a warm smile, a crisp nod, and a peck on the cheek.

The wedding party jumped to their feet applauding and cheering, but Avery didn't hear them. He wanted to hug his mother, but by the time he had the thought, she had slipped out of his hand and crossed the room to the bride.

When they started practicing the waltz, the bride apologized to Avery about her mother and gushed to him about his dancing. A short, plump girl, she had to tilt her head way back in order to look him in the face. Her eyes were wide. "Did your mother really teach you how to dance from the time you could walk?"

"Yeah," he said. "I can't remember a time when I couldn't dance."

Once he'd tightened up their frame and corrected her steps, Avery explained to the awestruck bride how, after focusing on posture, poise and balance, Jill had taught his sisters and him the basics of ballet and tap. Most of Jill's teaching, however, focused on ballroom, starting with the waltz and Viennese waltz, then the Foxtrot, Quickstep and Tango. Next came the Latin-American dances like the Salsa, Rumba, Samba, Cha Cha Cha, Mambo, Merengue, and the Paso Doble, which made learning the more freestyle dances easy. Besides the classic ballroom dances, Avery could do the East- and West-Coast Swing, Rock 'n Roll, Lindy Hop, Charleston, Nightclub Two-Step, and even the Texas Two-Step.

"Wow," the bride said. "That's amazing. So, are you gonna be a professional dancer like your mom?"

"No way," he said. "I only do this for my mother."

"But … you're so talented!"

Avery shrugged. "I might be good at it, but it's not what I want to do with my life."

She stepped on his toes. "Oops, sorry."

"It's all right." He smiled at the bride. "Let's focus on the waltz, okay?"

She was right about him having great aptitude for dance, but developing that natural ability had been an awful lot of work. After fourteen years of practices with his mother and serving as her assistant for the past three, Avery had absorbed the dances to the point that they were second-nature. He didn't have to think about steps, holds, turns, lifts, etc., and he didn't want to think about that stuff anymore anyway. Since he'd turned thirteen, dance had taken a back seat to his other interests: Boy Scouts, cross-country skiing, weight training, tennis, and other sports.

Truthfully, he had enjoyed dance a lot more when he was a boy because he got to spend time with his mother doing something he was really good at, and for which his mother lavished him with praise and affection. But when he was in 6th grade, a group of bullies found out that Avery had partnered with his sister in a ballroom dance contest and they teased him mercilessly, calling him a "fag," "homo," "pretty boy," and (the worst) "twinkletoes faggot." After that, Avery had kept his dancing skills a secret. Only his best friends Mallory, Lee, and E.B., who had sworn themselves to secrecy, knew about this ability of Avery's. In this sense, dance was his secret superpower, which he only revealed at out-of-state dance competitions or the occasional wedding reception or family reunion.

Looking at the wedding party sitting against the wall, Avery could tell that the Maid of Honor and some of the bridesmaids were hoping to dance with him today. He sighed.

Double Sausage

It was 7:37 on Monday morning—the first morning of February Break—and Jill was driving Avery to the school to go on his class trip to Washington, D.C. Since it was a joint trip between Avery's high school, Hancock, and their archenemy, Vanderbush, anything could happen. Avery had pleaded with Jill to arrive early so he could get a good seat on the bus, but she was late as usual. Making matters worse, they were in her piss-yellow Chevy Impala—a sedan the size of an oil tanker with a gaping hole in the muffler audible for miles. Avery's pleas to Jack to loan Jill the nicer car for the day had been disregarded.

They crested a hill with a view of the parking lot. The coach bus hadn't arrived, and there was a mob of people—his classmates and their parents—waiting with luggage on the school sidewalk. Avery would sooner be disemboweled by a pack of wolves than have his classmates see him alighting from Jill's jalopy.

"Don't pull in," Avery said. "Please."

"What?" she said. "Don't be silly. I have to."

"The bus isn't there yet. I'm begging you—drop me at the deli across the street, and I'll walk over."

"Avery Craig, it's ten degrees out there. You'll get sick. And it's dangerous—the traffic…"

Avery considered adding that he went over to the deli all the time, but he didn't want to get off-topic. The priority was his mother not dropping him off in the school parking lot.

"Please," he said. "The muffler … it's mortifying."

Glancing at the parking lot herself, Jill compressed her lips and nodded.

"I'll get some breakfast," Avery said. "They know me in there."

She turned into the plaza and parked in front of the Full Belly Deli. The female staff didn't know his name, but they treated Avery as a regular. Jill kissed his cheek.

"Have a good time, honey," she said. "Think you'll do any dancing during the trip?"

"Like school dances? I doubt it."

She shrugged. "Well, if they do, you can impress the girls with your skills." She brushed his bangs off his forehead. "My handsome boy. Have fun."

"Thanks."

Avery yanked the door handle and got out. He grabbed his suitcase from the back seat, waved to his mother, and stepped inside the deli. Fortunately, there was no line this morning. Wendy and Jolene, the two 20-something women working the grill and the register, chatted while a boombox played ♫"(Keep Feeling) Fascination."♫[6] Avery put down his suitcase, danced to the beverage cooler, grabbed a can of V8 vegetable juice, and danced to the counter. When the girls beamed at him, he put his can down and did a little 360° spin.

"Jo," Wendy said, nudging her coworker, "look who it is— Mr. Double Sausage, Egg, and Cheese on a Roll. Howdy, good lookin'. Long time, no see."

"Good morning, ladies. How are you lovely gals today?"

They giggled. Wendy was an attractive young woman with light brown hair, but Jolene was a knockout. Blessed in the chest and wearing a pair of white-framed horn-rimmed glasses, Jolene was the spitting image of nerdy Marilyn Monroe in *How to Marry a Millionaire*—a classic movie Avery had watched on VHS with his grandparents. While Wendy was putting his food on the grill, Jolene gazed into Avery's eyes.

"Mm … wow, those eyes of yours are something," she said. "Promise me you'll only use 'em for good, not evil."

"Nope," he said, grinning, "no promises."

---

[6] A boombox was a large, powerful portable radio, or combination radio/cassette player. Gradually, boomboxes were supplanted by the Sony Walkman and other brands of portable radio/cassette players with lightweight headphones instead of open speakers.

Jolene tittered, flipped her butter-blonde hair, and nodded at his bag. "Goin' on a trip?"

Avery replied that he was going on a school trip to Washington, D.C., and his bus was leaving soon. Wendy joked about Avery taking them with him, and Jolene sniggered and added that she'd rip her apron off right now and sit on Avery's lap for the whole ride to the capital.

"I'm so tiny," Jolene added, "you wouldn't notice me."

She raised an eyebrow and leaned partway across the counter, dipping low enough that Avery could see her kick-ass cleavage.

"You'd have to share your bed with us, though," she said. "And Wendy and me don't have any clothes packed, so we'd have to sleep in the buff. Hope that's okay."

Wendy gasped. "Jo!"

She and Jolene threw their heads back and laughed. The unexpected image of these two women nude and in bed with him gave him an erection so hard, he swore he could hear the zipper creaking on his tight Lee jeans. As the women laughed uproariously, Avery used the distraction to adjust himself. He redirected his tumescence from its cramped quarters in the crotch to along his inner thigh instead.

"We're only joshin' you, handsome," Jolene said.

"I know," he said.

"Mmm … mostly." She winked.

Wendy wrapped and bagged his sandwich and brought it back to the counter. The sandwich and V8 came to less than three bucks, so Avery gave them a fiver and told them to keep the change. He picked up his suitcase and headed for the door.

"Great seeing you, ladies. Bye."

"Thanks … *Double Sausage*," Jolene said breathily.

The girls were giggling as he walked out the door.

While waiting for a break in the traffic, Avery wolfed his food and thought about Wendy and Jolene. Why were they so aggressively flirtatious today? They'd flirted with him before, but today's banter seemed more serious—like if he'd said, "Yeah, sure," they would have torn off their aprons and left with him.

Naked and Smiling

When he walked into the parking lot, the coach bus was pulling in, and Steven "Doc" Holliday, Avery's buddy from Biology and the winter swim team, was getting out of his mother's station wagon. Avery greeted him with his best Bugs Bunny impersonation.

"'*Ehhhhh*,'" he said, "'what's up, Doc?'"

"Ace? Did you *walk* here?"

"No, I got some breakfast over at the deli."

Mrs. Holliday rolled down her window. Avery hadn't seen her since mid-January when she was constantly driving him and Doc to swim practices and meets. She was a mousy-looking redheaded librarian, and although she was shy with most people, she always had something nice to say to Avery.

"Avery," she said, "it's wonderful to see you, dear. I like your outfit—leather bomber jacket, sweater, jeans, penny loafers. Very handsome."

"Thank you," he said. "And may I say, Mrs. Holliday, you're looking quite fetching yourself."

Mrs. Holliday blushed and patted her hair. "Have a good time in our nation's capital, boys. Avery, please keep Steven out of trouble."

"I'm afraid that's impossible, Mrs. Holliday." He smirked. "I'm counting on your son to keep *me* out of trouble."

She laughed, kissed Doc goodbye, and drove away. Doc gave Avery his suitcase to put in the cargo hold and boarded the bus to save them a seat. The bus driver was cramming everyone's bags in, and as Avery waited his turn, he became aware of some girls inside the bus with their faces smushed against the windows. He didn't look directly back at them, but he could tell they were staring at him and whispering in each other's ears. They had to be Vanderbush girls, because he didn't recognize any of them.

Uncomfortable with being stared at, Avery looked away and his eyes met those of a girl from Hancock—a fellow honors student from junior high school. He couldn't remember her name. It began with a "jeh" sound (Jenna? Jessica?), and her last name was plain, like Smith or Johnson, and that's all he could remember about her.

♫"Raspberry Beret"♫

She wore a long charcoal wool coat, white earmuffs, and an actual raspberry beret, like the one Prince mentions in his song. She was a strikingly tall girl (like 5′10″) with long beaver-pelt brown hair and an attractive, unadorned face—smooth skin, high cheekbones, and an elegant nose.

She smiled tentatively. Avery smiled back and waved, which caused her to laugh and expose a mouthful of braces. Without the metal-mouth and those gigantic "bug-eye" glasses, she'd be a serious looker. Avery was relieved when she handed over her suitcase and boarded the bus; he was afraid she'd say hello to him, and then be insulted when Avery didn't remember her name.

When Avery reached the driver, he handed over his and Doc's bags. For some inexplicable reason, the bus company had a leprechaun theme, and the unfortunate driver, who was grossly overweight, had to wear a tight Kelly-green uniform. To say it was unflattering was an understatement.

Avery pulled a fiver from his pocket and palmed it to the man. He'd seen his grandfather do this for doormen in the City, and it looked cool. Also, the girls on the bus were still staring at him, and he wanted them to see how classy and generous he was. The driver pinched the bill by the corner and gazed at Avery. The man had a lazy left eye.

"What's this?"

"A gratuity, sir," Avery said. "My grandfather taught me it's what you do for drivers."

The man nodded. Avery read the name tag on his jacket: "HERB."

"You know what?" Herb said. "I been doing this job eleven years, and you're the first person to give me a tip. Ever. You got class, kid."

"Thank you for driving us, Herb."

Avery climbed aboard the bus and started down the aisle. Directly behind the driver was a woman teacher; at least Avery thought it was a woman; she looked like one of those female Soviet powerlifters. Across the aisle from her was Avery's English teacher, Ms. Wharton (who claimed American novelist Edith Wharton as a distant ancestor). She was reading a novel while a pudgy and grumpy-looking man consulted a clipboard. Avery had never seen him before and decided he must be a teacher from Vanderbush. After two rows of parent chaperones came the students. The girl with the raspberry beret was reading a book and didn't notice him. Damn, she had a pretty face; shame about the glasses and braces.

He continued slowly down the aisle looking for Doc. A few people on the bus he recognized from his Honors Social Studies class—Eric Park and Louis Zane, Johanna Glück and Kristen Brooks, and Bill Winters and Tara Mullally. Avery nodded and gave a thumbs-up to Eric and Louis; Johanna and Kristen rolled their eyes at him and turned away; and as for lovebirds Bill and Tara, they were sitting with their heads touching, oblivious to everyone and everything. The majority of the students, however, were from Vanderbush. The girls that had been staring at him through the window and whispering to each other stared and whispered some more as he passed their seats.

Most of the Vanderbush guys wore Wayfarers attached to their necks by neon-colored Croakies, and noticeably expensive ski jackets with the collars popped.[7] Dangling from their jacket zippers were old ski lift tags. They seemed like rowdy douches. One of them, a short kid with heavily gelled hair, jutted his chin at Avery.

"Hey, dude, nice jacket! What'd you do, steal it from grandpa?!"

Everyone looked at Avery.

"Nope," he said. "It was in your dad's closet this morning when I left your mom … naked and smiling."

The bus exploded in laughter. The guy's seatmate elbowed him.

"Oh, *burn!*"

♫"Love Theme From St. Elmo's Fire (Instrumental)"♫

Avery looked up and beheld a vision: a petite girl in a button-down pastel blue sweater. She had sparkling lilac eyes and chin-length hair the color of a fawn's coat in early summer. Her features were refined and delicate—especially her nose; she looked like a pretty doll. And when she looked up and their eyes met, a jolt passed between them.

---

[7] Wayfarers were a style of Ray Ban-brand sunglasses popularized in the 1983 teen romp *Risky Business*, and Croakies (often just an ostentatious accessory) were a brand of neoprene elastic straps that kept the wearer from losing his sunglasses.

3

A FEW rows back, Doc was standing and waving a hand. "Yo, Ace!" Before Avery walked away from the girl, she smiled. Avery smiled in return, continued down the aisle, and put his jacket in the overhead compartment.

He had wanted the window seat for the drive to D.C., but when Doc hitched over, leaving him the aisle seat, Avery didn't protest. He was in a daze and didn't care where he sat; all he could think about was that girl. Teachers stood and made announcements, but he didn't hear them. The bus began to move. For the first half-hour of the trip, Doc was yammering about something, but Avery didn't hear him either. Out of politeness, Avery nodded as Doc continued to talk.

"Watch out," Doc said, nudging him, "I think one of those Vanderbush girls has the hots for you."

Avery looked over the seat back. Two rows ahead, the fawn-haired girl and her seatmate, a blonde with a different earring dangling from each ear—a crucifix earring, like Madonna wore, and an earring with the Van Halen logo, "VH"—were peeking over their seat back at him. Avery gave the fawn-haired girl another look. She was considerably smaller than her seatmate, and compared to Dina Tempestilli, the girl with whom Avery had been flirting for three years, she was much less shapely. She wore a lot less makeup too—only a whisper of blush and pastel-blue eyeshadow—but her fine features, including her nose and her prominent cheekbones, were so naturally beautiful, Avery was glad they weren't caked with makeup. The two girls giggled and dropped out of sight again.

"Ace, you know them?" Doc asked.

"Nope."

"The blonde's hot," he said. "I wouldn't kick her out of bed, know what I'm sayin'? What about you?"

"She's hot, but I'm more interested in the other one."

The next time the girls looked at Avery, it was by leaning out into the aisle. The fawn-haired girl had her head on its side, her hair dangling, and her girlfriend's head was above hers. Avery smiled. The girls giggled and ducked behind their seat again.

Word Magic

Avery was frozen, unsure what to do. The girl seemed to be interested in him, but how could he start a conversation with her? What should he do? Stand in the aisle and talk to her? Ask the seatmate if she'd be willing to trade seats?

Avery closed his eyes. What would his idols do here? James Bond, Remington Steele, Steve Austin, Han Solo, Indiana Jones? Whatever they did, they'd be suave about it. They'd play it cool. Heck, Bond, Solo, and Indy? They'd simply ignore her.

Avery was longing and terrified to go up there. He wanted to introduce himself and suggest a seat change, but he was scared of being turned down—to his face. After a few deep breaths, he decided to forget about the girl.

"I'm going to rest for a bit, Doc."

"Sure, dude."

Avery reclined in his seat. He had drifted into what promised to be a delicious sleep when something jabbed him in the leg. Avery opened his eyes. The kid in the seat in front of him was passing him a note.

"Don't get the wrong idea, bud." The kid lifted a Walkman headphone off one ear. "It's not from me. It's from the two girls up there."

The girls peeked over their seat back and waved by wiggling their fingers. Avery took the note and smiled, and the girls submerged again. He opened the sheet of looseleaf. The note read,

> *Hi, I'm Caitlyn Cray! My friend Penny Aston wants to know your name!*

Avery had read in one of his father's books on salesmanship that you only get one chance to make a first impression. Even though Penny had only asked for his name, he wanted his response to be funny. He took out a "clicky" ballpoint pen and twirled it through his fingers, then pulled out his hand grip-strengthener and squeezed it in his other hand as he wrote.

> My given name is Zebulon, but my friends call me Zeb. I was born in a dilapidated doghouse in the rugged, misty mountains of West Virginia. Pappy ran moonshine. Grandpappy harvested birch bark. I was raised by raccoons, but now I'm an orphan.
>
> No, that's all a lie. I write stories, and Zeb is one of my fictional characters. My name is plain old Avery, which is an Old English name that means "elf king." My surname is "Craig," which is Scottish and means "crag" or "a high rock." So, my name, Avery Craig, means "Elf King on a High Rock."
>
> Please don't ask me what my middle name is. Only my mother uses my middle name, and she only does it when she's angry with me. You'll laugh at it, and then I'll be depressed for the whole trip.
>
> Which of you is which by the way?

Avery leaned into the aisle and tapped the shoulder of Walkman Dude, sitting in the seat in front of him. He held up the folded note.

"Would you mind?"

"Mm, I don't know, man." He looked over his shoulder. "I wanna listen to tunes."

"Tell you what," Avery said, "you like O'Grady's potato chips? I've got a *mondo* bag. Pass the notes, and the chips are yours."

"Deal."

Avery handed Walkman Dude the note, and as soon as the note reached the girls, Avery dropped the bag of chips over the seat back.

Two rows ahead, the girls broke out into uproarious laughter. Avery figured their hilarity was caused more by their teenage girl hormones than by the humor in his message (it wasn't *that* funny). Avery's years of training with other girls—listening to Lara Smith prattle endlessly on the phone for hours; joking and flirting with Dina Tempestilli; and writing erotic stories for Inge Ibsen—were about to pay off. To appear nonchalant about the upcoming note-exchange, Avery read a James Bond novel he'd brought—*Icebreaker*.

He was immersed in the book when Walkman Dude thrust his hand over the seat back. This time, the note had two sets of handwriting: the original one, Caitlyn's—where the letters looked like soap bubbles—and Penny's, which was the most exquisite penmanship Avery had ever seen: perfectly rounded small cursive with lots of flourishes, and every sentence arrow-straight and precisely within the lines. Avery was impressed.

> *HAHAHAHAHAHAHA! Penny says your hot stuff, Zeb! She's majorly into hillbillies! Got any of your pappy's moonshine on you? Yee-haw!*

> Hi, Avery, this is Penny. That was really funny. Caitlyn's nuts because her boyfriend couldn't come on the trip. You asked which of us is which. Caitlyn's the aggressive blonde, and I'm the quiet one with reddish-brown hair. You go to Hancock, right? Where do you live? What else do you write? What else do you do for fun?

> *Hey, ELF KING! Penny wants to have your babies! She said, "Caitlyn, I'm gonna marry him and have baby elves!"*

> Avery, it's Penny again. Don't believe a thing Caitlyn says. All I said was, when you got on the bus and we looked at each other, it was really intense. P.S.: You have amazing eyes.

Avery sensed an opportunity here. He decided to answer her questions by creating a dossier for himself:

<u>Dossier, Avery "Ace" Craig</u>:
School: Hancock High, 10th grade.
Age: 15 years, 11 months (my birthday's later this week).
Residence: Outskirts of Troutkill Junction, in a Quonset hut.
Height & Weight: 6 feet tall, about 185 pounds.
Writing: The Adventures of Jack and Zeb (Secret Havoc-In-Action Team), other stories, Scout Troop chronicles, crappy poems.
Hobbies/Interests: Reading, writing, weightlifting, cross-country skiing, swimming, tennis, Scouts, hiking, fishing, football, chess, computers, movies, pool (billiards), and others.
Sports: Competitive X-C skiing, fall tennis team, winter swim team, winter track.
Other Interests: A beautiful girl on a bus bound for Washington, D.C.
Health Concerns: Possible fainting if he makes eye contact with said girl.
Distinguishing Marks: Large, ferret-shaped birthmark on left butt cheek.

Soon after he handed the note forward, there was a deafening squeal—*"A ferret?!"*—and a peal of laughter. The girls were so loud, a teacher shushed them. Soon, the note came back to Avery. The original sheet of paper had been replaced by an elaborately folded one; it looked like a piece of *origami* that a Japanese girl exchange student had made for him last year. Each fold was numbered and labeled, with arrows pointing at which corners to open next. As Avery opened each leaf, there was a new message—either in Penny's precise, arrow-straight handwriting, or Caitlyn's soap bubbles. The message on the first fold was from Caitlyn.

> *Can I see your birthmark, "Ace"? HAHAHAHA! I'm kidding. (Or am I?) Heeeeeeeeeres Penny!*

Then, on fold number two, Penny chimed in:

That was hilarious, Avery! But what the heck is a
"Quonset hut"? You do live in a house, right?
So, a beautiful girl on the bus? Who is she? And
what's your middle name? I'll tell you mine if you tell
me yours.

Avery grinned. A scene from *Star Wars* popped into his
head: while chasing Luke Skywalker down the Death Star trench,
Darth Vader says in his sinister baritone, "I have you now." Avery
opened to the fold labeled, "Your Reply Goes Here, Studly." He twirled
his pen in his fingers, then dashed off a reply:

Sorry. I said, "girl," but I meant woman. I was
referring to the teacher sitting in the front row, behind
the bus driver—the one with a mustache who looks like
a Soviet powerlifter. I'm into women with mustaches.

The moment the note reached them, they screeched with laughter.
The male teacher who'd recently shushed them stood up.
"Girls, please! If you won't quiet down, I'll separate you."
Doc nudged Avery's arm. "Whatever you're writing, it must be
good. Workin' that Avery Craig word magic?"
"It's some of my best stuff yet, Doc." Avery twirled the pen in his
fingers. "I might be joining her up there."
Doc's eyebrows practically sprang off his face. "And the other one?
She'll come back here?"
"She might," Avery said.
"What's the other one's name?"
"Caitlyn."
"*Caitlyn*." Doc pursed his lips and nodded. "Nice."

Grappling with a Problem

When the note came back, it was on a new sheet of paper:

Hey, "ACE" … guess what? That woman up front?
That's Mrs. Gould, our gym teacher! I don't think she's
into boys, but I'll ask her if you want!

> Avery, Penny here. That was so funny! You're making this bus ride much more fun than I thought it would be. But you didn't answer my questions! What is a Quonset hut? And what's your middle name? OK, Caitlyn wants to say something…
>
> *Avery, we're bored! Your SO FUNNY! Tell us a story! This ride is so boring, and your so good at it!*

Caitlyn's incorrect use of the possessive pronoun "your" instead of the contraction "you're" ("you are") was super-annoying. But the girl knew exactly how to stroke his ego. Avery would overlook her poor grammar.

Okay, Ace—showtime. He clenched his eyes shut and thought hard for a story idea. First, he needed a location. The hotel where they were staying—in Bethesda, Maryland, outside of D.C.—came to mind. Next, he needed a problem. Before the trip, the chaperones had mentioned that the boys would all be staying together on one floor of the hotel, and the girls on another floor.

Hmm … this sounds like a job for Jack and Zeb.

Most of the time when Avery began a story, he didn't know where it was going. This uncertainty made him uncomfortable, so he often didn't finish stories he started, or if he did finish them, they were extremely short. In four or five years of writing stories and reading them to friends on the school bus, he'd thought of them like amusement park rides: Avery had to go where the ride was taking him. This was especially true whenever he tried to write anything funny. Once the story got rolling, he kept adding new stuff, exaggerating more and more, trying to see how far he could stretch it and keep it believable. Avery tore off the back cover of the trip itinerary and started writing:

> **"Grappling with a Problem"**
> by Avery "Ace" Craig
> The fax came into the Secret Havoc-In-Action
> Team headquarters at five o'clock in the morning.
> When the machine beeped, Jack swaggered out to the

communications center sipping a mug of coffee. He tore off the fax and read the message. Zeb wandered sleepily out of his suite, poured himself some coffee, and read over Jack's shoulder.

Some kids from Hancock and Vanderbush high schools were on a field trip in Washington, D.C., but when they arrived at the 15-story hotel, the teachers cruelly separated the guys and the girls. The girls were all put on one floor, and the guys all had to stay on the floor below.

"Well, *that* sucks," Jack said. "We've gotta help 'em, Zeb."

"All right. I'll go warm up the truck."

"And let's bring plenty of those thick-cut O'Grady's potato chips. Last time we ran out mid-mission."

"We sure did," Zeb said, "and my stomach was rumblin' somethin' fierce!"

"You take care of the truck and the O'Grady's," Jack said. "I'll pack the grappling hook cannons."

That night, one of the students, a super-cool dude named Avery Craig, contacted Jack and Zeb on a CB radio he'd smuggled down to D.C. in his suitcase. At lights-out, Avery gave them the go-ahead. Jack and Zeb fired the grappling hook cannons at the balcony railings on the girls' floor.

The grappling hooks caught the railings within a second of each other, clanging loudly and dangling 50 feet of strong rope down to the guys' balconies. All at once, the guys came out of their rooms, the girls came out of theirs, and the guys shimmied up and kissed the girls and went into the girls' bedrooms with them.

Jack and Zeb were watching the whole scene from the truck bed of their F350 king-cab pickup truck. They were sitting in lawn chairs, peering through binoculars, and munching O'Grady's Au Gratin potato chips.

"Well," Jack said, "another successful mission. Those kids can get it on for twelve hours if they want."

"Mm-hm," Zeb said. "Hope they brought enough prophylactics!" He overturned the bag of O'Grady's. The bag was empty. "Let's hit an all-night diner, Jack. My stomach's rumblin' again—somethin' fierce!"

"Good idea," Jack said.

They got in the truck and started it up. The ripping opening guitar riff of ZZ Top's "Legs" blasted out of the speakers as they roared away.

Grenada!?

Finished with the story, Avery glanced at his watch. He'd been writing back and forth with the girls for two hours. In one of his father's books about sales, the author described a technique called "The Close." Eventually, you had to come right out and ask for the sale. Avery's funny notes had been his sales pitch, but now it was time to *close* this baby.

> Girls—
>
> Listen, my arm's getting tired from writing (war injury, Grenada).[8] How about if Caitlyn and I switch seats? That way, Penny and I can talk more. Caitlyn, my friend Steven "Doc" Holliday is back here. He's a descendant of Doc Holliday, the Old West hero, and he called you a "hot blonde."
>
> How about it, girls? If we switch seats, I'll tell Penny about Quonset huts, my middle name, and anything else she wants to know. —Ace

He sent the notes—theirs and his—forward. A moment later, there was loud giggling from the girls' seats.

"Grenada!?" one of them chirped.

When their reply came back, it was written on the back of his story.

> *Wow! Great story! Looks like we're trading seats!*
> *AVERY "ACE" CRAIG ... COME ON DOWN!*

---

[8] On October 25, 1983, the United States invaded this tiny island nation in the Caribbean after a left-wing military group seized power.

Avery, I loved the line, "I'll go pack the grappling hook cannons." Do they really exist, or did you make them up?

Ace, I still want to see your birthmark! I think we could fit in the bathroom together! Wink-wink!

Avery put the note, his book, Walkman, and other things in his bag, and grabbed his coat out of the overhead compartment.

"Holy crap, Ace—you did it?" Doc said.

Avery nodded. "I love it when a plan comes together."

"And Caitlyn's coming back here?"

"Yup." He stood. "And I told her you thought she was hot."

"Oh, *man!*"

Crazy Good

A moment later, Caitlyn Cray was walking down the aisle holding a hobo purse and a Navy peacoat covered with rock band badges. Caitlyn was tall and slender, except in the chest where she was precociously developed beneath a skintight ¾-sleeve Scorpions' *Love At First Sting* T-shirt. Printed across her chest was the album cover, which featured a brunette tilting her head back, getting her neck kissed by some faceless guy, while, right in the center, was a generous dose of the brunette's ample side-boob. The hem of Caitlyn's T-shirt was short too, exposing her midriff.

♫"Rock You Like a Hurricane"♫

As the song's thundering preamble plays, Caitlyn sashays up the aisle in slow motion. A spotlight beams down, and smoke from dry ice wafts around her ankles. Her lips glisten, her makeup sparkles with glitter, a breeze flutters her hair. Avery gulps and forces himself not to stare at her chest, which is basically impossible because when she drops her things, she plants her fists on her hips, arches her back and swivels her torso, as if deliberately taunting him with the mouthwatering eyefuls. Avery has never been stared down by a beautiful girl before, and it's unsettling. He admires her hair instead.

Blonde with platinum highlights, Caitlyn's hairstyle is the same as actress Markie Post's on TV's *Night Court*: a medium-length mullet, full and wavy on top; shorter on the sides but longer in back, where it grazes her shoulders. Styled with gel, her hair forms a latticework of overlapping tresses.

A devilish smirk flowers on her face. The smirk is a half-smile made with her lips only, where one corner of her mouth is higher than the other. Intensifying the smirk's effect are her lips. Cotton-candy pink and pillowy plump, they evoke a fantasy of receiving an hour-long blowjob from her.[9] Her lips shimmer with lipgloss slathered on so copiously, Avery can smell its piquant cherry flavoring from a foot away. He gulps down some air and moans under his breath. His highly tuned instincts about people—instincts developed from moving a dozen times as a kid—tell him that as terribly sexy as she is, everywhere this girl goes, Big Trouble follows in her wake.

"Hi," she said, "I'm Caitlyn."

"Avery."

In a pair of lace-up granny boots with two-inch heels, Caitlyn was almost as tall as him. Her nose had a sassy little upward tweak at the tip, giving her a haughty mien. She craned her lips toward his ear and said, "Well played, Avery Craig. You're a trip, dude."

"One tries, Miss Cray."

No sooner did Caitlyn give him a fresh smirk, than a boombox in the back of the bus blasted Van Halen's rendition of ♫"Dancing in the Street."♫ One of Avery's favorite tunes, the up-tempo song opened with a wicked dose of synthesized guitar by Eddie Van Halen and a cowbell-infused drum beat by his brother Alex. Caitlyn danced down the aisle snapping her fingers with her hands raised over her head. Spinning around, she danced back toward Avery, wriggling her torso and wagging her butt to the beat.

"Woo, Van Halen!" She danced up against him. "Dance with me, Avery! *If* you can dance that is."

---

[9] American English dictionaries still refer to this sex act as a "blow job," but this two-word spelling is laughably outdated. The time has come for this (and its carnal cousin "hand job") to be a single compound word. Therefore, for all nine episodes of *Bodaciously*, these two sex acts will be denoted by their idiomatic one-word spellings: "blowjob" and "handjob." Lexicologists can bite me.

The way she said this, with a goading squint and head-bobble, she seemed to expect Avery to chicken-out. Avery's reservations about revealing his secret superpower—mostly worries about being teased or bullied—popped into his head, but in a split second he evaluated the situation and came to a decision. First, most of the students on the bus were from another school, so they didn't know him, and they probably wouldn't see him again after this trip. Second, Avery wasn't a skinny kid that guys could bully anymore; he was almost 16 years old and super well-built from working out daily. Third, the girl asking him to dance was crazy hot. That settled it.

"All right, Caitlyn," he said. "I'll dance with you."

Avery tossed his things on the seat, peeled off his sweater and plunked it down atop the pile of stuff. While Caitlyn ogled his physique, Avery scanned the narrow bus aisle. There was no room to move laterally, but a certain dance would work here.

"Do you know the Nightclub Two-Step?" he asked.

"I haven't done it in a while, but it'll come back to me."

"We don't have much space," he said, "so we'll do the in-place variation. We'll start with that, then go into freestyle, okay?"

The person controlling the boombox cranked the volume. Avery backed up to the last row of seats, and as David Lee Roth crooned, Avery swagger-danced like the legendary rocker toward Caitlyn. He stopped in front of her and smiled.

"We'll start in *close* hold."

Avery slipped his right hand under her left armpit, placed it between her shoulder blades, and pulled her bodily against him so her breasts squished against his chest. Her eyes dilated. She held his shoulder with her left hand, and Avery took firm hold of her right hand in his left, forming a frame, and they took their first step. They danced halfway down the aisle toward the front of the bus, then Avery did a spot turn with her, and they danced to the back again.

Once he and Caitlyn made a few passes up and down the aisle, the students sprang to their feet and clapped along. The male Vanderbush teacher was glaring at them, but Ms. Wharton had a hand on the male teacher's arm. Avery knew he had maybe 30 seconds before the male teacher shut them down.

Caitlyn broke out of the frame and danced up against him. Moving to the beat together, swaying forward and backward on their heels, they stared each other down with their chests touching. A girl squealed, "Caitlyn rocks!" Then, as Caitlyn pivoted to dance away from him, a cool finishing move came to Avery: a wrap and then a classic dip. He waited until she had stretched away from him as far as their arms reached, then gave her hand a quick tug toward him, coiling her up his arm until their cheeks touched. Pausing to savor the feel of her body against his, he did another wrap with her, this time stepping partway into a seat and catching Caitlyn in his arms as she toppled backwards toward the floor. Caitlyn panted and beamed. The entire bus of students clapped, hooted, and hollered. The male teacher next to Ms. Wharton shouted from the front.

"All right, you two!" he said. "Show's over! You with the boombox—shut it off!"

Avery and Caitlyn were at the back of the bus. Caitlyn—flushed, grinning—bowed to the applauding students and poked Avery's pectoral muscle.

"You're a crazy good dancer," she said.

"Thanks. You're not bad yourself."

Caitlyn said she'd been taking lessons in Queenstown for like ten years, at the Adele & Alfredo Dance Academy, and she'd been a part-time dance assistant for a year or so.

"How'd *you* get so good?" she asked.

Avery shrugged. "I just kind of picked it up."

"Well … hopefully we'll get a chance to dance again sometime."

"Yeah, sure."

As Avery headed down the narrow aisle, Caitlyn didn't move out of the way, forcing him to step to the side and squeeze past her. There wasn't enough clearance, however, and his chest ended up plowing across hers. Looking him in the eyes, she glanced down as it was happening and looked back up at him with that glistening smirk of hers.

"*Bye*, Avery," she said. "See ya later."

"Bye, Caitlyn. Nice meeting you."

Avery grabbed his things off the seat.

The First Plunge

When he got to Penny's row, she was in the window seat, gazing out at the New Jersey Turnpike. At first glance, she seemed nonchalant, but then he noticed that her hands were trembling. Avery stowed his jacket on the overhead rack but kept his bag with him. He rapped gently on the seat arm.

"Knock, knock," he said. "May I join you?"

She nodded. He sat. Penny bit her lower lip and said, "Boy, that dance you and Caitlyn did was really something."

"Thanks," Avery said. "Alright … wanna know my middle name?"

"Yes."

"It starts with 'C.' Guess."

She shrugged. "Charles? Chester?"

"Nope. And come on—do I look like a *Chester*?"

She grinned. "No, not at all. Those are the only 'C' names I could think of right now."

"Where'd 'Chester' come from?"

"One of my teachers. It's the girls' nickname for him because he's super creepy. You know … like 'Chester the Molester'?"

"You think I look like a *molester*? Thanks a lot."

She giggled. "No, I didn't mean it like that."

Avery made Penny swear not to tell anybody his middle name, because the only people who knew it were his family and now her. Then he prefaced it by saying that while it sounded like a girl's name, it was Scottish, and in Scotland it was a common name for a boy. Penny's eyes were wide with anticipation. Avery beckoned her closer, and when she leaned toward him, he whispered in her ear.

"It's 'Christy.' Spelled 'C-H-R-I-S-T-Y.'"

She sat up. "'Christy'?"

"Go on, laugh," he said. "Get it out of your system."

As she giggled, their shoulders touched. Wow, did she smell wonderful—much different than Dina's perfume and marijuana smell; Penny smelled like a mixture of powdery antiperspirant and roses in bright sunshine.

"I'm sorry," she said, "I think 'Christy' is a fine middle name."

"All right, your turn. What's yours?"

"It's so blah. I hate it." She sighed with a little whimper at the end. "All right … it's Jane."

"I love it," he said. "It's beautiful. And is Penny short for Penelope?"

"Yes. I don't like Penelope either. It sounds like an old lady's name."

"I disagree. 'Penelope Jane Aston'—it sounds genteel."

"'Genteel'?" she said.

"Like refined, elegant."

"Really?" She canted her head to the side.

"Yes. And your last name is the coolest. Aston? My favorite car is the Aston Martin DB5."

"Aston Martin?" Her face crinkled up.

"It's a car James Bond drives. Haven't you ever seen *Goldfinger*?"

She shook her head. "I don't know what 'Aston Martin' is, but you'll like this. My father's name is Martin Aston."

"That's so cool." He held out his hand. "Penelope Jane Aston? Avery Christy Craig."

She gave him her hand. Hers was much smaller than his—and delicate. It was so soft and adorable that Avery wanted to kiss it, but he stopped himself. As they gently shook, she smiled, and pleasure trickled out of his brain, down his spine. Now that he was holding Penny's hand, he didn't want to let it go; he decided to invent a reason to keep holding it.

"Have you ever had your palm read?" he asked.

She shook her head. Avery rummaged through his memory for the tidbits his older sister Julia had taught him about palm-reading. He turned Penny's hand over, palm-side-up, and held it in his.

"Okay," he said. "Hm … let's see … ah … yes, that's good."

"What? What's good?" She wriggled in her seat. "Tell me!"

"Your lifeline. That's here." He traced it with his forefinger up to her wrist. "See how it's a long, deep groove?"

"Yes," she said. "What's that mean?"

"That you'll live a long, healthy life. I estimate about … ninety years."

"Come on," she said, "you can't tell that from my hand."

"Yes, I can," he said. "I'm a trained palm reader."

As he rested his eyes on hers, he was hit with another electrical jolt. His breathing quavered. The jolt was now a constant current that seemed to pulse between them with each beat of their hearts—from him to her, and from her to him.

"What else, Avery?" She was gazing into his eyes.

"Your love line," he said.

"What about it?"

Avery skated his fingertip along it. Penny's chest heaved.

"It says … you will meet the guy of your dreams on a bus."

She giggled. They continued to stare at each other. Avery turned her hand over again, palm side down, and caressed her knuckles. She didn't stop him. His heart pounded. He was tickling the soft inside of her wrist when something jabbed him in the shoulder. It was another note from Walkman Dude.

"What's it say?" Penny asked.

"Come closer."

Avery spread out the note on his bag and read it aloud, doing his best impersonation of Caitlyn.

> *Well, well, well … Avery and Penny, sittin' in a tree … K-I-S-S-I-N-G! I haven't heard any noise up there in a while! What are you up to? THIRD BASE?*[10] *HAHAHAHAHA!*

Penny chuffed.

"You okay?" Avery said.

"I guess."

"You don't like my impression of her? People say I'm a pretty good mimic."

"Forget it, keep reading."

---

[10] Bizarrely, the types of base hits in the game of baseball were often used by teens in the '80s to describe their sexual experience, or to describe how sexually active a girl or guy was. If a person got to 1st Base with someone, that meant s/he kissed the other with tongue (a French kiss); 2nd Base meant the couple felt each other up and pleasured each other with a hand; 3rd Base meant that the couple engaged in oral sex (cunnilingus and/or a blowjob); and finally, a Home Run meant the couple had sexual intercourse.

Hey Avery ... something I didn't ask you ... do you have a girlfriend? Because if your going out with some Hancock slut and you don't tell Penny and you hurt her, I will cut your nuts off! Understood?! Please reply. Thanks!

"Well, at least she's direct," Avery whispered. "And she's protective of you, which is nice. But will you please teach her the difference between 'your'—Y-O-U-R—and 'you're'—Y-O-U-apostrophe-R-E?"

"Funny, I've never noticed that about her writing before." She smiled and nudged him. "Well, how about it? Huh? Do you have a girlfriend?"

There was his now-ancient flirtation with Dina, but in no way did she qualify as a girlfriend. She didn't know Avery liked her because he'd always been too chicken to ask her out. Sure, she'd laughed at every single thing he'd uttered since seventh grade, but she had a boyfriend and had always had one.

There was also Inge Ibsen, his 19-year-old alcoholic neighbor with whom he'd made out a little bit, but they had a falling-out last summer and hadn't spoken since. She didn't qualify as a girlfriend either.

"No," he said. "The closest thing to a girlfriend I've ever had was this girl Lara Smith in eighth grade. We never even kissed. She moved away last year."

The bus hit a pothole, Penny's hand landed in his, and their fingers magically interlaced. He and Penny leaned their heads back against the seats and looked at each other. There was excitement in her eyes, tinged with fear. The last time Avery had seen this look on a girl's face was with his older cousin, on a rollercoaster, moments before the first plunge.

4

FOR THE next hour or so, Avery and Penny talked and got to know each other. He listened to her sweet voice and caressed the soft fleshy skin between her fingers. Penny responded by resting her head on Avery's shoulder and talking even more.

Penny's parents were divorced. Her mother was a nurse at New Netherlands County Hospital, and her father worked for IBM. She had an 11-year-old sister who lived with her and her mom. She'd played field hockey in junior high, and to earn money, she did some babysitting.

When it was his turn, Avery said that his parents worked for IBM, his mother as an executive secretary, his father as a sales manager and trainer. Avery added that he'd moved a lot when he was younger. After mentioning his younger sister Sabrina (a talented dancer and volleyball player), Avery proudly told Penny about his older sister Julia, who'd gone to the Culinary Institute of America, and was now a chef at Spago—Wolfgang Puck's famous restaurant in L.A.

Then, seemingly in the blink of an eye, the bus stopped. They were at a rest area. After using the men's room, Avery and Doc walked into the food court, where they joined Penny on line at the McDonald's counter. Weary travelers standing on the endless line glared at Avery and the other students. Avery and Doc ordered lunch for the girls while Caitlyn hooked Penny's elbow and dragged her toward the bathroom.

"Come with me, *you*," Caitlyn said. "Tell me everything."

Lingering Squeeze

When the food was ready, Avery and Doc took the trays to a booth and sat down across from each other. Avery opened one of his Big Macs. He'd gotten two Big Macs, two large fries and a large vanilla shake. He'd considered having a "McDLT"—McDonald's new "lettuce and tomato" burger—but he'd had one before, and not only did it bear no resemblance to the enormous, picture-perfect McDLT shown in the pictures but its packaging was complicated—a Styrofoam tray with two compartments: one for the hot burger half, and one for the cold lettuce, tomato and mayonnaise half, to "keep the cool side cool, and the hot side hot," the ads said.

Shut up, dickweeds.

While Avery wolfed his first Big Mac, Doc, a quasi-germophobe and future dentist, made himself a placemat out of napkins. When his food was precisely arranged on the napkins, Doc unboxed his Quarter Pounder with cheese. He ate the way Avery imagined a dentist would eat—chewing deliberately, ever-vigilant about his teeth.

"Well, thanks for nothing, dude," Doc said.

Avery jammed a straw into his shake. "What did *I* do?"

"Caitlyn's got a boyfriend. Did you know that?"

"I think Penny mentioned it," he said. "They might still have the notes if you want to check the record."

"No, I don't want to '*check the record.*'" Doc picked up some French fries and jabbed them at Avery. "I ought to stop giving you my bio notes."

"Look, Doc, I might be wrong," Avery said, "but Caitlyn strikes me as a girl who devours boyfriends."

"So?"

"So … her boyfriend isn't here, and she might be looking for some fresh"—he pointed at Doc's hamburger—"meat."

Doc paused his chewing. "Good point."

Across the dining area, the girls skipped out of the ladies' room hand-in-hand.

"They're coming," Avery said. "I'll sing your praises to Caitlyn."

"Fine," Doc said. "You still get my notes. For now."

The girls arrived, and Penny motioned to sit next to Avery.

"Uh-uh," Caitlyn said, yanking her off the seat, "*I'm* sitting there." While Caitlyn slid into the booth, Avery put the carton containing Penny's Happy Meal (chicken McNuggets, small French fries, small soda, bag of cookies and a toy) in front of her.

"Where's *my* food, boys?" Caitlyn clapped twice briskly, like she was Cleopatra calling for the next course of a banquet.

"Sorry, Caitlyn," Doc said. "Here."

He pushed a tray across to her. Caitlyn dumped out her fries, tore open ketchup packets with her teeth and smothered the fries in ketchup as she talked. "What were you boys saying about us while we were gone? Hm?" She bumped shoulders with Avery and smirked.

"Nothing," he said. "We were busy foiling a robbery. Doc was, actually." Penny giggled and sucked on her straw. "I'm not kidding," Avery continued. "Three guys tried to hold up the McDonald's, and Holliday here smoked 'em from his seat. Didn't you hear the gunshots from Doc's six-shooter?"

"Ace's full of crap," Doc said.

"Is 'Doc' your real name?" Penny asked him.

"No," he said, "that's Ace's nickname for me. My real name's Steven."

Avery explained that he'd given Steve the nickname of "Doc" because his last name was Holliday, and like the notorious Old West gunslinger "Doc" Holliday, Steven wanted to be a dentist.

"Why do you keep calling Avery 'Ace'?" Caitlyn asked.

Doc looked at him and shrugged. "I don't know. It's what his best friend Lee's always called him."

Caitlyn popped a fry in her mouth and turned to Avery. "Okay, *Ace*—what's the dealie-o?"

"My initials are A-C-C," Avery said. "Three or four years ago at Scout camp, my friend Lee started calling me 'A.C.,' after the character 'T.C.' on *Magnum, P.I.* Then the older guys shortened that to 'Acey,' and then when I got on the tennis court and blasted aces past everybody, it got shortened to 'Ace.'"

"Cool," Caitlyn said. "But what's an ace in tennis?"

"It's when you serve so hard and fast, your opponent can't put his racquet on the ball," Avery said.

"I see." Looking askance at Avery, Caitlyn swiped a fry through a puddle of ketchup and popped it in her mouth. She dusted her fingers and nodded at Doc. "Can Ace do that?"

"Yeah." He nodded at Avery. "Dude, don't you have the school record for aces?"

"Two records," Avery said. "The number of aces in a match and in a season."

"Okay, 'Ace' it is then," Caitlyn said. "But if your initials are A-C-C, what's the middle C stand for?"

Avery smiled and shook his head. "I'll never tell."

"What's it stand for, *Doc*?"

"I don't know. Nobody does."

"Mm, that's okay," Caitlyn said. "I'm sure he told Penny. I'll get it out of her later."

"No, you won't," Penny said.

Caitlyn squinted and smiled at Penny. "Uh, yeah … I will, and you know it." She jutted her chin at Doc. "How do you and Ace know each other?"

"He sits behind me in Bio," Doc said, "and leeches my notes."

"*What* does he do?" Penny asked.

"Ignore him," Avery said.

"Oh, Avery," Penny said, "what's a Quonset hut?"

"It's a metal shelter that looks like a can cut in half lengthwise." Holding the Big Mac in one hand, Avery pulled out a pen and did a quick sketch on a napkin. "The military uses them a lot. My family lives in one. Except for the fact that there are no interior walls, it's super comfortable."

Penny carefully dipped a Chicken McNugget in Sweet 'n Sour sauce. "I can't tell if you're serious or not. Okay, what about grappling hook cannons? Are those real things?"

"Yup," he said. "The Army Rangers used them on D-Day in World War Two, when they scaled the cliffs at Normandy. I want to go there someday. Anyway, the cannons shoot out like a hundred feet of rope with grappling hooks on the end."

"What made you think of them when you were writing the story?"

"I don't know. It's the way my mind works—I'll notice or read some cool detail or mannerism or something, and I'll file it away. Sooner or later, when I'm writing a story or telling one aloud, it comes back to me."

"Doc," Caitlyn said, gesticulating with a French fry, "does Avery have a girlfriend at Hancock? Excuse me, I mean *Ace*."

While Doc and Penny were distracted with her fry-waving hand, Caitlyn slithered her other hand down and caressed Avery's thigh. Avery couldn't believe this was happening and that neither Penny nor Doc noticed it. He was too stunned to stop her.

"No, I don't think so," Steve said, squinting at Avery. "He's reading all the time."

"Reading?" Penny said. "You mean like in class?"

"Yup," Doc said. "He's kind of famous for it. Mr. Crain—that's our bio teacher—every day he asks Ace what he's reading and lets him read."

"I read a lot too," Caitlyn said. "Romance novels mostly." Under the table, she continued to rub his quadriceps muscle. "And what do you read, Ace?"

"Uh, lots of stuff. Fiction mostly."

"So, like, light reading?" Her fingers lightly brushed the inside of his thigh. "Nothing too *hard*?"

Avery took another bite out of his sandwich, reached down subtly with his free hand, and smacked Caitlyn's fingers.

As she smiled and ate her fries, Caitlyn slowly withdrew her hand, slithering it up his thigh and pausing at his groin, where she cupped his bulge and gave it a gentle, lingering squeeze. Startled by her boldness, Avery coughed, and some of his food went down the wrong pipe. Caitlyn dipped more fries in ketchup as Avery coughed.

"Ace, are you choking!?" She thumped him on the back.

A couple worrisome seconds later, Avery finally expelled the chunk into a napkin. He wiped the tears out of his eyes and glared at Caitlyn. She smirked and shrugged.

Penny reached for him across the table. "Are you okay?"

"Yeah, I'll be all right," Avery said.

A pudgy teacher with a mustache—the one who had halted Avery and Caitlyn's dance on the bus—walked from table to table, his eyes fixed on a clipboard. He stopped in front of their booth.

"Bus leaves in ten minutes, people," he said. "Finish up and get outside for attendance."

"Yes, Mr. Nelson," Penny said. "We will."

"Thanks, sweetheart," he said. "Keep these miscreants in line."

Penny's eyebrows clenched. "Miscreants?"

By the smug expression on the man's face, Avery could tell that Mr. Nelson thought he had a profound vocabulary, and, like Avery's adult nemesis—his geometry teacher Mr. Knox—he enjoyed lording it over his teenage students. Avery decided to take the guy down a notch.

"Troublemakers, Penny." Avery closed his eyes and saw synonyms for the word in his mind. "Also known as 'scoundrels,' 'malefactors,' 'reprobates' or 'lowlifes.'" He swallowed and squinted at the teacher. "Are you saying Caitlyn, Steven, and I are *lowlifes*, Mister Nelson? Because that hardly seems fair. You don't know us. And by the way, sir, you shouldn't call your female students 'sweetheart.' Some of them might take offense."

Mr. Nelson sucked his cheek and walked away. Caitlyn gave Avery a playful nudge in the ribs.

"Whoa, check out *Ace*! Droppin' the righteous vocab. Bet you wailed on the P-S-A-T's."

"The Verbal section I did," he said.

"Awesome." Caitlyn nudged him. "I'm *so* glad you showed him up like that. I can't stand that porker. Thinks he's so smart."

"Well, *I'm* not glad about it," Penny said. "I have Mr. Nelson for Social Studies, Caitlyn—you don't."

Avery sighed. "He won't be upset with you for something I said."

"He might." Penny gazed across the food court and glanced at her watch. "Whatever. I have to use the bathroom again."

"Same here," Doc said. "I hate the one on the bus."

"I know," Penny said, "it smells awful."

Caitlyn glanced at Avery. "It wouldn't be if these guys knew how to *aim*."

"Eww, Caitlyn … gross," Penny said.

You Passed the Test

When Penny and Steve walked away toward the bathrooms, Avery opened his second Big Mac. He glared at Caitlyn.

"What the hell was that!?"

"What was what?" She pouted and opened her eyes wide. They were sparkly gray. He'd never seen a person with gray eyes before, and they were so striking that he almost forgot what he wanted to say.

"Before," he said. "Molesting me under the table like that. I could have choked to death, you … you…"—he was about to say "bitch" when a better insult came to him—"…nymphomaniac!"

She scowled. "'Nymphomaniac'?! What the hell is that?"

"A woman with abnormal or extreme sexual desire," he said. "It's *not* a compliment."

"Oh come on, you're fine." She grabbed a drinking straw and slammed her fist down on the tabletop, stripping the paper wrapper off the straw. She shoved the straw through the slot on her soda cup lid, took a long suck, and let out a long "ahhhhh!" Putting down her drink, she said, "Let's be clear about something. The only reason you didn't choke is because *I* saved you."

"Well," Avery said, "if you hadn't grabbed my crotch, I wouldn't have choked. But never mind that. Why'd you do it?"

She rolled her eyes. "Do I have to say it? I think you're cute. I liked dancing with you. Didn't you like it?"

"Sure, and I think you're super pretty, Caitlyn, but you don't see me trying to squeeze your *boobs*."

Caitlyn glanced at the bathroom doors, pivoted in her seat, and leaned against his side. One of her breasts grazed his ribs.

"Maybe you should," she said. "They're *very* nice."

Her words, spoken while her breast was squished against him, made him tremble. His breath faltered.

"Caitlyn, you can't do this."

She put her lips close to his ear and twirled her fingers in Avery's hair. "Penny wouldn't have to know. This is a sucky trip for me. Me and my boyfriend are fighting and—"

"It's 'my boyfriend and I are fighting.'" Avery recoiled from her. "Never mind … move, I'm leaving."

Avery grabbed his coat and bag and slid to the side, shoving Caitlyn bodily out of the booth. When he was standing, he put on his coat, threw his bag over his shoulder, and stuffed the rest of his food into a McDonald's bag.

"Caitlyn, you're gorgeous," he said, "but I like Penny, and I don't want to mess things up with her. Can't you understand that? I mean … you're her best friend, and you've already got a boyfriend. Why are you hitting on me?"

Caitlyn's lips curled into a smile. Her nose wrinkled.

"Congratulations, Ace. You just passed the test."

"What test?"

"'The best friend comes on to you, and you turn her down test,'" she said. "Now I don't have to worry about you cheating on her."

"All right, but what do you mean by *cheating* on her? I just met her. All we've done so far is hold hands."

"Look, Ace, I've never seen her like this before. She's totally smitten with you, I can tell."

This surprised him. "You think so?"

"Mm-hm. I have a good feeling about you two."

Caitlyn slipped on her coat—a Navy peacoat covered with rock band badges: AC/DC, Joan Jett & The Blackhearts, Duran Duran, Heart, Mötley Crüe, Loverboy, The Tubes, The Police, Rush and many smaller ones that Avery couldn't read. They were fabric patches like the ones on his Scout uniform. The largest one, "VH," was the unmistakable logo for Van Halen.

She approached and was about to slide in next to him again, but Avery shook his head. Caitlyn pouted and plopped down across from him. Avery had hoped that Penny and Doc would be back by now, but there was no sign of them. Caitlyn was smirking at him but not saying anything.

"Van Halen, huh?" Avery pointed at the badge. "They're my favorite band."

"Yeah, they were mine too," she said. "But not anymore."

They looked at each other and said, "Sammy Hagar."

They sighed and shared a nod; in their love of the old Van Halen and their hatred of the band's new front man, they were comrades.

"Yeah," he said, "I know what you mean. They're coming out with a new album next month. Not only am I *not* buying it, I'm not even listening to the songs on the radio. I don't want my ears getting infected with stupid Sammy Hagar."

"Exactly," she said. "I hate him. I hate his *face*. But let's not talk about it. Van Halen is dead to me now."

Robot Assassin

For the rest of the bus ride to Washington, D.C., during the long wait in the lobby of the Bethesda Colonnade while they were checking in, and while unpacking his bag and exploring the hotel, Avery Craig's brain was engulfed in a fog: his first opiate-like feelings for a girl—Penny Aston—as well as scalding pangs of lust for another girl—Caitlyn.

That first night, the teachers and chaperones threw the students a pizza party in a hotel meeting room. Avery and Penny ate with Caitlyn and Doc, and then the hotel staff wheeled in a giant projection TV and arranged the chairs into rows, converting the meeting room into an *ad hoc* movie theater. Avery and most of the other students cheered when they learned what movie the teachers were showing that night: *The Terminator*, in which a robot assassin travels from the future to kill the mother of the unborn leader of the human resistance. It was a movie Avery had seen four times since it came out in 1984; he was astonished the teachers and parent chaperones were showing it.

He and Penny sat near the front and held hands. Five minutes into the film, when the naked Terminator (played by bodybuilder Arnold Schwarzenegger) says to a group of hooligans, "Your clothes. Give them to me," and then kills them, Penny whispered that she'd never seen the movie and that it was much more violent than she'd expected. She rested her head on Avery's shoulder and let him put his arm around her. He loved feeling petite Penny beneath his arm—so warm, so soft, so dainty. He couldn't believe his good fortune: a dark room, a sci-fi action movie, a bag of strawberry Twizzlers licorice, and a pretty, sweet-smelling girl snuggled against him. He could have died at that moment and died happy. Penny cowered against him through most of the movie. (Thank you, director James Cameron!)

Afterwards, the teachers reminded the students that tomorrow was a full day. Since they would be visiting several sites and needed to sleep, lights-out was at ten o'clock sharp. Penny and Avery squeezed each other's hands goodnight and went back to their rooms.

Of Course It's Water

At 10:30 P.M., Doc and Avery were in their room with the lights out. Doc was asleep, but Avery—keyed-up to a fever pitch by the attention today from girls—was doing his bedtime push-ups and crunches on the floor in the darkness, trying to exhaust himself and clear the fog out of this head. He had finished his 100th pushup when the phone rang.

Doc sprang up in bed and answered it. He handed the phone to Avery. There was screeching and giggling over the line; Penny and Caitlyn squealed that there was a water fight on their floor. They gave their room number and asked Ace and Doc to hurry upstairs. Avery said he'd be right there and hung up.

"What's going on?" Doc asked.

"Water fight." Avery grabbed his clothes. "Come on, the girls need us."

"Caitlyn asked for me?"

"She said, 'Get up here, guys!' C'mon, Doc—let's go."

Avery looked around for a weapon suitable for a water fight. In his suitcase was a Hefty trash bag for ♫"Dirty Laundry."♫ He ran into the bathroom with it, turned on the tub faucet full blast, and put the bag under the spout. Doc came in, squinting against the bright light.

"I don't know, Ace," he said. "We could get sent home, man."

"Stay here then. I'm going," Avery said. "If those clowns want a water fight, I'll give them one."

When Avery shut off the faucet, the garbage bag was heavy— like three gallons. *Nice.* Twisting and knotting the bag shut, he slung it over his shoulder, slowly opened the door to the hallway, and slipped out.

The hallway was empty, but there were teachers' voices coming from the stairwell nearest his room. With his bare feet soundless on the carpet, and the bag of water sloshing on his back, he jogged to the other end of the hall. He went into the stairwell and lunged up the stairs two at a time. He doubted Penny was in any real danger, but he wanted to rescue her anyway.

The girls' room was on the corner of the building. There was a commotion at the far end of the long hallway—boys, wielding squirt guns, chasing girls around—but this part of the floor was quiet. The girls' door was open.

Avery knocked on the doorjamb and leaned inside. When Penny and Caitlyn ran to the door, they were wearing pajama bottoms and T-shirts, and their T-shirts were soaked across the chest. It was a pleasant sight to behold, and Avery happily beheld it. He loudly cleared his throat.

"So … what's this about a water fight?"

Caitlyn's eyes widened. She put her fists on her hips. "Some guys from our school brought squirt guns."

Penny stood silently with her arms crossed over her chest until she looked around Avery's shoulder.

"Avery, what's that on your back?" A startled look came over her face. "Is that a bag of *water?!*"

"Of course it's water," Caitlyn said. "We called and said there was a water fight up here. You cried 'help,' and Ace brought *water.* What did you think he would do? You can be a major dipstick sometimes, Penny."

"Easy, Caitlyn," Avery said. "Be nice."

The floor shook with heavy footsteps, and a fat kid clomped around the corner brandishing a rifle-sized squirt gun. He was the kind of tubby kid a loving mother would euphemize as "big-boned" or "husky"—even though he had man-boobs that undulated under his T-shirt. He neared Avery and the girls, raising the gun. The girls squealed and ducked behind Avery. Tubby halted a safe distance away, made a goofy grin, squirted Avery five times in the face and shirt, and ran back around the corner. Avery started after him when Penny grabbed his arm and pleaded with him not to get in a fight. Standing behind Penny, Caitlyn gave Avery a sympathetic eyeroll, winked at him, and went back into the room. Tubby's unexpected assault had made Avery's adrenaline spike, but when he looked at Penny, her face was so angelic that Avery couldn't defy her.

"Okay, I won't. For you."

"Thank you, Avery."

She bounced on her tiptoes and kissed his cheek. Her lips touched his skin only for an eyeblink, but the warmth of them caused Avery's heart to pound.

"See you in the morning. Good night." She smiled again as she closed the door.

Successful Ambush

Avery sauntered back toward the stairwell in a trance. Yes, he would return to his room and forget about this foolish water fight business. Penny must really like him; she'd kissed him out of nowhere!

As soon as Avery got the heavy fire door open, Tubby rounded the corner at the far end of the long hallway. His squirt gun rifle dripped on the carpet; his eyes darted around; he was hunting for a fresh victim.

When their eyes met, Tubby accelerated down the hall, the floor pounding with every footfall. Avery considered his promise to Penny for all of a nanosecond before deciding to take Tubby down.

Having read so many espionage novels and watched every episode of *MacGyver* and *The A-Team*, Avery knew how to pull off a successful ambush. Backing into the stairwell, he chuckled to himself. Tubby would never see this coming. Once he was in the stairwell with the door clicked shut, Avery positioned himself in the corner of the landing, about six feet from the door. Heaving the Hefty bag off his shoulder, he swung it like a pendulum. He kept swinging it as he waited.

By the time the door banged open and Tubby rushed in, Avery had a sweet arc going. Tubby was peering over the railing when he spotted Avery. He was swinging around and raising the squirt gun to his shoulder when Avery let the Hefty bag fly. The undulating, amorphous blob sailed across the landing and collided with Tubby's chest. The squirt gun barrel pierced the Hefty bag, drenching him, and the impact slammed Tubby into the railing on the wall. He collapsed to the floor.

"You jerk," Tubby croaked. "I'll kill you."

"Nighty-night, dickweed."

Avery stepped over him and padded downstairs whistling the theme to *The A-Team*. Just as he was exiting the stairwell, Mr. Nelson's voice echoed from above: "What happened to you?" Avery silently shut the stairwell door and sauntered into an alcove that had vending machines in it. Exuberant with victory, he got himself a bag of Doritos and a Coke Classic and returned to his room. Doc met him inside.

"What happened?" he asked.

Avery sipped his Coke and thought hard for a good line. He wanted to say something witty like Bond's line in the *Goldfinger* teaser: "Shocking … positively shocking," but nothing came to him. After another sip of Coke, he shrugged.

"Let me put it this way, Doc. It was soaking. Positively soaking."

5

∽

THE NEXT morning, Avery awoke at five o'clock. Between Penny, Caitlyn, and the anticipation of his first day in the nation's capital, he'd been so wound-up that he'd barely slept. Back home, he regularly woke around this time to work out before school, but this morning he *had* to work out so he could burn off some of his excess energy. Avery put on workout clothes and splashed water on his face; grabbed his Walkman, headphones and jump rope; and went down to the hotel gym.

By any fitness enthusiast's standards, the "gym" was a total joke: an ancient treadmill, a rickety-looking rowing machine, and one of those bizarre, useless stationary bikes with handles, where you simultaneously pedaled on pedals and hauled on handles to power a giant fan. The place looked like photos he'd seen of the gymnasium on the *Titanic*.[11]

A pull-up bar jutted from the wall, and heaped in a dusty corner were a stretching mat, a medicine ball, and two 10-pound dumbbells. Ugh. His makeshift gym at home was better than this. Avery put his things down and started with pull-ups. He leapt, grabbed the bar with his palms facing himself, and cranked out twenty. Then he tossed down the stretching mat, put on his Walkman and moved on to crunches and push-ups. He'd brought several cassette tapes on the trip, but this morning he played "ACE'S ULTIMATE WORKOUT MIX,"

---

[11] The enormous "unsinkable" transatlantic ocean liner sank in April 1912. In 1985, its wreck was found on the ocean bottom by Robert Ballard and a team of undersea explorers.

which included high-energy songs like ♫"Panama," "Got Me Under Pressure," "Immigrant Song," and "Eye of the Tiger."♫

He was finishing a set of fifty push-ups, his triceps quivering, when two images flashed into his head: Caitlyn cupping his groin under the rest stop table, and how incredible her breasts had looked in that soaked T-shirt last night. He got a burst of energy and kept going. He pushed himself to sixty-two push-ups and collapsed.

After catching his breath, Avery used his new jump rope, then moved on to the rowing machine, strapping his feet in and rowing as hard as he could. There was a fan attached to the machine's flywheel, and with each pull on the handle chain, the fan revolved faster and faster, making a pleasant breeze and a satisfying buzzing sound. Every fifth or sixth stroke, the machine made a mysterious click, but he ignored it and kept going. By the time four songs finished playing, the sweat was pouring down his face. His back, shoulders, biceps, and forearms were on fire and his palms were slick with sweat. Still, he kept thrusting with his legs and heaving on the handle with all his strength, striving with each stroke to make the fan buzz louder: *Wuhhzzzzz. Wuhhzzzzzzzzzz! WUHHHHZZZZZZZZZZZZZZ!*

Then ♫"Overture (*Rocky II*)"♫ came over his headphones. Avery hadn't listened to this mixtape in a while, and he'd forgotten this song was on here. With the swelling orchestral music blasting in his ears, Avery imagined he was rowing against another scull, one rowed by Tubby, and the prize in their race was Penny. Avery pulled harder on the rowing handle. No way was he losing to that fat turd. Then Tubby became Eddie—a bully from Avery's past, a bully he would have to confront this fall, when the douche graduated to Hancock. God, how he wished that sawed-off were here. As strong as he now was, Avery could kill Eddie with a single punch to the windpipe.

There was that mysterious click again, and then, all at once, the chain snapped, and Avery careened backwards on the rowing seat. Because his feet were strapped in, when the seat reached the end of the slide, his torso hinged violently at the waist, and his back and head hit the floor behind the machine. Avery's Walkman and headphones flew off, but somehow he managed to hold on to the rowing handle. He sat up, unstrapped his feet, and snaked the broken chain back into the machine housing. He balanced the handle precariously on its holder and picked up his Walkman and headphones.

Helsinki Women

After he showered and dressed back in his room, Avery grabbed his bag and went down to the lobby. He sat on a sofa facing the elevators, so he'd see Penny and Caitlyn when they came down. A house phone sat on the end table beside him, and he considered calling them.

No, they were still sleeping, or getting ready. Avery imagined Penny standing in a towel, her shoulders steamy wet from her shower, a second towel wrapped in a turban around her head, holding two outfits against her chest and asking Caitlyn's opinion on which one she should wear today. Speaking of outfits, Avery hoped his own looked all right. He was wearing a typical winter school getup: Nikes, Levi's, an AC/DC "Back in Black" long-sleeved T-shirt, his new forest green commando sweater, his vintage leather bomber jacket with the fleece around the collar, and his trusty musette bag over his shoulder. The reason he was unsure of himself was that most of the Vanderbush guys were more stylishly dressed, with their neon ski jackets, Izod Lacoste polo shirts, and Ray Ban sunglasses.

He glanced at the revolving doors. It was getting light out. He got up and walked outside. Dark clouds were gathering to the west, but the temperature was in the 40s. It would rain later, not snow, and Avery hadn't brought an umbrella.

Inside at the front desk was a woman with a pearl complexion and shimmery coal-black hair—shoulder-length and straight, with her bangs cut straight across. A radio on the credenza behind her was softly playing the recent hit ♫"Rock Me Amadeus,"♫ and the woman was swaying to the beat. She was in her late 20s and exotic-looking. In all, she was the most beautiful flesh and blood woman he'd ever seen. Such gorgeousness definitely merited closer inspection.

She wore a cobalt blue and gold dress, with two rows of gold buttons down the front, and wide, thick shoulder pads that gave her a somewhat stiff carriage, like the android chick in *Blade Runner*. Her name tag read, "IRINA," and she was staring at the countertop, writing something. Recalling Penny's comment that he had "amazing eyes," Avery rested his forearms on the counter and opened his eyes wide.

"Good morning, Irina," he said.

However mesmerizing Avery's eyes might have been, Irina's—wide-set and glacier blue—trumped his entirely. She fixed hers on his and smiled. It was like he'd been blinded by the sun. He looked away.

"Yes, young man," she said, "how may I help you?"

Avery pointed at the revolving doors and asked if she knew today's weather forecast.

"Rain," she said. "Heavy at times."

She shook her pen, frowned, and muttered something in a language Avery didn't understand. While she was looking for another one, Avery produced a click ballpoint pen from his bag and handed it to her.

"Thank you, young man."

"The name's Craig, Avery Craig, but my friends call me 'Ace.'" He grinned. "I'm here with the group from New York."

"It is nice to meet you, Ace." She narrowed her eyes. "I hear about water fight last night. You are involved in this?"

This woman was at least ten years older than him and stunning. Since she was way out of his league, Avery decided to let fly with the flirting.

"Absolutely not. Those were *boys* from Vanderbush, and as you said yourself, I'm a young man. We Hancock guys are much more mature."

She raised an eyebrow. "Oh?"

"Yes, well, at least I am. More self-disciplined too. I was working out in your gym at five o'clock."

She looked him over with a faint smile on her lips. "This I believe. You are, how they say, well-built."

Avery rolled his eyes down her chest. "You're pretty well-built yourself."

She sniggered and wagged a finger at him.

"Irina, I need to ask a favor," he said. "Does the hotel have an umbrella I can borrow? I need a big one, like a golf umbrella—one big enough for two or three people."

"I see," she said. "One large enough to fit you and your many girlfriends?" She winked, the floodgate opened between his legs, and a rodney sprouted down his pant leg. Thankfully, he was standing close to the high counter, so Irina wouldn't spot it.

"Hmm," she said, tapping her forefinger against her lips, "we host insurance convention last week, and the company gives away big red umbrellas. I think we have some left over. I check."

Avery crossed his fingers as he watched her walk into the office. Her legs were long and shapely, and the skirt of her dress fit her like a (lucky) second skin. Across the lobby, the elevator dinged. Some students got off and shambled toward the dining room for breakfast.

Irina minced out of the office hiding something behind her back. With a flourish, she raised it toward the ceiling. It was a red umbrella about four feet long, so Avery knew it would be huge when opened. Irina's eyes were wide and full of merriment.

"Travelers Insurance," she said. "The last one."

She sidled up to the counter and held the umbrella out to him flat across her palms, like it was King Arthur's sword, Excalibur. Avery took hold of it by the handle and brandished it under the bright overhead lights.

"Thank you, Irina. It's perfect."

She put a hand on the counter and drummed her fingertips on the marble. Her nails were bright red and meticulously manicured. "I am— how you say?—green with envy?" She glanced at the lobby windows and pouted. "You will be seeing the sights while I am stuck inside."

Avery shrugged. "Well … you could always play hooky."

"'Hooky'? You mean 'hooker'—to be prostitute!?"

"No, no," he said. "'Hooky' means to skip school or work. Mark Twain coined the word, I believe."

She gave him a vaguely panicked look. "Mark Twain?"

"The great American writer?" Avery said. "Wrote *Tom Sawyer* and *Huckleberry Finn*?"

She shook her head.

"I take it you're not from the United States," he said.

She lowered her eyes. "Finland. I have green card to work here. My English is not so good."

"You speak better English than many Americans." Avery recalled the tiny bit he knew about Finland from a *World Book* encyclopedia entry. "Where in Finland are you from? Helsinki?"

"Yes!" She beamed. "You have been?"

"No, but I've heard it's a beautiful city." *Icebreaker*, the Bond novel he was reading, was set in Finland. "And I've read that Helsinki women are the most beautiful in the world."

Irina's ivory cheeks and neck turned pink. She giggled and tossed some hair over her shoulder. Avery leaned over the counter and whispered.

"If you decide to play hooky today," he said, "I'd be happy to squeeze you under the umbrella with me."

Irina grinned. "Have fun with your girlfriends, Ace."

Looking Good, Louis

Across the lobby, an elevator dinged. Avery hustled back there with the umbrella and plopped himself down on the sofa. A pair of businessmen carrying suitcases stepped off chatting and strolled around the corner toward the phone booths. When Penny finally got down here, he wanted to look casual. He wanted her to think that she was the furthest thing from his mind, when in actuality he'd done nothing *but* think about her since last night.

Avery took out the paperback of *Icebreaker*. He leaned back against the sofa armrest, stretched his legs out with his ankles crossed, and read his book. In no time he was transported to MI6 in London, where Bond was getting his new assignment.

Avery read a few pages before the elevator dinged and two guys from his Honors Social Studies class stepped off: Eric Park and Louis Zane. Avery and Eric traded silent nods of respect; Avery respected Eric because at 16, the prodigious Korean-American was an accomplished concert violinist and on track to become the class valedictorian. Louis he respected because not only was he a smart, good-looking guy (he resembled black comedian Eddie Murphy) but he was an impeccable dresser. Today Louis wore shiny tasseled loafers, jeans, an Oxford shirt and tie under a sweater vest, a navy-blue blazer, and, capping off the outfit, a fedora. They gave each other their usual once-over and went through a familiar ritual, quoting lines from the comedy *Trading Places*. Avery nodded at his natty classmate.

"Looking good, Louis."

"Feeling good, Ace."

Years ago, Louis had looked at Avery in such a way to suggest that he liked boys, and that he might have a crush on Avery. The first time it happened, back in seventh grade, it unnerved Avery, but after that he decided it didn't matter. So *what* if Louis liked boys, and so what if he found Avery attractive? Avery knew that he himself only liked girls, that he had no interest in Louis that way. Besides, secretly Avery was a little flattered; Louis Zane was among the best-looking guys at Hancock.

Another elevator dinged, and Doc stepped off with a group of other Hancock honors students. They were all huddled around the girl Avery had seen yesterday—the one with the raspberry beret. They were watching her manipulate a Rubik's Cube blindingly fast.[12]

A Staggering Treasure Trove

One of the guys was checking his watch as she twisted the sides and rotated the cube in her hands. She paused briefly, then resumed her manipulations faster. Five seconds later, she'd solved it; each side of the cube (which was comprised of nine smaller squares) was a solid color: red, yellow, blue, or orange.

"Thirty-one seconds," said the kid with the watch.

"Awesome," Doc said.

With a faint smile, the girl tossed the Rubik's Cube to a boy and adjusted her glasses. "Not my best time, but I'll take it."

Avery smiled and waved broadly at the girl; she smiled and waved broadly back.

"Ace," Doc said, "you know Gemma Jones, don't you?"

Gemma. That was her name.

"Come on, Doc—of course I know Gemma," Avery said. "We went to Van Wilder together."

---

[12] A multicolored 3-D combination puzzle, the Rubik's Cube was invented in 1974 by Hungarian sculptor and professor of architecture Ernő Rubik. It was immensely popular worldwide during the 1980s.

"Hi, Avery."

"Hi, Gem." A Canon 35mm camera hung from a strap around her neck. He gestured at it. "What's the deal there?"

"Photography is a hobby of mine," she said. "I'm in the Yearbook club, so I'm getting photos of the trip for the yearbook."

"Cool."

The guys walked away. Gemma followed them, smiling at Avery over her shoulder.

"Bye, Avery," she said.

"Bye, Gemma."

A moment later, the elevators dinged again. Avery held his breath, hoping Penny would be on this car, and was disappointed when the doors opened and the two most annoying teachers' pets in his class flounced into the lobby: the pretentious class treasurer Kristen Brooks and the haughty and humorless West German exchange student Johanna Glück. At nearly 6'0", Johanna was the star player on Hancock's women's volleyball team, and taller than most of the boys in the class—but not Avery.

When she had come to Hancock in September, Avery had found her attractive: her long tawny hair, her svelte athletic body, and her piercing eyes. But not anymore. As the two best debaters in their section of Honors Social Studies, Avery and Johanna routinely took opposing sides during class discussions and became bitter rivals. Outside of class, Johanna gushed incessantly about West Germany's superiority to the United States. She would wag her lush hair around and brag about her father (a vice president of Volkswagen) and how much more advanced her high school in Germany was compared to Hancock. Unwilling to tolerate further bashing of his school or country, one day in class Avery retorted, "I'll tell you one thing Germany isn't superior in, and that's war. We crushed you—*twice*. And the next time Germany gets uppity, we'll level your entire country." This had triggered jingoistic fist-pumps and chants of "ooh-ooh-ooh!" among his classmates. The conceited West German was silent for days.

After that, Avery needled Johanna by speaking in a cartoonish German accent when she was around, but it soon stopped being funny, so he took his pestering up a notch. Over Christmas break, while watching the German dialogue scenes in the movie *Patton*, Avery had gotten an idea. Borrowing some German language tapes from the library, he memorized two dozen German non sequiturs to annoy her with.

Avery put down his book. He hadn't done this to Johanna since early January, right after Christmas break, so it would totally blindside her. His and Johanna's eyes met as she and Kristen strolled past his sofa. Avery opened his mouth and was about to bark at her in German when he realized that without his classmates around to see it, the whole thing would be wasted. Better to wait until he had an audience.

"*Guten Morgen*, Ace," Johanna said warily.

When he saw a whisper of a smile on her face, Avery gave her a gossamer smile of his own, adding, "Good morning, ladies."

Johanna rolled her eyes; the girl couldn't help herself. She whispered to Kristen, and the two strolled away.

One of the elevators dinged, the doors opened, and a carful of rowdy Vanderbush guys jostled out, elbowing each other, laughing, swearing. A male Eastern Airlines pilot and stewardesses holding cups of coffee waited to board the elevator. In his uniform and cap, the pilot commanded respect. He scowled at the Vanderbush boys and said, "Settle down, fellas. There are women present. This is a hotel, not a locker room." The guys went silent. The pilot held the elevator door, waved the women aboard, then boarded himself. The second the doors closed, a Vanderbush guy said, "Settle down, fellas! This is a hotel, not a strip club!" They laughed and swaggered down the hall. *Vanderdouches.*

Avery was reading his book when snickering and shushing sounds echoed down the hallway. The Vanderbush guys were huddled around an open doorway down the hall from the front desk. The doorway had a Dutch door with the bottom half of the door closed, and the guys were checking the hall, then peering over the lower door. They reminded Avery of the guys in the movie *Porky's*, who peep into the girls' showers. Whatever they were gawking at, it was captivating enough that they were shoving each other for a look. Avery closed his book and hustled down the hall to investigate.

When he reached the huddle, the group's leader—a string bean of a kid wearing a junior varsity basketball letter jacket—nudged Avery and whispered loudly, "Vamoose, *Hand*cock. We were here first."

"Let me look," Avery said, "or I'll report you Vander*douches* to the hotel manager."

The leader groaned; his exhaled breath caused Avery to recoil. The guy hadn't brushed his teeth this morning—if ever.

"Fine … a quick look," Stringbean said, "then beat it."

He snapped his fingers and gestured for the other guys to make a hole; they stepped aside. The doorway Avery was looking through had an unobstructed view into the office behind the front desk. In a flash, Avery understood why the Vanderbush leader was guarding the find so jealously.

Not twenty feet away, Irina stood in front of a Xerox machine with her back to the doorway. Her butt in the snug cobalt dress was facing them, a small boombox on the credenza was playing ♫"Legs,"♫ and she was wagging her butt to the music. She wore dark stockings and a pair of red stiletto heels. It was clear that, between the music and the photocopier noise, Irina couldn't hear anything behind her.

As the song continued, Irina's butt-shaking became outright sexy dancing—her bending over and retrieving pages from the photocopier tray, dancing to the side to collate and staple the pages, swinging her hips and shimmying her torso to the music, then dancing back to retrieve more pages and so on. It was incredibly sexy because she seemed to have no idea they were watching.

One of them whispered over Avery's shoulder: "Oh … my … *God*. See you at breakfast, guys." He broke out of the huddle and booked it down the hall and into the men's room.[13] The kid's buddies snickered knowingly.

---

[13] "Booking," a slang term for leaving or departing quickly, was popular in the '80s for some reason, used in sentences like the following: "Sorry, dude, can't stay; gotta book." Often the word "it" was added to the verb to form some variation of "book it," like the following: "I saw him earlier, booking it down the hall" or "Come on, Jane—we've gotta book it, or we'll be late!"

Ace the Fashion Cop

Irina danced a new stack of pages to the collating station, straightened, and stapled them. Then, shimmying her hips, she raised her hands, treating Avery and the other guys to her ten long, pristinely polished, shiny red fingernails. During that brief interval, while Irina danced to ZZ Top's space-age guitar licks, Avery and the Vanderbush boys ceased to be archenemies and became instead a brotherhood of admirers of womanly beauty. Stringbean poked Avery between the shoulder blades.

"All right, man—time's up."

"Sure." Avery spied a phone on the wall near the copier. He backed away from the doorway. "But I've got a question for you."

Stringbean resumed his position in the center of the doorway and stared over the Dutch door. "Yeah, what?"

"Do you plan on brushing your teeth this morning?" Avery said. "Because dude … your breath *stinks*."

His buddies sniggered.

"Shut up, *Hand*cock," he said. "Now get lost."

Avery smiled and strolled back to the sofa by the elevators. He picked up the house phone, dialed the hotel operator and asked for the office behind the front desk.

"Bethesda Colonnade, front office. Irina Vacker speaking. How may I help you?"

"Legs" and the clacking of the photocopier made a racket over the line. Avery identified himself and said there was a group of Vanderbush boys watching her this very moment. There was a brief ruckus by her doorway, and then the entire band of them ran past him. None of them noticed Avery lounging on the sofa, talking on the phone. Irina asked him how he knew they were peeking in at her, and Avery described where he was—on a sofa near the elevators, with a view of the hallway.

"I see," she said. "And did *you* watch me at all?"

"No way. I'm a gentleman."

She lowered her voice and said, "I would not mind if you did."

"Well … I *glanced*."

"And what did you think?" she asked. "Am I good dancer? I love the American rock-n-roll. I never hear that song before."

"That was 'Legs' by a rockin' little band from Texas called ZZ Top," he said.

"'Legs,' Texas, Zee-Zee Top," she repeated solemnly.

"And as for whether you're a good dancer, you're better than the girls in the music video, that's for sure."

The banter with Irina was venturing into foreign territory, but Avery, ever the fearless, aspiring explorer, ignored his fears and boldly forged ahead. He paused, then added, "The models in the video—you're sexier than them too, Irina. *Much* sexier."

Irina giggled. "Ace, I am hotel employee, so it is not proper for me to say so, but … you are most charming and handsome young man. Your girlfriends are most lucky."

The elevator in front of Avery's sofa dinged.

Avery had gotten so caught up in flirting with Irina that he forgot he was waiting for Penny. Every muscle in his body tensed. The doors opened and three Vanderbush dudes in ski jackets stepped off, followed by Caitlyn and Penny. The girls were laughing as the guys walked away. Avery flushed under his sweater. It looked like they were laughing at something the Vanderbush guys had said.

Penny was beautiful—even more beautiful than when she kissed him at her door last night. Her face glowed, her eyes glittered, and her perfectly color-coordinated outfit gleamed. She wore a pink argyle sweater, a short pink skirt, pink argyle socks and flats, and an oversized pink argyle bow at an oblique angle on her head. Avery's throat cinched; his breath faltered.

"Hello, Ace?" Irina said over the phone. "Are you there?"

Avery stared at Penny until he became aware he was staring, then shifted his gaze to a spot on the ceiling. He cleared his throat and spoke loudly into the phone. Without saying her name, he told Irina that "Legs" was on ZZ Top's *Eliminator* album. He said he had an extra cassette he could give her and that he'd swing by and give it to her later.

Caitlyn ribbed Penny. "Check out Ace—the wheeler-dealer."

"Thank you," Irina said over the phone. "I love all things American. Have wonderful day. I enjoy talking to you, Ace."

"We'll talk later," he said. "Have a great day yourself."

Avery hung up and grinned. "Good morning, ladies. Who's ready for breakfast? I know I am. I've been up since five, working out." He put his book away, grabbed the umbrella and stood. "You look beautiful, Penny. I love your outfit."

She grinned. "Thank y—"

"Hey," Caitlyn screeched, "what about *my* outfit?!"

Nudging Penny aside, Caitlyn twirled in front of Avery, put her hands on her waist, and shimmied like she was dancing to ♫"Into the Groove."♫ She was the spitting image of Madonna in last summer's *Desperately Seeking Susan*: a black headscarf tied in a bow on her head, a dangling crucifix earring, a sheer crop-topped blouse that showed her midriff and flaunted a black bra underneath, a black miniskirt and black fishnet tights, and black boots.

"Penny thinks it's too sexy," she said, "that the teachers will make me change. What do *you* think, Ace?"

She twirled again, and with one hand on her head and the other on her waist, she wiggled her hips. Avery gulped. He wished he could tell her the unvarnished truth—that her outfit made him want to do her in a phone booth down the hall. But with Penny here, he had to be a bit more restrained in his reply.

"I think it's a bold outfit that will give some guys whiplash," he said. "But Penny's right—it might be a tad too sexy. And cold. It's only like forty degrees outside, Caitlyn. You're wearing a coat today, right?"

"Yes, I'm wearing a coat … *Dad*." Caitlyn huffed and nudged Penny. "I'll go get us a table so you can be alone with Ace the Fashion Cop." She sneered at him.

"Okay," Penny said.

"Don't be angry, Caitlyn," Avery said. "Your outfit is awesome. I was only being honest."

"Whatever." Caitlyn smirked, playfully bumped him with her butt, and sashayed down the hall. Avery turned around so he wouldn't ogle her ass as she walked away.

"Don't let her bother you," Penny said. "That's just how Caitlyn is. She always wants to be the center of attention."

"I'm figuring that out." He took Penny's hand. "It's so nice to see you. You look beautiful today. Did you sleep well?"

"Thanks. Yes, okay, I think."

She yawned. Her yawn was adorable, and Avery would have liked to have seen it again.

"I had trouble getting to sleep," she said, "and then Caitlyn was on the phone with Shane at six this morning."

Avery asked who Shane was, and Penny explained that he was Caitlyn's boyfriend. He couldn't come on the trip, so he was calling the hotel constantly to check on her.

Avery took a moment to appreciate how small and delicate Penny's hands were. "I couldn't get to sleep last night either." He brushed the hair away from her ear, leaned close and whispered, "All I could think about was you."

Penny stared at the floor, then raised her eyes slowly to him. "I dreamed about you."

An Impossibly Tight Squeeze

The elevator dinged and all at once a group of gabbing teenage girls swarmed into the lobby. Penny yanked her hands out of Avery's and took a step back.

"Pennn-eeeeee!" said one of the girls. "Who's your boyfriend?"

Penny blushed. Her hands bunched into fists. A heavyset girl stepped to the front of the brood. She had dark eyeshadow applied across her eyes in such thick streaks, she looked like an overweight superhero wearing a mask.

"Hey, Hancock! What's your name?!"

"Hancock," Avery replied. "My parents named me after the school. Smart, right?"

Penny and a few of the other girls chuckled.

"No, for real," Eyeshadow said. "What's your name?"

"Zeb."

"Okay, Zeb. You two made out yet?"

"Sorry, girls, that's private."

A skinny brunette beside Eyeshadow looked over her shoulder at the others. "Oooh, it's *private*. Little Penny's got a boyfriend!"

The girls laughed, and Penny glowered at them as they sauntered away. Avery sensed that he'd just seen a preview of Penny's temper—a scary 8′, 800-pound Sasquatch that hid inside a pretty 5′2″, 100-pound teenage girl. Now she was glaring at him.

"Why couldn't you ignore them? Now I'll never live this down."

"Live *what* down?" he said. "That we like each other?"

She shrugged.

"What's the problem?" he said. "I didn't say anything that makes you look bad."

"Yes, you did. When they asked if we've made out, you said, 'Sorry, girls, that's private.'" She groaned. "Terrific. Now that's all I'll hear for the entire trip."

"Okay, what should I have said? 'No, girls, we haven't even kissed'?"

"You shouldn't have said anything. Forget it. I need to get down there and spend time with Caitlyn. She's been on my case because I spent yesterday with you."

"I'm sorry it was such a hardship."

"Oh, Avery, that's not … please don't be angry. Please." She looked around the empty lobby, sprang up on her tiptoes, and kissed his cheek.

"Hey," he said, "I want to show you something."

Avery took her hand and walked her down the hall. At the last phone booth on the end, a phone booth in which the inside light wasn't working, Avery pushed the door open. He guided Penny in backwards and followed her inside. It was dimly lit and cramped. If Penny weren't so petite, it would have been an impossibly tight squeeze.

"There." He closed the door behind them and leaned the umbrella against the glass. "Penny?"

"Yes?"

"I want to kiss you now," he said. "On the lips."

She was silent. The only sound in the booth was of her shaky breath. Avery regretted *announcing* that he wanted to kiss her, instead of simply kissing her the second they'd slipped in here. It was a rookie mistake, but an understandable one; he liked her and didn't want to do anything that would make her uncomfortable. Although Avery had kissed only two girls—most recently Inge Ibsen, before last summer's falling-out—he was confident he could lay a great kiss on Penny.

"Avery … I don't think—"

"Don't think. Close your eyes."

As she did, Avery cupped her cheeks, tilted her head gently to the side, and planted his lips on hers. At first, she tensed up, and then she relaxed and collapsed limply against him. She pressed her chest against his and whimpered. She was warm and quivering and smelled like talcum powder and soft perfume. Avery uncoupled his lips from hers long enough to take a breath.

"I love your lips, Penny Aston," he said.

"I love yours, Avery Craig."

They kissed some more. Penny's hands were idle on his shoulders, but as soon as Avery's hands brushed her pert backside in that skirt (oh God, the soft curve of her tush and the crisp edge of those skirt pleats!), Penny hungrily squeezed his arms, then slipped her hands into the back pockets of Avery's jeans.

Although Avery was pretty sure no one had walked by outside, he didn't want this great kiss ruined by getting caught, so he decided to quit while he was ahead. He finished with his first-ever playful nibble on a girl's earlobe and eased them apart.

"I don't want those mean girls to see us," he said.

"That was wonderful." Her arms were wrapped around his waist now. She bit her lower lip mischievously like she had at her door last night.

"What do you think?" she said. "Am I a good kisser?"

"You're an amazing kisser. A natural."

Penny bounced on her tiptoes and wriggled with pleasure. "So are you, Avery."

"I'll slip out first and signal if it's all clear." Avery reached for the door handle, but before he could open it, Penny laid a hand on his.

"Wait." She closed her eyes. "I want to remember this feeling. My heart is beating so fast."

She smiled, then pulled his hand off the door handle and pressed it to her upper chest, above her breasts. She put her hand on his chest, and they stared into each other's eyes until their heartbeats slowed and synchronized.

Avery stroked her hair and kissed her one last time. He grabbed the umbrella and stepped out. The hallway was empty. He waved for her. Penny darted out of the booth.

"You go first," he said. "I'll wait a minute so it's not obvious we were kissing."

Penny gazed at him in the dim light of the lobby. "I can't believe this is happening. After one day."

"Go ahead," he said. "I'm sure Caitlyn and Doc are waiting."

Penny sprang up on her tiptoes and kissed him. Then she spun around, her hair and skirt whirling in her wake, and hurried down the hall.

6

RIGHT AFTER breakfast, Avery retrieved his extra ZZ Top *Eliminator* cassette and brought it to Irina. She met him at the Dutch door, thanked him profusely, and shocked him with what she did next. Leaning over the narrow countertop, she glanced up and down the hallway and screwed a slow, moist kiss into Avery's cheek.

"Have fun today, Ace." She minced back into the office.

Avery was like stunned prey: he couldn't move, couldn't breathe. He watched Irina's swaying hips and taut backside. Had Irina, the totally gorgeous front desk clerk, just kissed him?

Back at the photocopier, Irina smiled sympathetically over her shoulder. "You should go now. Your bus leaves soon, yes?" She smiled. "I see you tomorrow."

Avery nodded and reeled down the hall. He had some time before everyone gathered for attendance in the front lobby, so he decided to use it to further explore the ground floor of the hotel. He'd reconned most of the place already, including the hotel restaurant, ballroom, meeting rooms, phone booths, newsstand, and shoe-shine stand, but he hadn't scouted out the pool.

He found it at the end of a long hallway. The door was locked, but inside he could see the glittering pool with a diving board, and a side door that led into a sauna. The teachers and chaperones had promised that if the students behaved for the entire stay, the hotel would make the pool available to them on their last night. Avery chuckled to himself about how much this deal resembled a scene in *Caddyshack*. Once a year for an hour, the country club opens its pristine pool to the caddies, who totally destroy it.[14]

Superheated Plasma

Avery turned around and headed back toward the lobby. There was a staircase on the side of the hallway that led down to a basement level. He had just passed the stairwell when he glimpsed Caitlyn at the far end of the hallway, marching purposefully toward the pool. Avery did an about-face and ducked into the stairwell. Hopefully, she hadn't seen him.

♫"One Way or Another"♫

At the bottom of the stairs, Avery found himself in the inner bowels of the hotel, near the laundry room. Women chatted in high-pitched tones over the whirring and thrumming sounds of the big machines. He waited until he was confident that Caitlyn was gone, then opened the stairwell door again. There, with her hip cocked like the hammer on a pistol, and her butt kissing the stair banister, was Caitlyn. She had her Navy peacoat hooked on one finger, and it draped down her back.

"Hiya, Ace. Got my coat—see?" She raised it then draped it over the stair railing. "What'cha doin' down here?"

"Nothing—just exploring." Avery steered around her. "We should get back to the lobby." He started up the stairs.

"Hey, dude, hold your horses." Caitlyn grabbed him by his belt and tugged him back down to the bottom. "Penny told me you two kissed earlier. And in a *phone booth* no less."

"What?! Why did she—"

"Oh, chill out. You've got style. And Penny says you're quite the kisser. Although ... since Penny's never kissed a guy before, she's not qualified to judge good kissing."

"What's your point?" he said.

---

[14] The classic comedy *Caddyshack*, which lampoons the game of golf and the pretense and elitism of white, upper-class country club society, takes place at the fictitious Bushwood Country Club. (And yes, "Bushwood" is a *double entendre*.) This comedy classic's influence on '80s teens cannot be overstated.

"My *point* is that I know Penny isn't the only girl who's kissed you today. I saw that front desk tramp kiss you in the hall a minute ago." Caitlyn wiped his cheek with her thumb and showed him the smeared lipstick. "I think I should tell Penny. And our teachers. That woman will get fired, and you'll get sent home."

"Come on, don't do that," Avery said. "It was a friendly peck on the cheek, that's all."

Caitlyn shrugged. "*Maybe* I could be persuaded to keep my mouth shut."

"Don't say anything, Caitlyn. *Please.*""

Avery cringed at his begging. Bond would never beg.

Caitlyn smirked, and in that instant Avery remembered a word from his Daily Vocab calendar back home: *inscrutable*, an adjective that meant "not readily investigated, interpreted, or understood; mysterious." That was it: Caitlyn's smirk was *inscrutable*. Was she happy, scheming, or what? Avery had no idea. He composed a sentence in his head using the word: "*Caitlyn Cray made her inscrutable smirk, a half-smile with one corner of her mouth that left Avery wondering what she was up to.*" With that smirk and those gleaming, slippery lips, Caitlyn wasn't just *inscrutable*; she was "inscrutalicious."[15] (Hm … that Ace-ism was pretty good. When he returned to Hancock next week, he might drop it into conversations, see if it caught on.)

Avery lowered his voice. "Caitlyn, I like Penny, and I really don't want to hurt her."

Caitlyn responded as if she hadn't heard him. She pouted and said, "I can't believe you don't like my outfit." She fingered the hem of her sheer blouse, then her skirt. "I wore it for *you*."

"Are you kidding" he said. "I love it."

"Do you think it's sexy?"

---

[15] Avery Craig had a talent for creating lingo and charming his peers into adopting his newly minted words and phrases. Like Lewis Carroll, mathematician and author of *Alice in Wonderland*, Avery effortlessly invented portmanteau words (*portmanteaux*). For example, "Fantabulous," a creation of Avery's from fourth grade, was the melding of the words "fantastic" and "fabulous." Mysteriously, another one, "succulicious"— formed from "succulent" and "delicious"—never quite caught on.

"Incredibly."

"Do you think *I'm* sexy?" she asked.

"What do you want, Caitlyn? I'll give you twenty bucks right now to keep quiet about the front desk clerk. I just gave her a ZZ Top tape. She was thanking me, that's all."

Caitlyn raised the timbre of her voice; she sounded like a newborn kitten. "I don't want any money."

"What do you want then?"

What happened next was so sudden, it seemed like everything happened all at once.

♫"Easy Lover"♫

Caitlyn wraps her arms around Avery's waist and pulls him close, cranes her lips to his, and kisses him. Between her luscious cherry-flavored mouth, her heady perfume, and her soft breasts squished against his chest, Avery's groin responds predictably. Because she's a tall girl with long legs, her pelvis is level with his, and she presses it firmly against his burgeoning bulge, exhaling a soft *"mmmmm"* as she kisses him. She glides her hands down his back to his glutes, which she cups and squeezes greedily. When she finally eases away from him, she primps his hair and stares into his eyes.

"Okay," she said, tilting her head back and cupping his cheeks, "I have to admit, Penny was right. You *are* a good kisser. You kiss better than my stupid boyfriend, that's for sure."

"I didn't kiss you," he said. "You kissed *me*."

"Yeah, but you were kissing me back … *hard*." She yanked on his waist, drilling his bulge into herself. "I can't believe you didn't try to feel me up." She clucked her tongue and whispered in his ear. *"Cuz I woulda let you."*

She kissed him one more time, swiping her breasts against his chest, and punctuated the kiss with a gentle flick of her tongue in his mouth. Then, without a word, she peeled off him, grabbed her peacoat, and walked up to the next stair landing. She applied some lipgloss and smirked down at him.

"Don't worry—I promise I won't say anything about this. I promise I won't tell Penny that you did *nothing* to resist me." She popped a cube of grape Bubblelicious in her mouth and stared at him as she jawed on the gum. "Oh, by the way, before this trip is over, I might kiss you again. Or make you kiss *me* next time. Bye, Lover." She climbed the stairs, and the stairwell door at the top banged shut behind her.

Avery took a moment to catch his breath and allow his blood to cool from its current temperature of superheated plasma. When he had stopped quivering from Caitlyn's adroit kisses, he plodded upstairs.

Moves and Countermoves

More dazed than earlier, Avery used the bathroom, doused his face with cold water, and put a wet paper towel on the back of his neck. He couldn't believe what had happened. *Did* it happen? Did Caitlyn Cray, Penny's supposed "best friend from elementary school," waylay him in the stairwell and kiss him? Kiss him so masterfully that, had she continued for another minute, Avery would have come in his pants?

It didn't seem possible. But when he glimpsed himself in the bathroom mirror and saw Irina's smeared lipstick, he knew he wasn't imagining it. He wiped off the evidence with the paper towel and threw it away. Not only had Caitlyn Cray kissed him but she'd also made it clear that she had the hots for him and would ambush him again sometime during the trip.

How should he handle this? He considered confessing to Penny about it, but he knew that Penny was subservient to Caitlyn. And after only one day of being around Caitlyn, he knew that she was a master manipulator and too cunning an adversary to attack head-on. Bond, Hannibal, and MacGyver would concur. If he told Penny about the kiss, Penny would talk to Caitlyn about it, and Caitlyn would twist the situation to make Avery look bad, saying something like, *"Yeah, it's true, Penny—we kissed, but Avery kissed me. I didn't want to tell you about it because I know you like him."*

Avery bowed his head and sighed. Ugh, he wasn't even *going out* with Penny, and he had a headache cogitating these intrigues with the opposite sex. This stuff was foreign to him, and he sensed that, head-to-head against Caitlyn, he was outmatched. The last time he'd been this bewildered playing out moves and countermoves was during a difficult chess game against his grandfather. He'd lost that game, as he always lost to Pa, but he'd learned something about himself:

his imaginative, lateral-thinking brain was incapable of calculating beyond four moves ahead. And unlike chess, where there were rules governing how the pieces could legally move, in relationships with girls, there seemed to be no rules. None.

Since the start of the school year, when he'd read *Othello* in English class, Avery had named the little devil that hung out on his shoulder Iago. The little prick spoke to him in a soft, seductive voice: *"Why don't you forget about Penny and focus on Caitlyn? The girl obviously likes you a lot, she knows how to kiss, and I'm sure she'll have sex with you a lot sooner."*

Avery patted his face dry with another paper towel and paced in front of the sinks.

"And don't forget about Irina," Iago continued. *"That was more than a friendly peck on the cheek, and you know it. She's a lonely, sexy foreigner who probably dances at home in her lingerie to American rock music. She loves all things American, and you, Ace, are as American as it gets. She's totally into you. I think she wants to take your virginity."*

"Shut up, Iago," Avery said.

A man's voice boomed from one of the stalls. "What!?"

"Nothing," Avery said. "Sorry."

Avery thought of his father, Big Jack, a reputed womanizer, an accomplished swordsman, a seasoned pro at "laying pipe," and knew exactly what he'd say.[16] Jack would tell Avery to *"Forget about prissy Penny and focus on the foreign brunette one, or the randy little minx. Heck, both of 'em, if you can swing it."*

The Revolving Door

But Irina and Caitlyn, because they were surely much more experienced than he, made Avery uncomfortable. By contrast, Penny's innocence was strongly appealing. Penny was like the South Pole before Amundsen reached it, or Mount Everest before Hillary and

---

[16] "Laying pipe" was an old-school euphemism for sex used by men of Jack Craig's generation. The trope was likely coined by a pipeline worker, a self-deceived (or freakishly well-endowed) workman who had decided that his erect penis resembled a length of the pipe he'd been laying that day. You may roll your eyes now, Dear Reader.

Norgay stepped foot on the summit: no guy had been there before. Penny was untouched virgin territory. Caitlyn was undoubtedly neither untouched nor a virgin, and Irina surely wasn't either.

No, it was clear: Penny was the right girl for him. As for how he should handle Caitlyn, all he could do was avoid being alone with her, and if she happened to ambush him again, he would resist her. And if she insisted on kissing him, he wouldn't kiss her back. Avery threw away the now-crumpled paper towel and went out to the lobby.

The students were clustered together in various cliques. The teachers were by the front doors taking attendance, making announcements about the sites they were visiting that day, and reviewing the rules, but Avery didn't hear any of it.

The three kisses—from Penny, Irina, and now Caitlyn—and the endorphin cocktail that followed each one had put his brain in a stupor, so the teachers' voices all sounded like the adults' in the animated *Peanuts* cartoons: "*Waaugh-waaugh-waaugh-waaugh-waaugh.*" Doc, Eric, and Louis were standing near him, raving about *The Terminator*, saying they hoped there would be a sequel, but even that discussion didn't engage Avery. The stupor in his head was part arousal from Caitlyn; part guilt and worry for having allowed himself to be kissed by Irina and Caitlyn; and part confusion, because those other two had stirred up feelings in him that he'd thought he had only for Penny.

Penny and Caitlyn were standing across the lobby, talking with the Vanderbush guys they'd ridden the elevator with earlier. Avery was too far away to hear their conversation, but Caitlyn was doing most of the talking, and she was shamelessly flirting with the guys, touching their arms and jutting her breathtaking boobs in their direction. The guys locked their eyes onto her bra beneath the sheer blouse and kept them there.

At one point when Penny was talking to a boy, Caitlyn gave Avery a sidelong glance and blew him a kiss. Then one of the Vanderdouches said something that made Penny laugh, and Avery seethed. An hour ago, he and Penny had been synchronizing their heartbeats; now it seemed like she'd forgotten him.

The second that thought came into his mind, Penny flashed him a weary smile. She pulled a note partway from her overcoat and pocketed it again. Avery motioned with his chin at the hallway corner near the front desk. Penny nodded.

"Be right back, Doc," Avery said.

While he was moseying over there, Tubby was skulking around the lobby perimeter, giving him the stink-eye. This was Avery's first clear look at him since the stairwell encounter. Tubby was only about 5'8" to Avery's 6'0", but tipping the scales at 200–210, the lardass outweighed Avery by as much as 25 pounds. Avery wasn't worried about Tubby attacking him—not with the adults around—but he was concerned that the kid might confront him about last night's ambush in the stairwell, and Penny would overhear it. Avery had promised her he wouldn't fight, then broken his promise a minute later. Avery didn't make direct eye contact with Tubby or give him any sign that he knew he was there.

When the teachers announced it was time to board the bus, Penny crossed the lobby toward the revolving door, palming the note in her right hand. Avery strolled alongside her, slipped sideways into the revolving door compartment with her, and took the note. When the revolving door belched them onto the pavement, Avery discreetly kissed her cheek, opened the note, and read:

> Avery, I'm back in my room and only have a few
> minutes to write this before Caitlyn comes, so please
> excuse me if my handwriting is messy. Not sitting with
> you at breakfast was torture. All I wanted was to be
> near you.
>
> Kissing you was incredible. I'm glad you think I'm a
> good kisser because you totally are! I hope you don't get
> the wrong idea about me and the kind of girl I am. I've
> never done anything like that before.
>
> I told Caitlyn about our kiss, but only because she
> pestered me. Please don't tell anyone. I doubt you will,
> but guys usually brag about this stuff.

While we're apart today, I'll be thinking about
you and our kiss. I hope you're thinking about me.
Until later…
Affectionately,
Penny

Avery pocketed the note with the deeply satisfying sense that, from this point forward, his whole life would be better. Breathing deeply of the cold air, he smelled the prickly hint of rain and the pungent stench of diesel fumes…

He looked up. Mr. Nelson was standing by the bus door, waving his clipboard. "Let's go, Mr. Craig! We're waiting!"

Avery ran across the parking lot and boarded the bus.

Double Ass

Their first sites were directly across the street from each other: Ford's Theatre, where President Lincoln was shot, and the Petersen House, where he died. Why had the teachers chosen to start their D.C. sightseeing with the two most depressing sites? With the umbrella hooked under his arm, Avery stepped off the bus and looked at the sky: dark overcast, but no rain.

On the sidewalk, he and Penny smiled at each other from a distance. He wanted to be with her, to spend at least part of the day with her, but besides Caitlyn there were other forces at work today preventing that from happening. Because the two sites were close quarters and full of fragile, priceless antiques, the students and teachers would be split into two groups: one would visit Ford's Theatre while the other visited the Petersen House, and then the two groups would switch. Avery was in the group that visited Ford's Theatre first, which included Doc and Gemma; Penny and Caitlyn were in the other group. Mr. Nelson was about to take his group over to the Petersen House when a Vanderbush girl asked him how to spell "assassinate." Mr. Nelson hemmed and hawed, so Avery answered for him.

"The way I remember it is," Avery said, "anyone who assassinates someone is a double ass."

The girl and her friends laughed.

"Seriously," he continued, "there are two 'asses' at the beginning of the word—A-S-S, A-S-S. '*ASS-ASSinate.*' Get it?"

"Now I do. Thanks!"

Avery's group was entering the theater. Avery caught up and held the door open for Ms. Wharton.

"My, what a gentleman. Thank you, Avery." She smiled and went inside.

Right in the center of the theater lobby, in a glass case, was Lincoln's bloody shirt—the one he'd supposedly been wearing the night he was shot. A Vanderbush girl saw it and said, "Ugh, grody to the max!" Avery noted to himself that the shirt with its rust-colored bloodstains was 121 years old. A while back, he had read an article in the science magazine *Omni* about the theoretical possibility of cloning. What if someone in the future stole this shirt and cloned Lincoln from these bloodstains!?

A Ford's Theatre tour guide gave them some history about the night Lincoln was assassinated, mentioning that the play, *Our American Cousin*, was never performed again. He then walked the group into the theater, pointed out the stage and Lincoln's private box, and explained that after John Wilkes Booth had shot the President, he leapt out of the box onto the stage. Because his boot spur had caught on some bunting, Booth broke his leg when he landed, but before he hobbled offstage, he brandished a dagger and shouted the state motto of Virginia: "*Sic semper tyrannis*'!"[17]

After the tour guide finished his story, the students were sent upstairs in pairs to peek into the fateful box itself. Avery was paired with Tubby. When he and Tubby reached the dark landing at the top, the two Vanderbush girls who had been sent up first galumphed back downstairs. While Avery was getting his bearings, Tubby glanced over his shoulder, made his goofy grin, and body-checked Avery into the wall. The wall was solid plaster and totally unforgiving, and Avery's elbow absorbed most of the impact.

Tubby chortled. "Told you I'd get you back."

---

[17] "Thus be it ever to tyrants!" Things didn't work out so well for Booth. Twelve days later, he was shot in the neck in a tobacco barn, and the barn was set on fire. He was pulled from the fire but, paralyzed, died hours later.

Avery rubbed his elbow. "Hey, what's your name?"

"Warren." He raised his chin defiantly. "Why?"

"Never mind, your name sucks. I'm sticking with 'Tubby.' Or would you prefer 'Fat Ass'?"

"Screw you."

"Hey, have a little respect, Tubby," Avery said. "President Lincoln was assassinated in the next room."

As they neared the doorway to the box, the two shoved each other to be the first one through. With his superior heft, Tubby won. They were standing at the edge of a vestibule, about ten feet from Lincoln's chair. The chair and the rest of the box were cordoned off by thick purple velvet ropes clamped to brass stanchions. Tubby maneuvered his bulk in front of Avery.

The feuding boys tacitly called a truce and gazed in silent reverence at the scene of America's greatest tragedy. During his reverie, Avery fantasized that he was here on that fateful night. If Avery had been Lincoln's bodyguard, the assassination wouldn't have happened—*period*. Avery would've rammed that derringer up Booth's ass and pulled the trigger, grabbed that sawed-off, second-rate actor by his waistcoat and mustache, and chucked him off the balcony—straight onto a soldier's bayonet. The next night, Lincoln would've given Avery a dinner at the White House, told one of his funny stories, draped a gold medal around Avery's neck, and declared April 14th a national holiday forever: American Hero Avery Craig Day. After that, Avery would've been the President's personal bodyguard and confidante, throwing out any lobbyists or office-seekers who overstayed their welcome.

With his revenge fantasy and imagined triumph dissipating like smoke, Avery returned to Abe's box and the question of what to do about Tubby. Tubby's thighs grazed the rope, and his knees were locked. This gave Avery an idea—a horribly cruel and sacrilegious idea. He just hoped the ghost of their slain 16th president would forgive him. Standing about three feet behind Tubby, holding the umbrella by its metal tip, Avery slowly extended the wooden handle until it was millimeters from the back of Tubby's knee. Avery closed his eyes, silently apologized to President Lincoln, and jabbed Tubby with the umbrella handle. The effect was as sudden and devastating as if Avery had amputated Tubby's leg with an axe. All at once, Tubby pitched forward, his arms flailing in vain for something to grab onto, his thick middle toppling across the velvet rope, the rope snapping taut, and the brass stanchions overturning and clanging against each other. The noise was deafening.

As soon as Tubby hit the floor (with a sequoia-sized thud), Avery hustled out of Abe's box, then slowed and sauntered down the stairs, casting an artfully puzzled glance over his shoulder. Halfway down, savoring the collective stare of two dozen students without once meeting their gaze, he paused unruffled and checked his watch—idly, precisely, like Bond after the explosion in the *Goldfinger* teaser.

The tour guide plowed through the students and ran up the stairs, his face in a panic.

"What happened!?"

"I don't know, sir," Avery said. "But the guy you paired me with is really overweight. He just collapsed. I think his knee buckled."

For the Second Time that Morning...

The tour guide nodded and hurried past Avery. Doc met Avery at the bottom of the stairs, and they walked over to the display case that contained Lincoln's shirt.

"'Knee buckled,' my ass," Doc said. "You shoved him, didn't you?"

"Shoved, no," Avery said. "Gently nudged the back of his knee with *this*?" He held up the umbrella handle. "Possibly."

Doc chuckled. "Is that the kid you gave a *soaking* last night?"

"Yeah, and he's not happy about it."

Across the lobby, Gemma Jones was reading a book and stealing glances at him. She was standing at the end of the line of students waiting to go upstairs. Tubby, shadowed by the tour guide, trudged down the stairs as red-faced as a steamed lobster. The girls tittered. Mr. Nelson, consulting a clipboard, said Doc and a kid from Vander-bush were up next.

Avery was strolling toward the bathroom when he caught Gemma looking at him again. Viewing her from the side, he could see most of her face, and her glasses were barely noticeable. Even her hair looked glossy and styled. The girl was striking—especially with that snug Guess jeans number she was wearing today under the wool topcoat, and that cute raspberry beret. Avery waved to her and veered away. Then, when she returned to her book, he snuck around the lobby, came up behind her and sang the title lyric from "Raspberry Beret."

"Avery, you startled me!" she said.

"Sorry. I saw you alone over here and wanted to say hello. What'cha readin'?"

"Not reading *per se*." She held up the book cover: *Brain Busters: 101 Word, Logic, and Math Puzzles*. She waggled her pen. "I'm doing a cryptogram. Super easy."

"Yeah, those are easy," he said. "Do you play Scrabble by any chance?"

"Are you kidding? *J'adore* Scrabble."

Avery explained that he'd gotten a travel Scrabble set for his birthday and brought it on the trip, but he had no one to play with.

"Happy birthday," Gemma said. "Sixteen or seventeen?"

"Sixteen."

"What about those girls you've been hanging around with?" She tapped his arm with the puzzle book. "Don't you want to play Scrabble with *them*?"

"Mm, they're not exactly word people, you know?" he said. "How about it? Back at the hotel tonight, wanna play?"

"I'd like that. By the way"—she pointed with her pen and lowered her voice—"what happened up there?"

"The kid I was paired with tripped. Clumsy." Avery smiled at her. "Hey, I love your outfit."

She blushed. "Thanks."

"Looking good, Gem." Avery made a finger-pistol with one hand, aimed it at her, and fired.

Gemma chuckled. "Feeling good, Ace."

Avery went into the bathroom and ducked into a stall. Using another page of his now-tattered itinerary, he dashed off a reply to Penny's note from earlier:

Penny,

I'm writing this in the Ford's Theatre bathroom, so I have to write fast.

1. Breakfast was torture for me too. I might have looked like I was having a great time, but inside I was dying. You were so close, but I couldn't be with you.

2. I know you haven't done anything like our kiss before. Neither have I.

3. I won't tell anybody, I promise. Other guys do brag about this stuff, but I won't.

4. I'm thinking about you, and I can't wait to be alone with you later.

—Avery

When he came out of the bathroom, everyone was filing outside. On the sidewalk, he scanned across the street for Penny. With the pink argyle bow in her hair, she was impossible to miss. Avery walked down the sidewalk until he was directly across the street from Penny. Waiting until she saw him, he signaled discreetly with his note. She grinned and revealed a note of her own.

Their groups started across the street simultaneously. Penny lined up across from him, then Stringbean and his gang of Vanderdouches cut in front of her and Avery lost her. He stopped, looked for the pink bow, and glimpsed it through a gap between Stringbean and one of his sycophants. Avery walked straight toward them. At the last second, they stepped aside.

"Hey, *Hand*cock," Stringbean said, "watch where you're walkin'!"

Avery ignored them. When he and Penny saw each other, Avery held out his note, clasping it tightly between his thumb and forefinger. Then he extended his empty hand and made a pinching motion with his fingers. Penny mimicked him, and the two exchanged notes. But Penny added a flourish. As their shoulders brushed against each other's, she turned her head and blew Avery a tiny kiss.

On the opposite sidewalk, while the rest of his group went into Lincoln's death house, Avery stayed outside and read the note. From Penny's crisp opening "A," Avery's heart beat faster.

Avery Christy Craig!

Don't worry, you're not in trouble. Far from it.

I mentioned to Caitlyn that I wanted to spend some time with you at the next stop, but she complained about being alone, so I need to stay with her today.

And tonight, I think we shouldn't kiss. I don't know what this is between us, but it seems to be moving too fast. I want to slow things down, OK?

But I'm thinking about you, Avery. A lot.

—Penny

Avery didn't feel like seeing the bedroom where Lincoln died, and Penny's declaration that "I think we shouldn't kiss" had depressed him, so he stayed put, leaning against the staircase, waiting for his group to come out. He considered dashing off another note, but without having kissing Penny to look forward to, he lacked inspiration. He clutched the umbrella and stared at the sky. Where was the rain?

His group and the Ford's Theatre group came out at the same time. Avery scanned the sidewalk across the street for the pink bow, and when he spotted it, Penny and Caitlyn were surrounded by what seemed like an entire ski resort of Vanderbush guys. When one of them tugged playfully on Penny's bow, she smiled at the guy. For the second time that morning, Avery seethed.

WHUHHPPPPHH!

At Lincoln Memorial, Avery gazed at the great man while a gust of wind blew at his back. Sitting in his immense chair, staring across the reflecting pool, Lincoln initially seemed displeased with him, but as Avery drew closer to the giant-sized sculpture, he noticed a faint smile of forgiveness on Lincoln's face. This was the guy who'd freed the slaves, who'd forgiven the South for rebellion; surely, he'd overlook Avery's stunt at Ford's Theatre. He might even appreciate it.

A park ranger joined them and launched into her spiel about the memorial and the statue sculptor. Avery was aware of Penny and Caitlyn standing next to a column to his right, but he didn't look at them. Penny smiling at that other guy had pissed him off. In the distance across the reflecting pool, a dark storm was rolling in, and nobody but Avery had an umbrella. Gripping it in his hand, he stared at Lincoln and spoke under his breath.

"Bring it, Abe, bring it," he said. "If anybody has an in with Mother Nature, you do. Make it rain, Abe, make it rain. Downpour! Cats and dogs, baby! Do it, Abe! Do it, do it, do it, *do it!*"

When the park ranger finished, the students were given time to read the inscriptions inside the memorial, and then Mr. Nelson said it was time to return to the bus. The moment he said this, a powerful gust blew into the memorial, and raindrops spattered on the top steps beneath the overhang. The rain blew in, and Penny, Caitlyn, and everyone else stepped back from it.

He looked at Lincoln's beautiful, weathered, homely face and whispered, "Thanks, Abe."

From the base of the statue, Avery walked toward the memorial entrance, toward the storm, passing through a gauntlet of stupefied students, teachers, and chaperones. In his periphery to the left, he spotted Penny's pink bow. It was impossible to miss. She was standing next to an outer column, close to the rain that was blowing in. Staring straight ahead, Avery reached down and unsnapped the umbrella tie. The memorial echoed with murmurs. At the edge of the rain line, he raised the umbrella and pressed the button on the handle. The sound it made springing open resonated through the memorial: *WHUHHPPPPHH!* Avery stepped underneath the umbrella and pushed it into the storm until the rain drummed on the fabric. He gave Penny a smug smile.

"Would you and Caitlyn care to join me?"

With the beaming look Penny gave him, you'd think he'd just rescued her from a burning building. She minced over and got underneath the umbrella beside him. Caitlyn slapped the arm of one of the ski dudes.

"Later, losers," she said.

Caitlyn got under the umbrella on Avery's other side. Avery put his arm around Penny, she put her arm around him, and then Caitlyn put her arm around him, and they walked down the stairs together.

"Totally bitchin' move, Ace," Caitlyn said into his shoulder. "You earned big points with this." She planted a quick kiss on his ear.

Once Avery delivered Penny and Caitlyn to the bus, he ran back to the memorial with his umbrella and returned with Gemma and Ms. Wharton. It was his Scouting good deed for the day.

A Friggin' M60 Belt of German Insults

Because it poured all day long and the schedule called for them visiting several outdoor sites, Penny and Caitlyn spent the rest of that morning and most of the afternoon with Avery, huddling against him beneath the giant umbrella at Arlington National Cemetery, including President Kennedy's gravesite with its eternal flame, and the Tomb of the Unknown Soldier. At Jefferson Memorial, everyone got a brief respite from the rain beneath the rotunda. And at the Smithsonian Air and Space Museum, they finally got to go indoors.

Once the group returned to the sidewalk in the National Mall and they formed a line to get back on the bus, Penny and Caitlyn got beneath the umbrella with Avery again. There was a lot of rain and street noise, and everyone was excited because it was time for dinner. On line in front of him were Kristen Brooks and Johanna Glück. Johanna was talking, and Avery decided to eavesdrop.

He couldn't hear most of what she was saying, but she mentioned the Air and Space Museum and then remarked that the United States wouldn't have made it to the moon were it not for the German rocket scientists. Avery bristled. While he knew from a PBS documentary that Werner Von Braun and some other Germans had played a significant role at the beginning of the space program, Johanna's suggestion (once again) that Germans were superior to Americans roused Avery's patriotic fury. With most of the other students watching, Avery knew this was prime time to unload a friggin' M60 belt of German insults—like Rambo at the end of *First Blood*, ripping the town apart with gunfire.

Johanna glanced in his direction. Seeing him with Penny and Caitlyn, she rolled her eyes and whispered something to Kristen, who sniggered. Getting into character, Avery stood up ramrod straight, clicked his heels together, and delivered some of the lines he'd practiced for hours in front of a mirror—practically shouting at Johanna so she would hear him over the rain and street noise.

"Johanna, *Fräulein!*" Avery barked. "*Kommen Sie hier, Fräulein, schnell! Wollen Sie heute Abend mit mir essen?! Wollen Sie heute Abend mit mir trinken?! Ja?! Bitte, Fräulein?!*"[18]

Avery's monologue was so fast, so sharp and forceful like a German officer's, that not only did Johanna and Kristen spin around to face him but a coterie of Vanderbush girls, including Eyeshadow, gave a start. Except for Johanna, as soon as the other students realized it wasn't a German soldier shouting but Avery Craig, they gaped in wonder. And when he finished, everyone burst out laughing.

Now with a captive audience, Avery narrowed his eyes at Johanna and unleashed another, saucier salvo: "*Johanna, du hast einen sehr schönen Körper! Ich möchte heute Abend mit dir schlafen! Bitte, Johanna!*"[19]

Although they had no idea what Avery was saying, the students nearby laughed, but as the only one who *understood* Avery, Johanna Glück's mouth went slack, her cheeks flushed; she was visibly mortified. She gazed at Avery in jaw-quivering shock. Avery was about to deliver the *coup de grace*—a choice line demanding that Johanna remove her wet and soiled clothes at once and tell him the location of the hidden base—but before he could, Johanna and Kristen stomped onto the bus.

"Nice one, Ace," Doc said over his shoulder.

Standing near the bus doors with a clipboard, Avery's English teacher, the trim and youthful Ms. Wharton, shook her head disapprovingly. Avery had never seen her angry before. It unnerved him.

"That's *enough*, Mr. Craig," she said. "Keep it up, and no one will be eating or drinking with you tonight. Never mind the other activity you mentioned."

Caitlyn nudged him and whispered in his ear. "What did you say to her anyway?"

"Shame on you, Avery," Ms. Wharton jabbed her pen at him and marched over. She was wearing a raincoat and one of those clear

---

[18] "Johanna, Miss! Come here, Miss, quickly! Will you eat with me tonight?! Will you drink with me tonight?! Yes?! Please, Miss?!"

[19] "Johanna, you have a very beautiful body! I want to make love to you tonight! Please, Johanna!"

plastic rain hoods that tied under her chin; it made her look about 70 years old instead of her actual age of 30-something. "Avery, Johanna is a *guest* in our country."

"I'm sorry, Ms. Wharton, but she deserved it. She's been hassling me in Social Studies all year."

"Avery," she said, "I'm disappointed in you. You have to be the bigger person. Johanna is all alone in this country. How would you feel if you were all alone in Germany and she did that to you?"

A shiver of shame trickled down his spine. The truth was, he did know how it felt to be alone. He'd moved a dozen times, and with every new community he moved into, he'd felt so alone that he might as well have been from the Soviet Union.

"Not good," he said.

"You should apologize to her. Tonight, when we get back to the hotel."

"I'll think about it," he said.

"Please do." Ms. Wharton walked back to the bus door and resumed her attendance-taking.

Penny squeezed his arm. "I didn't know that you spoke German."

Avery was about to tell her that he didn't speak the language, that he'd simply practiced a bunch of phrases in front of a mirror, and then a thought struck him: *Dude, you know who else practiced in front of a mirror? Hitler.*

Avery shrugged. "I'm not fluent or anything, but, yeah, I speak a little bit."

"Your teacher's right," Penny said. "You should apologize. That must have been super embarrassing for her."

"Penny, you don't understand. That girl—"

"It was clever, Ace," Eric Park said softly behind him. "And Johanna deserved it, but..." Louis, Bill, Tara, and the other Hancock kids nearby turned and leaned toward Eric. The moment reminded Avery of a TV commercial for E.F. Hutton investments, where everybody in a restaurant stops eating and leans in to overhear what old E.F. is saying, and the narrator delivers the tagline, *"When E.F. Hutton talks, people listen."* Because Avery respected Eric so much, he, too, leaned toward the diminutive Korean-American.

"But," Eric continued, "you might want to consider easing up on her." The line to board the bus shuffled forward. "I think Johanna is homesick."

"I didn't know that," Avery said. "I will give your counsel thoughtful consideration, sir."

They nodded at each other. When Avery turned around again, Caitlyn was clutching his arm that held the umbrella and leaning seductively against him. She made a contemptuous snort.

"Screw that, Ace," she said, barely above a whisper. "I think it was hilarious. And if the girl can't take a joke, let her go back to friggin' Germany."

She glanced over at Penny. A second later, as they shuffled forward together, Caitlyn slid a hand into the back pocket of his jeans and squeezed.

<h1 style="text-align:center">7</h1>

Back at the hotel, they were ushered straight into dinner—a bacchanalian buffet of hamburgers, hot dogs, French fries, meatball sandwiches, hero sandwiches, fried chicken, Mozzarella sticks, unlimited soda, and several desserts—and nary a vegetable in sight.

Avery sat with Penny, Caitlyn, and Steve while eating his first plate of food, but when he got up for seconds and spotted Johanna sitting alone and poking at her dinner, that shiver of shame chilled him again, and this time it was worse. Ms. Wharton was right: Johanna was all alone in this country. And more than anyone else, Avery knew what that felt like. *Okay, Ace, let's do this.* He walked over and sat down across from her.

Johanna's jaw clenched, like she was about to shout at him.

"Easy, *Fräulein*." He raised his hands like he was being robbed at gunpoint. "I'm here to bury the hatchet."

She gave him a quizzical look.

"An American expression," he said. "Look, I'm sorry." Then, remembering the German phrase, he smiled and said, *"Es tut mir leid."*

She smiled back at him. She was wearing an expensive-looking cream cashmere turtleneck sweater that hugged her modest curves and lithe arms nicely. Her long tawny hair rested on her shoulders in heavy-looking heaps.

"Where's Kristen?" he asked.

Johanna frowned. "Calling her parents."

"Ah," he said. "Well, the reason I came over is, I want to apologize and negotiate a truce between us. What do you say?"

"A truce, yes." She nodded. "Zis is goot."

"If you'll stop talking about how terrible America is compared to Germany, and if you'll stop rolling your eyes when I talk—"

"I do not roll my eyes when you talk." She gazed blankly at him for a second, then rolled her eyes.

"There, you just did it!"

"Yes, yes, I notice now. *Tut mir leid.*"

"Okay," he said. "If you'll stop that stuff, I'll stop talking in German, I'll stop embarrassing you, and I'll stop being a dick toward you in general."

When he said, "dick," Johanna covered her mouth and giggled. Wow. When the girl wasn't as stern as vice-principal Staunton, she was beautiful.

"You have a lovely smile, Johanna," he said. "You should show it more often."

She blinked at him and moved food around on her plate.

"The truth is," he continued, "I think you're an impressive person—smart, beautiful, athletic—and I thought so from your first day at Hancock."

"*Danke sehr.* I think same about you." She took a breath, let it out and gave him a hesitant smile. "I too would like peace between us."

Grade-A American Awesomeness

They declared a truce and shook hands. Ms. Wharton, who had been watching them, nodded and smiled at Avery. He took a bite of a meatball sandwich. "It seems you're eating with me tonight after all."

"Yes." Johanna returned to her meal.

Avery put his sandwich down. "Listen, Johanna, I've been thinking." He said that if Johanna wanted a different perspective on the United States, she needed to talk to him and his friends sometime. Kristen, he said, was pretty snooty—hardly an example of a quintessential American teenager.

"*Quint ... essential?*" she said.

"Like the ultimate example of something."

"Ah, yes."

"The bottom line is," Avery said, "if you want to experience real American teen life—I mean like grade-A American awesomeness—what it's really like to live in the United States, then you need to hang out with *me*."

Johanna nodded and giggled. "Yes, Ace, I would like this."

As he and Johanna chatted and ate, Avery kept glancing across the dining room at Penny and Caitlyn. Enticed no doubt by the girls' outfits—Penny's pink preppy ensemble, and Caitlyn's sexy homage to Madonna—the Vanderdouche Peeping Tom Patrol was encroaching on their table. Dorky Stringbean had commandeered Avery's chair, spun it around, and straddled it, gawking at the two girls over the chair back. Meanwhile, Avery had left Doc there to ward off any male interlopers, but what was the guy doing? Spearing friggin' tater tots and staring into space. He liked Doc, but sometimes the guy could be a total milquetoast. Avery needed to get back over there—fast.

Across the room, Gemma was sitting alone, reading from a paperback, and eating—or trying to. Because her eyes were on her book, half of each forkful fell off the fork before it reached her mouth. The only other person Avery knew who ate like this was his genius friend E.B.; now that he thought about it, Gemma was probably a genius too. He decided to introduce Johanna to her.

"*Kommen Sie mit mir, Fräulein.*"

"*Gerne. Wohin gehen wir?*"

"*Du wirst sehen,*"[20] he said.

They picked up their trays and crossed the dining room. Avery was watching Penny and Caitlyn, and as soon as they were looking his way, he leaned into Johanna's shoulder—like he was sharing a secret with her. "By the way ... *wundervolle...*" Avery was pleased with himself for the addition of "beautiful": first, because he'd spontaneously used a German word; and second, because it made Johanna giggle, and Penny and Caitlyn saw it. "I did mean *one* thing I said to you today," he continued. "*Du hast einen sehr schönen Körper.*"

"*Danke, Ace,*" Johanna said. "*Und du hast einen sehr stark Körper.*"

---

[20] "Come with me, miss." ¶ "Gladly. Where are we going?" ¶ "You'll see."

Avery canted his head and smiled. "Now '*stark*'—does that mean 'strong' or 'built,' I hope?"

Johanna nodded enthusiastically. "*Ja. Sehr gut!*"

"So, to be clear … you're *not* saying I have a puny *poindexter* body."

"*Nein, nein.*"

"*Gut, mein kleiner Strudel.*"

This time, she laughed outright. When they reached Gemma's table, Avery said hello to her and introduced them.

"Gemma Jones," he said, "may I introduce Johanna Glück?"

Gemma looked up from her book. "We're in Honors Bio together, Avery. Hi, Johanna."

Avery chatted with the girls while he finished his meatball sandwich, and once they were chatting about Europe, he knew his matchmaking work was done. He got up quietly. As he was walking away, Gemma called to him, asking if he still wanted to play Scrabble tonight. Avery replied that he was looking forward to it.

"*Auf Wiedersehen*, Ace," Johanna said. "*Danke.*"

"*Auf Wiedersehen, Fräulein.*"

Stretched Like Taffy

Carrying his tray back over to his table, Avery stopped when he was behind Stringbean. Penny and Caitlyn looked at him. He put the tray down, removed his leather jacket and sweater, draping them over the back of a nearby empty chair, and smoothed out his T-shirt, the arm holes of which strained over his biceps.

To the group of Vanderbush boys he said, "Okay, guys, time to go. You've bored these girls long enough."

"Oh, for Chrissake—beat it, *Hand*cock," Stringbean said.

His buddies chuckled at the epithet. Penny went pale. Caitlyn bit her lower lip, and her eyes, flicking eagerly between Avery and Stringbean, became enormous. The tables around them went silent. Stringbean threw Avery an arrogant glance over his shoulder.

"Relax, *Hand*cock. We're just talking here."

"Not anymore." Avery tapped his watch. "Time's up, Stringbean."

Caitlyn sniggered.

"And that's *my* chair you're sitting in," Avery said.

Stringbean let out a long moan and stood up. He was at least four inches taller than Avery, but ridiculously skinny; the kid's clothes hung off him like they were on wire coat hangers. Avery had a good twenty pounds of muscle on the guy, easy. Stringbean simpered, spun the chair around, and dusted off the seat—as if cleaning it for Avery—then sat down on it again. In a final act of defiance, he put his Air Jordans on the tabletop, crossed his long legs at the ankles, and said, "*Ahhhhh.* So, where were we, girls?"[21]

Avery took a breath. He couldn't afford to get in a fight here, but he couldn't let this scrawny dweeb emasculate him either. Making matters worse, Mr. Nelson was eyeing them, so Avery was also under time pressure; he had a minute at the most to defuse the situation. He needed to do something that would establish his dominance, display his strength, and be funny and non-violent—all at the same time.

Stringbean was wearing a multicolored sweater that was so baggy on him, the collar drooped over the chair back. With a smile to the girls, Avery nonchalantly clutched Stringbean's collar in one hand and, tugging on it, walked away from the table. The sweater stretched like taffy, well over a foot, and the elastic tension pinned Stringbean to the chair back. Unsure what was happening, Stringbean flailed his arms, and his legs were dragged off the tabletop. "Let go of me, jerk!"

While the rest of the Douche Patrol looked at each other panic-stricken, unsure what to do, Avery continued to drag Stringbean slowly across the room, the muscles flexing in his arm and shoulder, the feet of the chair squeaking ludicrously on the floor. The students tittered, then chuckled, then laughed hysterically as Avery halted at the corner with his payload.

He spun Stringbean around so he was facing the wall, and yanked the stretched-out collar down over the seat back, pinning Stringbean's chest and arms and preventing him from standing up. Stringbean bucked in the chair, grunting and squealing like a bound hostage. This triggered *more* laughter—from the entire room now, including, Avery noted with glee, Gemma Jones.

---

[21] Air Jordans, manufactured by the sports apparel company Nike, were red and black high-top basketball sneakers endorsed by Michael Jordan—the then-new Chicago Bulls superstar.

The acclaim from the audience, especially from the girls, was intoxicating, and Avery upped the ante. Humming ♪"Beat It"♪ to himself, Avery did some of Michael Jackson's dance from the music video around Stringbean's chair—the kickout, the bounce step, the shoulder-roll, the arm-slice, and the wrist-shake. Admittedly, he didn't have M.J.'s lightning speed, but his moves were fluid enough that the students recognized what he was doing and howled with laughter. There were camera flashes while he was dancing, and when he finished, Avery bowed to the entire room, nattily waving one hand as he dipped at the waist.

"Thank you, thank you!" he said. "You're too kind!"

"That's enough, Mr. Craig." Mr. Nelson walked over and released Stringbean. "From now on, you're to stay far away from each other. Is that clear?"

"Fine by me, Mr. Nelson," Avery said. "Stringbean never brushes his teeth, sir!" The students laughed again.

"Shut up," Stringbean said. "And stop calling me 'Stringbean'!"

"I mean it, boys." Mr. Nelson emphasized his point by jabbing his clipboard at them.

The second Mr. Nelson turned around, Stringbean gave Avery the finger; students who saw it gasped. But instead of retaliating, Avery waved to Stringbean and moonwalked away from him across the smooth floor—netting Avery more laughs.[22] He then spun on his heels and swagger-danced to his table.

The Vanderdouches were gone. Doc, chuckling, gave him a thumbs-up. Caitlyn was beaming at him and faintly shaking her head, with her elbow on the table and her chin in her palm. Avery was concerned that Penny would be angry with him—that she'd regard what he'd done as fighting—but she too was smiling. Avery put his

---

[22] On March 25, 1983, in a taped musical revue show *Motown 25: Yesterday, Today, Forever,* pop star Michael Jackson unveiled his signature dance move, the moonwalk. To do a moonwalk, a dancer glided backwards across the floor by putting his weight on one leg, pushing off the ball of that foot, allowing his other foot to slide smoothly backwards, and then repeating the process for the other foot. After seeing M.J.'s moonwalk, Avery Craig had practiced it until he perfected it.

tray on the table, pulled up his chair, and sat down. Penny tapped him in the leg with a shoe.

"You handled that well, Avery. Thank you. I don't like those boys."

"Yeah, nice job, Ace," Caitlyn said. "Hey, those are some gnarly guns you're sportin' there, dude. How'd you get 'em?"

Avery flexed his arms, then speared a piece of lemon meringue pie and popped it in his mouth. "I work out—every day."

"*Every* day?" Caitlyn said.

"Yup. I was using the hotel gym at five o'clock this morning."

Caitlyn smirked and nodded.

Right after dinner, the hotel staff set up the dining room for that night's movie—*Superman II*. Although it was one of Avery's favorites, he wanted to hang out with Penny and Caitlyn tonight. They had planned to meet in the hotel game room, which had Asteroids and Ms. Pac-Man console video games, but when Avery went down there, they weren't around.

He called the girls' room from the house phone in the lobby, and when he got Penny, she said that she and Caitlyn were exhausted and had changed their mind. Disappointed, Avery hung up. On his way back to the dining room, he bumped into Gemma. She asked if he'd like to watch the movie with her.

"*Superman II* is one of my favorites," she said.

"Same here," Avery said. "Sure, we can watch some of it. But I'd rather we played Scrabble. I brought a cool travel set with me, and I don't have anybody to play with."

She smiled. "I'd like that. Come on, let's go watch the movie."

8

WHEN AVERY woke the next morning at 4:30, he went into the bathroom to change into workout clothes and brought the travel Scrabble set with him. He and Gemma had started a game in the stairwell before lights-out, and he wanted to see where he stood.

On Avery's last turn, he had played the word "AXIS" for 11 points and was inordinately pleased with himself until Gemma put "PR" in front of his word, forming "PRAXIS" and netting her a Triple Word Score of 45 points. Avery didn't know what "praxis" meant, but he didn't want to reveal his ignorance by challenging her on the word, and he hadn't brought a dictionary with him anyway. He'd mistakenly assumed that because he could hold his own in Scrabble against his Ph.D. grandfather, he would wipe the floor with anybody his own age. Gemma, however, was his equal. When they resumed their game this evening, Avery would have to try harder.

He put on his Adidas track suit and running shoes and tiptoed into the bedroom area where Doc was still sleeping. He tucked his billfold, room key, Swiss Army knife and *Icebreaker* in his bag and slung the bag across his chest. He grabbed a ski cap and gloves too; this morning he planned on running a couple of miles outdoors before his workout in the hotel "gym." He slipped out of the room and rode the elevator down to the lobby.

Nobody was manning the front desk, so Avery walked right out the front doors and jogged down the sidewalk. He really wasn't supposed to be doing this; a clause in the trip "contract" he'd signed forbade him from leaving the hotel alone, and he could be sent home for breaking the rule. Being confined to the hotel was really getting to him, though, and he needed to run. Besides, no one had seen him, so no one would know.

The sidewalk was empty and well-lit from streetlights. The businesses were closed, their signs turned off and their windows dark. Ahead on the corner was a newsstand. An old man cut the string on a bundle of *Washington Post* and stacked the newspapers in front of the stand. Avery jogged in place and glanced at the headlines. Apparently, NASA had made some headway into its investigation of the Space Shuttle Challenger explosion of three weeks ago.

On January 28, Avery had been home "sick" from school. It was late morning, and he was eating a bowl of Honeycomb and watching the Challenger launch on TV when the explosion occurred—73 seconds after takeoff. NBC Anchor Tom Brokaw guardedly reported, "It appears something has happened to the Shuttle." Avery coughed up his cereal and shouted back, "No shit, Tom! The Shuttle just blew up!"

Here on the sidewalk, jogging in place in the cold, Avery shook his head at the newspaper and kept going. Although he was wearing a hat and gloves, by now Avery had misgivings about leaving the warmth of the hotel. But when he deliberated some more, he was cheered by his flouting of the rules and the fact that he would surely get away with this. He continued his run.

He passed shadowy lumps huddled in doorways. Avery often saw homeless people when he went with his grandfather to arbitration cases in Manhattan, but it was disturbing to see them when he was alone on a dark street in a strange city. It was cold, and these poor people had nowhere to go. Meanwhile, it didn't seem fair that Avery had a hotel and a breakfast buffet to return to.

He warmed up as he ran, and the horizon turned grayish pink with the first signs of dawn. He was like Rocky in the fighter's pre-dawn workout scenes. Avery didn't have little kids running with him, and shopkeepers weren't standing outside their shops cheering him on, but he had thoughts of Penny to encourage him.

At the end of the next block, the lights of a 24-hour convenience store glared into the darkness, bathing the sidewalk in bluish light. Inexplicably, Avery was consumed by a craving for hot chocolate.

Maybe they had one of those automatic machines. The door chimed, and he walked into a wall of blaring music: Whitney Houston singing ♫"How Will I Know."♫

Inside, he got a hot chocolate, two packages of Twizzlers, and a bouquet of pink roses for Penny. When he went to the front counter to pay, a homeless black man was arguing with the clerk. The man was middle-aged and wore a jacket with corporal's stripes on the sleeve; he was probably a Vietnam vet like Jack. The man was trying to buy a donut and a cup of coffee, but he didn't have enough money. Avery looked at the vet's boots; there were holes in them.

Four years ago, Avery's winter boots had had holes in them, and as the holes got bigger, instead of buying him a new pair, Jack and Jill made him use plastic bags as boot liners, and Avery was relentlessly teased for it. Finally, his Scoutmaster, Mr. McDougal, "found" an extra pair of boots in Avery's size and gave them to him. Avery nursed a grudge toward his parents over the boots because they'd claimed they didn't have money to buy him new ones, yet they were going out to bars a few nights a week.

Here in the convenience store, Avery decided to make this his Boy Scout good deed for the day: he "found" a ten-dollar bill on the floor and said the man must have dropped it. The man's eyes got misty.

"God bless you, son," the man said.

Avery saluted him. "My father served in Vietnam, sir. Have a great day." Avery paid, and on his way out the door, he glanced at his watch: five-thirty. If he hurried, he could be the first person in the hotel gym.

Icebreaker

Back in his room, Avery put the flowers in water, dropped off his bag, grabbed his Walkman, and went downstairs. As he neared the gym, light splashed into the dim hallway and there was the whirring sound of the treadmill. Crap. Somebody had gotten here before him. He entered the room warily.

A tall, skinny man in his sixties was walking about two miles per hour on the treadmill. He eyed Avery haughtily over a pair of metal-framed glasses. The glasses kept slipping down his nose, and every time they did, he pushed them back up with precisely one finger. Wearing tight red Dolphin shorts with white stripes on the sides,[23] a tight white T-shirt, and a red headband; with no muscle tone whatsoever and the swollen belly of a famished African child, he looked like one of the fitness rejects in Olivia Newton-John's music video for the song ♫"Physical."♫ The man took a sip from a can of Fresca, scowled at Avery, and increased his speed on the treadmill. Avery didn't know anything about this guy, but he detested him: for being the first one in the fitness room, for his twiggy build, and most of all for his swaggering, shoulders-back posture, which only accentuated his hideous belly, as if he was proud of the thing.

Avery put on his headphones, played his workout tape, and faced the wall. He loathed this so-called gym; he missed his little home gym, where he always got a good workout. He shrugged and decided to make the best of it. He warmed up with fifty jumping jacks, did twenty slow pull-ups, then got down on the exercise mat and went into his real workout—push-ups, crunches, leg lifts, handstand push-ups, etc. The next time Avery looked around, Headband Belly Man (Avery's nickname for him) was gone. Avery was lying on his back on the mat panting and sweating. His Walkman had stopped. It was 6:49.

Up in his room, Avery showered and, because they were touring the Capitol and the White House today, put on the one dressy outfit he'd brought: a navy-blue blazer, white Oxford shirt, a highly patriotic red, white, and blue-striped tie, khakis, tan socks, and penny loafers. He took out two of his new handkerchiefs, meticulously folded one of them, and slid it into the breast pocket of his blazer so the top ½" peeked out. He tucked the other one in his pants pocket. He now had one handkerchief "for showin'," as Pa had said, and one "for blowin'."

Before he left, he glanced in the bathroom mirror. With his face pink from his workout, and the super-classy pocket square, he looked damn good. He decided not to bring his musette bag; it would clash with the dashing look he was going for today. He tucked his billfold and the packages of Twizzlers into his blazer inside pockets and made

---

[23] These classic '80s athletic shorts were worn slightly higher on the waist and had small, curved side-slits along the outer thigh. The shorts generally came in three colors and patterns: red with white piping; white with navy piping; and navy with white piping.

sure he had his room key. Finally, on his way out the door, he draped his raincoat over one arm and grabbed the roses in the bathroom. He rode the elevator down to the lobby and sat on the sofa with the house phone beside it.

At seven o'clock exactly, he called Penny's room. When she picked up, he said he was in the lobby and had a surprise for her. Two minutes later, the elevator doors opened, and Penny stepped off. She had a grave expression on her face. As if indicative of her mood, she wore a long-sleeved white blouse buttoned to her throat and a cameo covering the top button, navy blue slacks, and black flats. With a flourish, Avery handed her the roses.

"Oh, they're wonderful, Avery!"

She smiled and sniffed them, then, with a glance around the lobby, she bounced up on her tiptoes and kissed his cheek. When she asked where he'd gotten them, Avery casually mentioned that he'd bought them at a convenience store during his run earlier.

"What?!" Penny said. "*You left the hotel!?* Avery, you could get in trouble!"

"I'm not getting in trouble. Come on, aren't you a *little* impressed? I doubt other girls are getting flowers from guys on this trip."

"I'm sorry," she said. "I love them, I do, and I think it was super daring and romantic of you. I don't mean to sound ungrateful. I just don't want you getting in trouble, that's all. Some guys from my school got sent home last night for having alcohol in their rooms."

"Well, that won't happen to me."

Penny said she would put them in her room and come back soon. She boarded the elevator and was sniffing the roses when the doors closed. Avery settled into the couch and pulled out *Icebreaker*. He was rereading the scene where Bond is alone on a road in northern Finland with towering snowbanks on both sides of the road, and two giant snowplows—one in front of Bond's car and one behind—try to kill him. Ever since he was thirteen years old, when he first read Ian Fleming's *Goldfinger* and knew he wanted to be a writer, Avery had reread scenes that intrigued him so he could figure out how they worked and why they kept him reading. Especially action scenes. In three years, he'd studied dozens of action scenes in books, and when he came across one with a unique device—like the dueling snowplows in *Icebreaker*—he would read it several times and write out the sentences he most admired.

While he was reading, he realized something so thrilling that it made him gasp. Bond's car in the novel, a silver Saab 900 SPG (Special Performance Group) Turbo, was the same car that Inge Ibsen had bought herself last year. He and Inge had had an epic fight last summer and hadn't spoken since, but if they made up when Avery got his learner's permit, she might let him drive it. He'd be driving James Bond's car!

He was immersed in the book when he became aware of somebody standing in front of his sofa. Avery glanced up from his book to see two short black high heels pinched together, a pair of trim calves in stockings, a sleek navy-blue sheath dress, a string of pearls, and the subtly made-up face of … Gemma Jones. Avery couldn't believe his eyes. A gray cardigan sweater was draped over her shoulders, and because the dress was sleeveless, Gemma's smooth, pale arms showed when she waved broadly to him.

"Hiya, Scrabble buddy."

She hitched up her camera strap on her shoulder and smiled. Gemma's hair, in a shiny, brushed-out ponytail, looked bouncy and fresh today, and the glasses she was wearing were smaller, tortoiseshell ones.

"Hi yourself." He pointed at his temple. "What happened?"

"Oh, a lens fell out," she said. "Good thing I had my spares."

Gemma looked him over. She lowered the tortoiseshell glasses with her thumb and index finger like they were a pair of Wayfarers.

"Looking good, Ace," she said.

"Feeling good, Jones," he said. "I was about to say the same to you. For a second, I thought you were Elle Macpherson. Seriously."

She squirmed and fingered the pearls. "Thanks. I figured since we're visiting the Capitol and the White House today, I should make an effort."

"Well, guess what?" Avery gave her two thumbs-up.

Gemma tittered and sat next to him on the sofa with her knees pinched together.

"The dress and pearls are my mom's," she said. "We're the same size. She's *incredibly* pretty though—stunning, actually—so they look way better on her."

"I doubt that," he said.

She looked at him askance. "You haven't met my mom."

Avery rested against the sofa armrest and crossed his legs. Gemma stared at the floor, then turned to him and smiled.

"I enjoyed our game last night. Shall we continue it later?"

"I'd like that," he said.

"What are you reading?"

Avery handed her the paperback, and then Gemma said some of the sweetest words he'd ever heard: "I don't know much about James Bond. Would you teach me about him sometime?"

Avery said he'd be glad to. She handed back his book and laughed out loud.

"What's funny?" he asked.

"I was thinking about how you handled that Vanderbush guy last night. That was hilarious."

"Stringbean? Oh, thanks." Although he said this nonchalantly, inside he was bursting with pride.

Gemma chuckled. "*Stringbean*?"

"My nickname for him."

"Why'd you have to do that anyway?"

"He took my seat and wouldn't give it back," Avery said.

"You're an incredible dancer. You make it look so easy. Your moonwalk at the end was just the best. Johanna and I were cracking up."

"I'll tell you a secret, Gem, because I think you can appreciate it. It's all about the floor. The floor has to have the perfect smoothness, and that floor was *primo*.[24] And there's another secret. Wanna see it?"

"I'd love to see it," she said.

"I haven't showed this to anyone else—I mean *nobody*." Avery patted the sofa cushion beside him. Gemma hitched closer until she was inches away and he could feel the warmth of her body heat. Avery

---

[24] A classic '80s slang term, and a favorite of Avery Craig's: **primo**, *adj.* Excellent, first-class. (Probably borrowed from Italian: *primo* [adj.] First, foremost, prime.)

took hold of his crossed ankle, tilted the sole in Gemma's direction, and pointed at a strip along the toe. Gemma leaned closer until their shoulders touched.

"Is that *sandpaper*?" she asked.

"Yup, super rough stuff—like twenty grit. I glued it on there."

"Brilliant." She cradled her chin in her palm and regarded his shoe. "When you're pushing off with the toe, the sandpaper digs in, and—"

"—because the sole of the other shoe is perfectly smooth, it—"

"—glides across the floor," Gemma said in wonder. "Amazing, Avery."

"There's technique, of course," he said, putting his foot down. "You have to shift your weight each time so like ninety percent of it is on your push-off leg. Anyway, that's my secret."

Gemma smiled. "I'll take it to my grave." She made an adorable zipping motion across her lips. "Oh, by the way—something I heard about Stringbean. He was one of the Vanderbush guys that got sent home last night."

"Oh? Not because of the thing at dinner?"

"No. He and some other guys had alcohol in their suitcases."

Avery sighed and shook his head. "How stupid can you get?"

"Turns out … pretty stupid."

They laughed together, touching shoulders, but the moment the elevator dinged, Avery snapped to attention. He'd forgotten that Penny was coming back downstairs, and it wouldn't look good if he was yukking it up with Gemma. When Eyeshadow and her skinny minions poured out of the car, Avery relaxed. Eyeshadow gave Gemma the once-over and jutted her chin at Avery.

"What's up, Ace?"

Avery glanced up. "Ceiling tiles, Doll."

Beside him, Gemma sniggered.

"Dork." Eyeshadow flapped a hand at him, and the pack of girls strolled down the hall.

Gemma stood. "It was great seeing you. Scrabble later?"

"For sure."

A Short Lease

Avery returned to *Icebreaker*, looking up every so often to greet classmates on their way to breakfast: Doc, Eric, Louis, Johanna, and Kristen. Everyone was dressed-up for the Capitol and White House today. He couldn't imagine what was keeping Penny. When he picked up the phone to call her room, Caitlyn stepped off the elevator.

She halted in front of Avery and struck a pose that she seemed to have struck a thousand times before: she planted her hands on her hips, cocked her butt to the side, smartly bent one knee, and swiveled her shoe on its toe.

"What do you think, Ace?"

Today's eye-popping number consisted of a clingy, leopard print tunic shirt, cinched around her waist by a chunky black leather belt; a black miniskirt that scarcely covered her butt; black leggings with black leg warmers over her calves; and leopard print pumps. The top had a plunging neckline, showcasing the pale crests of her breasts.

"It's stunning," Avery said.

"Really?"

"Yup," he said. "But don't let President Reagan see you like that."

"Why not?"

"Because you're liable to give the old dude a heart attack."

She smirked. "Well … maybe I'm a commie spy and that's my plan. But don't worry, I'll be wearing my coat … *Dad*."

"Where's Penny?" he asked.

The other elevator dinged, and Penny stepped off with some other Vanderbush girls.

"Pen," Caitlyn said, "I'll see you down there. I've got my usual *entrance* to make."

As Caitlyn whirled on her toes, her miniskirt rode up her butt slightly, giving Avery a brief but unobstructed view of her leggings. The things were so snug that the outline of her butt crack was distinct. Avery moaned under his breath.

Penny asked if she and Avery could go someplace private to talk, so he led her to an empty meeting room near the gym that he'd noticed earlier. The door was open, and the lights were on. When he got them inside, Penny said that she'd heard "some disturbing rumors." A Vanderbush boy who'd been sent home last night—a husky kid named Warren—had claimed that Avery had soaked him with a garbage bag of water during the water fight the first night, then shoved him when they'd visited Ford's Theatre. Penny crossed her arms over her chest. "Avery, you promised me you wouldn't fight. Did you throw that garbage bag at him?"

"Yes," Avery said, "but only because he attacked me. I was going into the stairwell, and he chased after me. But as for Ford's Theatre, he said I shoved him? That's a lie, Penny. He's a fat, clumsy kid. He tripped, plain and simple, and he's too embarrassed to admit it. What did I do that was so wrong?"

Tears filled her eyes. "Are we fighting, Avery?"

"*I'm* not fighting."

"You raised your voice at me," she said. "My father used to yell all the time. It's why I hate fighting so much."

Her coat slipped out of her hands and onto the floor. She started to cry. He picked up the coat.

"Oh, Penny, I'm sorry. Come here." Avery hugged her and stroked her hair. "We're not fighting, honest. And I'm sorry I raised my voice. I'm not angry with you."

He pulled out a handkerchief and handed it to her. She dabbed her eyes and wiped her nose, then rested her head on his chest.

"Avery, let's not fight again—ever."

"I told you—I wasn't fighting." Avery picked up her coat and draped it over a chair back. "It's like Michael Jackson says"—he gently kicked the door shut—"'I'm a lover, not a fighter.'"

He embraced her, holding her so close that her body was dripping off his. Holding her was so natural, as if their bodies had been made for each other's: Avery's arms were the perfect length to envelop her; Penny, standing on her tiptoes, was the perfect height to be kissed by him. He leaned in to kiss her, but she leaned away.

"Avery, this is moving so fast. I don't think we should kiss again."

"What do you mean? We've kissed *once*."

"I know, but we only met two days ago."

"Two days, two months—what's the difference? I like you."

"I like you too." She sighed. "I think I'd feel better if I knew what was going on here. I mean, is this a vacation fling for you? Will you go back to Hancock and forget about me?"

"No way. What about you? Will you go back to Vanderbush and forget about me?"

"There's no way I can forget you," she said. "But I don't want us kissing anymore unless I know this is serious."

"It's serious."

They were kissing when the door whisked open. Penny sprang away from him like he was a rattlesnake. Irina walked in and kicked a doorstop under the open door. Avery introduced her and Penny.

"Irina's from Finland, Penny," he said. "She doesn't know who Mark Twain is, but I'm pretty sure she's not a Soviet spy."

Irina narrowed her eyes at Avery and drummed her fingertips against her skirt. "Your boyfriend is quite clever and handsome. You should keep him—how you say ... on short lease?"

"Actually, Irina," Avery said, "the saying is 'a short *leash*.' Like a leash for a puppy."

"Ah, yes ... short *leash*." She nodded thoughtfully. "Yes, this makes sense. You remind me of cute pup."

Penny picked up her coat and tugged on Avery's arm.

"Have a good day, Irina," Avery said.

In the hallway, Penny remarked that it seemed like Irina had been flirting with him. Avery said she wasn't—that she was European and they were all friendly like that. Besides, the woman was like ten years older than him.

"Do you find her attractive?" Penny asked.

What was Avery supposed to say here? Of *course* he found Irina attractive—what guy wouldn't? But deep down he knew that a glamorous older woman like her was far out of his reach.

"Sure, she's attractive," he said. "But she's twice my age. In fact, she reminds me of a woman in one of my favorite Bond movies. Would you like me to tell you about it?"

Penny scrunched up her face and shook her head. Avery sighed and walked them to the dining room.

9

After breakfast, Mr. Nelson made announcements. He reviewed the sites they would be visiting that day—the Capitol, the White House, the National Gallery, and George Washington's home, Mount Vernon—stressing that everyone had to be on their absolute best behavior today.

Then he described what had happened overnight: a group of students had been caught with alcohol, and they'd been sent home early this morning with a parent chaperone. Mr. Nelson reminded everyone that they had signed a contract agreeing to rules of behavior during the trip. He reviewed the rule about no alcohol or drugs, then went through the other ones. When he got to the rule forbidding students from leaving the hotel unsupervised, Penny looked at Avery and gulped. But Avery knew nothing would come of it; nobody had seen him leave.

"All right, everyone," Mr. Nelson said, "the bus leaves in fifteen minutes. Grab any last-minute things from your rooms, use the bathroom, and get out to the bus."

Avery arranged to meet Penny on the bus, then used the bathroom off the lobby. On his way outside, he passed the hotel solarium. A hand reached out from the doorway and tugged him inside.

Inscrutalicious

Caitlyn pulled Avery deep into the room. The solarium was empty and quiet. There were deck and lounge chairs on fake indoor grass carpeting, and a bunch of huge potted plants—small trees really. Gray light filtered in through a massive skylight. The place was like an indoor jungle.

"There," she said. "A little privacy for us."

"Caitlyn, we're going to miss the bus."

"Re-*lax*." She flapped a hand. "Nobody gets left behind. They've got those clipboards."

"I should have expected an ambush," he said, "from the inscrutalicious Caitlyn Cray."

"Is that another insult, like 'nymphomaniac'?"

"No, it's a compliment. I made it up."

Caitlyn straightened the lapel of his raincoat. They were surrounded by several Ficus plants, rubber trees, and an avocado tree. Avery felt like Indy at the beginning of *Raiders*, when his rival, the French archaeologist Belloq, corners him in the jungle outside the temple and demands he hand over the golden idol. Caitlyn remarked that she'd seen Penny's roses and asked where he got them.

"At a convenience store," he said. "During my run this morning."

"Well, the roses are your second totally bitchin' move. I wish my boyfriend was romantic like you."

She unbuttoned her coat and let it drape off her shoulders. Then she backed Avery up against the wall between two giant pots.

"Caitlyn, what are you doing?"

She stepped closer and opened his raincoat and blazer as one would part curtains. The leopard print fabric of her top was clingy; her breasts, prominent. "But, Ace," she said softly, "you know what *wasn't* a bitchin' move? Flirting with that nerd from your school. A little bird told me about the two of you in the lobby this morning."

"Don't call her a nerd. And who told you that—Eyeshadow?"

"'Eyeshadow'? That's what you call her?" Caitlyn's eyes narrowed into amused slits. "That's hilarious."

"Listen, nothing happened, so you can forget about—"

"Whoops!" Caitlyn tipped forward. Her hands were on his waist, her breasts against his chest. In the pumps, she was as tall as him.

"Stop, Caitlyn—before you do something we'll regret."

Her eyes gleamed with delight. She whispered like she was thinking aloud. "*Damn*, the body you're hiding under there." Holding his waist, she pressed her thumbs hard against his stomach, dragging them over the abdominal ridges under his shirt and T-shirt.

"Are those your *abs*?! I guess you do work out every day." She gazed into his eyes. "Look, I won't tell Penny about that other girl."

"Good, because there's nothing to tell."

Avery pushed on Caitlyn's shoulders, which only caused her to tighten her grip on his waist.

"But," she said, "I want another kiss. Pretty please?"

One of the rubber tree leaves kept brushing his face; Avery snapped the branch off.

"I'm *not* kissing you."

This was what he said, but the instant Caitlyn had breathily broached the idea of a kiss, he got an erection.

"Fine," she said. "I'll kiss you."

♫"Rock You Like a Hurricane"♫

As Caitlyn closed her eyes and leaned in toward him, Avery curled his lips inward and compressed them tightly together, so there was no exposed lip-flesh for her to kiss. But when she rubbed her breasts against him, Avery gasped involuntarily and one of her cherry-flavored lips breached his bilabial barricade. As if sensing his capitulation, while kissing him Caitlyn deftly took hold of his hands and placed one on her butt and the other on her breasts.

With Caitlyn working her magic on his lips, Avery found himself in a trance, mindlessly tracing the contours of her butt through the smooth fabric of her leggings, and cupping and gently squeezing her breasts. His groin throbbed, and he immersed himself in the kiss— drilling his bulge into her, moaning into her mouth, kissing her hard in reply. He was rhythmically grinding his bulge against her when Caitlyn leaned away and uncoupled her lips from his.

"If Penny wasn't my best friend, I'd steal you from her like"—she snapped her fingers—"*that*. And if it doesn't work out between you two, I'm dumping Shane and scooping you up." She primped his tie and tenderly straightened his bangs with her fingertips.

Avery frowned. "You're making a big assumption, Caitlyn."

"Yeah? What's that?"

"That I would let you 'scoop me up.' I like Penny."

"Mm-hm … well, I think part of you likes me more." She glanced down at his groin. "Uh-oh, you've got a problem there." Her eyes got girlishly wide.

"Yeah, a problem *you* caused."

Caitlyn reached in her purse and rolled Maybelline Kissing Potion on her lips until they were greasy with the stuff. She creased and wiggled her lips in thought, then yanked the raincoat off him and draped it over his forearm.

"*Voilà!* Now, no one can see your rodney." She sniggered and kissed him again. "God you're tasty!" She peeked out. "Okay, all clear. You go out first." Before he could leave, she grabbed his arm. "You'd better not say anything to Penny about this. If you do, I'll tell her about Irina and the other girl."

"I won't."

She didn't seem to have heard him.

"This was fun, Ace," she said. "You can bet your sweet patootie we'll be doing it again."

Sahhjent-at-Ahhms

Avery and Penny sat together on the bus and held hands during the ride to the Capitol. It was snowing hard outside, and the Washington Monument appeared vaguely in the distance as a colossal phallus. As the bus crept through the snowy rush-hour traffic, everyone, including the teachers and chaperones, was in high spirits, but Avery was preoccupied with something else. Ever since his torrid mini-make-out session with Caitlyn earlier, Avery had been nauseated, and his groin ached terribly.

At a Scout meeting once, Avery had overheard Clutch, Wacker, Griff, and the other older guys speaking in hushed, fearful tones about an agonizing phenomenon called "blue balls." According to the guys, when a girl got them revved up without release, the fluids and pressure that built up in a guy's scrotum got backed up in there, making him sick. The guys had grumbled that it was excruciating, but until this morning Avery hadn't believed them. Several times during the bus ride, however, Avery was sure he would vomit. When

Penny glanced at him and asked if he was all right, he said that he'd overeaten at breakfast and his stomach needed to settle.

When they arrived at the Capitol, they had to empty their pockets and pass through metal detectors. Avery was glad he'd left his bag with his Swiss Army knife back at the hotel. Mr. Nelson's review of the rules earlier had ensured that everyone (especially the remaining Vanderbush boys) behaved when they were led into the National Statuary Hall (the Old Hall of the House of Representatives). The group was met by a congressman from their district. The guy, James something, had round, chubby cheeks and looked like an adult-sized version of the Ivory Snow baby.[25] To go with his face, he had a high-pitched baby voice that made the girls giggle. Pointing at a statue of John Quincy Adams, he told them a canned story about how Mr. Adams had returned to the House after serving as President, and later died on the House floor. Avery raised his hand.

"Excuse me, congressman."

"Yes?"

"When you say he died on the House floor, did he, like, collapse on the floor, or did he just kind of slump over his desk?"

"Hm, I'm not sure. Good question. I'll ask my staff to find out."

Avery looked around at the other statues and noticed that Caitlyn was making eyes at him. While the congressman yammered on, Caitlyn stared straight at Avery and glided the tip of her tongue across her upper lip. Avery fantasized about humping her in an empty cloakroom.

He wished Mallory, Lee, and E.B. were here. Especially E.B., who interacted with the world like it was one giant videogame. The dude had the unique ability to ferret out the most interesting things on a tour—stuff behind the scenes or on the periphery that no one else noticed. If E.B. were here, he'd do something cool like find an old dumbwaiter, and they'd descend to a crypt beneath the building. A Jack and Zeb story started to form in his mind. Avery was writing down the idea when there was a tug on his sleeve.

---

[25] The Ivory Snow baby was featured in commercials and print ads for Ivory Snow soap products.

"Avery," Penny said, "we have to catch up with our group."

They found their group down the hall, at a sign that read, "SENATE GALLERY." An arrow pointed upstairs. Their guide, a skinny dweeb with a smudge of a mustache—probably some senator's ne'er-do-well nephew—spouted some history, but Avery ignored him.

Penny whispered in his ear: "What happened before? You, like, completely spaced out."

"Nothing. I was thinking of something. One second."

He took out his notebook again and jotted down another idea. It would be his best Jack and Zeb adventure ever.

"You looked a million miles away," she said. "You're not mad at me, are you?"

He wagged the notebook and put it away. "Story idea, that's all."

The guide opened the stairwell doors and said, "You mustn't make a sound upstairs. Understood?"

There were solemn nods and murmurs. They filed up the stairs.

In the gallery, the tour guide and Mr. Nelson stood inside the doorway with fingers to their lips. The guide pointed at the row of seats down front, with a view over the railing. Avery and Penny took the two seats in the far corner.

The first thing that struck Avery about the Senate chamber was the amount of dark, rich wood and gleaming marble. But the second thing that struck him was how *nothing* was happening. The president *pro tempore*—the guy who sat in the big chair at the front when Vice President Bush wasn't here—was flipping through a newspaper. Groups of men stood around chatting, like his grandparents' guests did during the pre-prandial cocktail hour, except in this case none of the men were holding drinks. Other men conferred at their desks, and some of the elderly ones openly slept in their chairs.

After five minutes of watching the senators do nothing, Avery decided that they didn't notice them up here. With school groups filing in and out all day long, week after week, year after year, students must look like wallpaper to them by now. He and Penny were partially hidden by a supporting column, which gave him an idea. He pulled out his pen and itinerary, jotted a note in tiny print, and handed it to Penny with the pen.

Penny, when we're about to leave, I want to kiss you.

She glanced over the railing at the Senate floor and wrote,

We can't. This is the Senate! I'd be so embarrassed if
we got caught. We could get sent home! I'm sorry, Avery,
but no way.

Avery took the pen and jotted a quick rejoinder:

Come on, one little kiss.

Penny sighed.

Okay, one quick kiss.

Avery scribbled,

All right, follow my lead.

He put the paper away, and when their group started filing out, he pretended he'd dropped something. When everyone was gone, Penny looked at him and swallowed. They leaned toward each other, closed their eyes, and kissed.

The sensation of Penny's lips was so new and pleasant that, like a new candy, Avery couldn't get enough of it. Before he knew it, what he'd originally intended to be a two-second peck had turned into a ten-second canoodling. Penny's hot breath bathed his cheek, and he forgot where they were.

There was a sharp whistle from the Senate floor. He and Penny sprang to attention and peered over the railing. Three men smiled up at them. One of them was stroking his forefinger across the other as if to say, "Shame on you two!"

"Senator Kennedy!" Avery said.

Penny turned the color of a stoplight. She sprang from her chair and ran out.

Avery leaned over the railing.

"I'm sorry, senator," he said. "It won't happen again."

Senator Kennedy and the other men laughed. "I hope not, young man," Senator Kennedy said. "The, ah, sahhjent-at-ahhms tends to, ah, diss-uh-*prooov* of teenagers necking in the Senate Gallery. Go catch up with your group, son."

"Yes, sir." Avery stood.

"And son," Senator Kennedy said. "You should apologize to your girl. I've never seen quite such a shade of, ah, red before."

"I will, senator. But before I go, may I make a statement in my defense?"

The senator grinned at his colleagues. "'Unanimous consent to, ah, revise and extend your, ah, ruh-mahhks'?" He chuckled. "Okay, son, what is it?"

"I only did it so we'd have a story to tell our grandchildren."

"Well in *that*, young man," the senator said, "you have, ah, succeeded."

Avery hustled out and followed the signs to the exit staircase. When he got downstairs, his group was way down the hall. Penny and Caitlyn were straggling at the end. He headed after them.

Two burly men in suits stepped out of a doorway. One of them raised a hand, halting Avery. "Hold it, son," he said. The other guy touched his ear. He had an earpiece—a cord went over his ear and snaked underneath the collar of his suit jacket; he was listening to something. He nodded and finally raised his hand to his mouth. He was holding some kind of miniature CB mike.

"Got it," he said into the mike. "We'll bring him down." He glanced at Avery. "What's your name, son?"

"Avery Craig."

"Avery Craig," he said into the mike. "Yeah. … Uh-huh. … Okay."

Now he'd done it. He'd been caught and was getting sent home.

"Am I in trouble?" Avery asked. "Like I told the senator—the kissing it won't happen again."

"Relax, son." The man who spoke into the mike put his arm down. "You're not in trouble. The senator simply wants to meet you."

"What?! So, I *am* in trouble."

"Take it easy," the guard said. "You're not in trouble, and your group will wait. What school are you with?"

"Hancock High School," Avery said. "West Troutkill, New York."

Meanwhile, the other man didn't say a word. He kept scanning the hallway. It was unsettling.

"Why does the senator want to meet me?" Avery asked.

The man shrugged. "No idea. Come on, let's go." He put a hand firmly on Avery's back. "This way."

The men walked down the cavernous marble hallway.

"Are you guys Secret Service agents?" Avery asked.

"No, we're on the senator's security and protection detail."

At the end of the corridor, there was another guard checkpoint, with a metal detector. A sign read, "OFFICIAL PERSONNEL ONLY BEYOND THIS POINT." Avery passed through the metal detector, and the senator's two guards led him to a towering wooden door at the end of the hallway. One of them rapped twice on the door and opened it.

"The young man you wanted to meet, senator. Avery Craig from West Troutkill, New York."

"Yes, ah, send him in!" the senator boomed.

One of the guards prodded him with a gentle push, and Avery stepped into a vestibule. Out a side door was an outer office. Secretaries were typing and talking on telephones.

"Straight through, son," the senator said.

Avery walked into a gigantic office of dark wood. Senator Kennedy stood behind a desk that was the size of Avery's dining room at home. The senator grinned.

"Come in, Avery Craig, come in! Don't tell me a young man so bold as to, ah, *neck* in the Senate Gallery is experiencing, ah, trepidation, at meeting a United States Senator." He extended his hand to Avery.

Avery was glad that "trepidation" was one of January's words from his Daily Vocab calendar.

"Trepidation? No, senator, I'm not feeling dread or apprehension, sir. I'm more embarrassed than anything." Avery shook the senator's hand; a whiff of whiskey was in the air. "I want to apologize again, sir. That was stupid and disrespectful of me."

"Forget it," Senator Kennedy said. "Would you like a, ah, cola, Avery? Or perhaps a root beer?" The senator said "beer" with a thick Boston Harvard accent, so it sounded like two syllables: "BEE-uh."

"Yes, sir. Thank you."

"Help yourself and sit down." He gestured to a sideboard, which had a mini fridge underneath.

Avery got himself a can of Coke Classic. Cracking it open, he breathed deeply of its smoky initial scent, held it to his ear, and listened to it fizz loudly in the can. For Avery Craig, this was the smell and sound of Freedom. He doubted any Soviet teenagers were doing this right now—hanging out in the office of a powerful political leader, drinking the world's finest soft drink. Seriously, how great was it to be an American? He took a sip, sat down, and crossed his legs. The senator was studying him closely. He smiled.

"You're a, ah, *fan* of Coca-Cola, I take it," he said.

"A big fan, sir. But I'm relieved they brought back the classic formula. Last year's 'New Coke' was an abomination."[26]

Senator Kennedy asked Avery if his surname of Craig was Irish or Scottish; Scottish, Avery said. He was taken aback at how attentive the senator was; he seemed genuinely interested in Avery's life. The senator squinted. "How old are you, son?"

"I turn sixteen in a few days, sir."

"Remarkable," the senator said. "You seem older. You've got a, ah, bigger frame than most young men your age. Anyway, the reason I wanted to meet you is, when I saw you up there, kissing your girl, you reminded me of my older brother Joe."

"Joe junior—the war hero?"

The senator sat up in his immense leather chair. "That's right."

"I'm honored, senator." Avery gushed momentarily about how his grandfather had been in FDR's administration, and both sides of his

---

[26] In 1985, the makers of Coca-Cola introduced a sweeter, less-fizzy version of Coke called "New Coke," and public backlash was severe. Within months, New Coke was yanked from store shelves, and the company released "Coca-Cola Classic Original Formula." Forty years later, it's still unclear whether this was a marketing blunder of epic proportions, or if it was an elaborate scheme designed to bolster sales of a soft drink that consumers had taken for granted. However, in-depth research of this matter—including interviews of ad men at Coca-Cola's advertising firm in the 1980s—has revealed that New Coke was actually a failed attempt at "hipification": making an old product "hip" for younger consumers. When presented with the "elaborate scheme" theory, one ad exec said, "Nope. They weren't that bright."

family had been lifelong, diehard Democrats. He wasn't sure if the senator heard him, though, because the man was staring wistfully into the distance.

"Kissing your girl in the gallery—that was something Joe *and* Jack would have done." Senator Kennedy smiled and shook his head. "Bold and fearless."

"In my case," Avery said, "it was more impulsive and thoughtless, but thank you, senator."

The senator chuckled.

"And in Jack's case," Avery said, "I doubt he would have been caught like I was."

"You're, ah, right about that," the senator said. "But if he was caught, he would have flashed that smile of his and gotten off the hook." The senator nodded at Avery. "You're a muscular, good-looking young man, like Joe was at your age. I imagine you have to beat the girls off with a stick."

Avery sighed. "The stick broke, sir, so I switched to an umbrella."

The senator laughed. "You're very well-spoken for only, ah, sixteen."

Avery crossed his leg and took a sip of the Coke. "Thanks. I think it comes from having to hold my own with the adults at the dinner table. My grandparents have these weekend get-togethers with some pretty impressive people and family friends, and I've had to work to keep up with them."

"Sounds a lot like my experience as a boy," Senator Kennedy said.

"Yes, I read a book about your family," Avery said, "how your father made you and your brothers and sisters debate at the dinner table. You were always competing. At least that's what I read, sir."

"That's the way it was all right." He leaned back in his chair, steepling his fingers. "How are you doing in school?"

Avery shrugged. "Okay, I guess. I get A's in English and A-minuses in other subjects—except for Geometry and Latin, that is. I'm on the verge of failing those. I *loathe* Latin."

"Tell me, Avery, are you interested in public service? Is that why you're here in D.C.? I ask because there are junior internships available and—"

"Senator," Avery said, "I want to be a novelist like Ian Fleming."

The senator leaned back in his chair and put a finger on his chin. "Interesting. He was one of Jack's favorites as I recall."

"That's right. Ian Fleming's books weren't selling in the U.S., and then President Kennedy said he was reading *From Russia with Love*, and Fleming became an overnight sensation. When you're president, sir, maybe you could do that for me."

The senator chuckled again. "Okay, Avery Craig. We have a, ah, *dee-uhl*."

"Oh, by the way, senator," Avery said, "congratulations on your niece's upcoming wedding."

The senator nodded. "Yes, Maria."

"I know what you might be thinking, sir," Avery said. "'Arnold Schwarzenegger? What the heck is this *bodybuilder* doing marrying my niece?' But I think he's a lot smarter than he seems, sir. I think he's got a big future in movies, politics even."

The senator nodded. "Yes, he's, ah, remarkably impressive, and a savvy businessman too. I agree with you about everything except the politics. I don't see how a man who speaks with such a thick accent could ever rise in the political world."

Avery put his Coke down and sat up in his chair. He looked the senator level in the eyes. "With all due respect, sir, lots of people think the *Kennedys* talk with a thick accent."

For a second, Senator Kennedy stared at Avery blank-faced, then broke into booming laughter. Emboldened by the senator's reaction, Avery stood and mimicked the senator's monologue to him from the senate floor earlier. "'The, ah, *sahhjent-at-ahhms* tends to, ah, *dissa-proove* of teenagers necking in the Senate Gallery.'"

The senator became red-faced, continuing to laugh. On a roll, Avery kept going. "'You should apologize to your girl. I've never seen such a shade of, ah, red *buh-fo-ah*.'"

With the senator laughing as hard as Avery had ever seen someone laugh, Avery stood up straight, raised his chin and gestured with his hands, as if he were standing in front of a lectern, finishing his brief performance with his best imitation of President Kennedy: "'We choose to go to the moon in this decade and do the other things. Not because they *aahh* easy, but because they *aahh haaahhhd!*'"

While the senator was doubled over slapping his desk, Avery sat down, crossed his legs, and sipped his Coke. The senator pulled a handkerchief from his pocket and dabbed his eyes. This was the first time Avery had made a person laugh so hard that he cried.

"You, Avery Craig," he finally said, "are a funny young man, and I could use some more, ah, *hue-muh*, in my life." He opened his desk drawer, took out a card and extended it to Avery. "I want you to have this, son. If you change your mind about one of the junior internships, give me a call."

"Yes, sir." He pocketed the business card. "Thank you. By the way, senator, my friends call me 'Ace.'"

"Ace, eh?" The senator smiled. "How did you, ah, get such a nickname?"

Avery was about to tell him when an intercom beeped on the senator's desk.

"Senator," a woman's voice said, "the Speaker of the House is on line three."

"Sorry, Ace, I have to take this," the senator said. "Son, do you ever get out to the, ah, Cape?"

"Cape Cod, sir?"

"Yes, Hyannis Port. If you're out there this *summuh*, you should, ah, drop in."

"Thank you, sir, I might do that. It was an honor meeting you, senator."

Senator Kennedy nodded and picked up the phone handset. "Tip? … Mm, I see. But it's in, ah, conference, isn't it?"

Avery went out the way he'd come in, quietly placing his empty Coke can in the wastebasket.

Majorly Boneheaded

Out in the hallway, he was met by the bodyguard who'd spoken to him earlier. "Your group's down in the rotunda. I'll take you."

As they walked down the long hallway, the guard said, "I don't know who you are, young man, but I've gotta tell you—you had the senator laughing his butt off. And let me tell you something else— you're young so I'm not sure if you can appreciate this, but one of the most powerful men in the country spent *fifteen minutes* with you. I've seen Senator Kennedy give other senators less time than that. What I'm saying is, you made a good impression on him, and he's a great man to have in your corner. What's your name anyway?"

Avery reached into his inside blazer pocket, peeled off a Twizzler, and took a bite.

"The name is Craig, Avery Craig. What's yours?"

"Jim." He chuckled and looked askance at Avery. "You must have the luck of the Irish in you. Make out with your girl in the Senate Gallery and spend time with a U.S. Senator? Unbelievable."

"It was an honor, Jim," Avery said. "Meeting the senator, that is— not making out with my girlfriend."

Jim chuckled again. They walked through an archway into the rotunda. "Good luck to you, Avery Craig … although I don't think you need it." He clapped Avery on the shoulder and walked away.

In the rotunda, everyone was staring up at the ceiling—except Penny and Caitlyn, who were commiserating. The tour guide said the painting on the ceiling had to do with George Washington, but Avery didn't care. As he was walking over to the girls, Caitlyn shook her head at Avery and waved him off. Even from fifty feet away, the embarrassment on Penny's face was obvious. When Avery looked up next, Caitlyn was walking toward him. She joined Avery against the wall, bumped shoulders with him, and clucked her tongue.

"'Smooth move, *Ex-Lax*.' Oh, Ace, a majorly boneheaded move."[27]

"Yeah, I guess," he said.

"You *guess*? Making out with Penny in the Senate Gallery?" Caitlyn leaned against him. "That's not something you do with Penny—a girl who gets embarrassed if she burps in a restaurant. That's something you do with *me*, someone who'd love to get caught by Senator Kennedy, and who'd tell everyone about it. Ace—what happened? You were going along great, making wicked cool moves. Now what do we do with you?"

---

[27] This TV commercial tagline for the laxative Ex-Lax was often used by cool, trendsetting teenagers like Caitlyn and Avery to express sarcastic disdain for a fellow teenager's botching of a situation. A similar, but less popular, '80s catchphrase was, "Nice play, Shakespeare."

Avery shrugged and said that at least he'd gotten to meet Senator Kennedy. When Caitlyn didn't believe him, he showed her the senator's business card.

"I should go tell Penny I'm sorry," he said.

Caitlyn smirked. "Give her time to cool off. Trust me."

"'Trust me'? Hey, that's my line."

"No, it's not," she said. "We both stole it from Indiana Jones."

Avery huffed. "Let me guess—she doesn't want to sit with me on the bus for the rest of the day."

Caitlyn shoved her hands in her coat pockets. "Not right now."

"Fine. If I write her a note, will you give it to her?"

"Sure."

"And do you promise not to read it?"

"Nope." Caitlyn looked around, then goosed Avery's butt. He jumped a foot. "Go write your apology, loverboy." She wove through the throng.

After the rotunda, they toured some other rooms in the Capitol, but Avery paid no attention. He was busy drafting his note to Penny in his head. By the time their group reached the Capitol gift shop, Avery knew what he wanted to say. He bought a notepad, went into the bathroom, and scribbled his note:

> Penny,
> I'm sorry. Caitlyn was right: that was a majorly
> boneheaded move. Please forgive me. Sometimes I don't
> think things through. It was impulsive and stupid of me,
> and I shouldn't have put you on the spot like that. If it's
> any consolation, I met Senator Kennedy afterwards, and
> we talked for like 15 minutes. I doubt he'll say anything
> about our kiss. As I understand it, he's made some pretty
> boneheaded moves himself.
> Sincerely,
> Avery

Avery emerged from the bathroom as the group was filing outside to the bus. It was snowing harder now, but a grounds crew was keeping the Capitol steps and sidewalk shoveled and salted. Kids made snowballs and tossed them at each other. Penny was standing by herself beside the bus with her hands in her pockets. Avery was approaching her with the note when Caitlyn cut him off.

"I wouldn't, Romeo. She's still fuming. Give it to me."

He watched her deliver the note to Penny. Then, without so much as a glance at him, Penny followed Caitlyn onto the bus.

When he boarded the bus, Gemma was sitting alone in the second row, reading a book. She looked up and smiled faintly. He smiled and sat down beside her.

A Primer on James Bond

Although their next stop on the tour—the White House—was technically only a short drive down Pennsylvania Avenue, because of construction detours and the fact that tour buses were required to use a special entrance, they had to take the long way around. Avery used the extra time with Gemma to give her a primer on James Bond.

Avery explained that Bond was created by the British writer Ian Fleming, who himself had worked for British Naval Intelligence during WWII. The novels came first, he said, with *Casino Royale* published in 1953; the first movie, *Dr. No*, was released in 1963. So far, only three men had played James Bond: Sean Connery, George Lazenby, and Roger Moore. Avery added that, in his opinion, Sean Connery played the best James Bond. Gemma asked him which Connery Bond movie was his favorite and without missing a beat, Avery replied, "*Goldfinger*. Totally."

He added that he owned his own VHS tape of the movie and had watched it over fifty times. When Gemma asked him what his favorite Roger Moore James Bond movie was, he said, "That's easy—*The Spy Who Loved Me*. And it has the most beautiful Bond girl ever."

Gemma scoffed. "'Bond *girl*'? Sounds pretty male chauvinistic if you ask me."

"It is, but the books were written back in the fifties."

"What's the name of her character?" Gemma asked.

Avery explained that she had two names. Because she served in the Soviet military, she was Major Amasova. But her spy code name was Agent Triple-X.

"*Triple-X?*" Gemma said. "You mean like she's in *sex* movies!?"

Avery was surprised Gemma knew what a triple-X film rating meant. Luckily, she hadn't asked him for other examples; if she found "Agent Triple-X" too racy, what would she have thought of "Pussy Galore"?

"No, it's just a racy-sounding name," Avery said. "Most of the Bond girls have them."

"And you've read all the books and seen all the movies?" she asked.

"Yup—some of them multiple times. My biggest dream is to write James Bond novels."

"So, what's stopping you?"

"I looked into it," he said. "I don't have the rights to the character. A writer named John Gardner does. No way is the publisher going to let a teenage guy write a Bond novel."

Gemma removed her glasses and stared at Avery. Her eyes, a rich coppery brown, were enormous globes.

"Someday you might," she said. "But if you can't, to heck with James Bond. Create your own spy character—an American."

"Maybe I will."

Gemma fogged her glasses and wiped them with a tissue. Her cheekbones were high and prominent and lovely. She held up her cleaned glasses to the window and put them back on.

"You should take a college course," she said absently.

"Why?"

"Because the stuff they teach us in high school is so lowest-common-denominator. I learned more about computers in one course at the community college than I'd learned in ten years before that."

Gemma had three computers: an Apple IIe, an Apple Macintosh, and, because her father worked for IBM, an IBM PC. Programming came easily to her, and she'd written some simple games using ASCII characters for graphics, and now she was taking an advanced course at New Netherlands Community College to learn how to do sophisticated bit graphics.

Avery sighed. "It sounds great, but I doubt my parents would go for it. They know I write, but they think it's only a hobby."

"Show them it's more than a hobby." She gently nudged his shoulder with hers. "Write a *novel*. That will show them you're serious."

"I might do that."

"Thank you for teaching me about Bond," she said.

"Anytime."

After half an hour of wending through the D.C. streets, the bus pulled up to the White House gate. The entire time Avery had been talking with Gemma, he hadn't thought about Penny or Caitlyn once.

That Kind of Pow-uh

When the bus stopped and the air brakes hissed, Mr. Nelson and Ms. Wharton got off, stood in front of the gatehouse, and talked with a Secret Service police officer. From where Gemma and Avery sat, they had a clear view of the scene outside.

The police officer flipped through pages on a clipboard and, shaking his head, showed Mr. Nelson the list. Ms. Wharton opened an envelope, removed a letter, and started reading it aloud. Another officer exited the gatehouse, took the letter, then reached in the window and made a call. He spoke on the phone for a minute, glancing down at the letter as he talked. Finally, he frowned, hung up the phone and talked to Mr. Nelson and Ms. Wharton. Avery could tell by their posture that the news wasn't good, and so, apparently, could the other students on the bus.

"Uh-oh," said a girl sitting in the seat behind him. "Looks like we're not getting in, which is complete bullshit cuz my parents voted for President Reagan *both* times." There was more grumbling and mutinous talk, which got louder when Mr. Nelson and Ms. Wharton conferred briefly and moped back toward the bus. Beside him, Gemma groaned softly and said, "There's obviously a problem."

Avery perked up in his seat. Here was an opportunity for him— an opportunity to be the hero and get back into Penny's good graces. He needed to do something here, something bold, but not so bold that it would embarrass Penny. The question was, what should he do? What *could* he do?

He could call Pa. His grandfather knew people who could call the White House and explain the situation. Important people like Mr. Worthington, a friend of Pa's from graduate school, who was, or used to be, an ambassador to South Korea. Avery peered over the seat and out the bus windshield; there was a phone booth up the block; Avery could run to it and call Pa. But if he got his grandfather on the phone, then what? Pa would then have to call the people he knew, and so on; it could be an hour before anyone reached the White House and explained things.

Then he remembered … Senator Kennedy. As Mr. Nelson and Ms. Wharton stepped back onto the bus, Avery showed them the senator's business card.

"What if I called Senator Kennedy for us?" he said. "I'm sure he can get us in."

"But Senator Kennedy doesn't represent our district," Mr. Nelson said. "There's nothing he can do. He doesn't have that kind of power. We're simply not on today's tour list, so I'm afraid that's that."

Looking at Avery, Ms. Wharton smiled and shook her head. "No, Mr. Nelson, I say we let Avery try."

"Fine, Ms. Wharton," Mr. Nelson said, "but *you* can argue with the officers this time."

"Okay." She waved Avery ahead of her. "Avery, dear—you're up."

Avery bounded off the bus with confidence, but when he hit the cold air and the falling snow, the doubts crept in. What if he couldn't get them into the White House? He could feel the students' eyes on him; they were counting on him to fix this. It was too late to turn back now. As if sensing his anxiety, Ms. Wharton patted his shoulder.

"Relax, dear," she said. "The worst that happens is, we don't get to do the White House tour. It's disappointing, but hardly a tragedy."

When they reached the gatehouse, Ms. Wharton requested that Avery be allowed to call somebody. The officer in the window handed Avery the phone handset and asked for the number to dial. Avery read Senator Kennedy's phone number off the card. A secretary answered. Avery identified himself and explained his situation: that he'd met with Senator Kennedy earlier, and now he and his classmates were at the White House, trying to get in for their scheduled tour, but their schools weren't on the list.

"Is this Ace?" the secretary asked.

Avery's jaw dropped. "Yes, ma'am, it is."

"The senator is about to start another meeting, but I'll try to catch him. Please hold."

The silence on the line while he waited was agonizing. He'd been on hold only for a minute, but with the Secret Service police officers studying their watches and glowering at him, one minute felt like an hour. Finally, the officer in the gatehouse window shook his head.

"Okay, son," he said, reaching for the phone, "that's enough."

Then Senator Kennedy's voice boomed over the line: "Avery 'Ace' Craig! My secretary says you and your, ah, fellow students are waiting outside the White House for your, ah, scheduled *too-uh*."

"That's correct, sir," Avery said. "I'm sorry to bother you, senator, but I don't have anybody else I can call. Mister Nelson—that's one of our teacher-chaperones—he said that because you don't represent our district, you wouldn't have the power to fix this. But my English teacher, Ms. Wharton"—he smiled at her—"she said, 'Avery, you should call Senator Kennedy. I bet *he* can get us in.'"

"Oh, she did, did she?" the senator said. "Is she attractive, this teacher of yours?"

"Very," Avery said, glancing at her. "She's standing right here, sir."

"Put her on, son."

Avery handed the phone to Ms. Wharton, and although he couldn't hear what Senator Kennedy said to her, he saw its effects—Ms. Wharton giggling, faintly wriggling, and cooing, "Oh, senator, you're most kind. Thank you." She was blushing when she handed the phone back to Avery.

"Ace," Senator Kennedy said, "I'll call the White House tours office right away. What's the name of your school, son?"

Avery told him his group was composed of two schools in New Netherlands County, New York: Hancock and Vanderbush. The senator laughed.

"You're joking!"

"No, sir."

"Relax, Ace. I'll have you and your, ah, fellow students inside the White House in five minutes. And you be sure to tell Mister, ah, *Nelson* that Senator Ted Kennedy of Massachusetts absolutely *does* have that kind of *pow-uh*."

"I'll do that. Thank you, senator. Thank you so much. If there's ever anything I can do for you—"

"Forget it, Ace," Senator Kennedy said. "Enjoy the tour. Tell the President I said hello." He hung up.

Avery gave the phone handset back to the officer.

"So?" Ms. Wharton said. "What did he say?"

"That he'd have us inside the White House in five minutes."

Ms. Wharton smiled and shook her head at him. "Avery, not only are you a terrific English student but you're poised, persuasive, and more than a little manipulative in real-life situations."

He shrugged. "I wanted to get us in. By the way, Ms. Wharton, what did the senator say to you?"

"I can't remember exactly, but he was quite charming. It was something like, 'You must be a great English teacher, because Avery Craig is one of the best-spoken young people I've ever met.' Then he jokingly asked if I gave private lessons in grammar and elocution."

"I don't think he was joking, Ms. Wharton."

"What makes you say that?"

"Because before I put you on, the senator asked me if you were attractive, and I said, 'Very.'"

Ms. Wharton wagged a gloved finger. "Avery Craig…"

"Well," he said with a smile, "it's *true*."

The phone rang inside the gatehouse. The officer who answered it listened without saying anything and hung up. He was shaking his head and faintly smiling when he addressed Ms. Wharton. "Okay, ma'am, we got the word. The students can start lining up."

Because he wanted to surprise everybody, Avery tried not to let his elation show. It was hard to remain stoic, however, because he was amazed with himself. As often happened when he experienced a great burst of emotion, he heard a song in his head—in this case the majestic inaugural horns of the theme from *Superman*. He walked toward the bus, humming the theme to himself.

♫"March from *Superman*"♫

Dark shapes press against the bus windows; the students breathlessly await the verdict. Avery bows his head and trudges down the sidewalk. He wants them to think he's failed. He plods up the bus stairs and stands next to the driver, Herb, who nods sympathetically and says, "Hey, kid, at least you tried." Mr. Nelson sits in the first row, next to the Soviet female powerlifter. The students are leaning over the seat backs. A few of them groan when they see the downcast expression on Avery's face, but most of them are silent, slack-jawed, barely breathing. Avery glimpses Penny near the back of the bus; she looks worried. Gemma, however, gazes at him with steely eyes and a proud smile; somehow, she knows he's been successful. Behind him, Ms. Wharton says, "Go on, Mr. Craig—tell them." Avery heaves out a sigh, then, after a pause, throws his fists in the air.

"We're in!"

The entire bus erupts in shouts, squeals, and chants of "Ace, Ace, Ace!" Avery poses in profile, like Christopher Reeve as Superman, with his fists on his hips and an imaginary breeze fluttering his cape. Gemma looks up at him and giggles. While the students are chanting, Mr. Nelson gets to his feet.

"Okay, that's enough, folks," he said. "Nice work, Mr. Craig."

"By the way, sir," Avery said, "Senator Kennedy asked me to relay a message. He said, 'You be sure to tell Mister, ah, *Nelson* that Senator Edward Kennedy of Massachusetts *does* have that kind of *pow-uh.*'"

Avery Craig was a hero.

It was the greatest moment of his life so far.

10

Dᴜʀɪɴɢ ᴛʜᴇ White House tour, Avery was in a fog of euphoria, only peripherally aware of the guide's monologues about each room. His fellow students monopolized his attention with their pats on his back and whispers of, "Way to go, Ace."

Because of the mix-up (Ivory Snow Baby had mistakenly scheduled their schools for the following week), and because Senator Kennedy had called on their behalf, the White House tours office extended their tour into the West Wing—something almost never done during a workday when the President was in residence. They got to peek into the Oval Office (it was smaller than Avery had imagined), and they saw the famous jar of jellybeans that President Reagan kept on his desk. Now they were in the main hall, waiting to be led to the next room, when six Secret Service agents, each the size of an Abrams tank, marched in and surrounded the group.

A moment later, a tall and beaming President Ronald Reagan strode down the hallway. Staff members flattened themselves against the wall as he passed. A gasp went up among Avery's classmates (even their young tour guide was awestruck), and they whispered until Mr. Nelson shushed them.

And then President Reagan, Leader of the Free World, was standing before them. His face was wrinkled, and his head shook minutely, but when he spoke, his voice was the same pleasing combination of comforting and powerful, folksy and resonant, that Avery had heard whenever the President's televised addresses interrupted Avery's favorite prime time TV shows.

The President welcomed them all to the White House, thanked them for showing an interest in the workings of government, and made Avery and the others feel like he was more honored to meet *them* than they were to meet him. Avery, a guy who'd never been star-struck, found himself off-balance in this man's presence. His grandfather, an economist who had served in FDR's administration, loathed Reagan's policies. Pa considered him a second-rate actor and a threat to the United States' economic future, but Avery had to admit, the man had charisma; even standing still, Reagan glowed. Avery was nodding stupidly at something the President had said when the President smiled again and swept his gaze across the group.

"Now"—President Reagan's voice became sonorous and soothing—"which of you is Avery Craig?"

Everyone swiveled to face Avery. He raised his hand.

"Right here, Mr. President."

"Ah," he said, "you're 'Ace,' is that correct?"

"Yes, sir."

"Senator Kennedy says you're a young man to watch. He says you'll be leading the Democratic party in twenty years."

Avery's first instinct was to mumble a platitude about how kind the senator was, but he nixed the idea; a humble comment would lie there like a wet dog. Avery had seen a Bob Hope special where Reagan was in the audience, so he knew the President liked a good joke.[28] Earlier today, Avery had made a U.S. Senator crack up; how cool would it be to make the President of the United States laugh?

"That's true, sir," Avery said. "But not the Democratic party."

The President frowned and glanced at an aide. "I don't understand. Senator Kennedy said you and your family are lifelong, diehard Democrats. When did you change parties?"

Avery smiled coyly and morphed his voice to sound like President Reagan's. "*Well*, Mr. President...," he drawled, "...about thirty seconds ago."

---

[28] Bob Hope, an American comedian and actor, was most famous for entertaining U.S. troops during WWII, the Korean Conflict, and the Vietnam War.

The President threw back his head and laughed. His aides joined in the laugh, and so did the students, teachers, and parent chaperones. And then the President did something Avery didn't expect: he shook Avery's hand with an iron grip, clapped him on the shoulder and said, "Ace, you'll fit *right* in around here."

The President shook hands with the adults and posed for a photo with the entire group. Avery and Gemma stood on one side of the President while Caitlyn insinuated herself on the other side. Finally, an aide sidled up to the President, whispered in his ear, and the President made his goodbyes. "Thank you, Mr. President," the students said in unison, and as the President was walking away, Avery, swept up in the euphoria, said one more thing—loudly this time.

"Mr. President!?"

President Reagan paused and glanced over his shoulder.

"Keep up the great work, sir!"

The President beamed again, gave a thumbs-up, and strode commandingly down the hall toward the Oval Office. It seemed to Avery that his last remark had made the much older man stand taller and walk more briskly.

Whose the Nerd?

After all the thanks and congratulations from his classmates (not to mention a hot stolen kiss from Caitlyn), Avery's elation was short-lived. The fact was, while Caitlyn had kissed him; while Ms. Wharton had patted his shoulder and whispered in his ear, "an A-plus-plus-*plus*, Avery"; while Louis Zane had punched him playfully in the arm and said Avery was "the man"; while Eric Park had called Avery's performance "a masterstroke"; and while even stoic Johanna had nodded and said, "*Sehr gut*, Ace"; Penny remained aloof, as she had been since the Senate Gallery.

The tour group ate lunch at a McDonald's on Pennsylvania Avenue, but Penny was silent and aloof there and at the Washington Monument. Since Penny was still avoiding him, Avery decided to hell with her. He went up to the top of the monument with Gemma and stood close to her, staring out at the view. The snow had stopped, and the sun had come out, giving them a magical view: the blanket of snow glittering on the National Mall.

Afterwards, they hung out at the Vietnam Veterans Memorial. As they walked in, Avery mentioned that his father, Jack, was a Vietnam vet, but he'd only told Avery about his boxing matches in the Marines, never about fighting in the jungles or anything. The monument was a gleaming black granite wall along a down-sloping walkway, with the names of killed and missing soldiers carved into it. Avery looked for a couple of Jack's childhood friends who were killed early in the war, but there were way too many names. The names were listed in chronological order, and by the time he and Gemma reached 1968— the height of the war—they were at the bottom of the walkway, with several feet of names looming above them. He and Gemma turned to each other and shook their heads; it was overwhelming.

During the ride to their next site—the National Gallery—Gemma told Avery about her family. Her father was a computer scientist who did research for IBM, and her mother was a painter, amateur pianist, and homemaker. When Gemma asked about his parents, Avery said that his mother, a former Rockette, was the executive secretary to the IBM West Troutkilll plant manager, and that his father worked for the company as a sales manager and trainer, and he traveled a lot.

Gemma continued to talk about her interest in computers and how supportive and encouraging her parents were. Then, out of nowhere, she nudged him and said, "My mother would love you, Avery. You should come over for lunch sometime. Mom's an amazing cook."

In the National Gallery, since he still hadn't received a note from Penny, Avery stuck with Gemma. While they wandered through the museum together, Avery was reminded of what had been a favorite TV show before it was canceled—*Remington Steele*. He imagined himself as the suave Remington Steele character and Gemma as brainy Laura Holt. When he mentioned the show to her, Gemma said that she, too, used to love it, and then they discovered they had two other favorite TV shows in common: the comedy *Night Court*, and the nighttime soap opera *Dallas*. He and Gemma were chatting about their favorite episodes when Doc handed Avery a note.

"It's from Caitlyn," he said.

"Thanks, Doc."

When Avery looked up, Caitlyn was scowling at him across the gallery floor. He read the note:

> *Hey, whose the nerd? Lose her and hang with us!*
> *We're bored!*

Despite Caitlyn's many charms, at the moment she infuriated him. Yeah, she had a body like Heather Locklear's,[29] and yeah, her kisses were friggin' magic spells, but even so, he was livid with her for calling Gemma a nerd. Having played Scrabble with Gemma last night and spent this afternoon with her, Avery had discovered that not only was Gemma Jones a cultured, world-traveled, and brilliant girl but she was also kind, sensitive, and very attractive. The fact was, Gemma might be a little nerdy, but she was hardly a nerd. And, unlike Caitlyn, Gemma surely knew the difference between the possessive pronoun "whose" and the contraction "who's." Avery crumpled up the note.

The tour guide had stopped them in front of *Niagara*—Frederic Edwin Church's magnificent painting of the Niagara River at the edge of Horseshoe Falls. While the tour guide blathered about the painting, Gemma appraised it with her head tilted slightly and her arms crossed. She spoke wistfully into Avery's shoulder.

"I've always wanted to go to Niagara Falls," she said. "Have you been there?"

"No. I've always wanted to go there too."

"We left the movie early last night to play Scrabble, so we didn't see it, but I love the scene in *Superman Two*, when Clark and Lois go there." Gemma stepped over to the next painting, a landscape by Andrew Wyeth. "This stuff is good, but my mother took me to the Louvre in Paris a couple of years ago, and the paintings just blew me away. You know the *Mona Lisa*?"

"That's the homely woman who looks like George Washington with a dark wig, right?"

Gemma giggled.

---

[29] Heather Locklear was a slender, shapely blonde actress popular in the 1980s into the '90s. Later in 1986, she would marry Tommy Lee, the drummer for the rock band Mötley Crüe.

"I'm familiar with it," he said, "but I've never seen it in person."

"Well," she said, "if you walk across the room in front of the *Mona Lisa*, her eyes *follow* you. It's creepy."

Avery and Gemma trailed farther and farther behind the group until eventually they were in the same room as the others, but at the very back. When the group strolled into the next room, Avery glimpsed Caitlyn and Penny off to his right: they were staring at him and whispering to each other. Avery nudged Gemma's arm.

"Can I get your thoughts on something?" he said. "An issue involving boy-girl relations?"

"Sure."

"Yeah," he said, "so … imagine you got caught kissing a guy in the Senate Gallery."

"Okay," she said soberly.

"And let's suppose that the person who caught you was Senator Kennedy."

Gemma's eyes flicked up and to the side. "Okay, got it."

"Would you be mortally embarrassed?"

"Question." She adjusted her glasses. "Did any of my friends witness this?"

"Excellent question, madam. No. Nobody."

"And who was I kissing? You?"

"Yeah."

Gemma bit her lip and looked at the floor. "I wouldn't have a problem with that. Now, who was this girl?"

"We met on the bus ride from New York."

"Let me get this straight," she said. "You met a girl on the first day of the trip, and you kissed her in the gallery of the U.S. Senate?"

"It was dumb of me, right?" Avery hung his head as they walked to the next room. Gemma touched his arm.

"Actually, it's quite romantic," she said, "but it also seems premature and a bit impulsive."

"Yeah, I know," he said. "I think there's something wrong with me."

"There is," she said. "It's called being a teenage guy. My father says the reasoning, judgment, and decision-making parts of your brain haven't fully developed yet."

Gemma explained that her father headed up IBM's A.I. (Artificial Intelligence) division, so he knew a lot about thought processes and brain development. She added that the A.I. models her father and his team had created were becoming unbeatable at chess, and within ten years or so, they'd be smarter than most humans.

He and Gemma were the stragglers in their group now. Ahead, Penny and Caitlyn glowered at him as they walked into the next gallery. Gemma was gazing thoughtfully at the floor and nodding. She turned and looked him squarely in the eyes.

"Did you apologize to this girl?" she asked.

"Yes, in a note." The girl's name was Penny, he said, and she hadn't replied yet. When Gemma asked him to point her out, Avery gestured subtly with his chin. "Up there, next to the statue."

Gemma raised an eyebrow. "The one that looks like Heather Locklear? *She* was embarrassed?"

"No, the girl next to her," he said. "The petite one."

"Oh, that makes more sense," Gemma said. "The other one looks a little … *fast.*"

Avery chuckled. Gemma's candor was delightful.

"You apologized, so the ball's in her court," she said.

Avery looked around. He and Gemma were alone. The tour had moved into the next room.

"Come on," she said, "let's catch up with the group."

The Best Part of the Trip

After the National Gallery, the tour bus drove them way out of town to Mount Vernon, George Washington's home. For the home of the country's first president, it was depressingly lame, with little to see because so many rooms were off-limits to the group. What most intrigued Avery about the place was how the mansion was built on a high hill overlooking the Potomac River. What was *underneath* all that earth? What if old George had kept a secret laboratory under there?

During the outdoor part of the tour, he and Gemma were chosen to enter George Washington's barred crypt and stand next to the First President's sarcophagus as the tour guide talked about

Washington. While the guy was yammering, Avery spotted a crack between the marble floor and the base of the sarcophagus, with light leaking out of the crack. Gemma discreetly tapped Avery's foot with hers and directed her eyes at it. Avery nodded. What was *down* there? It was as though the gargantuan sarcophagus could be slid to the side, revealing stairs down to a bomb shelter or George's lab.

As the guide led the group back to the bus, he spoke pompously about how "magnanimous" Washington had been by freeing his slaves after his and his wife's deaths. Avery glanced at his friend Louis—the only black guy on the trip. He could tell that Louis was miffed by the guide's monologue, and as they crunched up the hill to the parking lot, Avery decided to say something.

"Excuse me, sir," he said loudly, "but how was that magnanimous?!" The students ceased their background chatter; the teachers and chaperones gawped at him; the squirrels in the trees stopped chittering. "I mean, Washington and his wife were dead, so it's not as if they needed their slaves anymore. Now ... if George and Martha had freed their slaves while they were alive—*that* would have been magnanimous. And while he was at it, Washington could have issued a statement against slavery, and if he'd done that, we might not have had the Civil War."

By now, they were in the parking lot, it was dark and cold, and the guide was smiling and nodding as the students filed onto the bus.

"You make a good point, young man," the guide said to him, "but history is full of these 'if onlys.' It was a much different time, and we can't judge the past by modern standards. Thank you for visiting Mount Vernon, everyone! Safe travels!"

♫"The Way It Is"♫

While they were filing onto the bus, Louis thanked Avery for speaking up to the guide.

"My parents and I went to Monticello last summer," Louis said, "and they gave everyone the same spiel. They, like, totally forget that these guys were slave owners."

"Yeah," Avery said, "meanwhile, tour guide dudes, guess who *built* these places? Slaves."

Louis shrugged.

"Things aren't perfect for black people today," he said, "but I've got it a lot better than my parents and grandparents. Like, if I was on this trip when my parents were in high school, I wouldn't be allowed in the restaurant we're eating at tonight. That, or I'd have to eat in the kitchen."

Avery had a sudden realization that left him slightly nauseous. He wanted to try to be a real friend to Louis, instead of a mere acquaintance, but he was unsure how to do that. The fact that Louis was black and Avery was white made it difficult because, at school during lunch for example, the races seldom mixed. Also, Avery was into girls, and he was pretty sure that Louis liked boys, so they had nothing in common there. The only thing they seemed to have in common is that they were both good dancers. Avery decided to change the subject.

"Speaking of food, I hope we get to the restaurant quick. I'm friggin' *starved*."

"Oh, Ace—always food and the weights with you."

When they got to the restaurant, an Italian place in Georgetown, Louis sat with Doc and Eric while Avery sat with Gemma at a table in the back. He had wolfed down his third slice of hot bread with butter when Caitlyn walked by and handed him a note. It was another piece of origami made from a sheet of lined looseleaf. Avery unfolded the note in his lap.

> Avery,
> What you did at the White House was so cool, but
> who is that girl you've been with all afternoon? Are you
> mad at me? I'm sorry I ran out of the Senate today, and
> I'm sorry I ignored you. Your apology was sweet. Can we
> meet when we get back to the hotel? I have a surprise for
> you. —Penny

Avery looked across the dining room. Penny saw him and smiled. Avery replied with a nod and continued eating his lasagna. Gemma twirled a wad of fettuccine Alfredo on her fork.

"As American Italian food goes, this isn't bad," she said.

Avery leaned into Gemma's shoulder. "Hey, I used to work in an Italian restaurant run by the Mob."

"You're kidding!"

"Nope. You know that place in Merlinsville, next to the IGA?"

"Primo Pizza? Sure, we get pizza from there all the time."

"Mafia," he said. "Honest to God."

"Wow." Gemma's hands drooped; her silverware hit her plate. "How do you know it's Mafia?"

Avery glanced over Gemma's shoulder. Across the room, Caitlyn was staring at him while wresting a loaf of Italian bread apart.

"Another time," he said. "Listen, in case I don't get a chance, I want to thank you."

"Thank me?" Gemma said. "For what?"

"For hanging out with me today, for your advice, for—"

Gemma sipped her soda and put the glass down. "Are you kidding? Hanging out with you has been the best part of the trip for me."

"Same here, Gem."

Crazy For You

Avery couldn't imagine what kind of surprise Penny had for him, but when they got back to the hotel and he went upstairs to the second-floor stairwell, Penny was there with her hands behind her back.

"What have you got there?" he asked.

She bounced on her tiptoes and handed him a flat paper bag.

"Here, open it. Sorry I didn't have a chance to wrap it."

Avery reached inside the bag. It was a paperback copy of *For Your Eyes Only*, a collection of James Bond stories by Ian Fleming. He had this book at home, but there was a bookmark in the bag too—a plastic-coated one with a photo of Ian Fleming smoking a cigarette, the smoke curling around his face. Avery remarked that he loved the gift, and Penny said that she'd gotten it today in a bookstore next door to McDonald's.

"But what about the book?" she asked. "Do you have it?"

"No, I don't."

"Read what I wrote inside."

He opened the book to the flyleaf.

> Avery,
> I know your birthday isn't for a couple days, but here's one of my presents for you. The other one can't be bought in a shop.
> Affectionately,
> Penny

"It's great, Penny. Thank you so—"

She threw her arms around his neck and kissed him aggressively. Had Caitlyn been coaching her in kissing technique? When they stopped a minute later, Penny hugged him and lay her head on his chest.

"And that's gift number two," she said. "Or three, if you count the bookmark."

"I love them," he said. "I'm sorry about this morning. I promise I won't embarrass you like that again."

They gazed into each other's eyes. Penny's pupils were dilated. She and Avery swayed in each other's arms, and then she sang softly against his chest. Avery asked her what the song was.

"Promise you won't laugh?" she said.

"I promise."

"♫'Crazy For You'♫—you know … Madonna?" She sang some of the lyrics aloud. The echo in the stairwell made her soft voice sound like a choir of angels, and then she abruptly stopped.

"Avery, who was that girl you were with all day?"

"She's a friend from Hancock. Her name is Gemma."

"Why'd you spend *all day* with her?"

"Because Caitlyn told me you were angry with me," he said.

Somewhere upstairs, a door squeaked open and banged shut. There were footsteps, and then it was quiet again. Avery said that Caitlyn had told him that Penny wanted space today.

"I'm sure it was just a misunderstanding," Penny said.

Somehow, Avery doubted that. He held Penny's head against his chest and stroked her hair.

"What time is it?" she asked.

Avery glanced at his watch. "An hour until curfew."

She yawned. "Mind if I go to bed? I'm totally beat."

"Go get your beauty rest."

"I'm crazy for you, Avery Craig."

Channeling Charles Ingalls

While Penny went out to the lobby to catch the elevator back up to her room, Avery decided to get in a pre-bedtime cardio workout by jogging up the stairs.

When he reached the landing for his floor, Avery heard crying coming from somewhere upstairs. The crying was high-pitched and sounded like a girl's. *Ugh.* Something told him he should go help her, whoever she was, but he didn't have the energy for this. The instant he grabbed the door handle, however, a heart-wrenching wail resounded through the stairwell. He groaned and trudged upstairs.

A girl was sitting on the landing above. Her knees were pinched together, her shoulders hunched, her fingers curled over the concrete step. Mascara dripped down her cheeks like black blood. Avery was about to do an about-face and skedaddle back downstairs when he took a closer look at the girl. It was Johanna. Avery recalled humiliating her outside the Smithsonian, and bile rose in his throat. Once again, Ms. Wharton's rebuke resounded in his head: *"Avery, Johanna is all alone in this country."*

As he approached, Johanna raised her head, muttered some-thing in German, and motioned to get up. Avery pressed a hand on her shoulder and smiled sympathetically.

"What's wrong, *wundervolle*?"

Johanna didn't say anything; she simply sat there, shaking her head and sobbing, with her face scrunched up in an ugly mess.

"You look like you could use a handkerchief," he said. "Check this out."

With a magician's flourish, he plucked his fresh, "showin'" handkerchief out of his blazer breast pocket and handed it to her.

"*Danke*, Ace," she muttered. "*Wunderbar.*"

"*Gesundheit.*"

This made her smile, albeit briefly, and Avery used the lull between her heaving sobs to sit down next to her. Johanna's crying was gut-wrenching—like somebody had died. He put an arm around her.

"Talk to me, Johanna," he said. "It's okay."

Through sobs, she explained that her boyfriend back in West Germany—the son of another Volkswagen executive—had dumped her. When she got back to the hotel tonight, a telegram from him was waiting for her.

"He broke up with you by *telegram*?" Avery said.

Johanna blubbered and nodded.

"What a douchebag."

This made her giggle. Avery was curious what language the guy's telegram had been in—German or English—and how it might have been worded, but this didn't seem like the best time to ask her. Right now, she needed consoling.

Not having any real-life experience in consoling girls, Avery rifled his brain for examples of how other men did it. His father, Big Jack, didn't handle crying women well at all; whenever his sisters or mother cried in Jack's presence, he would storm out of the room. Pa was slightly better, embracing and patting them for a moment, but swiftly changing the subject to something less uncomfortable. No, *the* role model for dealing with crying womenfolk was TV's Charles Ingalls on *Little House on the Prairie*; whether comforting Ma, Mary, Laura, or Carrie, he was simply the best—America's dad. As Johanna wiped her eyes and blew her nose, Avery rubbed her back and channeled Charles Ingalls.

"There, there … it's all right; it's going to be all right. It's okay, Johanna … get it *all* out."

He would be there comforting her for another hour.

11

～

THE GYM was empty early the next morning. After some stretches, Avery played the workout mixtape on his Walkman, jumped on the treadmill, cranked up the speed to 8 mph, and ran.

The girl situation was awkward to say the least. He liked Penny but he also liked Caitlyn—a girl who seemed not to give a crap what other people thought, and who loved kissing him. Spending yesterday with Gemma had been great too; in a few short hours, Avery had come to deeply admire and respect her.

Caitlyn worried him the most; he was uncertain how to handle such a tricky balancing act. No more stolen kisses or mini make-out sessions; he had to avoid her for the rest of the trip. Once he and Penny were back home, none of this would matter.

After a 30-minute run, two sets of 50 push-ups, two sets of 50 crunches, and 20 handstand push-ups, Avery stood and caught his breath. His face was hot and he was sweating, and when he turned around, Caitlyn was lurking in the doorway. She wore a Duran Duran ♫"Rio"♫ T-shirt, tight vanilla short-shorts, and white Keds without socks, and she leaned against the doorjamb in a feline pose with that inscrutable smirk on her lips. She pushed herself off the doorjamb with her butt and slinked over. Avery cradled his headphones around his neck but kept the Walkman playing.

"Hey, Ace," she said, "you said you worked out first thing every morning, so I decided to come work out with you."

"How long have you been watching me?" he asked.

Van Halen's "Panama" came over his headphones.

Gotcha, Ace

"I don't know … a while." She nodded at his Walkman. "'Panama,' huh?"

"Damn right. It's my favorite workout song. It's about a race car."

Caitlyn smirked. "Sorry to burst your bubble, but it's about *sex*. They all are."

"Look," he said, "'Panama' is about a race car. I read it in *Rolling Stone* magazine a while back. You know the part of the song where there's an engine revving in the background? That was the exhaust of Eddie Van Halen's Lamborghini. They backed it right up to the studio doors and revved the engine. The song is *not* about sex. When it comes to Van Halen, there isn't a friggin' thing you know about them that I don't, got it?"

"Okay, dude, chill out."

"But since you know so much about the meanings of songs," he said, "maybe you can tell me what *this* one is about."

Avery fast-forwarded the Walkman and played Duran Duran's "The Reflex." Caitlyn rolled her eyes.

"Oh, Ace, I'm losing respect for you. It's about masturbation."

"What?! No way."

She made a fist and wagged it in front of her groin. "Jerking off. Choking the chicken."

"I'm familiar with the concept," he said.

"I'm sure you are."

"There's no way it's about that."

"Think about the lyrics." She rattled off a few lines that supported her argument. "Come on—it's obvious."

Avery walked to the mat beneath the pull-up bar and gave her examples of lyrics that contradicted hers. Caitlyn shrugged and moistened her lips.

"Hey," she said, "take your shirt off before you do pull-ups. Lemme see that smokin' hot bod you're always hiding."

"I'm not taking my shirt off," he said.

"Do it," she said, "or I'll tell Penny that you kissed me in the solarium and the White House yesterday, and in the stairwell the day before that."

"But you kissed *me*," he said. "All three times."

Her stare was unwavering.

"Fine." Avery peeled off his T-shirt and jumped for the bar. He grabbed it with his palms facing him to accentuate his biceps and launched into pull-ups. Caitlyn stood right beside him, slack jawed.

"Holy crap, Ace! Lemme feel your arm."

By the time he told her no, she was already squeezing it. Avery did his best to ignore her caresses, continuing to crank out pull-ups swiftly and precisely.

"Damn, Ace—you're so strong." Her hands slithered off his arm and onto his tensed chest and abs.

"Those aren't my arms," he said.

Caitlyn positioned herself beside Avery and spoke barely above a whisper, so at the bottom of each pull-up, his ear was next to her mouth. At the top of each pull-up, however, Avery missed a word or two of her monologue. She ran her fingers over the ridges of his abdominal muscles as she talked.

"This incredible … on Penny," she said. "Ace … virgin? Because the only … inside Penny … marry her."

"Shut up," he said, "I'm trying to concentrate."

He was inching toward the top of the bar for his twenty-seventh pull-up, straining with the effort, when Caitlyn's right hand slid down his abs. Before Avery realized what was happening, her fingers had slithered under the waistband of his shorts and touched his pubic hair. Avery let go of the bar and swatted her hand away.

"Damn it, Caitlyn, you nympho! You can't do that! What the hell is wrong with you?!"

She glanced at the pull-up bar and frowned. "That's it? That's all you've got? I thought you were going to show off for me."

"What do you mean, 'That's it'? That was twenty-seven pull-ups." He put his T-shirt back on. "Most guys can barely do ten. I'll bet you can't even do *one*."

"Let's see."

Caitlyn shucked her T-shirt over her head. For a split second, Avery thought that she was topless underneath, but it turned out she was wearing a flimsy white tank top without a bra. She wiped her palms on her shorts and positioned herself under the bar.

"Can you help me, Ace? I can't reach it. I need a boost." She pouted. "*Please*?"

Avery got behind her and held her by the waist.

"Jump on three," he said. "Ready? One … two … three!"

Caitlyn sprang off the floor and grabbed the bar with a litheness that surprised him. It was obvious that she hadn't truly needed his help, so he let go of her.

"Hold on to me," she said.

"Fine, but I'm not helping you. Start pulling."

Arms trembling, Caitlyn hoisted herself up. Avery's hands were on her bare midriff.

"That's it, you're doing it," he said.

And then she let go of the bar. Avery's hands slid under the tank top and clamped onto her bare breasts. Now on the ground, Caitlyn smiled over her shoulder.

"Gotcha, Ace."

Her breasts were high, firm, and wonderful to hold. Caitlyn softly moaned, and that's when Avery realized that he was massaging them, lightly squeezing her nipples between his fingers. He recoiled from her, triggering a chain reaction of stumbling. His heel banged against something, he keeled backwards, and fell on the floor. His funny bone sang. Caitlyn yanked down her tank top and hurried over to him.

"Oh, I'm so sorry, Ace." She giggled and extended a hand. "Here, let me help you."

"Get away from me," he said.

Out in the hallway, footsteps approached. Caitlyn scooped up her T-shirt, hastily slipped it on, and stood. Penny walked in. Avery lay on the floor, rubbing his elbow and wincing.

"What's going—oh, Avery, are you okay?!" Penny knelt beside him. "What happened?"

"Ace was showing me how to do pull-ups," Caitlyn said. "He tripped on something and fell."

"Why are you here, Caitlyn?" Penny said. "You hate Phys Ed."

From where Avery sat on the floor, he had a front-row seat to Caitlyn's squirming; he sat back and enjoyed it. Caitlyn's eyes darted around.

"I was hungry, so I … I came downstairs. Breakfast wasn't ready, so I … wandered around and saw Ace in here doing pull-ups. He helped me do one, and the next thing I knew, he was on his ass."

Avery got to his feet, and Penny hugged him.

"I'm glad you weren't hurt," she said.

"Ace, you're sure you're okay?" Caitlyn said. "You fell pretty *hard* there."

"I'm fine."

"Penny, I'm going up to the room." Caitlyn gave Avery a lingering stare from the doorway. "I need to take a long, hot shower. I love how *hard* the water pressure is in the hotel." She winked at Avery and vanished into the hall.

When Avery turned around, Penny had wandered over to the pull-up bar.

"Hey, will you show *me* how to do a pull-up?"

"Sure." He lifted her by the waist, and she grabbed the bar. While Avery kept a firm hold on her, she pulled with all her might, her lips sputtering from the effort. Gradually, Avery supported more and more of her weight until he was hugging her around the hips and doing squats with her in his arms. Penny continued to grip the bar as her chin cleared the bar effortlessly—five, six, ten times in a row.

"You're doing it, Penny, you're doing it!" he said.

Laughing hysterically, Penny went limp on the bar and slid out of his arms to the floor. Avery kissed her, and she hugged him and rested her head on his chest.

"I can't believe this trip is almost over," she said. "When we go home, we'll never see each other."

"It'll work out," he said. "We'll have the weekends and vacations, and the time apart will make the time we're together more special."

"That's how it is with me and my father," she said. "Since the divorce, I only see him every other weekend and for two weeks in the summer, but we always have fun. I can't wait for you to meet him. My mom too. I think you're going to like them."

"See?" Avery raised her chin. Penny's eyes were shiny in the fluorescent lights. "Let's enjoy every minute today."

"All right," she said.

Rogues' Gallery

Before boarding the bus, Mr. Nelson said that Ivory Snow Baby's office had called to apologize for yesterday's mix-up at the White House. To make up for his mistake, the congressman had arranged for them to have an extended tour of FBI headquarters later in the day.

They first went to the National Archives, where they saw the Declaration of Independence and the Constitution in their bulletproof, fireproof, and bombproof cases, and then the Treasury building, where they were shown a sheet of $100 bills and a $10,000 bill.

They ended the day at FBI headquarters—the sandy brown and daunting J. Edgar Hoover Building—and were greeted in the lobby by a man in a dark blue suit. "Hello everyone. I'm FBI Special Agent Dan Sloane, and I'll be showing you around today."

In a hummingbird's heartbeat, most of the girls swarmed to the front and mooned over Agent Sloane. The mid-30s man was 6′2″, and his arm and shoulder muscles bulged beneath a navy-blue suit. He had a chiseled jaw—the kind of jawline you only saw on movie stars—and when he got talking and moved a certain way, his suit jacket bloused, revealing a holstered gun under his armpit.

"All right, guys and gals, listen up," he said. "Before we begin our tour, there are only two rules. One, stay with the group at all times. Two, don't touch anything unless I say it's okay. Everyone ready? You're about to learn what we do here at the Bureau."

They followed him across the lobby, with Avery and Caitlyn leading the pack. Caitlyn smirked at her Vanderbush girlfriends and spoke softly: "Do you think the 'no touching' rule applies to Agent *Sloane* too?" The girls giggled. "By the way, girls, did you see? No wedding band."

"Are you friggin' *mental*?" Eyeshadow said. "He's so old."

Caitlyn scoffed. "I'd totally do him."

Penny sniggered and said, "Caitlyn, you're awful."

Special Agent Sloane began the tour by showing them the Rogues' Gallery—a hallway with framed posters on the walls of the FBI's Ten Most Wanted criminals. He encouraged them to commit their faces, names, and crimes to memory. The group was then led through an office bullpen, where agents sat at IBM PCs and talked on telephones. Agent Sloane said they were working on active investigations.

From there, he took them to a fingerprinting station and explained a diagram of the three types of fingerprints—arches, loops, and whorls. He then fingerprinted an all-too-willing Caitlyn, and after examining her prints, he said, "Young lady, some of the most notorious criminals have whorl fingerprints. I hope you're not contemplating a life of crime."

"I think you're too late, Agent Sloane," Avery said.

Caitlyn smirked at Avery, spun around, and fanned out her blackened fingers. "Dudes, check out my *whorls!*"

Next, Agent Sloane took them downstairs and led them to a set of fishbowl windows. Inside were various instruments and chemistry apparatus, where men and women in lab coats were performing scientific experiments. A lab technician talked about forensic science and crime scene investigation techniques, and then Agent Sloane continued their tour.

Their last stop was at a giant window built into the wall. Behind the glass was an indoor firing range. A huge agent, a black man in his mid-forties, walked out of a side door carrying a .45 Thompson submachine gun, or "Tommy Gun." He spoke briefly about how the Chicago Mob had used it extensively during Prohibition (earning it the nickname "The Chicago Typewriter"), then put earmuffs over his head and made everyone jump out of their skin when he blasted a paper man target downrange. Flames spewed from the gun's barrel, and the paper man was shredded beyond recognition.

Their tour ended in the main lobby. Ms. Wharton thanked Agent Sloane, and the students clapped and cheered.

Out of nowhere, a vision for his life popped into Avery's head, and the vision was so clear, it was as though it was a memory of something that had already happened. Like Ian Fleming, Avery would work in the clandestine services (in his case, the CIA) and eventually write novels based on his experiences.

Agent Sloane smiled and waved to the group, then strolled away. Avery walked after him.

"Agent Sloane, may I ask you a question, sir?"

"Sure, son. What is it?"

Avery introduced himself, told him his plan, and asked him if he knew anybody at the CIA that Avery could talk to.

"*CIA?* You're sure?" Agent Sloane grimaced, like he'd just seen a week-old dead body. "Not the Bureau? Don't you want to catch criminals and bring them to justice?"

Avery explained that while he loved the Sherlock Holmes stories, and the TV shows *Columbo* and *The Rockford Files*, solving crimes didn't interest him. He believed he would be better at gathering intelligence in the field as a covert operative for the CIA.

"I think I'd be awesome at it," Avery added.

Agent Sloane chuckled. "Awesome, huh? Well, from what I've heard, you don't approach them; they approach *you*. Tell you what, I'll call a few people I know and tell them about you. I can't promise anything, but someone might contact you."

"Thank you, Agent Sloane."

"If you don't hear anything after a few months, give me a call." He handed Avery a business card, shook his hand, and walked away.

When Avery rejoined the group, Penny asked what Agent Sloane had given him.

"His business card," he said.

Caitlyn addressed the group: "Oooh, ladies, check it out! Ace got Agent Studly's *phone number!*"

"Can I see it?" Doc asked.

Avery let him examine the card, then put it safely in his billfold behind Senator Kennedy's. Mr. Nelson announced a ten-minute bathroom break before the group returned to the bus and then the hotel. Avery waited until Penny and Caitlyn went into the bathroom together, then hurried over to Gemma.

"Hey," he said, "mind if I call you later?"

"This isn't more girl trouble, is it?"

"No, it's about my future, and I'd really like your opinion. Tonight, at curfew—may I call you?"

"Sure, that's fine."

Across the lobby, Penny and Caitlyn exited the bathroom.

"I'll call you tonight, Gem," he said.

Perfect Specimens All

On the bus, Mr. Nelson announced that even though some students had been sent home for "violating terms in the class trip contract," he, the other teachers, and parent chaperones had decided to keep their promise of a swim night in the hotel pool. The students cheered and chattered all the way back to the hotel.

Penny remarked to Avery that she hadn't brought a swimsuit, so she wouldn't be going. Yawning, she added that she was exhausted anyway and wanted to take a nap before dinner. Avery said he understood, and that they'd have dinner and watch that evening's movie together. He split the last of his Twizzlers with her and let her get a head start on her nap by resting against his shoulder.

As he was getting off the bus, he felt a hand slide into his jacket pocket, and then Caitlyn walked by. She winked at him over her shoulder, said to Penny, "Come on, let's put you down for a nap," and disappeared inside the revolving doors.

Avery plucked the note out of his pocket. Sure enough, it was in Caitlyn's soap bubble handwriting: *"Hey, Ace. Penny might not have a swimsuit, but I do, and wait 'til you see it! IT'S SOOOOOOOO FRIGGIN' SEXXXY! I'll be wearing it for YOU. Your gonna love it. XOXO -C."* Avery crumpled up the note and threw it away.

It was late on a weekday afternoon in February, and the hotel lobby was quiet. Everybody headed up to their rooms to get changed. Avery was walking toward the elevators when Irina, at the front desk with another staff member, smiled and waved to him. She pointed around the corner. When Avery reached the office Dutch door, Irina was standing there with a boombox.

"I am on break now," she said. "I have something to show you. Would you like to see?"

"Sure," he said.

She led him down the hall to an empty meeting room, waved him inside, and shut and locked the door.

"My dancing," she said. "I have been practicing."

She plugged in the boombox, pressed play on the cassette player, and danced to "Legs." At first, the situation weirded him out, but then he focused on her dancing. It was less natural than the other day at the copier when she hadn't known anyone was watching her. After watching her for a bit, Avery complimented her on her progress and gave her notes.

"It's good," he said, "but you need to be yourself more. You need to feel the music and flow with it. Like this."

Avery gave her a five-minute demonstration and lesson. When he finished, Irina shut off the boombox and put a hand on his arm.

"Ace, how old are you?"

Avery decided to exaggerate slightly. "Uh … seventeen, why?"

She planted her hands on her hips and looked him squarely in the eyes. "How old do you think I am?"

Avery examined her closely. Today Irina was wearing an ice-blue suit that brought out her striking eyes. Under the jacket was a silky white blouse with two buttons undone, showing a hint of cleavage. She wore considerable makeup, but compared to women like Ms. Wharton, who had little wrinkles on her forehead and at the corners of her eyes, Irina's face was perfectly smooth.

"I don't know," he said. "In your mid-twenties?"

"I am nineteen. Only two years older than you."

"Wow. You're so sophisticated."

"Ace," she blurted, "I like you."

"I like you too, Irina. You're officially my favorite Finnish woman."

No sooner did Avery flash his unintentionally devastating smile than Irina collapsed into his arms. She confessed how much she would miss Avery when he went home tomorrow.

"I am so lonely here. You are nicest American young man I meet."

She told him that the only American men who seemed to like her were fat, middle-aged men only interested in sex. Avery comforted her, but it was impossible to do without getting aroused. Her body was womanlier than Penny's or even Caitlyn's, and she smelled fantastic—a beguiling mixture of musky perfume, lavender, and talcum powder. Predictably, his johnson responded with enthusiasm. As pleasant as this was, though, a tightness in his chest and a heaviness in the pit of his stomach told him it was wrong. Then again, what was wrong about it? He wasn't making out with Irina; he was merely consoling her; he could consider this his Boy Scout good deed for the day.

While hugging Irina and rubbing her back, he gradually drew back his pelvis so she wouldn't feel his erection. In reply, Irina put her arms around his waist and pulled, drilling his bulge back into her. His blood thrummed in his ears; his breath rasped in his throat. Irina muttered that because she was off tomorrow, this was the last time they would see each other. Her hug was more of a desperate cling than a romantic embrace. For a long moment, Avery was outside of his body, watching himself hold this gorgeous Finnish hotel desk clerk, and the surrealness of it was dizzying. Then Irina asked if they could talk on the phone sometime.

Initially, Avery was going to tell her that he didn't think that was a good idea, but she looked so sad and was faintly trembling like a frightened bunny in the grass. Irina seemed deeply depressed. If he told her no, the woman might swallow a bottle of sleeping pills or jump in front of a D.C. Metro train. What would it hurt to talk on the phone with her once in a while?

"Sure, that would be great," he said, "so long as you call me. My parents are always complaining about long-distance calls and how expensive they are."

He suggested they write letters to each other too—an idea that appealed to Irina, who wanted to improve her English.

"We will become good friends then?" she said.

"Sure, good friends. Look, Irina, I should go. It's swim night and—"

She kissed him. The rapturous sensations of her lips and her womanly chest pressed against his made him instantly lightheaded, and had he not been holding onto her, he would have fainted. His hands went into autopilot mode, gliding down Irina's back and caressing her butt, then up her hips and ribs to her breasts.

Perfect specimens all.

Irina's breathing was rapid and shallow. Avery continued to kiss her and was about to glide his hands down to her butt again when she spoke breathily out of the side of her mouth.

"Ace? We should stop. If I am caught, I lose job."

Hot tar choked his throat. He coughed to clear it.

"Sorry," he said.

"Do not be sorry. I kissed you first."

"Yeah." Avery fumbled in his pocket for his notepad and pen. Once they had exchanged addresses and phone numbers, they walked to the door holding hands.

"Farewell, Ace. I call you soon, yes?"

"I'd love that."

"You are wonderful kisser. Your girlfriend is smart to keep you on short leash."

"Thanks." He handed her the boombox and opened the door for her. "Farewell, Irina."

While wiping his mouth with a handkerchief, he watched her womanly butt recede down the hall.

Another One Bites the Dust

What was happening? Before this trip, Avery had been the guy equivalent of Saran Wrap: girls looked right through him. But ever since the start of this trip, he'd been deluged with girls: Penny, Caitlyn, and Irina, not to mention Jolene and Wendy at the deli back home. And there was Gemma, whom he enjoyed and who seemed to enjoy him. Avery didn't understand his newfound popularity with the opposite sex, but he liked it. He liked it a lot.

After he caught his breath, and his blood had cooled some, Avery rushed up to his room and took a cold shower. He put on his new Jams swim trunks, a T-shirt, and flip-flops; grabbed his Adidas track suit, a towel, and his room key; and went down to the pool.

Before he opened the door, Avery heard girls shrieking inside. A boombox was playing a song by Queen: ♫"Flash"♫ from the movie *Flash Gordon*. Somebody cranked the volume on the boombox.

The swimming pool roiled and churned. A red rubber ball, like the ones used in dodgeball but smaller, sailed past Avery's head, whanged off the wall, and dribbled down the pool deck. What Avery was seeing wasn't quite the mayhem of the pool scene in *Caddyshack*, but it was damn close. While the relentless drum and bass of "Flash" blasted around the pool room, Avery assessed the situation.

There were no adults around, which explained the chaos. While a few girls sat in lounge chairs around the perimeter of the pool deck, most of them were in the water, herded into the shallow end by four college-aged guys brandishing red balls. The girls were huddled together and cowering against the guys' barrage. The balls made loud, wet smacks and *tunnnnggg* sounds when they hit; the girls shrieked like they were meeting Madonna; and the balls left pink welts on their skin. Meanwhile, the guys from Hancock and the few remaining Vanderbush ones were treading water off to the side, avoiding the onslaught altogether. Clearly, none of them were going to intervene; it was up to Avery.

He strode over to Gemma's chaise. She was wearing a Princeton T-shirt and gym shorts and snapping photos with her camera.

"Mind if I leave my stuff here?" he asked.

"No, go ahead," she said.

He dropped his things and kicked off his flip-flops. One of the girls in the pool broke out of the defensive huddle. It was Caitlyn. Waving and calling to Avery, she waded to the side of the pool and heaved herself halfway out. The water sluiced gorgeously off her smooth shoulders and half-covered breasts. Her swimsuit was a scanty pink bikini, and as promised it was *"SOOOOOOOO FRIGGIN' SEXXXY."* Avery couldn't see the bottoms, but the bikini top looked exactly like Heather Thomas' on a poster Avery had on his bedroom wall at home. Like H.T.'s, the strings that connected the bra cups and tied around Caitlyn's neck and back were precariously overtaxed; they looked flimsier than overcooked spaghetti.

"Hey, Ace! In case you didn't notice, we could use your help here! Get over here and—"

A ball smacked her in the face. From the startling yelp she made, Avery could tell she was hurt. He glared at the guys. They were laughing and heckling her. Avery ran over and hauled her out of the pool. Before he could get her fully onto the deck, another ball smacked her in the ass. Caitlyn squealed, which caused the guys to cackle louder. The ball bounced down the pool deck.

"I've got you," he said.

Another ball whizzed past them and rolled under a chair. Avery led Caitlyn to an empty chaise and sat her down. There was a welt on her back, another one on her butt, and a third one on her cheek. Her nose was bleeding. He peeled off his T-shirt and gave it to her.

"Pinch this on your nose and tilt your head back."

With blood dripping down her lip, Caitlyn looked up at Avery.

"Get them for me, Ace. *Hurt* them."

"I will."

Caitlyn shouted to the guys in the pool: "Boy, are you assholes gonna get it now!"

"Flash" ended, and the pool room swelled with the thrusting bass line from Avery's favorite Queen song, ♫"Another One Bites the Dust."♫ Spotting two balls at the end of the pool deck, Avery ran for them, shouting at the Hancock and Vanderbush guys as he passed: "Spread out! Get the balls and feed them to me! One of you watch for teachers! Go!" They scrambled out of the pool.

Down the pool deck, one of the college guys was climbing out of the pool. His and Avery's eyes met, and then the guy saw what Avery was running toward—two balls next to a chaise lounge. Before the guy finished climbing the ladder, Avery blew past him, scooped up the balls, and spun around.

About the size of a grapefruit, the rubber ball was perfectly sized for Avery's big hand and inflated with a slight amount of give, so he could grip it. As the guy charged him, Avery set his feet and drew his arm back. The guy's face fell like he'd just stumbled into a grizzly bear. He skidded to a stop and tried to turn away, but it was too late.

Into this throw, Avery put every scintilla of his strength. With the guy maybe ten feet away, Avery, gritting his teeth and aiming straight at the guy's face, unleashed his hardest throw ever—a fastball like he was striking out Reggie Jackson. In the blink of an eye, the ball left his fingers and collided with the guy's nose. He squealed and doubled over, blood gushed, and he turned away cupping his face.

"My nose! You broke it!"

Wounding the guy had ignited Avery's killer instinct. The skinny wimp was stooped over near the pool edge, with his back to Avery.

"*Shut up, dick.*" Avery kicked him into the pool.

"Yeah, Ace, deck 'em!" Caitlyn shouted. "Watch out, behind you!"

Instinctively, Avery ducked before turning around, and when he did, he was faced with a bigger guy gripping a ball. This one appeared to do some weightlifting. He darted left and right, feinting with the ball, trying to close the gap before he threw. He seemed to expect Avery to run away, but instead Avery rushed *him.*

Weightlifter threw the ball wildly and ran back down the cement deck. Bouncing his ball off his bicep first, Avery wound up and hurled it at the retreating guy's head. It was a line-drive throw like a laser beam—on par with one he'd seen the legendary Dave Parker make from the right field fence to home plate—and it pegged Weightlifter in the back of the head so hard, it was as though Avery had punched him. The guy stumbled and crashed onto an empty chaise lounge. *Another one bites the dust!* While his classmates laughed and cheered, Avery did a few M.J. moves from the "Beat It" music video.

"Ace!" Doc tossed him a ball.

One of the college guys was running down the pool deck toward the exit. Because his back was to Avery, there was no way Avery could hit him in the face directly, but a glimpse of the guy's reflection in the glass door gave Avery an idea for a bank shot. If he could do this, it would be a one-in-a-billion throw—possibly better than "The Egg."

Shuffling to the side, Avery aimed at a spot on the door, made a last-second adjustment, and rifled the ball. It whistled past the guy's shoulder, ricocheted off the door glass, and drilled him in the balls. He took one more step and crumpled to his knees, cradling his groin. The students let out another laugh and cheer.

Meanwhile, Nosebleed, cupping his nose, was wading up the steps out of the shallow end, followed by the fourth guy—a fat-faced dope with giant ears.

Across the pool deck, a Vanderbush kid was holding two balls. "Hey, Ace—catch!" He flipped a ball to Avery.

As Nosebleed scurried for the exit and Fat Face sloshed up the steps, Avery and the Vanderbush kid converged on them. Vanderbush hit Nosebleed solidly in the neck, causing him to bawl and beg for mercy. For his final throw, Avery spotted an all-too-tempting target: Fat Face had slipped on the steps and was beached on his stomach on the pool deck. His swim trunks had fallen partially down, exposing several hideous inches of ass crack.

Avery sprinted down the pool deck to the diving board and sprang off. While in midair, he fired at Fat Face's ass. When the ball hit, the soaking wet *THWAAACK* against his bare cheeks was ten times louder than the one that had hit Caitlyn. Avery splashed into the pool, and when he resurfaced, Fat Face was squealing and scrabbling for the exit. Nosebleed, pinching his nose, and Weightlifter, doubled over cupping his balls, staggered to the door and tried to open it, but they blocked each other. The fourth guy threw a ball and hit Avery in the ribs; it ricocheted and landed in the water near him; he picked it up.

"Ace! Over here!" Johanna, Hancock's Amazonian star volleyball player, was jogging down the pool deck toward the door. She gestured with her fingertips for Avery to "set" the ball in front of her.

Avery's toss was a perfect "alley-oop"—high and about six feet in front of her. With her back arched, knees bent, and a clenched fist over her shoulder, Johanna leapt high enough in the air to dunk a basketball and hung there for a second, her eyes glued to the ball as it fell, and then her arm, torso and legs jackknifed together, and her fist slammed down on the ball. She spiked it, smacking Weightlifter squarely in the throat.

Then Caitlyn, holding Avery's T-shirt to her nose, streaked across the pool deck with a life preserver ring and slung it at them as they were tussling to get out the door. The ring hit one of them in the head, caromed off, and whacked another one in the mouth. The four of them jostled against each other squealing like cornered animals, and finally shoved their way out the door.

Doctor Craig

For a moment, the pool room was silent, and then Queen's song ♫"We Will Rock You"♫ came on. Avery smiled and muttered, "I love it when a plan comes together." He wished he had a cigar to light like Hannibal did on *The A-Team* at the end of every successful mission. He shut off the boom box, told everyone to hide the balls, and hung the life preserver back up. The adults would be here any second.

When he climbed out of the pool, Gemma was snapping photos of him. Avery's wet bangs were in his eyes. Slicking his hair back, he spotted a bunch of Vanderbush girls huddled protectively around Caitlyn. Rhonda (a.k.a., Eyeshadow), her skinny sycophants, and a few others he didn't know wheeled around and checked him out.

"You know what, Hancock?" Rhonda said. "You're all right."

"Thanks."

"And your bod's friggin' *mint*," she added.

The other girls giggled and murmured in agreement. Caitlyn told them she wanted to talk to Ace alone. They drifted away, chirping their allegiances.

Caitlyn was trembling. Avery fetched his towel, draped it over her back, and guided her to a chaise. He took his T-shirt from her and dipped it in the pool, then had her hold it over her nose while lying on her back. Avery sat on the edge of the chaise beside her.

She removed the T-shirt. "Ace, it's not broken, is it?"

Her cheek was pink, but her nose appeared undamaged. He had her wiggle it, and since she could do it without pain, Avery said he doubted it was broken.

"I think it's just a nosebleed," he said. "But the guy *I* hit in the face—*his* nose is probably broken."

"Good." She flashed a smile. "And that guy you got in the nuts? On a *rebound? So* choice."

Avery shrugged. "When they hurt you, something in me just snapped."

"I know, I loved it. You were like a caveman." She ran a fingernail just under his waistband. "Are these Jams?"

He nodded.

"Nice," she said. "Not the suit. Your buns." Caitlyn squeezed his hand. "Thanks, Doctor Craig."

He patted her shoulder with his other hand. "You're a little shaken up, but you'll be okay."

When she looked up at him and their eyes met, she was smiling but her eyes were wet. "Ace, I need to talk to you. Can we go someplace alone?"

Mr. Nelson rushed in wearing a gaudy Hawaiian shirt and swim trunks, followed by Ms. Wharton sporting a kaftan and a wide-brimmed sun hat. Mr. Nelson glared around the room with his arms effeminately akimbo.

"*What* is going on in here!?" he said. "We could hear you down in the lobby! There's *blood* on the floor out there for Pete's sake! Somebody had better explain what happened in here—right this second!"

Caitlyn removed the T-shirt from her nose. "Mr. Nelson, if you'll chill out, *I'll* explain." Matter-of-factly, Caitlyn said that everyone had been minding their own business when "a gang" of college guys came into the pool area and harassed the girls. She then turned the entire situation around on Mr. Nelson.

"Where were *you*, Mr. Nelson?" she continued. "Those stupid frat guys were attacking us girls, and you and the other adults weren't around. You'd better hope my mother doesn't hear about this. Let me tell you, if Avery Craig hadn't been here, more of us girls could have been badly hurt. As it is, they hit me in the face and gave me this bloody nose."

"We should get you to the hospital," Mr. Nelson said. "It might be broken."

"No." She smiled at Avery. "It's just a nosebleed."

"All right," he said, "I'll talk to the hotel manager about the college kids. The pool was supposed to be reserved for us." He grabbed the door handle, and, in a bad impression of Arnold Schwarzenegger as the Terminator, said, "I'll be *back*." He left.

Students groaned and whistled.

"What a dweeb," Avery said to Caitlyn.

She snorted. "Totally."

Ms. Wharton clapped and chirruped, "All right, people, we have the pool for another hour, so let's enjoy ourselves."

12

A VERY SWAM a few laps, checked to see how Caitlyn was doing, and chatted with Gemma, Doc, Louis, Eric, and the other guys. Then, when everyone was heading back to their rooms to change for dinner, Avery went into the locker room, rinsed off, and changed into his Adidas track suit. It was loose-fitting, and he was going commando in it which made him a little uneasy, but he liked the feeling of the smooth fabric against his cool, damp skin.[30]

He was some distance down the hall when the pool room door whooshed open behind him.

"Hey, Ace!" Caitlyn was standing in the doorway, spinning his blood-spotted T-shirt in her hand. Her hair had dried and was a lighter blonde than usual. "Where ya goin'?"

"Back to my room to dress for dinner. I'm starving."

Aside from a pair of dangling gold "C" earrings, a threadbare hotel towel over her shoulders, and the skimpy pink bikini, nothing else covered Caitlyn's long, supple body.

"Wait up," she said. "I'll walk with you."

♫"Her Strut"♫

She slinks out of the doorway and approaches him in a confident strut. She makes flouncing, exaggerated steps on the balls of her white Keds, and her hips rock like she's sashaying down a catwalk.

---

[30] "Commando" is a slang term for a state of dress in which a person isn't wearing any underwear. The word's etymology is unclear, although it might derive from WWII commandos who, because they often had to go on missions at a moment's notice, didn't have time to put on underwear.

Brimming from the bikini cups, her breasts jiggle with every step. The bikini bottoms, cut high on the sides, expose her filly-trim legs all the way up to her hip bones. *Jeeeziss.* Her bikini is indeed the same one as Heather Thomas' in his poster back home. In fact, in this year's *Sports Illustrated* Swimsuit Edition, supermodel Elle MacPherson also wears a bikini like this one; the style is called "high-leg" or "French-cut."

Avery cleared his throat and averted his eyes. If he gazed at Caitlyn's body any longer, he'd fire up a full-on lightsaber in his pants.

She halted abruptly in front of him. "Follow me, Ace. I know a faster way." She tugged him toward the doorway into the stairwell. "Besides, we can't have me going out in the lobby like *this*." All at once, she spun around, yanked her towel open, and thrust her hip to the side—*POW!*

"No." Avery coughed. "Definitely not."

She smirked. "Trust me."

Ohhhhh ... Yeah

"Here, catch." She tossed him his T-shirt. "Don't need it anymore. Bleeding's stopped."

She hurried down the stairs; Avery followed. At the bottom, she held the door open for him, then marched them down the basement hallway and slapped an elevator button at the end. She nudged his shoulder with hers.

"Our own private elevator," she said.

"Isn't this the service elevator?"

"Yeah, so?"

"I don't think we're supposed to use it," he said.

"Dude, it's an *elevator*—it takes stuff up and down." She smacked the button again. "And it's the friggin' slowest one on the planet."

Avery was making a concerted effort to keep his eyes on her face, however her breasts and butt kept distracting him. Underneath her bikini bottoms was a small cylindrical bulge.

"What's that on your butt?" he asked. "Under the suit?"

Caitlyn was watching the lighted number panel above the doors. She gave him a sidelong glance and clucked her tongue.

"Ace ... are you *ogg*-gling my ass?"

"What!? First of all, it's pronounced '*oh*-gling,'" he said. "Second, I wasn't ogling anything. Third, don't act like you're offended; we both know the only reason you wore that bikini was to get my attention."

"I don't have any pockets," she said with a pout, "so I've got my room key under there. And this."

She fished out a lipgloss, rolled it across her lips, and put it back. The elevator arrived, and the doors clanked open. With a flourish, Caitlyn waved him aboard.

"Heroes first," she said.

♫"Let's Go All The Way"♫

Avery steps into the car. It's huge inside. The doors clank shut, and the second he turns around, Caitlyn pounces on him. She shoves him against the wall, swathes his thigh with her bare leg, and kisses him, sousing his mouth with a gush of cherry flavoring. Avery stops breathing. His flabbergasted fingers brush her ribs and lower back. Her bare skin is so pleasantly cool and smooth, it doesn't seem real. Caitlyn presses the button for the top floor, and the elevator rises. "I'm chilly, baby," she says. "Lemme warm up on you." She unzips his track suit jacket and slides her arms inside, then stabs her breasts into his chest while she claws his bare back. Unwrapping her leg, she stands on the balls of her feet and kisses him, practically gnawing his lips with hers. Far away in his mind, like a muffled cry from a well, his conscience says he shouldn't be doing this, but Caitlyn's allure is an invisible natural force, like magnetism or gravity, and Avery is irresistibly compelled to touch her. He glides one hand down and slips his fingers under her waistband. The second his fingers caress her bare butt, he shivers; it's the smoothest thing he's ever touched. When he fondles her breasts with his other hand, Caitlyn leans back and regards him warmly with a sigh.

"Oh, Ace … I'm gonna miss you when we go home. You protected me down there. Shane—that's my boyfriend—he'd never do that." Her jaw clenched. "He's such a friggin' loser."

"I shouldn't be doing this. You shouldn't either. Penny's your best friend."

"I know, I know, but I've been thinking about this a lot, so listen to me for a sec."

In a rapid monologue, Caitlyn said that Penny was wrong for Avery, and that he was making a mistake with her. For starters, Penny was way too concerned about what other people thought. Also, Penny's parents were jerks—especially her father, whom Caitlyn called "a total A-hole." Finally, if Avery was with Penny, he could forget about anything sexual; he wouldn't be getting anything for "a long … long … long time."

"You and me, on the other hand"—she kissed him again—"are *purrrfect* for each other. We're leaders. You know, whatchamacallits."

"'Alphas'?" he said.

"Yeah, Alphas, that's it," she said. "Damn you're smart—that's another thing. How you made the President laugh? Ohmigod, *such* a turn-on. What I'm saying is, we're leaders, each in our own way. Like how you totally took charge down at the pool? *Totally* awesome. And what about how well we danced together on the bus? I've gotten so many compliments about that. Besides, Ace, I really like you."

The elevator was still going up. Caitlyn had been right: it was the slowest one on the planet. She leaned back and smiled—an actual smile, not a smirk.

"So, do you like my bikini?" She thrust her chest out and swiveled her torso; Avery nodded; she giggled. "*Told* you it was sexy."

"Caitlyn, we're gonna get caught."

"No, we won't. It's after-hours. Nobody uses this elevator after five o'clock."

She kissed him again, with tongue this time, and buffed his chest with her breasts. She slid a hand down his abs, cupped his bulge, and massaged it. They were kissing and writhing in each other's arms when the elevator clunked to a stop.

"Now what are you doing?" he said.

"*Nuthin'…*"

The elevator doors opened.

"Come on, Lover," she said. "This is where we, uh … *get off.*"

She tugged him into a small vestibule. Across from the elevator was a steel door with a sign that read, "Stairs to Roof." The elevator doors closed behind them. The vestibule was cold, and the only sound was the low whistle of air blowing under the door to the roof. Caitlyn guided him into the corner, looked into his eyes, and pouted.

"Doctor Craig? Would you examine something else for me?"

Before Avery grasped what was happening, Caitlyn had untied her bikini neck strap and peeled off the cups.

♫"Oh Yeah"♫

Her breasts spill out and settle with a mesmerizing quiver. Loosed from the bikini, their fullness on her slender frame makes them seem even larger. Avery's jaw drops, his lungs collapse, and his brain grapples with the idea that the breathtaking sight in front of him is real, not a photo in *Playboy*. Firm yet faintly pendulous, Caitlyn's bare breasts are the first ones he's seen on a flesh-and-blood woman. They're impeccably shaped with peachy-pink areolas and delicately puffed, bijou buttons for nipples. Caitlyn's boast to him the other day that her breasts were "*very* nice" wasn't an exaggeration but an understatement. More arousing than Patti McGuire's, Terry Nihen's, Justine Greiner's, or any other *Playboy* Centerfold's, they send Avery reeling, like boxer Mike Tyson has just walloped him in the jaw.[31]

Caitlyn rubbed his bulge over his track pants and lifted his chin with her other hand. She arched an eyebrow. "Hmm ... *oh*-gling my *boobs* now, baby?"

With a smirk, she cupped them in both hands and playfully jiggled and slapped them together. Avery's eyes sprang out of their sockets like a cartoon character's; he was surprised not to hear an accompanying air-raid siren.

She swiveled her torso and gazed at him. "So... whaddaya think?"

"They're amazing, Caitlyn. You're so beautiful."

"They're thirty-four *deeezzzz*, Ace. Do they turn you on?"

He nodded stupidly. "They're gorgeous. *You're gorgeous.*"

"Wanna hold them?"

He put a hand over each one and kneaded them.

"Mmm," she said. "Your hands are so big and strong ... so *boss*."

---

[31] At the time, Mike Tyson was an up-and-coming young boxer infamous for his ferocity and powerful punches. Later that year, he would knock out Trevor Berbick to become the youngest Heavyweight Champion of the World in history.

Avery massaged them while lightly pinching her nipples in the fleshy webbing between his fingers. The contradictory way they felt in his hands was fascinating. How could they be so soft yet firm, so sculpted yet malleable?

"Oooh, that feels good." Caitlyn closed her eyes for a second, then opened them wide. "Sorry I tricked you into holding them yesterday."

"Mm … I forgive you," he said.

She giggled and rubbed his bulge faster. "Poor Acey. You're gonna stab a hole through your pants." She glanced down. "Tsk, tsk, Mister Boy Scout. Talk about pitching a *tent*." She kissed him. "Caitlyn's gonna give you some relief." Before Avery could take another breath, Caitlyn slipped her hand under the waistband. Avery had always been confident in the size of his equipment, but for a split second he had doubts. What if Shane or other guys Caitlyn had been with were hung like the Budweiser Clydesdales?[32]

Clouds Parted, Sunbeams Shone

As it turned out, Avery's worries were for naught. The moment Caitlyn's slender, silky fingers curled around his erection, her eyes squinted, her lips puckered, and she exhaled a long "*hoooooooh*" of contentment.

♫"Moving in Stereo"♫

"*There* we go." She stroked him gently. "How's that, baby?" Her eyes flashed, becoming enormous and full of wonder for a split second before returning to their inscrutable almond shape. She kissed him softly on the cheek. "Nice?"

Avery could barely breathe. It was an effort just to swallow and nod. Caitlyn glanced down and smirked.

"Commando, dude? Kinda grody, don'tcha think?"

"I *thought* I was going straight back to my room," he said.

---

[32] The Budweiser Clydesdales were enormous work horses featured in print and TV ads for the Anheuser-Busch brewing company. They were often shown pulling wagons with kegs of Budweiser beer. In some ads, the horses' schlongs could be seen, and the things were so absurdly oversized that they almost dragged on the ground. Eventually the marketing arm of Anheuser-Busch noticed this and swapped out the male Clydesdales for mares.

She giggled. Avery leaned his head back against the wall and relished the sensation. Relished it, that is, until Caitlyn abruptly stopped and withdrew her hand.

"Ugh, hold on. Sorry, baby."

She stepped to the side, shaking her wrist. For a panicked second, Avery worried she'd decided to quit, leaving him with dreaded blue balls again. He winced recalling the horrible ache in his scrotum, the waves of nausea. But when she snuggled against him again, this time at an angle alongside him, he realized that Caitlyn's change of position had been for his benefit. Now, she could better hinge her elbow and grip him more pleasurably. She re-curled her fingers around him and resumed her heavenly handiwork.

"How's that?" She was resting her head on his shoulder. She smiled and kissed his neck. "Better?"

"It's incredible."

Could he be dreaming? This was way better than any wet dream he'd ever had. He considered pinching himself, but decided if he *was* dreaming, he didn't want to wake up. Less than a week ago, he'd been trekking through a blizzard, pining for Dina Tempestilli; now he was getting the first handjob of his life, from a gorgeous girl he barely knew. Come to think of it, this situation was a lot like the erotic stories in *Penthouse Forum*.[33]

When Avery let out a little moan, she sucked on his earlobe and rubbed his butt with her other hand. The only sounds in the vestibule were the low whistle of air under the roof door, and the rhythmic swish of her fist rubbing against the inside of his polyester track pants. Avery let go of her breasts and watched them. They quivered hypnotically with every thump of her hand. Ecstasy washed over him like gentle, foaming surf on a beach.

Then, as Caitlyn continued to stroke him, she mewed, "Ace, do you care about me?"

---

[33] *Penthouse Forum* was a magazine of erotic stories published by the men's magazine *Penthouse*. The stories in each issue of *Forum* were allegedly true, but readers knew they were fiction. After all, how often did you see, or even hear of, couples having sex in elevators, phone booths, hot tubs, changing rooms, car washes, photography darkrooms, plane cockpits, or submarines?

Avery opened his eyes and took a breath. He wasn't capable of answering questions at the moment, much less questions about his feelings. Care about her? Like, did he *love* her? If that was the question, then the answer was no. But he couldn't say *that*, not now. He didn't want her to stop and bring the waves of pleasure to an end.

"Yes, very much," he said.

"I knew you did," she said. "You *rescued* me down there. No guy's ever done that for me before. You're wonderful, Avery."

"I'd do it again. I'd never let a guy hurt you."

Down in his pants, her grip on him loosened, her pace slowed, and the piston-like thumping transitioned to a gentle spiraling motion. A newly unique sensation of pleasure engulfed him.

"Oh, Caitlyn … thank you for this."

She regarded him amusedly, her eyes drifting across his face, his chest, his abs.

"Avery, has any girl done this for you before?"

He shook his head.

"Wow," she said. "I'm your first?"

"Uh-huh."

She kissed his ear. "Would you touch me while I do this? You turn me on so much."

"Sure, anything." Avery swallowed. "Touch you where?"

Sniggering, she removed one of his hands from her breast and slid it down the front of her bikini bottoms, positioning his middle fingertip on a little button down there and moving it around. The whole region was steamy and felt like how her lips looked—positively lubricious. Avery discovered that her little button was magic: when he wiggled his fingertip on it, Caitlyn gasped and tugged him faster.

"Ohhhh … yes. Caitlyn likey."

The way their arms were tangled and interwoven made their pleasuring each other awkward, like a game of Twister, but as horny as Avery was for her, he didn't care. Caitlyn didn't seem to mind either. With her eyelids fluttering open and shut, Caitlyn hummed the melody of "The Reflex," then grinned and sang half of the first lyric; Avery reflexively replied with the rhyming second half.

As Avery and Caitlyn pleasure each other, the sprightly pop-rock sounds of ♫"The Reflex"♫ swell in the background. Steam wafts around the vestibule, a strobe light flashes, a breeze flutters their hair. Lots of split-screen shots and jump cuts. Close-ups of Caitlyn's lipgloss-greasy lips and her plenteous side-boob against Avery's bare chest; Avery's fluttering eyelids; Caitlyn's hand bobbing fiercely in his track pants; Avery's hand moving briskly in her bikini bottoms; Caitlyn's "C" earrings waggling and her head tipping back in ecstasy. The song increases in key and tempo, racing headlong toward the crescendo. Avery and Caitlyn's manipulations become faster and faster, and then the song cuts out.

Caitlyn stood on tiptoe and thrust her breasts toward Avery's mouth. "Kiss my boobs while you touch me, baby?"

He did. They tasted strongly of chlorine. The bitter taste must have shown on his face, because within seconds Caitlyn was slathering her nipples and mouth with Maybelline Kissing Potion. The piquant smell of cherry flavoring hung in the air, choking his brain in a fog of lust. The lipgloss made her breasts much tastier, and Avery licked them, swirled his tongue around, and nibbled them softly—all while wiggling his finger. Then Caitlyn kissed him on the mouth.

"I want to look at you now," she said.

Caitlyn smiled with tenderness in her eyes and used her free hand to play with Avery's hair and caress his cheek. They synchronized their pleasuring of each other and gazed into each other's eyes like it was a staring contest. Caitlyn ground her vulva against Avery's finger and wriggled on the balls of her feet. She kissed him, sucked air through her teeth, shivered—"Ohmigod, it feels *so* good." As for Avery, his breathing was now so rapid and rasping that he was on the verge of hyperventilating. With every exhale, he let out a warbly moan. His capacity for speech was gone.

Caitlyn stroked him with an awestruck look on her face. "You're *so* handsome, Ace—your eyes, your hair, your nose. And Rhonda's right—your bod's friggin' *mint*." She kissed his chest. "I wanna feel your naked body so bad!" She yanked his track suit jacket off one shoulder and pressed her bare breasts against his ribs, letting out a little hiss, like her nipples had gotten scorched on his skin.

"Ace, am I your sexy little doll?"

Avery nodded and grunted.

"You're getting close, baby," she said. "Keep looking at my face and boobs, and you'll come"—she licked her lips—"lickety-split."

He nodded and drank her in.

"Touch me faster," she said. "I want to come *with* you."

He did as ordered.

"Oooh, yes, that's it." She gasped. "Am I sexy, baby? My boobs, my butt, my legs, my lips?"

He nodded.

"*Say it*, Ace. I need to hear it."

"Everything about you is sexy. Your lips especially. You're … *inscrutalicious*."

"What's…"—she panted—"that mean?"

"Mysterious and delicious, Babydoll."

She gasped again. Clenching his finger between her thighs, Caitlyn shuddered on the balls of her feet and made muffled little squeals. Her face and neck flushed pink, and she tossed her head back and sighed like she'd just received some deeply relieving news.

"Oooh, Ace, you made me come so hard!" She kissed him, flicking her tongue wildly in his mouth. "I can't believe you've never done this before. Now it's your turn. I'm gonna make you come super hard. Ready?"

Avery nodded, or at least he thought he did; he was teetering on the edge of passing out. A look of single-minded focus came over Caitlyn's face. She resumed her handjob—faster and with a firmer grip. "Feel nice, baby?"

He nodded.

"You like Caitlyn's soft hand stroking your hard cock?"

He nodded again. The pressure in his head was so strong, he was certain an artery was about to burst.

"By the way…" She mashed her warm, slick lips against his cheek. "*Happy birthday*." And then she tilted her head back and smiled. Clouds parted, sunbeams shone, and the gates of heaven opened before him. It was Caitlyn's broadest, warmest smile yet, without a trace of that devilish smirk. Her teeth were so straight and white—why didn't she smile more often? Avery could have blissfully gazed at Caitlyn's mouth until his dying days, but when she moaned and climaxed a third time, his sensory apparatus was overloaded. Every muscle in his body tensed, like he was having a seizure. He was paralyzed as overwhelming pleasure swelled inside him. He grunted involuntarily to release some of the intense pressure in his head.

"Oooh, Ace," she said, "come for me!"

Caitlyn tightened her grip, jerking him so ardently that Avery worried she might yank it off. Gasping for breath, he couldn't hold back any longer: his hips bucked, his legs spasmed, his groin clenched into a knot, and then, finally, there was sweet release. Gone was all the pent-up tension of the week, all the sexual frustration he'd ever felt with girls, and all his worries—about school, Scouts, sports, SATs, college, his parents, his friends, his future, everything.

The succession of grunting broadsides, the multi-salvo barrage of knot and release, seemed to last for hours. Then, as the smoky ecstasy cleared out of his head, he returned to reality. Caitlyn slowed her hand to a stop and collapsed against him, her bare, piqued breasts smushed against his naked chest, and her breath sultry on his cheek.

Purrrfect Together

They held each other and caught their breath. A moment later, Caitlyn let go of his penis. The inside of his track pants felt sodden and gluey.

"Well … *somebody* came." Caitlyn kissed him and raised an eyebrow. "Big time." She carefully withdrew her hand and wiped it on his towel, then reached back into his pants with the towel and wiped him off. "We came together, baby."

"That's good, right?"

"No, that's *wonderful*." She was faintly trembling. "I feel so close to you, Avery. Do you feel close to me?"

He was still so shell-shocked that he couldn't feel much of anything, but the way she was clinging to him told Avery that she needed to feel loved.

"Yes, honey." He rubbed her back. "Very close."

"You called me 'Babydoll' before. Am I your sexy Babydoll?"

He squeezed her butt. "You bet."

She kissed him while speaking out of the side of her mouth. "You don't regret it, do you?"

"A little bit," he said.

"Like, you feel guilty? About Penny?"

He nodded.

"You shouldn't. We're just, like, *crazy* attracted to each other. We can't help ourselves." She kissed his neck. "Don't worry. I won't tell Penny." Her gray eyes were liquidly soft. "I swear."

"I won't tell anyone either."

"Come on," she said, "you'll be bragging to your buddies the second we get downstairs."

He held her head in his hands. "No, I won't. It's none of their business. I would never dishonor you like that."

She beamed. It wasn't quite the smile that had triggered his orgasm earlier, but it was close. She zipped up his jacket.

"Promise me we'll see each other again?" she said. "Just you and me? No Penny?"

He kissed her. "I promise."

They got their clothes resituated and walked to the elevator. Caitlyn surprised him by lashing out with her leg and punching the button with a karate side kick. Below, the elevator whirred. She hugged him.

"I think when you get home," she said, "you're gonna figure out pretty quick that you and Penny aren't right for each other. But you and me?" She ran her fingers through his hair. "We're *purrrfect* together."

When the elevator arrived, they stepped inside. Caitlyn pressed the button for Avery's floor and snuggled into his arms. They were going down. For a moment, the only sound was the whir of the elevator, and then Caitlyn sniggered.

"What's funny?" he said.

"*Nuthin'*. I was thinking about the mess I caused in your pants."

"Wonderful."

She tilted her head back and smirked. "Hey, dude … I just gave you a *handjob*. I doubt any other guys on this trip are getting handies. How about a little gratitude?"

"You're right. Thanks."

She kissed his cheek. "I'm kidding. *Yeesh*, lighten up."

The elevator shuddered to a stop, and its doors clanked open loudly, like it was disgusted with them and couldn't get rid of them fast enough. It was his floor. Caitlyn pressed the button for her floor and walked him off the car, holding the elevator door open with her butt. She put her hand on his jacket and rubbed his chest.

"I want you to know," she said, "if you were my guy, I'd satisfy you every time we saw each other." She stared into his eyes and caressed his cheek. "Every … time." She pushed him away. "Later, Lover."

She smirked and finger-waved, the elevator doors closed, and she was gone. With the towel bundle covering his crotch, Avery hustled down the hall to his room.

13

FORTUNATELY, WHEN Avery got to his room after his tryst with Caitlyn, Doc was out. Avery wasn't reeling anymore, but he had a headache. He stumbled into the bathroom, stripped, and turned his track suit pants inside-out. He washed and rinsed the pants in the tub, wrung them out, and hung them on the towel rack to dry. After a shower, he examined his face in the mirror. He needed a shave. Until recently, he'd only had to shave once a week, but now he had to do it every few days. The alternative was to go around with a *Miami Vice* stubble-beard, and no way was he doing that. He filled the sink with hot water, splashed his face, spread shaving cream on his cheeks and neck, and got started.

While he shaved, he thought about the girls in his life. His first thought was of the kiss with Irina. The kiss itself had been amazing, but he was weirded out by her confession about how lonely she was. Avery couldn't fathom why a gorgeous young woman like Irina didn't have a boyfriend. Avery paused his shaving and stared at himself in the mirror. There *had* to be something wrong with her. Not that it mattered. Chances were, she'd forget about him by tomorrow, and he'd never hear from her again. In the meantime, he'd gotten to kiss a stunning Scandinavian woman and caress her womanly body.

Finished shaving, Avery got dressed, opened the window curtains, and gazed down at the four-lane highway in front of the hotel. It was lightly snowing, the snow falling invisibly out of the darkness and only coming into view when it reached the warm glow of the streetlamps.

After four days of being kissed, touched, and tempted by Caitlyn, Penny, and Irina, Caitlyn's handiwork earlier had been such a relief. She'd said that if Avery were her guy, she'd satisfy him *every time* they got together, and because she'd stared unwaveringly into his eyes when she said it, Avery knew she meant every word. He hated to admit it, but the promise of regular sex with Caitlyn was irresistible and having to wait a "long … long … long time" for anything sexual with Penny was crushing. He had to make a choice, a much harder choice than Coke or Pepsi.[34] Who did he want as his girlfriend: Penny or Caitlyn? Penny was pretty, sweet, and innocent. Caitlyn had a beautiful face and a mind-blowing body, but most of all she was exciting. How she'd pounced on him from across the elevator car. The way she pursed her lips when she took hold of him. Like her pink bikini, Caitlyn was "SOOOOOOOO FRIGGIN' SEXXXY," and they turned each other on—big time.

Avery gazed at the river of car headlights below. After a minute or so, he nodded. Caitlyn was right: she and Avery were perfect for each other. The question now was, when and how should he break the news to Penny?

Unexpectedly Sexy

The telephone rang. Avery crossed the room and picked up the phone.

"Hi, Avery, it's me," Penny said. "Can we talk before dinner?"

"Sure," he said. "What's up?"

"No, not on the phone. Can we meet down in the lobby?"

"Yeah, okay."

"See you in a few. Bye." *Click.*

Avery stared at the phone handset before replacing it in the cradle. He slipped on his blazer, grabbed his room key and billfold, and left. He was beyond confused. Penny had sounded bubbly on the phone, like she was pleased with him. But how could she be pleased with him after the pool fight? Maybe she hadn't heard about it yet. Impossible; she must have.

---

[34] Pepsi had Michael Jackson and Madonna in its "Pepsi: The Choice of a New Generation" TV ad campaign, but the soft drink was too sweet for Avery's taste.

In the lobby, he stood by the sofas near the elevators. Tonight's dinner was in the main ballroom, and the happy chatter of his fellow students was drifting down the hallway. As he waited for Penny, he paced and glanced at his watch. Ten minutes passed. Was she at dinner already?

♫"Someone For Me"♫

He starts toward the ballroom when an elevator whirs and dings, and the doors slowly open. Penny is alone in the car, and the first thing Avery notices are her legs. She's standing on the ball of her foot with one knee bent, poised to dash out of the car the second the doors fully open. There's a pink ribbon in her hair, tied in a big bow. She wears a snug, short-sleeved pink sweater; a short gray pleated skirt with pink and gray argyle knee socks; and penny loafers. Between her skirt hem and the tops of her socks are six scrumptious inches of her trim and creamy thighs. And then Penny does something unexpectedly sexy—she bites her lower lip, plants her hands on her waist, and shimmies, causing her skirt pleats to waggle against her thighs like a bell. With her hands clasped behind her back, she skips off the elevator. As she crosses the marble floor with her ponytail waggling, Avery is seized by a giant fist squeezing his chest and stomach; clearly, this is punishment for what he did with Caitlyn earlier. How could he do that to sweet Penny?

When Penny reaches him, she glances around the quiet lobby, stands on her tiptoes, and kisses him. He's certain that Caitlyn is secretly coaching her on kissing technique because Penny squeezes his butt, arches her back, and buries her breasts into his chest. Hers aren't nearly the size of Caitlyn's, but they're firm and eager, and equally effective. She finishes the kiss by wriggling against him and rubbing his nose with hers. She takes hold of his hands and gazes up at him with shining eyes.

"You're incredible, Avery!"

Apparently, Caitlyn and the other Vanderbush girls had gushed to her about how Avery was "a total hero" at the pool earlier.

"I don't understand," he said. "Why aren't you angry with me? Technically, I was fighting."

"Not really. It was a *pool* fight. You didn't punch anybody."

"No, but I might have broken a guy's nose. He was bleeding, and I *did* kick him into the pool."

Penny grimaced. "Oh, my."

"Why are you suddenly okay with me fighting?"

"I guess because you were defending my friends," she said. "Avery, are *we* fighting?"

He sighed. "No, I guess not."

"Can we go to dinner now?"

Avery nodded.

Under the Table

When they walked in, most of the students turned their heads and whispered to each other. Louis, a fedora perched jauntily over one eye, gave Avery the nod. Everybody was seated and eating dinner.

Doc and Caitlyn were at a table in the center of the ballroom. Caitlyn was standing and waving to them like she was signaling a rescue plane. She greeted them in adult fashion, kissing them on both cheeks. Her makeup covered the pink spot where she'd been hit by the ball earlier, and she was wearing a black knit tube dress that hugged her body, dark stockings, and crimson heels. For the umpteenth time this week, seeing her made Avery shiver like he was freezing to death. Obviously reveling in the distress her outfit was causing him, Caitlyn asked if he liked her dress, then twirled and wriggled.

Dinner was a fancy buffet with a carving station—a choice of roast beef, ham, or turkey—and about a dozen side dishes. Caitlyn had chosen their seats: Avery next to her, and Penny and Doc across the table from them. Although sitting beside Caitlyn made Avery nervous (what if she hinted that they'd fooled around?), his appetite was unaffected. The pool fight had exhausted him, and ever since the tryst in the elevator, his brain had felt foggy. His head, which had faintly ached earlier, was now throbbing. As he ate, a vague worry gnawed at him: what if Caitlyn had given him such an intense orgasm that it ruptured a blood vessel? The pressure in his head before he released had been severe—more severe than the first time he'd bench-pressed 200 pounds. What if he wasn't as sharp or clear-headed ever again? What if he'd damaged his brain!? God, he hoped not.

While Caitlyn and Penny discussed the trip, and how sad they were that it was ending, Avery and Doc discreetly and efficiently shoveled in food. When Avery returned to the table after getting a second plateful—ham, spinach, and mac & cheese—he saw Caitlyn kick off one of her high heels under the table.

Nodding wide-eyed at something Penny was saying, Caitlyn crossed her legs. A moment later, her stockinged foot caressed Avery's calf until it reached the sensitive area under his bent knee, where she poked her toes in and out of the gap. Avery jerked his leg away. Then Caitlyn reached for the saltshaker, a tall one, sprinkled some salt on her food, and nudged Avery with her foot under the table. When Avery looked at her, she was talking to Penny and idly stroking the saltshaker with her fingertips. Avery hitched his chair over to keep her frisky foot out of range. Penny squinted at Caitlyn, then Avery; she seemed to sense that something was going on between them.

Watching Penny and Caitlyn talk with each other, Avery knew he had to choose, and since this was the last night of the trip, he had to choose tonight. Tomorrow they'd return to their schools, their friends, and their lives at home, and the fantasy world of this trip would disappear. Unless he chose one of them tonight, Avery would go home without a girlfriend.

There was an assortment of desserts on the buffet table, and Avery chose three that he never got at home: Key Lime pie, lemon meringue pie, and cheesecake with strawberry sauce. Penny and Doc each got blueberry pie, but Caitlyn didn't get a dessert. Instead, she hitched her chair next to his and annoyingly sliced off slivers of *his* desserts.

After dinner, there was supposed to be another movie, but the hotel's projection TV was broken. As a *mea culpa* for this and the pool mishap earlier, the hotel hired "Dr. Funkenstein," a tall black DJ, to give the students a dance party. Initially, Avery was skeptical of the top hat-wearing DJ, thinking Dr. F. would spend most of his time making annoying chatter, but he turned out to be all business. Holding headphones next to one ear, he grooved to his selections—an outstanding set of dance tunes—and didn't say a word to interrupt the party all night.

Electrifying Moves

♫"I Feel for You"♫ kicked things off, drawing most of the students onto the dance floor. Avery, Penny, Caitlyn, and Doc danced to the song as a group. They danced together to ♫"Let The Music Play"♫ and did some "robot" moves to ♫"The Safety Dance,"♫ but when ♫"Burning Up"♫ came on, Caitlyn steered Avery away from the group, lip-syncing Madonna's racy lyrics as they danced.

During ♫"P.Y.T.,"♫ Avery drifted away from Caitlyn and danced on his own, stitching together his best Michael Jackson moves while mouthing the flirtatious lyrics to the girls. Louis tossed his fedora to Avery, who donned it by rolling it up his arm like M.J. and moonwalked across the dance floor.

And then the opening hiss and dreamlike synthesizer of ♫"For Your Eyes Only"♫ washed over the room, Penny flashed into his mind, and Avery went to her. As they danced to Sheena Easton's ethereal voice, Avery gazed into Penny's adoring eyes, not once thinking of Caitlyn. When the last synthesizer notes faded out, and he and Penny smiled at each other, Avery was certain Penny was the right girl for him.

Certain, that is, until ♫"I Didn't Mean To Turn You On"♫ came over the sound system, and Caitlyn, looking like a panther in her black tube dress, locked eyes with him. Wagging her shoulders to the beat, she slinked across the floor and yanked him away from Penny. From the moment Avery put her in a frame, they were lockstep, gliding around the ballroom. The other students formed a circle and clapped to the beat. Caitlyn had some electrifying moves. Avery's favorite was when she danced away from him, and he yanked her back toward him. Spinning on the toe of one shoe, Caitlyn turned, threw her head back, and raised one red heel off the floor in a super-sexy *piqué*.

All at once, Avery got a vision for a sexy dance for her to this song. He showed the moves to Caitlyn, and in seconds she was doing them flawlessly: hip shimmy and hand flap, twirl, right knee kick and push-out, half knee-kick, change direction, strong left knee-kick with head thrown back and splayed fingers at sides, step out, double-arm crisscross, power pose and point at the audience. As she repeated the little routine, Avery marveled at her dancing ability. He put her back in a frame, they danced to the rest of the song in a Foxtrot, and Avery finished their dance with a majestic dip.

When he lifted her to her feet, the other students clapped and cheered. He and Caitlyn smiled at each other and panted. Their dancing had been practically effortless. Maybe they were "*purrrfect together*" like she'd said. After they danced the East Coast Swing to Wham's ♫"Wake Me Up Before You Go-Go,"♫ they led everyone in a dance to ♫"Footloose,"♫ then sat out a few songs to rest.

But when ♫"Thriller"♫ began to play, Avery showed everyone how to do a scaled-down version of the dance from the video, focusing on three elements: the sharp, angular arm and hand movements, the Zombie Hop-Shuffle, and, most importantly the signature move— the Zombie Walk, with its stiff jerky leg movements, its mechanical head movement, and its slightly off-balance steps. Caitlyn and Louis picked up the dance right away; Gemma, Eric, and Ms. Wharton got it after some personal attention; but Penny and Doc were hopelessly flummoxed. When the DJ saw what Avery was doing, he played the song again, and for five glorious minutes, some forty Hancock and Vanderbush high school students, normally sworn enemies, were dancing in unison to "Thriller." For the final minute of the song, Avery stood at the front facing everybody and admired his work. Jill and maybe even Michael Jackson himself would be impressed.

After "Thriller," Avery lost track of Penny and danced with Caitlyn for the rest of the evening. Caitlyn was the only girl who could keep up with him to ♫"Sussudio"♫—a fast, concussive, drum-heavy number. They were in sync throughout the entire song, and the magnetism between them was palpable. They danced millimeters apart and gazed into each other's eyes to ♫"Stand Back"♫ and then ♫"Relax."♫

When they sat down to take a break, Caitlyn asked one of her friends where Penny was; she said Penny wasn't feeling well and had gone back to the room. Avery got sodas, and when he returned to the table, Caitlyn gulped hers, slapped the cup down, and leaned into Avery's ear: "Meet me in the jungle room, Ace."

He nodded. She walked to the ballroom door, made sure no one was looking, and slipped out.

Easy, Tiger

Avery followed a minute later, his footsteps echoing in the empty lobby. No one was at the front desk either.

♫"Make the Move"♫

His heart pounds. He can't wait to kiss Caitlyn again, to hold her improbable body in his arms. He quickens his step, slowing down when he nears the entrance to the solarium and sees a faint glow through the French doors. He can make out the shadowy outlines of the giant plants inside. He gulps down a breath, slips into the room, and eases the door shut behind him.

Caitlyn's voice resounds from somewhere in the room: "Over here, Lover." Avery wends his way through the maze of potted plants, past a trickling fountain, down a narrow gravel walkway through the long solarium, into an open marble-floored area surrounded by more plants. Caitlyn is sitting on an armless padded patio chair with her legs crossed, her elbow resting on her thigh, and her chin in her palm. When their eyes meet, she smiles.

"Ohmigod, I loved dancing with you tonight," she said. "It got me *so* hot. Get over here and kiss me."

Thinking of how Bond handled situations where a beautiful woman seductively bade him hither, Avery sauntered toward Caitlyn. He even paused to glance at his watch when what he really wanted to do was run to her and hump her against the wall. When he reached her, Caitlyn stood, shoved him into the chair, hiked her dress up to her hips, and straddled his lap. While they kissed, she skated her fingernails through his hair.

"Ace," she said, "*we* need to be together, not you and Penny."

"Yeah. I realized it when we were dancing."

"We're so in-sync," she said. "We *have* to be together. Can't you see us at our school dances? We're gonna tear it up. We're gonna *rule* both our schools."

"But, what about Shane?"

She sniffed. "What about him?"

"He's your boyfriend."

Caitlyn smirked. "Not anymore."

♫"Physical Attraction"♫

She spreads her legs a little wider and wriggles up close to him until her groin grinds against his bulge. In no time, they're staring into each other's eyes, and Caitlyn is riding his lap, making sexy little whimpers as she gyrates her hips. Her breasts, jutting out conspicuously in the black dress, jiggle with her gyrations. Then Caitlyn slows down and rotates her hips. Avery's bulge drills into a steamy area, and by the now-familiar way that she gasps and smiles, Avery knows he's struck oil against her little button. Caitlyn rides him, kisses him, and flicks her tongue in his mouth. Avery is precariously close to coming in his pants. He puts his hands on her breasts and kneads them.

"Easy, tiger," she said. "You can rub them, but don't squeeze."

"I thought you liked me massaging them."

"I do, but not in this dress. I don't want to stretch it out. It's one of my favorites."

They resumed for a minute or two, and then a disturbing vision popped into his head: Caitlyn making out like this with one of the Vanderbush ski douches.

"Stop, Caitlyn." He opened his eyes and clutched her waist.

"What's wrong, baby?" she asked.

"If we go out together, are you going to be faithful to me?"

Caitlyn made an "X" on her chest. "Cross my tits and hope to die."

"That's not good enough," he said.

She sighed. "Look, Ace, I won't flirt or fool around with other guys because I'm totally into you, and I don't want to screw it up. I know it's only been a few days, but sometimes a girl just knows. Looks, bod, brains, talent—I know I'll never find another guy like you. I'll be a good girl, I promise."

"And you'll dump Shane?"

"The second I get home. But I need to know something first. How do you feel about me?"

"When I'm with you, I can barely breathe," he said, "and the physical attraction is like an electromagnet."

Caitlyn's eyes became dreamy. "That's exactly how I feel. But what about *me*—you know … on the inside?"

Avery said that he didn't know her yet, but he wanted to get to know her, and Caitlyn said the same thing. They stared at each other.

"What do we do now?" Avery said.

"You mean, how do we tell Penny?" She swallowed. "I'll do it. It'll be easier if it comes from me."

Caitlyn said she would tell Penny right away and call Avery after curfew to tell him what happened. She stood and pulled Avery up, then smoothed her dress and primped her hair.

"Before I go," she said, "this thing between you and me—tell me it's not just physical. I mean, you care about me, right?"

He knew he cared about her, but he wasn't sure how much.

"Yes, I care about you," he said. "Deeply."

Caitlyn smiled and walked out, her heels clip-clopping on the marble floor. She brushed through some plants at the end of the room and was gone.

The Parapet

Shortly after Caitlyn left, Avery returned to his room. He took a shower and got ready for bed. Doc, already in pajamas, was folding his dirty laundry and stacking it neatly in a garbage bag on the top layer of his suitcase. He had laid out clean clothes for tomorrow; the pristine pile sat on the chair by the window.

Avery was in the middle of doing push-ups when Doc sat on the bed.

"Hey, Ace," he said, "can I ask you a question?"

"Sure, go ahead." Avery moved on to crunches and leg lifts.

"It's more of an observation actually." Doc said that everybody was talking about how Avery and Caitlyn had been "all over each other" tonight.

"We were only dancing," Avery said.

"Dude … the way you were looking at each other tonight, it's obvious there's something going on between you two. I saw it, Penny saw it, everybody saw it." Doc took a deep breath. "There's something else. When I was sitting with Caitlyn on the bus the first day, all she did was ask me a bunch of questions about you, like where you lived, whether you had a girlfriend, a bunch of stuff like that. She claimed she was finding out for Penny, but I got the feeling that she was really asking for herself."

"Weird," Avery said. "Well, there's nothing going on between us."

For some reason, Avery was too exhausted tonight to continue his bedtime calisthenics. He crawled onto his bed, leaned back against the headboard, and laced his hands behind his head. Doc yawned, went to his bed, and pulled down the covers.

"Wanna get breakfast in the morning?" he asked.

"Yup."

"Mind if I shut out the lights?"

"I'm waiting for a call," Avery said, "but sure, go ahead."

Avery sat alone in the dark with the LED clock radio on the nightstand as his only company. He thought about how he'd crapped out during his workout tonight; that had never happened before. What was different tonight? Sure, he'd danced a lot, and there was the battle royal in the pool this afternoon, but … *oh, the handjob.*

In Health and Biology, Avery had learned that the body used a lot of energy to create semen, and after ejaculation, the body put most of its energy into restoring semen reserves. Caitlyn had pumped the energy out of him so to speak, but it'd been worth it. He smiled in the darkness. One night of no calisthenics was a small price to pay for his first handjob—something Avery was certain he'd remember vividly for the rest of his life.

Meanwhile, Caitlyn still hadn't called him. Every so often, he glanced at the glaring numbers on his red LED travel clock—11:17 then 11:39 p.m.; 12:10 then 12:33 a.m. Why hadn't she called? She'd said she would call him "later," after she spoke to Penny. Or had he misunderstood her? Maybe she was planning to talk to him in the morning.

As he sat awake in the darkness, Avery brooded over Doc's comment that it was obvious to everybody that he and Caitlyn were into each other. *Was* it obvious? They had danced together a lot, and they were attracted to each other, but they didn't kiss at all during the dance, and no one had seen them kissing during the trip. He supposed that someone might have seen Caitlyn playing footsie with him under the table, and then a sickening thought came over him. What if Penny had left the dance early because she knew about him and Caitlyn? She'd eyed them suspiciously during dinner. Avery had heard of "woman's intuition"; that might be how Penny knew. He sighed and shook his head. When he looked at the clock again, the LED read, "1:07 A.M.," and he knew Caitlyn wasn't going to call. It was stifling in the room, and he desperately needed air.

Ten minutes later, he was on the hotel roof. The air was refreshingly cold. It was lightly snowing, and there were a few inches of it on the roof. Avery crossed to the parapet and peered down at the street. The divided highway in front of the hotel was quiet; only a few cars whisked softly past.

Tomorrow, the trip would be over, and he'd go home to his ordinary life as a sophomore at Hancock High. His life would be a lot better (theoretically, at least) because he'd have a girlfriend, Caitlyn Cray, who promised to satisfy him sexually "every time" they saw each other. But somehow her promise was less enticing than it was worrying. Now that he'd tasted her charms, he craved her physically and wanted *more*. After their brief, post-dance make-out session, even after an ice-cold shower, his entire groin area throbbed. The blue balls were *back* ... and worse than ever. As Caitlyn had likewise expressed to him in the rooftop vestibule, he wanted to feel her silky, naked body against his skin. And if they danced that well together, imagine how great the sex would be! He wanted her so badly, he could scream.

So much about Caitlyn appealed to Avery: her kaleidoscopic gray eyes; her wavy and wild blonde hair; her slender yet fully blossomed body; and her pillowy-lipped smirk. During the pool melee, when she was attacked and cried out for Avery's help, it had kindled a powerful protective instinct that he'd never felt before.

♫"Burning Heart"♫

Avery stared over the parapet watching the falling snow. More than sex, he wanted a girl to love him, to think he was amazing, to hang on his every word and declare it the greatest thing she'd ever heard. Love. Was Caitlyn capable of real love? That was the problem with her: aside from the couple of times he'd seen her smile, most of the time she was a friggin' sphinx, so Avery had no idea what she was truly thinking and feeling. Could he ever love a sphinx?

Avery shoved his hands in his jacket pockets and strolled alongside the parapet. He hated how he'd treated Penny. All right, so she cared too much about what other people thought? She was sweet and thoughtful, and so what if she wasn't as physically developed as Caitlyn? With that fawn-colored hair, those lilac eyes, and that adorable nose, she looked like a beautiful doll. And in that short, pleated skirt and knee socks, she showed she could be sexy too.

Penny or Caitlyn? As far as sex with Caitlyn went, he didn't like that if he eventually did get inside her, some other guy or guys would have been there before him. Avery grimaced. This was how the British explorer Scott must have felt when he finally reached the South Pole, only to discover that Amundsen and his team had already been there and planted the Norwegian flag. With Penny, Avery might have to wait a "long … long … long time," but when they finally did it, Avery would be like Sir Edmund Hillary on the summit of Mount Everest: he'd be the first guy there—a place no man had ever been before.

Avery paced along the parapet some more to calm himself, and as he was riding the elevator back downstairs, he said a silent prayer asking God for two things: a sign showing him which girl was best for him, and to make his blue balls go away.

<h1 style="text-align:center">14</h1>

To the blue balls part of his prayer, Avery received an answer in the night, but it wasn't the answer he'd expected.

Shortly before dawn, the hotel room door opened and clicked shut. There were shushing sounds and giggling female voices. Avery was disoriented, unsure of where he was, and then he groggily recalled that he was on his class trip to Washington, D.C. Two shadowy female figures moved across the room, shedding clothes on their way toward his bed, and the next thing he knew, his bedcovers came off and two warm bodies cuddled against him.

"What the hell!?" He switched on the bedside light. Caitlyn and Irina were in bed with him and totally nude. Avery glanced at Doc's bed. It was made-up and empty. "Where's Doc?"

Caitlyn rolled her eyes and nudged Irina. "Ohmigod, the dude's got two majorly hot babes in his bed, and he wants to know where friggin' Doc is."

"What are you two doing here? And together? I don't understand."

"After you went to bed," Caitlyn said, "I wandered downstairs and bumped into Irina, and we hit it off. Anyway, we got talking, and we decided that since we're attracted to each other and you, we both want to give you a *sweet* birthday present."

"We give you blowjob together," Irina said. "You would like, yes?"

"Duh! Of course he would like." Caitlyn rolled lipgloss on her lips. "Two majorly hot babes wanna suck his rod. What's not to like?" She squeezed him. "Mm, you've got a righteous stick of wood goin' here, Ace." Caitlyn motioned with her head. "Okay, Irina. Hit it."

"'Hit it'!? I do not want to hit Ace's penis!"

Caitlyn groaned. "No, not his penis. 'Hit it,' as in, start the music."

"Oh, yes."

When a Plan Comes Together

There was a boombox on the nightstand, and Irina pressed play on it. The screaming opening guitar riff of ♫"Woke Up With Wood"♫ blared out of the speakers, and Irina danced back to the bed, rocking her hips robotically. "My dancing is better, Ace? Yes?"

"You're looking great, Irina."

"All right, let's go." Caitlyn kicked the blankets off the bed, and the two girls lay on their stomachs in the V between Avery's legs, friskily waggling their feet in the air. Caitlyn went first, using her slow teasing lips and tongue, then passed him to Irina. Avery soon blacked out from the waves of ecstasy. When he regained consciousness, he glanced at the foot of the bed.

The boombox was gone, and in its place was the actual band ZZ Top, with their guitars, drums, long beards, and Wayfarer sunglasses, continuing to play "Woke Up With Wood." Gemma, Penny, Jolene, and Johanna were sitting next to each other on the edge of Doc's bed. They were all in white lab coats, holding clipboards and pens, making notes and sharing them with each other, and wagging their feet in unison with the music. Their lab coats were open, and underneath they were wearing white lace bras and panties. Gemma removed her lab coat, placed her fist under her chin and leaned in for a closer look. Caitlyn announced she was about to make Ace ejaculate.

"Watch and learn, ladies," she said.

Caitlyn kissed the underside of his erection then rubbed it zestfully against her smooching lips. When Irina positioned her mouth next to hers, Caitlyn rubbed him against both of their lips. Unable to hold back any longer, Avery released in geyseric spurts; it was like a fountain of liquid cinnamon roll icing. Caitlyn shook her head maniacally.

"Woo! I love it when a plan *comes* together!"

While the other girls squealed, Gemma was silent, clinically observing everything and scribbling copious notes on her clipboard.

When Avery was finally spent, Caitlyn lit a cigar like Hannibal did on *The A-Team*. She took a few puffs, then she and Irina kissed each other. Caitlyn handed Avery the cigar, and she and Irina crawled up the bed and lay on either side of him, rubbing against him and kissing him while he smoked it. The girls on Doc's bed removed their lab coats, bras, and panties, crawled onto his bed, and rubbed and kissed him as well. Finally, like they did at the end of all their music videos, ZZ Top gave Avery three thumbs-up and dematerialized before his eyes.[35]

A Slab of Tree Bark

Avery basked in the relief, not caring a whit about the soaked feeling around his groin. He was falling asleep with the harem of beautiful young women cuddled around him when the phone rang. It rang a second time.

"I'll get it," Gemma said. She was nude except for her tortoiseshell glasses. She crawled over the other girls' writhing bodies, plopped down on Doc's bed, and answered the phone. Bizarrely, the voice that came out of her mouth wasn't hers, but Doc's: "Hello? … Yeah, he's here. I'll get him. … Ace?!"

There was a jolt against his shoulder, then another, and out of the distance, Doc's voice rose to a shout, piercing the misty boundaries of his dream. "Ace!"

"What? What?!" Avery squinted his eyes open; the bedside lamp was on. Doc was hovering over him, shoving the telephone handset in his face.

"It's Caitlyn," he said.

Avery took the phone handset. The dream mist lingered in his head, and he could faintly see the ghost of Gemma on Doc's bed, sitting back with her legs crossed and twirling a foot, which made her breasts quiver. Avery rubbed his eyes and took a breath, and Gemma faded away entirely. He spoke into the phone: "What's wrong? Why are you calling so early?"

---

[35] In their music videos, ZZ Top often showed up to help a poor schlub get the hot girl, and at the end of the video, once their mission was successful, they just faded away—vanishing into thin air.

"We need to talk. Meet me in the coffee shop downstairs?"

"All right," he said.

"See you in fifteen minutes."

Click.

The alarm clock read, "5:13 A.M." What was the problem? Why was it so important they meet right away? He rolled over, put the phone handset in the cradle, and felt the wetness in his shorts. He shut off the bedside lamp, swung his legs out of bed, and shuffled to the bathroom cupping his groin. Cleanup after a wet dream was always humiliating, and never festive, but at least he wasn't dealing with the nausea of blue balls anymore.

Avery cleaned himself up, threw on workout clothes, grabbed his billfold, room key, and Walkman, and went down to the lobby. The hotel coffee shop, off the main hallway on the lobby level, was an old-timey deal, like ones in the City that he'd been to with his grandfather. There were big picture windows in front, and inside were ancient pink Formica tabletops, a lunch counter, and a few 2-person booths. Caitlyn was sitting in a booth facing the entrance.

Avery was shocked by her appearance. Whenever he'd seen her this week, she had been made-up and sexy, but this morning she looked as haggard as a bank hostage. She wore a ragged Adele & Alfredo Dance Academy sweatshirt; she had no makeup on, so the pink welt on her cheek was visible again; and there were dark circles under her eyes. She sipped a cup of coffee and motioned to the seat across from her. A waitress took his order: a black coffee and a chocolate glazed donut.

"Take your coffee black, huh?" Caitlyn said. "How manly of you."

Avery nodded, but the truth was, he'd never had coffee before. He was only having it because Caitlyn was. Her free hand was on the tabletop, peeking out of her sweatshirt sleeve. Avery made sure none of their classmates were around (only a businessman at the lunch counter), took her hand, and stroked her fingers and the webbing between them. Caitlyn's eyes welled up. Her jaw trembled.

"What's wrong?" he asked. Because Avery was in workout clothes, he didn't have a handkerchief. He plucked some napkins from the dispenser and handed them to her. She dabbed her eyes and sniffled.

"Tell me what's wrong," he said.

"I'm gonna miss you."

"Miss me? We'll see each other next week."

The waitress brought his food. Avery broke off a piece of donut and ate it. Then he tried the coffee. It tasted burnt and bitter, like a slab of tree bark had been charred, ground up, and brewed.

Caitlyn groaned. "I couldn't do it, Ace."

"You didn't talk to her?"

"No, I talked to her—all night in fact. It was awful."

Caitlyn gave him a synopsis of her sleepless night. After she left Avery in the solarium, she went back to the room, fully intending to give Penny the bad news, but Penny was curled up in a ball on the bed, "crying her guts out." Caitlyn said she spooned Penny for hours and swore to her that there was nothing going on between her and Avery. Once Penny had finally fallen asleep, Caitlyn, feeling guilty and unsure what to do, lay awake the rest of the night.

"I couldn't do it." Her shoulders slumped. "Penny's been my best friend since third grade, and I couldn't break her heart. Can you understand?"

Avery ate some more of his donut. He tried another sip of the coffee, thinking the chocolate and sugar would make it more palatable, but it didn't. He put the cup on the saucer and shoved it away.

Caitlyn gestured while clutching the napkins. "Well? Are you gonna say something or what?"

Avery closed his eyes to gather his thoughts. He couldn't pinpoint what he was feeling. He thought about how he'd hurt Penny, how Caitlyn had done a complete 180 overnight, and how the consistent sexual gratification Caitlyn had promised him was being snatched away. He opened his eyes.

"What about everything you said to me this week?" he said. "How you and I are more compatible, how Penny is all wrong for me and *we* need to be together instead? How handsome and funny and smart you think I am? How attracted we are to each other, how well we dance together, how *'purrrfect'* we are for each other? Was that all bullshit? I guess you didn't mean any of that, right?"

Tears ran down her cheeks. "No, I—"

"What? *Like* me? You like me, but you don't want to see me anymore, is that it?"

"No, Avery." She reached across the table and took his hands. "I want to see you. But I can't hurt Penny. What if we go home, you date Penny, and we see each other on the side? What's wrong with that? Then, when you figure out she's all wrong for you, you can break up with her and we can be together. Why can't we do that?"

Avery pulled his hands away. "Isn't this just putting off the inevitable? I mean, if you want us to be together, why not do this now? We hurt Penny either way."

"Why can't we keep things between us casual for a while?"

"While you continue to have your *friggin' loser* boyfriend!?" The businessman glanced at them over a newspaper. Avery lowered his voice. "I get you part-time, when you feel like it, is that it?"

"No, it's not like that."

"I won't be any girl's 'boy toy,' and I'm not sharing you with another guy." He dropped a five-dollar bill on the table. "Goodbye, Caitlyn." He shoved the rest of the donut in his mouth, grabbed his things, and walked out. He was halfway down the hall when Caitlyn called out behind him.

"Ace, please … wait!"

The anguish in her voice was like a pair of talons, ripping chunks of flesh out of his back. He stopped in front of an empty meeting room. When Caitlyn scurried up and hugged him, Avery led her inside the room and shut the door. She stood on tiptoe and kissed him.

"I do care about you, Avery. So much." She squeezed him so tightly that he thought his ribs would break. "The fact is, I'm falling for you, and it scares the crap out of me. I've never felt like this about a guy. You're all I've thought about this week. But there's no way you could ever love me. You're too good for me. You're…" She kissed him again, threw the door open, and ran out.

The Doctor is In

Driven half-insane by Caitlyn and Penny, Avery went to the gym to work out; he needed to forget them for a while. Fortunately, the place was empty. He played "Ace's Ultimate Workout Mixtape" on his

Walkman. The first song was a favorite of his—Led Zeppelin's intense "Immigrant Song"—and Robert Plant's martial wails inspired Avery to push his body to the limit. He ran four miles on the treadmill, then did so many crunches, leg lifts, pull-ups, and elevated push-ups that he lost count.

As he worked out, thoughts of Caitlyn and Penny kept popping into his mind. While he was running, when his breathing and stride were in perfect sync and he felt as if he could run forever, the memory of Caitlyn riding his bulge last night came back to him so vividly that he stumbled and gasped to catch his breath.

In the middle of crunches, he recalled the feeling of petite Penny in his arms during last night's slow dances, and the way her lilac eyes had glittered in the lights. Avery shut off the Walkman and put it on the floor with his track suit jacket.

Now he was doing his 17th handstand pushup when there was a *click* from the hallway.

A pair of baby blue Keds sneakers with white laces came through the doorway. The Keds were on a pair of long, smooth legs, a pair of legs he was certain he'd seen before. Upside-down with sweat trickling into his eyes, he traced up the girl's legs to a pair of baby-blue shorts, and up those shorts to a close-fitting white Izod polo shirt, and up that polo shirt to a long and lovely neck and a pretty, studious face wearing tortoiseshell eyeglasses.

It was Gemma Jones. Her hair was in a smart-looking ponytail, and she was holding a 35mm camera and working the film advance lever with her thumb. She put the camera on a chair, smiled at Avery, and walked briskly on the treadmill while reading a book.

Ignoring the pain in his deltoids and triceps, Avery forced himself to do another three handstand push-ups—finishing with an even 20. He kicked himself away from the wall and back down to the floor.

For the first time in days, his mind was like a tranquil pond. He was at peace, face-down on the mat and panting. Across the room, the treadmill stopped, and the water cooler gurgled. Then Gemma touched his shoulder.

"Avery, are you okay?" Gemma was kneeling beside him, holding a plastic cup of water.

Avery rolled on his side. "Yeah, I'm fine. Thanks." He sat up and chugged the cup of water. Gemma got him another cup, and he chugged that one too.

She sat down next to him. "Gosh, after all that dancing last night, how do you have the energy for an early workout? That was so much fun, by the way. Like, when you taught us all how to do the 'Thriller' dance? You're an incredible dancer, Avery."

"Thanks." He glanced at the wall clock. It was seven o'clock—time for breakfast—which was great because the turmoil with girls hadn't affected his appetite one bit. He glanced at Gemma's legs and remembered his dream of early this morning.

"You were in a dream I had last night," he said.

"Oh?" She adjusted her glasses. "What was I doing?"

"Wearing those glasses and a lab coat, studying me, and making notes on a clipboard."

"*Studying* you?" Gemma chuckled. "Like you were a subject in a science experiment?"

♫"She Blinded Me With Science"♫

Avery smiled recalling his wet dream. "You could say that."

She stood. "Well, I have to change for breakfast. See you later."

"May I walk with you?" he asked.

"Sure." She got her book and camera and met him in the hallway, where she handed him a brown paper bag. "Happy birthday."

"You didn't have to get me anything."

She shrugged. "It's kind of dumb because I had no idea what to get you, and I couldn't wrap it or anything."

He opened the bag. She'd given him a birthday card and a Scrabble word book with lists of acceptable words in the game.

"I figured you could keep it with your travel set, and we'd use it when we play."

"I love it, Gem. Thanks." He asked about her other book, and learned it was about the history of computers.

"You're really into computers, aren't you?" he said.

"Mm-hm," she said. "I'm getting my Ph.D. in Computer Science. I'll be known as 'Doctor Jones,' like my father."

"Your father is a 'Doctor Jones'? That's so cool," Avery said.

In the lobby, a throng of people waited in front of the elevators. Avery pointed at the stairwell and suggested they take the stairs.

Gemma coughed. "That's a dozen flights!"

"Come on, Doctor Jones"—he winked and tapped her shoulder—"live a little."

They jogged the first two flights. The floor numbers were painted on the walls at each landing. When they reached the fourth floor, Avery had to slow down so Gemma could catch up.

"Hey, when we were at the FBI yesterday," he said, "I had a vision about what I want to do for a career. Mind if I tell you about it? I'd love your opinion."

"Sure."

While they continued up the stairs, Avery told her that he wanted to become a covert operative for the CIA, then, following in Ian Fleming's footsteps, write novels based on his experiences. Gemma looked at him with wide-open eyes and nodded as he talked. When he finished, she smiled.

"I think it's solid," she said. "You as a CIA operative? I can totally see it. Agent Sloane said the FBI has high physical and athletic standards, so I imagine the CIA's standards are even higher. But, based on the display of athletic prowess I just saw"—she made a fist and punched him gently in the shoulder—"I think you'll easily qualify there. How are your grades?"

"English, Biology, Computer Programming, and Social Studies, A's and A-minuses. Latin and Geometry, D's."

"Uh-oh." She wiggled her lips. "You'll need to improve those two for sure. How'd you do on the PSATs?"[36]

Avery told Gemma that he'd scored a 780 on the Verbal section, but only a 480 in Math.

"Your Verbal's awesome," she said, "but your Math needs work. Before the SAT, you need to do a ton of practice exams. I have some books you can borrow. We could even study together."

---

[36] The Practice Scholastic Aptitude Test (PSAT) was a rehearsal for the real thing (the SAT), which would be administered during Avery's junior year. There were two sections on the exam, Verbal and Math, with a maximum high score of 800 in each section, or a combined perfect score of 1600.

"That'd be great," he said.

"Whoo." She hauled herself up by the railing. "I'm not sure this was such a good idea." She tromped up a few more steps and pushed her glasses up her nose. "Hey, you seemed upset about something while you were working out." She looked at him askance. "Why so down, Charlie Brown? Talk to me. The doctor is in."[37]

Avery groaned. "I don't want to trouble you with it."

"Does it have something to do with Penny and Caitlyn?"

"Yeah," he said. "How'd you know?"

Gemma continued climbing. "It's pretty obvious. You and Caitlyn were dancing a lot—and super close—and everybody saw how upset Penny was when she left. So, I have to conclude that your current state of upset has something to do with them."

"You are correct on all points, Doctor Jones," he said. "Are you sure you don't mind listening to this?"

"No, I'd like to help if I can."

They continued up the stairs. Without getting into great detail, Avery explained how, during the trip, he had become involved with Penny and her best friend, Caitlyn. He hadn't intended to get involved with Caitlyn, he said, but she'd pursued him. Last night, they'd decided they would be a couple, and then this morning she changed her mind. Avery said he liked each girl for different reasons. He knew he needed to choose, but he wasn't sure which girl was best for him.

When they reached the stairwell door to Gemma's floor, she leaned back against the wall and panted with her hands on her knees. Her cheeks were a steamy pink.

"Would you like to hear … what I … think?"

"Yes," he said.

Once she'd caught her breath, she stood up straight and gave him a grim look. "Frankly, I think you're working from a faulty assumption—that either of these girls is best for you—when the fact is, *neither* is best for you. If you want to go to a top college, you need

---

[37] In the *Peanuts* comics by Charles Schulz, the character Lucy Van Pelt occasionally offers psychiatric help to her fellow characters. A sign reading "The Doctor Is In" hangs on her booth—an obviously repurposed lemonade stand.

to get your GPA and SAT scores up. And because both girls go to a different school, you won't see either of them very often. Oh, and if you get involved with Caitlyn, you'll constantly be worried that she's making out with the entire Vanderbush football team."

"Jeez … harsh," he said.

Gemma shrugged. "Sorry. The point is, I think you have a lot going for you, Avery. Why throw it away over some girl?" She glanced at her watch. "However, I realize that guys have"—she grimaced and made air quotes—"*needs*, and that you don't want to go back to Hancock *sans* girlfriend…"

Avery grinned at Gemma's use of "*sans*," the French word for "without."

"So, perhaps the idea of neither girl isn't practical," she continued. "But that doesn't mean you have to do the choosing."

"What are you saying?" he asked.

"I'm saying you make *them* choose." Her enormous coppery eyes caught the light from the wall sconce and glinted with mischief. "When we get on the bus after breakfast, make sure you're the first one on. Then, whichever girl sits beside you, *she's* the right girl. And if neither one sits with you, neither is the right girl. Got it?"

Avery nodded. "Gemma, you're the best. I mean totally awesome."

She smiled. "Have a good day, Avery."

"You too … Dr. Jones."

Avery opened the exit door for her. Gemma whisked through the doorway, and the heavy door clicked shut. Her scent—a powdery-smelling antiperspirant and fragrant apple shampoo—hung in the air as Avery went down one flight to his floor.

15

ONCE THE students had assembled in the lobby with their suitcases, the teachers made announcements and took attendance. Avery positioned himself next to the revolving doors, so he'd be the first one on the bus. He didn't look around for Penny or Caitlyn; he was taking Gemma's advice about making them choose.

He still had the giant red umbrella Irina had given him. He considered giving it back, but when he looked outside and saw it was raining, he decided to keep it. The umbrella didn't belong to the hotel anyway; the insurance company had left it behind.

When they were finally dismissed, Avery gave his suitcase to Herb with a tip and boarded the bus. He chose a seat, put his bag and umbrella on the overhead rack, and hitched over against the window.

The blurred reflections of students drifted across the glass, and the bus filled with voices. Which girl would sit next to him— Caitlyn or Penny? What if neither girl sat with him? They might have mutually decided that Avery was nothing but a foolish fling, and that neither wanted him for a boyfriend. Their friendship might be more important to them than he was.

Somebody settled into the seat beside him. Avery was facing the window and couldn't make out the person's reflection. A hand clasped his hand. A small hand. Penny's hand.

♫"Take Good Care of My Heart"♫

"Hi," Penny said.

"Hi."

Her eyes gleamed in the gray light from the window.

"Sorry about last night," she said.

"Sorry for what? You don't have anything to be sorry for."

"How I ran out before the dance was over."

She rested her head on his shoulder and said she'd been jealous last night about how much Avery and Caitlyn had danced, and the chemistry between them. But she said she was over it now; Caitlyn had stayed up all night with her, assuring her that nothing was going on with Avery.

"She said your feelings for me haven't changed," Penny said. "Is that true?"

If he wanted an out with Penny, this was his chance. All he had to do was tell her that his feelings *had* changed, and he could be with Caitlyn. But having Penny against his shoulder stirred an unfamiliar sensation deep in his gut. It was totally unlike the primal, unquenchable lust that Caitlyn provoked in him.

"No, honey," he said, "my feelings haven't changed."

He put his arm around her and held her close. Penny relaxed against him. She glanced over her shoulder and leaned toward him. They kissed, and the bus headed out.

A Bait and ... Whatchamacallit

The trip's last stop was the National Zoo, and during the short drive Avery listened to Penny prattle on about the dance, how much she was looking forward to them going on their first date together when they got home, and how much she would miss him until they saw each other again. Avery listened to her, remarking to himself how much he liked the sound of her voice, how pretty and musical it was.

Avery still had the giant red umbrella Irina had given him, and when they reached the zoo, because it was drizzling outside, Avery brought it with him. No sooner had he opened it than Caitlyn sidled up and asked if she could squeeze underneath with him and Penny. Fully made-up now, Caitlyn looked her hot self again, instead of the bank hostage of early that morning.

Like he had at Lincoln Memorial, Avery held the umbrella handle with one hand and put his other arm around Penny, while Caitlyn hugged his umbrella arm, and the three walked through the zoo huddled together against the rain. Avery was confused. He knew that Caitlyn had talked with Penny and assuaged her worries about him and Caitlyn, but what was going on?

The walkways were clear, but there were a few inches of half-melted snow in the animals' display areas, and while the lions seemed annoyed by the weather, the penguins were overjoyed—squawking, flapping their stubby wings, and diving off a rock into a wide, black pool.

"It's so cute to see the animal couples, isn't it?" Penny said, squeezing his hand. "It's like they're in love."

Caitlyn shivered. "I'm friggin' cold, Penny. Let's warm up on Avery. *Share* him with me, Pen?"

Penny giggled. "Okay."

On one side of him, Caitlyn unbuttoned her peacoat, pressed her breasts against his side, and hugged him around the waist. On the other side of him, Penny held his arm and leaned against him. When the group started toward the panda exhibit, Caitlyn slipped a hand in the back pocket of Avery's jeans and squeezed.

The panda exhibit was a disappointment. Ling-Ling, the panda bear gift from China, was hidden behind a rock, with only her hind legs and a shaking cane of bamboo visible. A notoriously shy female panda, she stayed hidden, and when their time was up, they had to leave without having seen her. Caitlyn let out a loud groan.

"That sucked ass!" she said.

Penny and other students around them laughed.

"Miss Cray," Mr. Nelson said, "watch your language."

"But that was a total rip-off! A bait and … whatchamacallit." Caitlyn nudged Avery. "Ace knows what I mean."

"'Bait and *switch*'?" Avery said.

"Yeah," she said, "a bait and switch. They lure everybody here with promises of seeing a cute panda, but when you get here, all you actually see are panda legs and some stupid bamboo."

Penny huffed. "You're right, Caitlyn. I was looking forward to it."

"Good thing we've got our own bear to hug," Caitlyn said.

"Right." Penny giggled again, and she and Caitlyn squeezed him at the same time.

In the parking lot, while they waited to board the bus, the rain became a downpour. Avery told the girls to get on the bus. Since he had the umbrella, Avery borrowed Louis' fedora and danced around the parking lot humming "Singing in the Rain." He'd watched this movie starring Gene Kelly and Debbie Reynolds half a dozen times with his grandparents and secretly loved it. Humming and whistling the signature tune, he skipped and danced around the parking lot in his best Gene Kelly imitation, splashing in puddles, twirling the open umbrella by its handle, spinning on a lamppost, throwing his arms out grandly, removing his hat and smiling into the falling rain.

The bus engine started. Mr. Nelson came to the bus door and shouted, "Mr. Craig, we're leaving!"

Avery danced to the bus, collapsed the umbrella, and boarded. Herb shut the door behind him.

"Nice, Ace," he said. "You're a regular Gene Kelly, son."

"Thanks, Herb."

Tossing the fedora back to Louis, Avery waded down the aisle high-fiving students. Gemma smiled at him over her book. Mr. Nelson scowled from his seat.

"Sit down, Mr. Craig," he said. "*Now.*"

"Trying to, sir. My fans won't let me."

When he finally stowed his things, he toweled off with a dirty T-shirt and sat down next to Penny. She asked him what everybody had been laughing about. Avery said it was nothing, only a little dance he'd done. She rested her head on his shoulder.

"I feel so close to you, Avery," she said. "I don't want to go home. I feel like I'm going to die if I can't see you."

"I'll miss you too."

"But we'll talk on the phone every day after school, right?"

"Sure," he said.

Avery pulled out a package of Twizzlers and tore off a few strands for them.

"And we'll write to each other every day too, right?" she said.

No way was Avery writing her a letter *every day*, but he didn't want to be a downer when she was so psyched.

"Yeah, sure."

Penny ate her Twizzlers, then yawned and cuddled against him. "I'm so tired. Would you mind if I slept on your shoulder?"

"That's fine," he said. "Here."

Avery took off his leather bomber jacket with its fleece lining, draped it over her, and kissed her cheek.

While she rested, Avery took out a legal pad and pen. As the bus droned along the interstate, Penny and many other students fell asleep, but Avery used the quiet to start writing the story he'd imagined in the Capitol the other day.

He wrote for a while, then put away his notebook and pen and basked in the warmth of Penny lying against him. As she slept on his shoulder, her breath fluttered some loose tendrils of hair near her mouth. With Penny against him and the rain outside streaming across the window, it was clear: Penny was the best girl for him. He didn't need Caitlyn. Heck, he wasn't sure if he even *liked* Caitlyn.

Round and Round

Soon after entering New Jersey, the bus stopped at a rest area, and they were given a half-hour meal and bathroom break. Avery ate with Penny, Caitlyn, and Doc, and used the bathroom afterwards. On his way out to the bus, he came around a corner and bumped into Caitlyn.

♫"Crimson and Clover"♫

She was alone in the hallway, holding her peacoat and purse over her arm. Because she'd been wearing the coat earlier, Avery hadn't seen today's sexy ensemble and he gulped at the sight of her in it: tight stonewashed jeans; Victorian-style granny boots; and a crimson turtleneck sweater, ribbed and snug, that accentuated her breasts and begged the question of whether or not she was wearing a bra.

Caitlyn hooked his arm and tugged him back around the corner into a janitor's closet. When it came to ferreting out secluded spaces, the girl was a savant. She left the door open a crack—Avery could hear girls and guys chatting as they passed by outside—and kicked a rolling bucket and mop out of the way.

"Caitlyn, this time you're definitely going to get us caught."

"Don't be angry with me." She took some things out of her purse. "I wanted to say goodbye and give you your birthday present."

She gave him a card and told him there was a letter inside that he should read when he was alone. Then she handed him a small box tied with blue ribbon. He opened the box, and inside was a thumbnail-sized lapel pin of a playing card—the Ace of Hearts. She tilted her head back and smiled.

"Allow me, baby." She pinned it on his jacket lapel. "There." She patted his chest. "The Ace of Hearts for the Ace of *my* heart."

His eyes were wet. "I love it."

She cupped his cheeks and kissed him. "I'm gonna miss you, baby. Will you miss me?"

"Terribly."

She wriggled against him. "Who's your sexy Babydoll?"

Avery kissed her and fondled her breasts over the turtleneck. Her nipples stiffened underneath; *if* she was wearing a bra, it was made of cheesecloth. She squirmed, but Avery locked his arms behind her back.

"Lemme go," she said.

"Not 'til you hear what I have to say."

She stopped struggling. "What?"

"I don't understand," he said. "What are you doing?"

"Read my letter. It's all in there."

His throat was thick. "Caitlyn, you're hurting me. This back and forth and round and round is torturing me. You need to *be* with me or let me go. If you truly care about me, you'll stop torturing me."

"Shh." She touched his cheek. "I care about you, Ace—more than you know. Read my letter." After a full-body hug and kiss, she tilted her head back, and her mouth bloomed into a luminous smile. She pressed her pelvis against his bulge. "Oooh, sorry I got you so excited, baby. I'd help you out, but this is *hardly* the time or place." She sniggered. "I promise I'll make it up to you. Think about how good it'll feel when we get each other off again." With her index finger, she tapped the pin, then his nose. "I'll see you soon … Lover."

Avery released her. Caitlyn peeked outside and slipped sideways out the door, blowing him a kiss as she disappeared. He trembled in her wake. He could still taste her cherry lipgloss, smell her perfume, feel her breasts. He dabbed his eyes with his handkerchief and slipped out to the bathroom, where he splashed cold water on his face.

Back on the bus, when he passed Caitlyn's seat, she and Rhonda were playing the card game Uno. Caitlyn didn't notice him.

Your First, Your Last, Your Forever

Soon after the bus started moving, Penny fell asleep on Avery's shoulder again. Once he was certain she was fast asleep, he opened Caitlyn's card.

♫"Just The Two of Us"♫

It was a girl's "Sweet 16" birthday card, but Caitlyn had crossed out "Sweet" and replaced it with "Sexy." Inside the card was a long letter, written on multiple sheets of Bethesda Colonnade stationery in Caitlyn's soap-bubble handwriting:

> Ace,
>
> I know your birthday isn't until tomorrow, but since we won't see each other for like a week or two, I wanted to give you this now.
>
> Sorry it's a girl's birthday card. I got it and your present in the hotel gift shop, and this was the only one they had. I hope you like the present.
>
> I'm writing this in the hotel coffee shop. We were arguing in here a little while ago. A guy at the front desk gave me this stationairy. I think your in the gym, working out as usual. I wish I could go down there, kiss you and make everything better, but I know I can't, so I'm writing to you instead.
>
> It's hard for me to express my true feelings, and the fact that I'm writing this and sharing it with you should tell you how much I care about you. I'm trusting you to not share this letter with Penny or anybody else.
>
> I've never cheated on my boyfriend before, and I only did the things I did with you because it felt so right. I'm physically attracted to you (majorly), but it's a lot more than that. Your special. You've got, like, this charisma, and unlike Shane, I can tell you care about me, your a great guy, and your going places in life.

Avery winced at her multiple incorrect uses of "your" instead of "you're," but he kept reading:

I hope you can forgive me for not going through with the thing I was suppozed to do last night, but everything I told you this morning was the truth, straight from the heart.

Ever since we danced on the bus on Monday, I started falling for you. I've been asking myself, "How can two people be so instantly in-sync?" When you look into my eyes, my entire body tingles, like an electric charge passes out of your eyes and into mine, and I can't think. This, like, <u>animal</u> <u>urge</u> comes over me. I want to feel your strong muscles against me, holding me, keeping me safe. I want to feel you inside me filling me up, and the two of us moving as one person.

I want to be your first, Ace.

<u>Your first, your last, your forever</u>.

Avery's heart pounded; an erection had surreptitiously reared up in his pants. He covered it with the letter, took a few deep breaths to calm down, and kept reading:

I guess what I'm trying to say is, I want you and I want to be with you. Please don't give up on me. You promised me that we'd see each other alone when we get home. I want that, I <u>need</u> that. I need you, Ace. I think if we can spend some time together, just the two of us, you'll see we can be super happy together. Meanwhile, I'll try and get the courage to tell Penny how I feel. But I won't say anything until you and I meet sometime soon. How about next week?

I miss you already and wish we could kiss right now (and a lot more). I'll be thinking about you all the time. And don't worry … I won't flirt with any other guys, I swear. I won't even kiss Shane when I get home. I'm saving all my kisses for you now. I'm all yours.

Dying to be in your arms again,

Your Loving, Sexy and Faithful Babydoll,

C. ♥ XOXOXOXO ♥

P.S.: I'll call you next week, but if you want to call me, my number's in the book. It's the only "C. Cray" in there. My mom's name is Cassie.

> P.P.S.: I took a ton of photos of you and me during the trip, and I'll send them to you as soon as they're developed. I think your gonna love them—especially certain ones of me. ♥

Finally, at the bottom of the page was a lipstick lip print with an arrow pointing at it and a message saying, "From my lips to yours, Ace!"

He was trembling again, and once more he was on the verge of tears. What should he do? If only he could discuss this with Gemma. He looked around the bus, but couldn't see her, and with Penny on his shoulder, he couldn't move anyway.

Pennyville or Caitlyntown

If he chose Caitlyn, he would surely be setting himself up for perpetual torment: she would constantly be tempting and teasing him, getting close and pulling away. Was he okay with being dragged into janitor's closets, stairwells, bathrooms, and elevators, and forced to live a secret second life?

No, he wasn't.

In the back of the bus, a boombox played ♫"How Will I Know."♫ Penny shifted on his shoulder. His jacket slid off her; Avery covered her up again and gazed at her sleeping face. Penny would never torment him the way Caitlyn did. And so what if she wouldn't do anything sexual for a "long … long … long time"? Sex wasn't everything.

But, God, the pull of Caitlyn was so strong. After last night in the solarium with her, all Avery wanted to do was slide under the sheets with her nude beneath him, get inside her, and *never leave*.

When the bus crossed the border into New York, Avery gazed out the window. He was hoping he'd see something that would make it clear which girl was right for him—like an exit sign for "Pennyville" or "Caitlyntown"—but there was nothing but the usual humdrum landmarks: the river, the New Netherlands Mall, and the IBM West Troutkill plant. They were only a mile from the Hancock High School parking lot. A few moments from now, the trip would come to an end.

After hours of mulling, Avery had come to a decision: he'd wait a few days, then call Penny and let her down easy. Then he'd be free to see Caitlyn.

The bus stopped at the red light in front of the high school. Cars were lined up in the parking lot with parents waiting on the sidewalk—some beaming like they hadn't seen their kid for a month, others visibly sighing and checking their watches. No sign of Jill's Impala with its mortifying muffler, thank God. On his shoulder, Penny stirred.

"Avery?"

"Yeah?"

She craned her lips to his ear. "I love you."

Avery flushed; Penny's words had blindsided him. He didn't realize how much he'd longed to hear a girl say those words. Moving from town to town so many times as a kid, he'd never let himself get close to anyone. Ever since 7th grade, when he met Dina Tempestilli, he'd thought that all he wanted from a girl was sex. But it turned out that was only a small part of what he wanted.

Penny was smiling with tears in her eyes. Avery kissed her.

16

AVERY HAD been back at school for two days but hadn't had a moment to himself until Biology today. He sat in his usual seat in the back and read.

All anybody wanted to talk about was how Avery had met Senator Kennedy; how he'd gotten the students into the White House, where they met President Reagan; and how he'd pummeled a "humongous gang" of frat guys in the hotel pool, sending several of them to the hospital. As students who were there recounted the battle to friends who weren't, and those friends told the tale to their friends, the number of frat guys increased from its true number of four to fourteen. Also exaggerated were the number of paramedics and police that showed up, the severity of the injuries sustained by the attackers, and the quantity of blood spilled during the melee.

Eric Park and other members of student government who'd witnessed Ace's leadership on the trip talked to Avery about running for Class President next year. Girls he barely knew who'd heard about his dancing prowess asked if he'd dance with them at the next school dance. And various current events that happened over February break had everybody freaked out about one thing or another.

Guys who smoked cigarettes were freaked out over an anti-smoking ad on TV starring Yul Brynner. Girls were freaked out because a woman had died of cyanide poisoning after taking a Tylenol capsule. Fashion-conscious girls were freaked out by a news report about Imelda Marcos, wife of overthrown Philippines President Ferdinand Marcos, and how she'd had to abandon her collection of 5,400 shoes when the couple fled to Hawaii. And a bunch of junior and senior guys were freaked out in a good way by the erotic movie 9½ *Weeks* because it featured blonde babe Kim Basinger nude. Older guys who had seen the sexy flick over vacation described it to their younger, less fortunate classmates.

Now 16, on Monday afternoon (his first day back) Avery took (and aced) his driver's written exam and received his learner's permit. Avery also met with Mr. Birdsong, Hancock's aging head guidance counselor, for his CPEC (Career Path Exploration Consultation). It was Avery's first meeting with the man, and as he told him about his career plans, he found himself feeling sorry for him. Mr. Birdsong was bald, a fact that his comb-over of a dozen hairs made glaringly obvious, and his suit was a pinkish-tan color and shiny with wear.

At first, citing Avery's A's in English and his "noteworthy" PSAT Verbal score, Mr. Birdsong tried to steer Avery toward "a more practical and attainable field," proposing that Avery instead become a journalist, English professor, or attorney.[38] However, once Avery insisted that he was set on his plan to work for the CIA and then write novels, Mr. Birdsong relented.

"Very well, Mr. Craig," he said. "I'll research which colleges and study track are best for someone interested in the clandestine services and journalism, and we'll meet again in a month or two."

Now Avery was sitting in the back of Biology, reading the copy of *For Your Eyes Only* Penny had given him for his birthday. It had been a few years since he'd read Ian Fleming's collection of James Bond short stories, and the plots engrossed him as if he were reading the book for the first time.

In the title story, Bond is given a mission to hunt down and assassinate an ex-Nazi who murdered two of M.'s friends. The ex-Nazi has gone into seclusion in the mountains of Northern Vermont. Bond,

---

[38] Mr. Birdsong had Avery browse a multi-volume reference book—the *Occupational Outlook Handbook* (published by the U.S. Department of Labor's Bureau of Labor Statistics), which gave the titles, descriptions, education requirements, salaries, etc. of hundreds of careers. It was like the Sears catalog of careers, and Mr. Birdsong made it seem like all Avery had to do to have a successful career was shop for the right career in the catalog.

posing as a hunter, crosses from Quebec into the U.S. through the forest and reconnoiters the villain's hideout. Avery loved this story and wanted to write something this suspenseful himself someday. He had submerged into the story deeply enough that he'd forgotten where he was, and then … a voice with the timbre of a hand-held air horn startled Avery out of his literary reverie.

"Ace!?" Mr. Crain said. "Ah, Ace?!"

Suddenly Avery wasn't international spy James Bond, stalking an ex-Nazi in the autumnal Vermont woods, but high school sophomore Avery Craig. He glanced out the window. Down in the parking lot was a mountain of dirty snow. Mr. Crain snapped his fingers and waved from the front of the class.

"Ladies and Gentlemen, it's time for our daily literature lecture from that infamous in-class reader, Avery 'Ace' Craig. So, ah, Ace, perhaps you could tell us a bit about today's book?"

Antithetically Sexy

Mr. Crain interrupted Avery's reading every day, probably hoping to shame him into paying attention in class. The thing was, Avery enjoyed being in the spotlight and was happy to comment on whatever book he was reading.[39]

"Well, Mr. Crain"—Avery held up the book to show the cover—"it's *For Your Eyes Only* by Ian Fleming."

"Hm … wasn't that a movie recently?"

"Correct, Mr. Crain, in nineteen eighty-one," Avery said, "but the movie's nothing like the book. The book is a collection of stories."

"And why read the book, instead of watching the movie?"

"An excellent question, sir. The book and the movie are completely different. It's mostly how well Fleming describes things. Like, listen to this passage." He read aloud Fleming's description of the sunrise creeping into the valley where Bond was staking out the cabin. "See? It's how clear and eloquent his descriptions are."

---

[39] So far, Avery had read 20-odd books in Mr. Crain's class. Besides novels, he read books on fiction writing, cross-country skiing, endurance swimming, mountaineering, military reconnaissance, espionage, performance driving, and outdoorsmanship.

"Fascinating, Ace," Mr. Crain said. "A fine analysis. Carry on."

Melody Bates spoke up from the front row, where she sat next to Lee. Melody had honey blonde hair flipped up at the ends and blue eyes that were wide not from curiosity, but a perpetual state of confusion. She also had a talking-doll voice that made Avery bristle every time he heard it: "Mr. *Kwain*," she said, "I don't get it."

Mr. Crain blinked his eyes several times. "What don't you get, Melody dear?"

"Why Avery gets to read in class. Why can't *I* read in class?"

At Melody's question, he let out a long sigh and said, "Do you *want* to read in class?"

"No, but—"

"Okay then, moving on! We were discussing photosynthesis."

Avery glanced across the aisle and moaned under his breath.

Dina Tempestilli. Clad in a black T-shirt, her bare slim arms folded on the desk, she lay with her head on its side and gazed at him dreamily, glassy-eyed. Clearly, she was stoned again. Avery had crushed on her since 7th grade English. Her feathered sable hair thicker than liquid chocolate, her sculpted breasts, and her Roman nose made her what Avery called "antithetically sexy." She smiled, and Avery's heart skipped a beat. Instantly, he was taken back to the last day of 8th grade, during locker cleanout. Somebody had been blasting a boombox, and at the precise moment that Journey's ♫"Any Way You Want It"♫ came on, Dina rounded the corner at the far end of the hallway. Standing tall, walking casually but purposefully through the gauntlet of guys rubbernecking from their lockers, shimmying faintly to the music, her feathered hair fluttering, her breasts jiggling, and her lips curling in an impish smile, she ignored the other guys but mouthed "Hi, Ace," to *him*, Avery Craig, before disappearing down the hall. The moment was burned into his mind forever. From then on, every time Avery saw her, that song's ripping opening guitar riff and exuberant title lyric echoed in his head.

As Dina shifted in her seat, Avery glimpsed "Def Leppard – *Pyromania*" bulging across her chest. She turned to face him, and her sable hair sluiced across and over the side of the desk. Avery sucked in a breath and smiled at her. Dina smiled and blinked slowly in reply.

A Long Way to Go

He opened his book to where he'd put Penny's first letter to him. Although sitting in the back row, he made sure no one was looking before carefully unfolding the sheet of looseleaf. He smiled at the teddy bear and rainbow heart stickers and read the letter again:

> This letter is <u>For Your Eyes Only</u>.
> Dearest Avery,
> Hi! I'm now in Social Studies, and it's boring.
> Mr. Nelson is giving a lecture about God knows what.
>   From what I know so far about love, I must be in love with you. Last night I laid in bed for at least an hour before I could fall asleep. All I could think about was you and me. Now is that love or what? I've never felt like this toward anyone before. I never thought I could be so happy. I hope that I always make you feel the same way.
>   You are the best thing that has ever happened to me.
>   ♥ Love Always, ♥
> Penny
>   P.S.: Yesterday, my mom dropped off my pictures from the trip at Fotomat.[40] Soon, we'll have lots of pictures of the two of us together!
>   P.P.S.: I can't describe how good you make me feel. Do you remember us feeling each other's heartbeats in the phone booth? I do.

God, did he remember. Their kisses in the phone booth, in the Senate Gallery. Although they'd spoken on the phone every day, he hadn't seen her in person—hugged her, kissed her, looked into her eyes—for, like, four whole days. What if he forgot what she looked like?

---

[40] In the 1980s, years before digital photography, cameras used rolls of film that had to be developed. Professional photographers often had their own darkrooms to perform this chemical process, but amateurs had to take their film to Fotomat or another film-developing company. Fotomat had innumerable tiny huts in shopping plaza parking lots, where customers dropped off rolls of film in paper envelopes labeled with their contact information and developing instructions. A couple of days later, customers received the prints and negatives of their photos.

With his next breath, he thought of Caitlyn—Caitlyn of the slippery, cherry-flavored lips. He mused about how good it had felt holding her in his arms while she straddled his bulge. And how amazing she'd smelled the last time they kissed—at the New Jersey rest stop. He wanted to be true to Penny, but Caitlyn was making it impossible.

Avery folded up Penny's letter, put it away and went back to the Bond story. When he finished it, he reread his latest Jack and Zeb story—the one he'd begun writing on the way home from D.C. Ugh, it was depressing. If he wanted to write as well as Ian Fleming, he had a *long* way to go. While "The Puzzle Game of Death" had some funny lines in it (e.g., *"Zeb, the trail's gone colder'n a witch's titty—brrrrrrrrr!"*), on the whole it was foolish. Sadly, it was time to leave Jack and Zeb behind. They were great when Avery was 11 years old and he would read their adventures aloud on the school bus, but he'd outgrown them. He wanted to write something more adult—something that not only had a good plot but great writing. There and then, Avery resolved that this was the year he'd start taking his writing seriously.

Avery put his story away. At the front of the classroom, Lee's blocky head turned slowly toward Avery like the Terminator's. His features—especially his head—had sharp edges, like the guy was constructed of LEGO blocks. He wagged his eyebrows, curled his bicep, and flexed it rhythmically—*buh-boom, buh-boom, buh-boom*—like there was a heart beating in the muscle. Avery flexed his own ample bicep in reply and picked up his book again.

When the bell rang, Lee walked to the back of the room, where Avery and Doc were packing up.

"Ehh … what's up, Doc?" Lee said.

"Not much, man. Gotta get to Home Ec."

Steven carefully tucked some papers into a pocket in his Trapper Keeper, picked up his books, and handed Avery two pages of notes in his meticulous handwriting.[41]

---

[41] The Trapper Keeper was *the* notebook and student work organizer of the mid to late '80s. Because it was expensive, it was something of a status symbol among students.

"Give these back to me after study hall?" Doc said.

"You got it, man. Thanks."

He left.

Lee whispered into Avery's shoulder: "We've gotta talk—you, me and the girls. It's about the quizzes."

Avery groaned under his breath; he knew what he and Lee would soon be discussing.

"Yeah, okay."

"Why the sad face, dude?" Lee said. "What, you miss *Penny*?"

"Yes. And don't tease me about it, dick."

Lee made his patented open-mouthed toothy grin and darted his eyes around. As they walked out together, Avery nodded to Mr. Crain, who was sitting on a stool pensively watching them leave.

"Have a good day, Mr. Crain," Avery said.

Lee made a thumbs-up. "Yeah, great class today, Don. Way to take it up a notch!"

"Ah, Ace and Lee—the Dynamic Duo. Good day, gentlemen."

Out in the hallway, Avery had to walk around a gaggle of girls huddled around one girl's locker. The girls were rapt listening to her describe catching her boyfriend at the mall with another girl. Avery waited until he and Lee were well past Mr. Crain's classroom before bringing up the issue with the quizzes.

"All right, what's this about the girls and the quizzes?" Avery said.

"They're tired of writing the answers on their shoes and arms."

"We'll just have to come up with something different." Avery bobbled his head. "I think we'll have to memorize the answers."

"Hey," Lee said, "did you see Melody's boobs in that skin-tight blouse today?!" He bit his fist, shook Avery by the arm, and laughed maniacally.

"Why don't you ask her out?" Avery said.

"I will—as soon as you ask out *Dina*. Meet you in the library."

While Lee booked it down the hall, cradling his binder in his elbow and weaving smoothly through the throng, Avery sauntered behind and mulled the problem of the Biology quizzes.

What they were doing wouldn't bother him if Mr. Crain was an A-hole like Mr. Knox, but Mr. Crain was funny, a good teacher, and he let Avery read in class. Then there was what Gemma had said about Avery getting into a good college. What if he got caught and ruined his chances? The fact was, he didn't *need* to cheat; he was helping Dina because he'd always liked her, and Lee was helping Melody because he desperately wanted to get into her pants.

Avery was in a daze thinking about this as he turned into the busy stairwell and shuffled down the stairs behind a group of basketball players. On the landing halfway down, he passed two girls leaning against the wall.

"Hey," one of them said, "are you Avery Craig?"

Don't be a Stranger

They were Alpha Girl seniors who had never spoken to Avery before. The brunette, Heather Doyle, could have been a model for *Seventeen* magazine; she always wore cute preppy outfits like today's—a long-sleeved white Oxford shirt with a skinny pink tie underneath a buttoned vest; khakis; and white sneakers. But he wasn't sure about the other girl—a redhead with an enormous mane of curled and feathered hair that looked like it took an hour to style—because she had a twin sister who styled her hair exactly the same way.

The second girl was either Scarlett or Shannon O'Grady. Mallory said that people secretly referred to them as Sweet and Sour because one was pleasant and the other was bitchy. The bitchy one, he remembered Mallory saying, was aptly named Scarlett, and the pleasant one was Shannon. Because this particular O'Grady sister was smiling at him and wearing a demure-looking outfit—pearls, a fuzzy cream sweater and matching skirt—Avery deduced that she was Shannon.

"I am." He smiled. "Shannon, Heather … what's up?"

"How do you know our names?" Heather asked.

With a surplus of girls interested in him now, Avery could afford to be bodacious in his reply: "Who *doesn't* know the names of two of the most beautiful and stylish girls at Hancock—Shannon O'Grady and Heather Doyle?" He smiled and was pleased to see them giggle. "What's up, pretty ladies?"

The late bell rang; Avery would be late getting to the library, and he didn't have a hall pass. Meanwhile, Shannon and Heather didn't flinch. Avery decided to play it cool like them, leaning back against the wall and crossing his ankles.

"We heard about your class trip to D.C.," Shannon said. "That stuff people are talking about, like the thing that happened in the pool. Is any of that true?"

"What did you hear?" he asked.

"Like," Heather said, "some guy *Ace* defended the girls from a bunch of creepy college guys. Ace—that's your nickname, right?"

"Yup."

"Is it true?" Shannon asked.

Two guys the size of soda machines entered the stairwell's upper landing. One of them was black, the other white, and they wore football team letterman jackets in the Hancock school colors of blue and gold. Walking abreast down the stairs, they took up the entire width of the staircase. Since starting at Hancock in September, Avery had seen them around school many times, and he always knew when they were approaching because other students plastered themselves against their lockers to make way.

"House, Wally!" Shannon waved them over and gestured at Avery. "This is Ace, the guy we were talking about at lunch."

They stopped on the landing and loomed over Avery. The black guy, House, did all the talking. Wally, even taller than House, was taciturn behind him.

"Stuff happened in D.C.," House said, "that true?"

"Yeah, pretty much," Avery said.

"We heard you gave those college guys a serious smackdown. Heard you sent a couple of 'em to the hospital."

"Not exactly, House. I might have broken a guy's nose, but that was the extent of it."

House gave him a deep nod and clasped his hand. "You're all right, man. Heard you got one helluva arm. You play football?"

Avery thought about how he'd played quarterback in Pop Warner, and how he always quarterbacked during touch-football games in his development. "Yeah ... some."

"Our QB's graduatin'," House said. "Gonna need a new one next year. Wanna try out?"

"Would you two be guarding me?"

"Damn skippy," House said. "Center and Right Guard."

"Okay, I'll do it."

"That's what I'm talkin' about." House slapped Avery's shoulder, rattling his entire skeleton. Avery pitied the poor bastards who got hit by this guy. When House headed downstairs, Wally nodded minutely at Avery and followed his teammate.

Heather nudged Shannon. "Ask him about the dancing."

"Oh yeah," Shannon said. "Everyone's talking about how you're an awesome dancer, like a pro. We heard you and some girl from 'Bush were totally *tight*."

"I'm not a professional," Avery said, "but the girl you're talking about … yes, we dance well together."

"Why haven't we seen you at any of our school dances?" Heather asked.

He shrugged. "I guess because you two are seniors, and I'm a sophomore. I just got here in September."

"You're only a *sophomore*? I thought you were a junior."

"Nope," he said. "Shannon, there's something I've always wondered about you."

"Yeah? What's that?"

He opened his musette bag and pulled out a small bag of O'Grady's *au gratin* potato chips.

"Are you related to the potato chip O'Gradys?"

She chuckled. "No, I wish."

"Too bad. I was hoping you could get me some free ones."

He snapped the bag open and held it out for them. They each took a chip.

"And Heather," Avery said, "are you related to Sir Arthur Conan Doyle? Author of the Sherlock Holmes stories?"

Heather snickered and shook her head. Shannon smirked at Avery as she and Heather headed upstairs.

"I keep a diary, ladies," he said. "Guess what tonight's entry will be?" They paused on the steps. "'Dear Diary, today two of the most beautiful and stylish girls at Hancock talked to me. If I die in my sleep tonight, I'll die a happy man.'"

They giggled and minced up the stairs. At the top, a grinning Shannon glanced over her shoulder, flipped her hair, and said, "Don't be a stranger … *Ace.*"

Callipygian

When he reached the library entrance, Avery checked his watch. He was late for study hall, and he didn't have a hall pass. If he went in the library without one, he'd be given detention for sure.

Avery glanced around the corner. The door to the reading specialist's classroom was open and the light was on inside. Miss Shipley was in her early 20s, and every day, whatever the weather, she wore silky blouses that showed a lick of cleavage, and thin, clingy skirts that mesmerized Avery with every swing of her hips. Her first day had been in the fall, and ever since Avery had met her, he'd routinely called her "Miss Shapely" by "mistake."

From deep in the recesses of his brain rose the blood-stirring tribal drums and riot-inciting guitar of Van Halen's ♫"Hot for Teacher."♫ Avery peeled off his sweater, revealing a snug Nike T-shirt that made his chest, arms, and abs look great. Caitlyn was right: he hid his body too much; he needed to start wearing nothing but T-shirts. He stuffed his sweater in his bag and walked into her tiny classroom.

Across the room, Miss Shipley sat on her desk with her legs crossed. She was correcting a stack of papers with a red pen. When she glanced at Avery, her hair—long, dark and wavy—waggled.

"Good afternoon, Mr. Craig. What brings you by today?"

"Hello, Miss Shapely. You look *terrific*. You must do aerobics."

The corners of her lips formed a faint smile. "Now, Mr. Craig. I've told you—it's Miss *Ship*ley, not 'Miss Shapely.'"

"Right. Duh." Avery rapped himself on the head. "Sorry."

"And yes, I do aerobics from time to time," she said.

He smiled. "Well, you're looking positively *shipshape*. Keep it up."

She giggled and tossed her hair over her shoulder, and then an embarrassed expression came over her face. It was as though she'd suddenly remembered that she was a teacher, not a college coed flirting with a guy in her dorm.

She put down her pen. "What can I do for you, Mr. Craig?"

"A couple of things, please, Miss Shipley." Avery pulled out Doc's bio notes. "First, I need a photocopy of these notes. I was hoping you could do it for me again."

"For your study group?" she asked.

"Exactly." He handed her the sheet of looseleaf. "The other thing is, I'm reading a new book, and the author uses a word in it I've never heard before."

"*You* have a question about a word, Mr. Craig? I've seen the books you read. And I seem to recall you telling me that you taught yourself to read when you were four years old."

"Three, actually," he said. "But I can't take all the credit. I was kind of a *Sesame Street* junkie, so I'm sure that had something to do with it."[42] He wagged his copy of *Icebreaker*. "I've got the word right here." Avery took a step toward her; now came the tricky part. While keeping his eyes on her, he "tripped" on a desk leg and dropped the paperback and binder, sending them sailing across her desk. They landed on the floor in the corner.

"Oh, dear!" She scurried to his side. "Mr. Craig, are you okay?"

"Yeah, I think so." Avery winced and rubbed his shin. "Could you get my things?"

Miss Shipley walked to the corner and hinged over at the waist. She was wearing a thin, powder blue crepe skirt, and the fabric stretched taut against her firm butt. When she turned around with his things, Avery grimaced again to sell his injury and hobbled over to her desk. She handed him his binder and paperback. "Now, what was the word you had a question about?"

"I can't remember where it was in the book, Miss Shipley, but the word is 'callipygian.' Cal-uh-pij-hee-en. I think that's how it's pronounced. It's spelled 'C-A-L-L-I-P-Y-G-I-A-N.'"

"Hmm." She wrote it down and tapped her lips with a finger. "Never heard of it." She reached for a *Webster's Collegiate* dictionary, flipped through it, frowned, and tossed it on the desk. "Not in there. Are you *sure* you're spelling it right?"

---

[42] *Sesame Street* was an educational TV show for preschool-age children. The program appeared on PBS (the Public Broadcasting System).

"I'm positive."

"We'll have to check the unabridged dictionary in the library. Follow me." She opened the door and led the way down a narrow hallway. Avery lagged behind so he could imbibe Miss Shipley's butt some more. They went through the far door and passed Mrs. Braun, the ogress at the library front desk.

"You're *late*, Mr. Craig," she said.

"Please excuse him, Mrs. Braun. He's with me." Miss Shipley waved the looseleaf paper of Doc's notes. "I'll make a copy of these, Mr. Craig. Wait for me by the dictionary stand."

"Thank you," he said.

A minute later, Miss Shipley handed him the original and photocopy, then, with a sexy double-tap on her thigh, bade Avery closer. She leaned toward him and whispered: "How do you spell the word again?"

"'C-A-L-L-I-P-Y-G-I-A-N,'" he said.

She flipped through pages and scanned the columns with a finger.

"Ah-*hah*, here it is," she said. "'Callipygian. Adjective.'" The girlish curiosity in her eyes vanished. "'Having well-shaped buttocks.'"

"Oh," he said, "so *that's* what it means."

She scowled. "Mr. Craig, I have half a mind to give you detention. How would you like to spend an afternoon cleaning my blackboard and erasers?"

"*Your* blackboard and erasers, Miss Shipley?" Avery made puppy-dog eyes. "I'd be happy to. Anytime."

She smirked, wagged a finger at him, and walked away. He might have been imagining it, but it seemed like she was swinging her hips even more now to taunt him.

As Avery was admiring Miss Shipley's sashay, he remembered the Bond Girl name he'd coined for Irina—Venus Mantrap—and mused about a possible name for Miss Shipley. What about … Jane Shapely? Or, what if he went over-the-top and made "Shapely" her first name? Like … Miss Shapely Assets? Not bad. Hmm … she wore skirts a lot— thin skirts. How about … Shapely Thinskirt? *Yes.*

The next thing he knew, Lee was shaking his arm: "Where were you, man? You spaced out there."

They sat down at a table in the reference section surrounded by bookcases. Avery explained that he'd been inventing Bond Girl names and told him a few. Lee leaned toward him snickering, his eyes wide and intense.

"Venus Mantrap? Shapely Thinskirt?" He clutched Avery's upper arm and laughed. "So, Miss Shipley ... *she's* Shapely Thinskirt?"

"Yup."

"Oh, that's good," Lee said.

Holding his hands in front of his face, Lee pressed his fingertips together and wiggled them minutely and fast, like his fingers were trying to start a fire by friction. Lee did this whenever he got excited by an idea. If he was *really* excited by an idea, his fingers would try to gouge his eyes out. To outsiders, this behavior was surely bizarre, but Lee only did it around Avery, Tom Mallory, and a few other guys. It was so funny that Avery and Mallory had adopted it themselves, but because the mannerism fit perfectly with Lee's personality, he was the best at it by far. Lee stopped his finger-wiggling, glanced at the door to Miss Shipley's room, and lowered his voice.

"That Miss Shipley's friggin' hot, isn't she?"

"Yup."

"You got her to bend over to pick up your books?" Lee said. "Seriously? C'mon, Ace—you're jackin' me."

"No, I did. And I got her to look up a vocabulary word for me."

"What word?"

"Callipygian."

Lee snorted. "What the hell does that mean?"

"'Having well-shaped buttocks.'"

"Ace!" He punched Avery's arm. "Holy crap! And you got her to *look it up* for you?"

"Yeah."

Lee grinned maniacally and shook his head. "Oh, Acey!" He sang "Danny Boy" with Avery's nickname: "'Acey Boy, Acey Boy ... the pipes, the pipes are calling!'" He drummed the tabletop, made some beat-box sounds, and went still.

"All right," Avery said, "what are we doing about the quizzes?"

"I don't have a problem studying," Lee said. "I like Bio. But I'd like to keep going with it. You know, for insurance. Plus, I think the girls need it. Melody for sure."

"We'll have to memorize the answers," Avery said. "I'll come up with something before lunch tomorrow."

"Awesome, Ace. Uh-oh!"

Lee's fingertips wiggled again, then accelerated and headed for his eyeballs. He tried to avoid his drilling fingertips by arching his back away from them, but his fingertips couldn't be stopped; they bored into his eye sockets.

"Ah! Ah! Ah!"

The bell rang. Lee scooped up his books and stood as if nothing had happened.

"So, tomorrow at lunch?" he said. "With the girls?"

"Yeah," Avery said. "Later."

17

IN THE hall outside the library, Avery thanked Doc and gave him his biology notes back, then he wove through the crush of students to his locker. Inside, slipped through a vent slit, was a note from Mallory.

> Hey, Ace!
> Screw the bus today—I brought the Capri! Meet me outside in 10, so we can get ahead of those smoke-spewing turds!
> I've got an adventure for us, bud. A good one. If you've got your Indy fedora in the locker, wear it.
> I am, Kind Sir,
> The Most Legendary Mallory

Avery put on his bomber jacket and fedora and packed his books and other things in his bag. He slammed his locker shut and ran down the hall clutching his musette bag to his stomach like Indy fleeing the temple with the golden idol in *Raiders*.

"Hi, Avery!" It was Gemma.

He backpedaled and approached her locker. She was back to wearing her giant plastic-framed glasses instead of the more understated tortoiseshell ones. They were so badly smudged that Avery was tempted to yank them off her face and clean them for her.

Avery said he was in a rush; his friend Tom Mallory was driving them home. Gemma said she knew Tom because she used to live up the street from him.

"Want a ride?" Avery asked.

"That would be great," she said, "but I've got to stop in the office first. Can you wait?"

"Sure. His car's a forest green Mercury Capri. Meet us in the student lot in five minutes—we have to beat the buses."

"Oooh, *forest* green?" She grinned, revealing her braces in all their glory. "I'll be there."

Vixen Ridge

Avery ran out to the parking lot. It was cold, but nowhere near as cold as it had been that morning, when it was like 12°F. Mallory was sitting on the car hood with his arms crossed, wearing his battered leather jacket and fedora. Swelling out of the car windows was the movie theme ♫"March from *Raiders of the Lost Ark*."♫

"All right," Mallory said, "let's beat those buses."

They got in and slammed the doors. They were about to drive off when Avery remembered Gemma. He told Mallory that he'd offered her a ride home. Mallory frowned at the buses across the parking lot.

"I sure hope she makes it," he said. "I hate getting stuck behind the buses. Hey, take a look in the glove compartment."

Avery opened it and pulled out a stack of materials: a Sierra Club book on Mount Washington and topographical maps of the Presidential Range of the Appalachians. Mallory said he had two sets of all the materials, so the ones Avery was holding were his to keep. Mallory nudged him.

"I want us to have one more adventure before I leave for Cornell. One big blowout. Are you in?"

"Of course I'm in," Avery said.

"Good. Make sure you read that book on Mount Washington and study the topo maps. We'll need to train, dude. It's no joke."

Avery flipped the book open to the introduction, a fact jumped out at him, and he shared it with Mallory: the highest recorded wind speed on earth was on the top of Mount Washington. On April 12, 1934, the wind got up to 231 mph.

"Yeah," Mallory said, "and the weather can change up there like *that*." He snapped his fingers.

"Damn," Avery said.

Mallory pointed out the window. "Crap—the buses … they're pulling out."

The *Raiders* theme was transitioning from its romantic sequence into its climax. Just as Mallory cranked the volume on the stereo, Gemma burst out of the auditorium doors and scanned the parking lot.

"Wait, Mal—here she is."

Avery jumped out of the car. The Capri was a two-door coupe, so he folded the front passenger seat forward and waved Gemma toward them. He cupped his hands around his mouth and shouted to her.

"Come on, Jones! Move, Jones, move! You can do it!"

She grinned and ran for the car, her knapsack jouncing wildly on her back. When she reached the car door, Avery took her knapsack, helped her into the back seat, folded the seat back, and jumped in.

"Indy—punch it!"

They took off.

The four-cylinder engine whined as Mallory shifted from first gear to second. They were racing across the parking lot toward the traffic light at the school entrance. The long convoy of buses was now barreling toward the same traffic light. Mallory shifted up to third gear and floored the accelerator. Parked cars whizzed by in a blur. Huddling in the cold, packs of students shot their fists in the air and cheered in solidarity; *everybody* hated the buses.

"Come on, Indy!" Avery shouted. "Beat those bastards!"

Mallory steered the Capri, tires chirping, through an opening in the median and cut diagonally across the entrance road. Avery glanced out the window. They had at least fifty yards on the buses.

"You got 'em, Mal. No problem."

Ahead, the traffic light turned yellow. Mallory zoomed to it and swung a right as it turned red. The buses, forbidden from turning at red lights, halted at the corner.

"Mal-o-REEEEE!" Avery drummed on the dashboard. "Nobody's better at beating the buses! Nobody!"

They slapped each other five. Mallory grinned and turned down the music. From the back seat, Gemma patted their shoulders.

"Dangerous but impressive, Thomas," she said. "I really appreciate the ride. Where are you going to school next year?"

"Cornell," he said.

Avery interjected that Mallory would someday be the Indiana Jones of civil engineering, building roads, tunnels, and bridges through jungles in the Third World.

"Sounds exciting," Gemma said.

"Yeah," Mallory said. "Someday, I'll be working in some banana republic somewhere, and I'll have to pay off dictators and hire mercenaries to protect us from rebels."

Avery asked Gemma what she'd had to pick up in the office earlier.

"A letter from the College Board." She touched Avery's arm. "I can't believe it. I'm a National Merit Scholar Finalist!"

"That's amazing, Gemma."

"That *is* amazing," Mallory said. "Congrats."

"Thanks. No one else knows yet. I can't wait to tell my parents."

"This calls for a celebration—*pronto*," Avery said. "Mal?"

"Yeah. How about some ice cream?"

"Gosh, I'd love that but my parents will want to take me out for dinner. Can we even *get* ice cream this time of year?"

"Carvel's open," Mallory said.

Avery flapped a hand. "Those sluts are always open." Then he remembered who was in the car with them. "Sorry, Gem. I meant—"

She giggled. "You called an ice cream chain 'sluts.'"

Mallory drove them to the Carvel in Troutkill Junction, where he and Avery ordered large vanilla soft-serve cones dipped in chocolate. They bought Gemma a hot fudge sundae.

Back in the car, they were on Woodside Creek Road, passing Van Wilder, their old junior high school, when Gemma leaned between the seats and pointed at the materials on Avery's lap.

"What's all that stuff?" she asked.

Mallory shut off the stereo. "Our next adventure. Mount Washington. Highest peak in the Northeast."

"Wow, I've never climbed a mountain before," Gemma said. "I've only been hiking once, and that was at computer camp like five years ago. Mountain climbing—isn't that dangerous?"

"It can be." Avery gulped down a huge glop of ice cream. "But Mallory and I are Scouts, so we've done a lot of it."

"What's the most dangerous part of mountain climbing?" Gemma asked. "Like, avalanches or breaking your leg?"

"No," Avery said, "fatigue."

"Yeah," Mallory said. "That and hypothermia."

"Mallory's right," Avery said. "Hypothermia's worse."

"Huh?" Gemma said.

Avery pivoted in his seat. "Hypothermia is when your core body temperature drops critically low. The most dangerous thing on a mountain is the weather. If a storm blows up and you get wet and don't get into shelter immediately, you can die."

"Really? Even during the summer?"

"Even then," Avery said.

"On Mount Washington," Mallory added, "it's not unusual for it to be snowing on the summit in July."

"Gosh," she said.

"You haven't heard the worst part," Mallory said. "Tell her, Ace."

Avery groaned. "It's something our scoutmasters pounded into us." Avery deepened his voice. "'If your hiking buddy shows signs of hypothermia, you have to strip him and get into a sleeping bag *naked* with him.'"

Gemma giggled. "Well, when you go, please be careful."

"We will," Mallory said. "We'll go sometime this summer. We have to train for it first."

"Don't worry, Gem," Avery said, "we'll say goodbye before we go. You know … in case we don't make it back."

Gemma slapped his shoulder. "Don't say that." She pointed at a street sign ahead. "Thomas, that's my street. 'Vixen Ridge Lane.' My house is at the very end."

Mallory made the turn. The road, thickly wooded on both sides, switchbacked up a long hill. Farther up the hill, they passed a few cleared lots, but there wasn't a single house on any of them; only blacktop driveways and concrete foundations. After they had driven a quarter mile, Mallory glanced in the rearview mirror.

"How far is it, Gemma?"

"At the top of the hill, at the end of the cul-de-sac," she said. "The development's brand-new, and our house is the only one built so far."

Gemma then launched into a story about the house. When her mother, Beverly, met with the builder, the man didn't have a name for the development yet. Apparently, he was so smitten with Beverly that he proposed naming it "Beverly Hills," but she thought it sounded snooty. Then, one day when Gemma and her parents were up on the ridge with the developer, choosing the lot for their house, a vixen and its kits came out of the woods. Beverly suggested "Vixen Ridge" instead. The developer liked it and used it.

♫"Uptown Girl"♫

They came out of another switchback on the crest of the ridge. The road ahead ended in a cul-de-sac, and there, in the center of a snowy lot surrounded by woods, was a house unlike any that Avery had ever seen before, and absolutely unique in New Netherlands County, epicenter of the plain vanilla raised ranch. After a mere glimpse of the place, Avery knew that Gemma's parents were loaded.

"Whoa," Mallory said. He stopped in the cul-de-sac.

The house was constructed of redwood, glass, black metal, and stone. Unlike the houses in Avery's development, which looked like rectangular boxes on bare lawns, Gemma's house, in two sections, blended seamlessly into the landscape. The lower section that faced the street was built into a wooded hillside, and the upper section, which included a square tower on the corner, rested on a plateau on top of the hill. Both sections had floor-to-ceiling windows. Without question, it was the most modern house Avery had ever seen.

"Damn, Gemma." Mallory parked in the driveway. "Nice digs."

"It's incredible," Avery said.

"Thanks, guys." She described the inside of the house a little bit, then pointed out the square tower, saying that it was her mother's painting studio. "The place took two years to build. We moved in back in December. Dad calls it our treehouse."

"Treehouse? Why's that?" Avery asked.

"Because when you're looking out the windows on the second floor, all you see are the treetops. You guys will have to come over sometime this summer. We've got an inground pool."

"A pool?" Avery said. "Awesome."

"Yeah," Mallory said.

"I know you're on the winter swim team, Avery," she said. "You can use it anytime you want."

The Fox

The front door opened and a tall brunette woman with an arresting figure stepped outside. She wore paint-stained jeans, snug and faded, and a red turtleneck sweater. Her hair, dark and lush, was in a loose pile on her head, and she had a wide mouth of fire-engine red lipstick. She leaned against the doorjamb, removed a cigarette from a gold case, put it in a cigarette holder, and lit it with a gold lighter.

♫"Twentieth Century Fox"♫

"Who's *that*?" Avery asked, trying to contain his excitement.

Gemma groaned. "*Mom*. Smoking again."

Mrs. Jones pinched the cigarette holder elegantly between her thumb and index finger, and because there was no wind, the smoke from the cigarette ember curled around Mrs. Jones' face. There was only one word for it: sexy. Unconsciously, Avery muttered, "Holy...," but he stopped himself; surely, Gemma didn't want to hear Avery rave about how hot her mom was. Meanwhile, this was Vixen Ridge all right, and Mrs. Jones was the fox.

"She only smokes a few a day," Gemma continued, "but it's *so* unhealthy. I've been after her to stop." Gemma thanked Mallory for the ride and asked Avery to come meet her mother. "I told her about how you got us into the White House. My mom really wants to meet you, Avery. Please?"

"Okay. Wait for me, Mal?"

"No prob."

Avery followed Gemma up the driveway. A low stone wall separated the woods from the lawn on one side of the driveway, and in front of the garage, there was a basketball hoop on the edge of the courtyard. Gemma led him up a walkway to the front door. As they neared the doorstep, Mrs. Jones' eyes dilated and she stood sharply upright, like she was seeing a ghost, and then she relaxed again and arched an eyebrow. The look reminded Avery of smoldering brunette Sylvia Trench in the Bond movie *Dr. No,* when, sitting at the casino table, she arches her eyebrow, inquires, "Mister...?" and triggers Sean Connery's legendary blasé reply: *"The name is Bond. James Bond."* Mrs. Jones even had seductive blue-gray eyes like Sylvia Trench's. She gave him a furtive smile and took a final drag from the cigarette. Then, plucking it from the holder, she squashed it under her paint-stained sneaker and put the stub in her pocket.

"Gemma," Avery said, "you didn't tell me you had an older sister!" She giggled and nudged him. They stopped in front of Mrs. Jones. "Gemma, dear … who is this positively *charming* young man?"

♫"West End Girls"♫

There was a faint English accent in Mrs. Jones' voice, and when it floated out of that flawless red mouth, it was as if Avery was looking at Sylvia Trench herself. Gemma was right: her mom *was* stunning. Sensing an erection was imminent, he took his musette bag, which had been hanging at his side, and redeployed it over his groin.

Gemma introduced Avery and told her mom that Avery and Mallory had given her a ride home. Avery pinched his hat brim and shook Mrs. Jones' hand.

"A pleasure to meet you," he said.

"Goodness, what a gentleman," Mrs. Jones said.

"Your accent, Mrs. Jones—are you originally from England?"

"Yes, darling—London, West End," she said. "Born there, moved to the States when I was sixteen. Simply never lost the accent." Mrs. Jones put an arm around Gemma. "So, *you're* the young man Gemma can't stop talking about."

"Mom … please."

"I'm afraid your reputation precedes you, Avery," Mrs. Jones said. "When Gemma returned from Washington, she told me about this young man named 'Avery Craig'—and how funny, handsome, athletic, talented and brilliant he was."

Gemma blushed so hard, Avery swore he could feel the heat radiating off her.

"Mom!"

Mrs. Jones' voice, so sexy and melodious, was mesmerizing. The expressions she used were American, but the faint English accent and the honeyed timbre of her voice gave everything she said a touch of exotic elegance.

"That's flattering, Mrs. Jones, but"—Avery nodded at Gemma—"your *daughter* is the brilliant one. Wait 'til you hear her news."

"What news?"

"I'll tell you inside, Mom."

"Avery," Mrs. Jones said, "would you and Thomas care to come in for a snack? I have a terrific new pizza stone."

"No, Mom," Gemma said, "if we have pizza, we have to order it from Primo over in Merlinsville. Avery used to work there. He says it's owned by the *Mafia!*"

Mrs. Jones arched an eyebrow. "You're *joking.*" She touched Avery's arm. "Avery, dear, is this true? Do tell."

"Another time, Mrs. Jones." He glanced at the car, where Mallory was frowning behind the wheel. "It's been great meeting you, but I have to go."

Mrs. Jones said he was welcome anytime. Avery thanked her and said that he would be back.

"If Mallory and I return alive, that is."

"Avery," Gemma said, "stop saying that!"

Mrs. Jones' eyes widened. "Return alive from where, darling?"

"Mount Everest," he said.

She squinted at him with her lips puckered; she was trying not to laugh.

"He's pulling your leg, Mom," Gemma said. "They're climbing Mount Washington in New Hampshire—but not until this summer."

"Well," Mrs. Jones said, "if you need a good Sherpa, let me know. I have connections."

Avery pinched his hat brim again. "It was nice meeting you."

Pixie dust snowflakes floated down. A few flakes settled in Gemma's and her mother's hair.

"It's getting cold out here. You ladies should get inside."

Gemma nudged him. "We don't want to get hypothermia. Right, Avery?"

"Hypo-*what?*" Mrs. Jones said.

"I'll tell you later, Mom."

"Please thank Thomas for getting Gemma home safely." She shook Avery's hand. "And thank *you*, dear, for not ma'am-ing me."

"Mom hates being called ma'am," Gemma said. "It makes her feel like an old lady."

"There was no danger of that, Mrs. Jones," he said. "I have a personal policy of never calling beautiful young women *ma'am*."

Avery gave Mrs. Jones a Steve Austin-caliber wink.[43] She made a little gasp and grinned. "It was a pleasure meeting you, darling."

"*Bye*, Avery," Gemma said.

Sleeping Bag

Avery hustled back to the car. His fingers were frozen. Thankfully, Mallory had the heat blasting inside. The windshield wipers flapped slowly as Mallory reversed out of the driveway.

"Getting yourself a backup girlfriend? Took you long enough."

"Sorry. Gemma really wanted her mother to meet me."

They coasted down the series of switchbacks. At the bottom of the hill, Mallory turned right onto Woodside toward Avery's house.

"How about that house, huh?" Mallory said. "Gemma's parents must be friggin' *loaded*. I'd be nice to that girl if I were you. Gemma's got a crush on you, bud. *And* the mom. Big time."

"No way. And definitely not the mom. She just met me."

"You're wrong about that." Mallory turned into Birch Knolls and crept through the development. "Remember that book on body language we read a while back? I was watching them—touching your arm, laughing at your half-assed jokes—"

"How do you know they were half-assed?"

"Gemma being like"—Mallory raised his voice two octaves—"'Avery, my mom *really* wants to meet you ... *please*?'"

"You're imagining things, dude."

They idled past the raised ranches in Avery's development and gazed out at the falling snow. It was starting to accumulate.

"Hey, bud," Mallory said. "You know what you were telling Gemma about hypothermia? The bit about getting in the sleeping bag naked with your buddy?"

---

[43] Steve Austin was the hero of the 1970s TV show *The Six Million Dollar Man*. His trademark flirty move with the ladies was giving them a playful wink. Avery thought the move was cool, so he used it himself occasionally.

"Yeah?"

"No offense, but if you get hypothermia when we're up on Mount Washington…"

"Yeah?" Avery said.

"Dude…," Mallory drawled, "…you're gonna *die*."

Avery nodded resignedly. "Same here. No naked sleeping bag shit for me either. Hey, speaking of…"

Avery ejected the *Raiders* soundtrack cassette and popped in ZZ Top's *Afterburner*. The song ♫"Sleeping Bag"♫ came on.

"Yeah!" Mallory cranked up the volume.

When they reached the cul-de-sac, Mallory pulled over next to Avery's mailbox and let the car idle. They did air guitar to the music, waving their imaginary guitar necks back and forth in sync, like the guys in ZZ Top did in their videos.

"Bet you'd like Penny to slip inside *your* sleeping bag," Mallory said.

Avery chuckled under his breath. *Not Penny so much as Caitlyn.*

"You're so lucky, man," Mallory said. "I wish I had a girlfriend."

"You will, Mal—soon. This is our year, I can feel it." Avery put the Mt. Washington materials in his bag. "Talk to you later?"

"Sure. Start reading the Mount Washington book, and we'll discuss."

Avery raised a fist. "Adventure!"

"Adventure!"

They clasped hands, and Avery got out of the car.

18

Avery checked the mailbox, hoping the tapes he'd ordered from the Columbia House Record and Tape Club had arrived, but the box was empty. Sabrina must have brought in the mail. He ran up to the house, and since the door was unlocked, he didn't have to use his key.

♫"Our House"♫

Inside, the air reeked of vegetable oil. Standing in the tiny entryway inside, Avery glanced upstairs above the stairwell. The family cat, Mr. Smithers, was perched on the pony wall, as he often was when Avery came home from school. The cat blinked as Avery climbed the stairs. "Good afternoon, Mr. Smithers. How are you today, sir?"

The cat made a silent meow, stretched, and padded along the ledge of the pony wall to the stairs, bunting Avery when he reached the top. Avery petted the cat. The living room TV blared with the baritone voice of Stefano DiMera, the colorful villain on the soap opera *Days of our Lives*. Avery loved his criminal mastermind character; DiMera was like a low-budget Bond villain.

He found Sabrina in the kitchen, cooking French fries in the deep fryer and poking at the bubbling oil with a slotted spoon. Because Sabrina was easily distracted, Jack and Jill had forbidden her from cooking with anything but the microwave oven. Avery gestured at the bubbling fryer.

"You should've waited for me to do that," he said.

She sipped from a can of Coke. "I was hungry, Ace."

"And don't drink my cans of Coke. Drink the two-liter bottle."

"But it's flat."

"You can have that one can," he said. "The cans are mine."

"Yeah, I know," she said. "Because *I* bought them for you."

While You Were Out

His sister's hair, the pale yellow of straw, was in braids today with baby-blue ribbons tied in bows at the ends, making her look like the girl on the Swiss Miss hot cocoa box. She was wearing a pair of round, pink-tinted sunglasses and a Bon Jovi T-shirt. Sometimes it irked Avery that his 14-year-old sister was taller, cooler, and more popular than he had been at 14. On the other hand, she was a great dancer and volleyball player, and she always covered for him.

Sabrina pouted over her shoulder. "Please don't tell Jack and Jill about the fries, Ace."

"I won't say anything," he said.

Sabrina grinned and did a brief Madonna-esque dance.

"Careful," he said. "Not around the fryer."

The cat's water bowl and dish of dry food were empty. While Avery filled them, the cat did figure 8's between his legs, but the moment he placed them on the tray again, the cat peeled away and chowed down.

"I waited like an *hour*," she said. "Why weren't you on your bus?"

"Got a ride home with Mallory. Did you bring in the mail?"

She pointed with the spoon. "On the table."

Avery rummaged through the pile. Besides bills for his parents, there was a *New Netherlands Gazette*, a *Pennysaver*, a *Time* magazine, and a letter from Penny, postmarked the day before.

"Did Penny call?" he asked.

"Uh-huh." Sabrina stirred the fries. "Four times."

"*Four?* How'd she sound? Angry? Worried?"

"Worried, yeah," she said. "You got three other calls too." Sabrina turned away from the fryer again and peered over her sunglasses. "From *three* other girls."

She unplugged the fryer, raised the basket from the oil, let it drain for a millisecond, and dumped the golden-brown fries on a platter covered with paper towels.

"Who were the other girls?" Avery asked.

Sabrina said the first caller, "Irina something," had "a weird accent"; the second caller, Inge Ibsen, had sounded "kinda tipsy"; and the third caller, a girl whose name began with C, was "a rude bitch."

"Caitlyn?" he said.

"Yeah, that's her," Sabrina said. "I wrote down all the numbers and put them on your desk."

Sabrina thumped the bottom of a Heinz ketchup bottle with the heel of her hand, plopping the ketchup over the fries.

"What do you mean *rude*?" Avery said. "What did she say?"

"Not much. It was how she said it—talking to me like I'm friggin' five." She affected a whiny voice: "'Now Sabrina, make sure you tell Ace I called. *Caitlyn Cray*. C-R-A-Y.' Crap like that."

"That sounds a little patronizing but not rude," he said. "She doesn't know how old you are."

"Whatever. I don't like her." Sabrina ate a French fry and walked into the living room. She sat cross-legged on the rug, about three feet from the TV, with the platter of fries balanced on her lap.

Avery grabbed a box of Cheez-Its and a can of Coke. He stood in the doorway and nodded at the TV. "What's Stefano up to now?"

"It's hard to explain."

"Did Roman and Marlena get back together? And what's the deal with Bo and Hope?"

"Tell you later." Sabrina peered at him over her sunglasses. "You'd better call Penny back. Hey, got any pictures of her? Is she pretty?"

"Yeah, she's pretty, and no, I don't have any pictures of her."

"Fine. You don't have to bite my head off."

Avery went down the hall to his bedroom. Four pink "While You Were Out" phone sheets were on his desk. Why the heck had Inge called? They hadn't spoken since their falling-out back in August—when he'd biked from Pa and Gram's in Wellington to Inge's grandparents' place near the river (like 30 friggin' miles!), only to get there and find her drunk, and the sex she'd promised they'd have never happened. He was sick of her constant drinking and chaos. Avery got enough of that crap here at home.

He tossed his hat onto the dresser, dumped his jacket and bag on the bed, and closed the door. For some reason, he glanced at his "Blown Away" poster, and imagined himself sitting in a similar armchair, getting a blowjob from Caitlyn Cray, and his hair blowing back like the guy's in the photo.[44] Avery sighed, put the food and Penny's letter on the desk and crossed the room to select some tunes.

Avery's stereo was *boss*: a 150W receiver, dual cassette deck (perfect for making mixtapes), and variable speed turntable. And now he had *four* Minimus-7 speakers for it. Each one was 40 watts and less than 8 inches tall, and they were mounted on wall brackets in the four corners of his room. With bands like Led Zeppelin and Pink Floyd, you could hear how they'd recorded certain songs for quadraphonic sound: the music "swirled" around the room.

Sometimes after school Avery liked to unwind by singing along with the Charlie Daniels Band's "The Devil Went Down to Georgia," and other times liked to put on Michael Jackson's "Billie Jean" and practice his moonwalk. But today he knew exactly what he wanted to hear: ♫"Rapper's Delight."♫ He popped the cassette in the stereo, turned up the volume, and walked over to the full-length mirror.

Rapping with the song, watching his dance moves in the mirror, Avery practiced the 7-minute song once, then rewound the cassette to practice it a second time. The phone rang. Chances were, it was Penny, but until he knew who was calling, he needed to answer the phone generically. He sat at his desk and glanced out the window; the snow was starting to pick up. Avery pulled the telephone base unit toward himself and picked up the handset.

Keep Your Options Open

It was Irina Vacker. After they'd said hello, she said, "I am glad to be hearing your voice again. I am thinking you do not want to talk to me anymore." Avery apologized, saying that he'd been busy with schoolwork and hadn't been around when Irina called.

---

[44] The "Blown Away" poster was a long, landscape-oriented photo of a man in an armchair in front of a stereo, with the man's hair, tie, and a lampshade being blown backwards, as if by the sound blasting out of the speakers. The 1978 photograph, by photographer Steve Steigman, was used extensively in ads for Maxell cassette tapes during the 1980s, probably because of its not-so-subliminal suggestion of sex.

She asked if Avery had been thinking about her, because she'd been thinking about him a lot—especially their kiss.

"Of course I've been thinking about you, beautiful," he said. "How have you been?"

Avery listened while Irina unloaded her troubles. The hotel had a new general manager who refused to promote her to assistant manager and was making her work the graveyard shift; a coworker—a married guy named Victor—kept hitting on her, trying to get her to sleep with him; and Irina's parents back in Helsinki were getting divorced.

When Irina finished telling Avery about the problem with Victor, she sniffled over the line. Out of nowhere, the urge to rescue her—like when Caitlyn was attacked at the hotel pool—swelled inside him. Avery told her that everything would be okay and that he sympathized with her about her parents. His own parents, Jack and Jill, had gotten divorced briefly when he was a little kid.

"Look at it this way," he said. "The next time you go home, you'll get to have *two* Christmases."

Irina sniffled. "Thank you, Ace."

"As for your work situation, there might be something we can do. Let me think about it."

"I cannot believe you are only seventeen years old. You are, how they say—wise before your years." And then, in a little girl voice, Irina said something that made Avery's entire being *twang* like a spring: "Ace, I know you already have girl, but maybe you would visit me?"

Avery stopped breathing. Stunned, he looked around his bedroom for a second, like there was a camera hidden somewhere and he was being pranked on *Candid Camera*.[45] "You mean come down to Washington, D.C. by myself?" Obstacles to a potential visit popped into his head, but he recalled a piece of advice that Big Jack had given him many times: *"Keep your options open. It's good to have choices."*

"My spring break's in April," he said. "Maybe I could come down on Amtrak. You know—the train?"

"Oh, Ace, that would be wonderful!"

---

[45] *Candid Camera* was a TV show in which pranks were played on unsuspecting people, and the pranks were filmed.

"Great, we'll plan on it then."

"I can get you room at Bethesda Colonnade cheap," she said. "Or … my apartment is plenty big, so you can stay with me if you like. I can be tour guide for you. If we even bother to leave my apartment, that is. We might never get out of bed." She giggled. "Ace, would you send me picture of you?"

Avery was still catching his breath after imagining Irina nude in bed with him. "I can do that. But could you send me a few sexy photos of yourself? Like, you in lingerie or a bikini or something?"

"I will do this."

"I'll make you a mixtape too," he said.

"What is 'mixtape'?"

Avery explained that a mixtape was a collection of songs with a common theme. The songs he'd put on the "Irina mixtape" would all remind him of her in some way. A few songs sprang to mind: "Legs," "She's A Beauty," and "Fresh."

"I cannot wait," she said.

"Call me again in a few days," he said. "I'll think about your problem and form a plan."

They agreed that she would call in the early evening. Avery said goodbye and was about to hang up when Irina added, "When you visit, I wish to dance for you in my bra and panties. You would like this?"

Avery moaned; Irina giggled.

"I cannot wait to do sexy dancing for you," she said. "You dream about me tonight, yes?"

"For sure," he said.

Her Fathomless Brown Eyes

When he hung up the phone, he glanced at Penny's letter and noticed his hands were shaking. Penny was basically his girlfriend, and here he was, making plans to travel hundreds of miles to see (and have nonstop sex with) an older woman he barely knew. Honestly, the prospect was a little frightening. Heck, Irina could be an international serial murderess who got her jollies by seducing teenage guys and killing them by slicing off their dongs. Maybe it wasn't such a good idea. Then again, stuff like that never happened, and what was wrong with him having sex with Irina? How would that hurt Penny? If Penny never found out about her—which she wouldn't because Irina lived hundreds of miles away—it wouldn't affect his relationship with Penny. Right?

Avery groaned. He spun in his desk chair and gazed at the posters on the walls and the other stuff in the room; everything passed by in a blur: Heather Thomas in her scanty pink bikini; Princess Leia in her copper and leather bikini from *Return of the Jedi*; the *Raiders of the Lost Ark* movie poster; the "Blown Away" poster; the picture of Robert Palmer from the cover of *GQ* magazine; the Huey Lewis and the News *Sports* album poster; the Van Halen poster; Sean Connery leaning on the Aston Martin DB5 from *Goldfinger*; Elle MacPherson on the cover of this year's *Sports Illustrated (SI)* swimsuit edition; the cutouts from *SI* of Norwegian cross-country skiing legend Johan Ødegaard and Avery's favorite tennis players (Bjorn Borg, John McEnroe, and Boris Becker); the dozen or so newspaper clippings about his various athletic feats over the years (e.g., "Avery 'Ace' Craig Shatters Hancock Tennis' Records for Aces in Match, Season" and "Hancock Sophomore Sets New 1500m Freestyle Swim Record"); the bulletin board with pictures of his favorite Bond Girls; the computer and printer; the stereo and the bookcase overflowing with books and records; Heather Thomas again, and—as the chair came to a stop—gorgeous Princess Leia.

When he'd gotten the poster three years ago, at first he simply enjoyed looking at it; Carrie Fisher was so sexy in the photo: that warm light on her face and bare belly; that white mist in the background; her pouty pink lips and long thick braid; her feminine repose as she lay half on her side with one knee bent; and most of all her fathomless brown eyes gazing down at him—regally, defiantly. Since then, Leia had become an omniscient presence in his room, Avery's very own human Magic 8-Ball, listening to him and dispensing wisdom.[46] He took a breath and looked into her eyes.

---

[46] The Magic 8-Ball was a toy that looked like a giant black 8-ball used in billiards. Popular in the 1970s and early '80s, teen girls would ask it a question, turn the ball over, and peer through a clear window on the bottom. Floating in liquid inside the ball was a multi-sided die with different answers written on each side (e.g., "Yes," "No," "Unclear," etc.).

What should I do about Irina, Princess?

Hmm, the Finnish girl with problems at work? Maybe you can play the hotel manager and the married guy Victor against each other. Let me think about it. Ask me again tomorrow.

I know Penny's my girlfriend, but Irina's like a Bond Girl. I feel like an opportunity with her is a once-in-a-lifetime thing. I mean, the woman is majorly hot. Do you understand?

I understand. Yes, she's sexy, but she also strikes me as psychologically damaged and desperate. The girl's not exactly a genius either. Be careful with her.

All right, Princess. Thanks for looking out for me.

Anytime, dear.

Avery glanced at Penny's letter on the desk. He decided to put on a little background music—something without distracting lyrics—while he read it. He flipped through his meticulously curated collection of LPs and chose a favorite: Tchaikovsky's *1812 Overture*. He slid the record out of its sleeve and put it on the turntable. Knowing that the song quickly went from inaudible to deafening, he made sure the volume was low, then sat at his desk and put his feet up.

When he spoke to Penny on the phone, the first thing she'd ask was if he'd gotten and read her latest letter. Sipping his Coke and eating Cheez-Its, Avery opened the letter and read:

> Dearest Avery,
> 12:15 P.M. I'm in Bio now, writing three things at the same time—this letter to you, a note to Caitlyn, and my bio notes. I hope I get a letter from you today.
> 12:25 P.M. I can't wait until this Friday! What movie are we seeing? Will we sit in the back row? (I hope so.)
> 12:42 P.M. I can't wait to see you on Friday. I am going through withdrawal from not seeing you. Well, the bell is about to ring, so I'd better start saying my goodbyes.
> When we have to say goodbye over the phone, isn't it heartbreaking? I can't put into words how strongly I feel for you. I'm literally dying to have you hold me again.
> ❤ Penny ❤

The phone rang. Avery took a deep breath and answered it.

It was Penny. Once they'd greeted each other, Avery heard soft breathing on the line. At first, he thought it might be Penny (or her sister, Dora), but the clarity and volume of the breathing told Avery that the eavesdropper was on *his* end. To confirm his suspicion, he glanced at the privacy monitor he'd connected to the telephone base unit. The tiny Radio Shack countersurveillance box could detect when someone was listening in on an extension or if someone outside of the house was listening in on the line. The LED was glowing red. Avery knew who the culprit was.

"Sabrina, get off the phone! I don't listen to your phone calls!"

Click. Avery waited a second, in case Sabrina was trying the fake hang-up gambit, but the line was quiet, and the red monitor bulb switched off and stayed off.

"Everything all right?" Penny said.

"Now it is." He ate some Cheez-Its. "Alone at last."

"When Dora does that to me, I could kill her, and she knows it." Penny huffed. "I've got some bad news."

She'd forgotten that this weekend was one of her weekends with her father, so she and Avery couldn't go on their first date as planned.

"I'm sorry," she said. "Are you disappointed?"

"Yeah, but I understand."

"I miss you so much. Do you miss me?"

"Very much."

"Tell me what we'll do—you know, when we see each other again?"

"I don't know," he said. "Go to a movie, I guess."

"No, I mean what will we *do* … like, *to* each other?"

"Oh." Avery twirled the long, coiled phone cord in his fingers. "Okay … you'll be wearing that gray pleated skirt that I love, and I'll kiss you, slip my hands under your skirt, and caress your perfect butt. It's so firm, like an unripe nectarine."

She giggled. "Keep going. What else?"

"After a while, I'll slide the fingers of my other hand under your skirt in front and caress you there."

"Oh, my." Her breath was ragged. "Avery, I'm going crazy not seeing you. I hope you're still attracted to me. What if you think I'm ugly?"

"Are you kidding? If anything, I'll be even more attracted to you."

"Mom'll be home any minute, I should go. I miss you so much, my whole chest hurts. Can a person die of heartache, Avery?"

"No," he said. "Only if the couple was separated for *years*, but we'll be okay. It's only about ten more days. Remember, I'm missing you just as badly."

"Okay. Can we talk again tomorrow?"

"Sure."

"Until then," she said. "Night."

Click.

Please Don't Bend!

Avery did a little homework and was about to go downstairs to work out when the phone rang again. This time, it was Caitlyn.

"*Hell-lo*, Ace."

"Caitlyn?"

"Catch ya at a bad time?"

"Yeah," he said, "I was about to work out."

"I thought you might be zipping up."

"Excuse me?"

She giggled. "I'd totally understand if you were … you know … *relieving* yourself. Penny told me about your sexy phone call before."

"I need to work out," he said. "Is there something you want?"

"I sent you a letter the other day. I'm guessing you haven't gotten it yet, 'cause you totally would have called me the second you opened it."

Avery said he hadn't received a letter from her.

"Are you *sure*?" she said. "It was in a plain envelope with no return address. You might of missed it."

"Hold on. I'll go check."

"You do that."

Avery put down the phone handset, jogged out to the kitchen, and sifted through the pile of mail. On the bottom, tucked inside a grocery store circular, was a bulging plain white envelope with no return address. Scrawled on the side and the back of the envelope in Caitlyn's soap-bubble handwriting was, "<u>PLEASE DON'T BEND!</u>" Avery ran back to his room and picked up the handset again.

"Got it," he said. "Does it say, 'Please don't bend' on the outside?"

"Mm-hm. Open that puppy up. But read the letter first. It's short."

He ripped open the envelope and yanked out a sheet of looseleaf. Some other contents slid back into the envelope.

> Dear Ace,
> Enclosed are the pictures I mentioned in my last letter to you. I'm only sharing these with you because I trust you, and I know you won't tell P. or anyone else about them.
> I miss you, Ace—a lot. I wanted you to have these pictures to remind you of the physical attraction we share. I'm dying to see you again soon, for you to kiss and hold me. I want to feel you between my legs. I said it before, and I'll say it again … Ace, I want to be your first. Your first, your last, your forever.
> Your Sexy Babydoll,
> V.
> ♥XOXOXOXOXO♥
> P.S.: I got your address off one of P.'s letters to you. In case somebody else gets this letter by mistake, I'm not writing my return address, and I used initials and not names.

"You signed the letter, 'V,'" he said. "Is that your middle initial?"

"Mm-hm … 'Veronica.'"

"Veronica, huh? She's my favorite from the Archie comics."

"No *shit* she's your favorite," Caitlyn said. "She's mine too. She's rich, she's hot, and she's got big tits."

"What about Betty? She's beautiful and big-breasted, and she's blonde like you, *and* she's sweet."

"But Betty's friggin' poor," she said. "Veronica's *rich*."

"Meanwhile, I don't get what those two see in Archie," Avery said. "He's a redheaded geek. He must have a super schlong."

Caitlyn chuckled. "They're stupid comics, Ace. Check out the photos already."

"Okay. Hold on."

"Take your time," she said. "I'm not going anywhere."

Avery put down the letter and slid a stack of photos out of the envelope. The first three photos were of him and Caitlyn: sitting next to each other and talking in the hotel lobby; standing on the Capitol steps together; and dancing during the D.C. dance party. In all three photos, the physical attraction between them was obvious. The fourth, fifth and sixth photos were of Avery alone: him in the hotel dining room telling a story; him doing pull-ups in the hotel gym; and him doing the moonwalk during the dance party. The final six photos—Polaroids that Caitlyn had taken in the hotel bathroom mirror—were of her alone.[47]

♫"Heart And Soul"♫

The first two Polaroids showed Caitlyn in outfits she'd worn during the trip: the Madonna *Desperately Seeking Susan* outfit, with the sheer lace blouse that ended at her midriff and the black bra underneath (she was sucking on a Blow Pop, too, like Madonna); and the black stocking dress that hugged Caitlyn's body and made her look like a shapely panther. And then he came to the final four photos— also taken in the hotel bathroom mirror with a burst of flash. They were the sexiest pictures he'd ever seen of a female body—including any of the women he'd seen in *Playboy* or *Penthouse*.

In the first one, Caitlyn was smiling and posing in the pink bikini. In the second, she was posing again, but without the bikini top. In the third, she was totally nude, facing the mirror at a slight angle, giving him a clear view of the golden V between her legs. And in the fourth photo, she was nude again, this time standing in profile, showing her breasts and butt (talk about *callipygian*), and blowing him a kiss. Forgetting he was on the phone with her, Avery lined up the Polaroids on his desk. He was in a trance imbibing her body and her smile. The next thing he knew, there was swelling along his inner thigh—like a

---

[47] Polaroid was the premier brand of "instant" camera in the 1980s. When the shutter button was pressed, snapping the photo, the camera clicked then made a high-pitched hum and whir, and ejected a 4"square photo. At first, the space where the photo would appear was black. Gradually, the shapes and colors would fill in, and in about five minutes, the picture would be fully developed. Compared to later innovations like digital photography, Polaroids are quaint; but at the time, when developing a roll of film could take a week or longer, five minutes was miraculous.

remora on a shark—and Caitlyn was loudly clearing her throat over the phone line, making the earpiece rattle.

"From your mouth-breathing," she said, "I assume you're looking at the nude ones."

"Uh-huh."

"So … what do you think?"

Avery was shaking. "You're incredibly sexy, Caitlyn."

"Thanks, Lover," she said. "You're pretty hot in the pictures yourself. Although I do wish I had a few of you in the buff—or at least in your Jams by the pool."

Avery couldn't stop staring at the Polaroids.

"Hey," she said. "So, guess where I am."

"I don't know. Where?"

"My bedroom, on my bed. And guess what I'm wearing?"

"What?" he said.

"*Nuthin'.*"

Avery gasped.

"I'm looking at the pictures of you," she said, "and of us together, and I'm naked under the sheets, and guess what else?"

"What?"

"I'm touching myself," she said.

♫"She Bop"♫

Avery's throat cinched up. He coughed.

"Talk sexy to me," she said. "Tell me what you'd do to me."

Avery was staring at the photos so intensely that it was a miracle he didn't burn a hole through them. He was severely tempted to take her up on her offer, but a tiny voice deep inside him said that he couldn't entirely trust her. For all he knew, Caitlyn might be recording their call so she could blackmail him sometime in the future. Well, two could play that game.

"Hold on a second, would you?" he said.

"Getting Vaseline and tissues, huh? Go ahead, I'll wait."

Avery put down the phone handset and unlocked the bottom drawer of his filing cabinet. This drawer was loaded with electronic gadgets; Avery considered the cache his own personal MI6 Q-Branch. Over the years, he'd received a lot of electronics as birthday and

Christmas gifts: a chess computer, a multimeter and soldering kit, a pair of CB-rated 40-channel long-range walkie-talkies, a pair of short-range headset walkie-talkies, a bulk-eraser, a bullhorn or megaphone, a speakerphone, and his handy little gem—a microcassette recorder with a suction cup microphone. Avery put a new blank tape in the recorder, licked the rubber hollow on the suction cup mike, and affixed it to the back of the phone handset. Then he plugged the mike into the recorder and pressed the record button. Time to get a little Caitlyn insurance.

"I'm back," he said.

"You know," she said, "if you want, I'll ride over there and give you a hand—my nice, soft hand. Remember?"

Avery gritted his teeth and watched the spindles rotate on the cassette recorder.

"Or what if I used my *mouth* this time?" she said. "I know you love my lips. Imagine me putting my soft, pretty lips over your hard—"

"What are you talking about, Caitlyn?"

She groaned. "I'm talking about the promise you made me on the trip—that we'd see each other when we got home. I miss you, Ace. When are we gonna spend some time together alone? My mom's at work—until midnight. Why don't you come over here?"

He didn't say anything. Caitlyn sighed.

"Hey, guess what I'm eating." A loud *pop* sounded in the phone earpiece. "A cherry *Blow* Pop. I've been sucking it for like an hour. Listen." For a good ten seconds, Caitlyn made loud sucking, slurping, popping, and other sundry throat noises into the phone. When she got back on the line, she was panting. "Does that make you hot? I bet it does. I bet you've got a wicked rodney right now."

Caitlyn's cockiness about the state of affairs in his pants annoyed him. He was about to indulge in some dirty-talking phone sex with her when he glanced across the room at his poster of Sean Connery as James Bond leaning against his Aston Martin DB5.

Discipline, Ace. Discipline.

"It makes me want a Blow Pop, that's for sure," he said. "A grape one. No … watermelon."

"Come on, the idea of me giving you a blowjob doesn't get you hard? Look at my firm, juicy tits in the photos I sent you. Don't you want to hold them again? Now imagine holding them while I suck you. My beautiful tits *and* lips, Ace? Haven't you fantasized about me, baby? I have about you." ♫"Burning Up"♫ played in the background on Caitlyn's end of the line. "Hear what I'm playing? Remember us dancing to this in D.C.? Have you ever listened to the lyrics?" The volume increased sharply.

Avery had never paid close attention to the lyrics of this song, and he had to admit, while not explicit, they were pretty damn racy. The volume lowered, and Caitlyn came back on the phone crooning like Madonna, as if she'd spent days singing along with the Material Girl.

"I want you to talk dirty to me, baby," she said. "But first, listen to what I'd do to you. Where are you by the way? Your bedroom, sitting in a chair, right?" She made a throaty sigh. "I'm rubbing myself under the covers and imagining you're here with me."

A pleasant memory flashed into Avery's mind: Caitlyn and him in the elevator vestibule, and her taking his hand, sliding it down her bikini bottoms, and placing it on her clitoris.[48]

"Close your eyes and imagine it, baby," Caitlyn said. "I walk into your bedroom wearing a trench coat. When I take it off, I've got nothing on underneath. Nothing but my naked body—hot, ripe, and ready … for *you*. I get on my knees and peel off your underwear. Then I rest my tits on your legs and inhale your throbbing love-stick. I give you a blowjob so amazing, you pass out when you come."

Caitlyn giggled, then continued. "Afterwards, I suck you again, and when you're super hard, I straddle you in your chair, lower myself onto you, and clench your cock with my tight little pussy. I'm facing you and my big, perky titties are rubbing against your muscley chest, and you're bouncing me like a ragdoll as we stare into each other's eyes." Caitlyn gasped. "Oh, you feel so good inside me. Oooh, baby…!"

---

[48] The day he'd returned from the trip, Avery did some research on female anatomy. Between Jack and Jill's copy of *The Joy of Sex*, an issue of *Penthouse*, and the *World Book Encyclopedia*, Avery figured out that the "button" he had successfully manipulated on Caitlyn was her *clitoris*. Intrigued, he read *The Joy of Sex* cover to cover in an afternoon.

"Caitlyn, enough! I can't do this. Goodbye."

Avery hung up the phone and shoved it away like it was radioactive. He was simultaneously aroused and repulsed by Caitlyn's dirty talk. Before her handjob, the most he'd done with a girl was some light making out with Inge Ibsen. The call was also shocking—shocking how good Caitlyn was at dirty talk. Avery's inner thigh looked like he was shoplifting a Hickory Farms summer sausage.[49] Once he'd caught his breath, he checked to make sure the recorder had worked. Damn had it worked; he was surprised the tape hadn't melted. He rewound and ejected the cassette tape, slid it in the envelope with Caitlyn's letter and the photos, hid the envelope in the back of his filing cabinet, and locked it.

All ... You ... Want!

Avery had to get his mind off Caitlyn and do something else—fast. Her simulated fellatio with the Blow Pop, and her vividly erotic story describing what she'd do to him, had instigated a chain-reaction and core meltdown that left Avery literally *burning up* with lust.

Avery stripped off his T-shirt and jeans and slipped on his Adidas track suit pants. They were the same baggy ones he'd worn in D.C. during Caitlyn's handjob. Liberated from the tight jeans, his wood wagged ridiculously inside the loose nylon pant leg. Shirtless, he held the track suit jacket in front of his groin, grabbed his Walkman, and headed downstairs.

"Ace, what'cha doin'?" Sabrina called to him.

"Working out."

"Can you help me with my algebra?"

"I will—later."

The unfinished basement, a suite of two rooms with exposed foundation walls and unfinished wood framing, was Avery's summer residence, and it served as his year-round home gym. He snapped the pull-chain on the overhead light, glanced at the space heater, and

---

[49] Hickory Farms, a retail store that sold gift boxes of cheese, cracker, and sausage assortments, was a fixture in many American malls during the 1980s. The store was especially popular as a place to buy last-minute Christmas gifts for dads.

threw the windows open instead. An icy gust enveloped his burning, naked chest. Caitlyn's phone call had been positively incendiary.

Avery lay on the weight bench. Picturing nude the various girls he knew—Caitlyn, Dina, Irina, Inge, and Miss Shipley—he bench-pressed the 200-pound barbell eleven times. Then he pressed play on his Walkman, and as Van Halen's ♫"Panama"♫ blasted in his ears, he went into a workout frenzy: push-ups, pull-ups, crunches, triceps dips, military presses, concentration curls, squats, hamstring curls, and calf raises—so many reps of each exercise that he lost count.

When he finally collapsed half an hour later, Avery was physically exhausted, but the fog of lust was as thick and intoxicating as ever. While sitting on the bench catching his breath, he eyed the phone book and rotary-dial telephone on the desk across the room. Why shouldn't he call Caitlyn and ask her to come over, or call a cab to drive him to her place? The girl was smoking hot, and if Avery was honest with himself, he wanted her as badly as she wanted him. Furthermore, Caitlyn was probably right that Penny wouldn't have sex with him until they were married. Ugh … Avery couldn't wait for sex until he was married; his scrotum would explode! And then a thought popped into his head that made him shiver: what if he passed up this chance to lose his virginity to a hot-to-trot, gorgeous girl like Caitlyn, and a similar opportunity never came his way again? The opportunity with Inge last summer—had already fallen through.

He went to the desk and flipped through the phone book until he found a "C. Cray" in Vanderbush Mills. Caitlyn had said her mom's name was "Cassie"; "C. Cray" must be her. He snatched up the handset, put his finger in the hole for the first number, and dialed frantically. The phone number was mostly 8's and 9's, so each revolution of the dial took a long time, and as the dial whirred, Avery critiqued what he was doing.

Dude, she's a sure thing. Penny might technically be your girlfriend, but all Caitlyn wants from you is sex. No love to complicate things. Caitlyn knows you need sex, and she's eager to give it to you. It'll be like in Trading Places—*where Don Ameche wags a bottle of whiskey and says to Eddie Murphy, "Whiskey! All … you … want!"—except in this case it'll be Caitlyn wagging a partially closed fist near her lip-glossed open mouth and saying, "Ace ... blowjobs! All ... you ... want!" Keep dialing, Ace! Half an hour, tops, and you'll have relief. Go! Keep dialing!*

But Penny's your girlfriend now. Don't do this. Besides, it's snowing hard out there. Caitlyn won't be coming over, and cabs won't drive you.

No, don't slow down. Don't stop! Oh, you putz!

He slammed down the receiver and pounded the desktop. Still shirtless, he ran out to the garage, slipped on his training gloves, and punched the heavy bag, making the chain clank. He worked fast, fierce combinations into the bag, and when he finally stopped, his face and chest were slick with sweat. Avery finished with one more punch—an Apollo Creed-inspired overhand right—then grabbed the snow shovel and went outside.[50]

Three inches had fallen since he'd gotten home, and it was coming down hard. The snow melted the second it touched his hot skin. Avery lay on his back in the snow and made snow angels, hoping it would cool him down, but his skin scoffed at the so-called cold. He got back up and went to work with the shovel, clearing the walkway in two minutes. Then he tackled the driveway. Starting at the garage, he jogged towards the cul-de-sac, pushing the shovel in front of himself and throwing the snow on the lawn when it became too heavy to push. While he shoveled, the falling snow melted on his skin and trickled icily into his pants, but even that did nothing to douse the fire in his loins.

A battle was going on in his mind, a battle between Lust and Reason, and Reason was getting its ass kicked. He should go inside and call Caitlyn, and if she couldn't make it over tonight, he could at least have phone sex with her. Or ... he had that sexy recording of her inside. That tape was just sitting up there, waiting to be played at his leisure. Avery glanced at his bedroom window. The glass glowed warmly. Caitlyn's scalding dirty talk and her Blow Pop-sucking echoed in his head, and then he gasped—those nude Polaroids of her! Avery walked up the driveway, accelerating with every step. Halfway to the house, he dropped the shovel and broke into a sprint.

---

[50] Apollo Creed was the nemesis of boxer Rocky Balboa in the early movies of the *Rocky* franchise.

The Perfect Curtain Line

After a much-needed shower, Avery got dressed, went out to the living room picture window, and gazed out at the falling snow.

Where the hell were Jack and Jill? As usual, they hadn't left a note or an answering machine message about where they were going or what time they'd be home.

Avery should have been used to this crap by now. From the time he was six or seven, he'd known his parents liked to party, and he, Sabrina, and Julia had spent dozens of nights staring out windows like this one, wondering whether his parents would make it home alive. A few years ago, he'd told Jack and Jill that he and his sisters worried about them, and they'd promised to be more responsible and considerate, to call in the future, but it didn't last. Inevitably, they broke their promises.

His parents had many good qualities—they were charming, charismatic, funny, and hard-working—but being doting parents wasn't one of them. Although they would claim otherwise, they had a fixed hierarchy of importance in their lives. They as a couple, inseparable Jack and Jill, came first; their work and partying after work came second; and Avery and his sisters came last.

Ever since Jack became a sales manager and trainer for IBM, his parents' after-work partying had graduated to cocktails and "working dinners," where Jack and Jill were schmoozing some executive in Manhattan or Westchester, but the result was the same: most nights, they didn't get home until late, and if Avery and Sabrina wanted any dinner, Avery had to cook it. He was starving. He hoped there was food in the refrigerator; sometimes there wasn't because Jill despised grocery shopping.

Avery spent some time *helping* Sabrina with her algebra homework (she was an expert at manipulating him into solving the problems for her), then shut her door and went out to the big living room stereo. The component system had a receiver, turntable, equalizer, dual cassette deck, and reel-to-reel tape deck. With the exception of the IBM PC in the corner (ostensibly the "family" computer), the stereo was the best piece of electronics in the house, and Avery loved blasting his music on it.

It had four 200-watt speakers, each of which, at four feet tall, was taller than the character Tattoo on *Fantasy Island*.[51] Avery popped in a mixtape appropriately labeled "Sheer Powah Mix," cranked the volume, and bolted into the kitchen—like a miner from a lit fuse on a stick of dynamite.

He was rummaging through the fridge when the syncopated bass and drums of ♫"Back in Black"♫ shook the kitchen walls. The shockwave from the first guitar strum caused him to whack his head on the refrigerator.

There was just enough in the fridge and the pantry to make a simple dinner: a two-pound slab of ground beef (which, miraculously, Jill had had the foresight to defrost); two boxes of Hamburger Helper; and a bag of frozen peas, carrots, and corn. Avery set up the electric skillet on the counter, browned the beef, drained the fat, and played spatula air guitar around the kitchen.

When everything was done, he shut off the skillet, made himself a big plate, brought a plate to Sabrina, and ate at the kitchen counter. Then Sabrina flashed past the doorway and the stereo shut off.

"Dammit, Sabrina, I was listening to that!"

"Jack and Jill are home!"

"Whatever."

Avery heard them before he saw them. The front door opened and thumped shut. He watched his parents climb the stairs. Jack wore a suit and tie, so Avery figured they had come from one of their schmoozing dinners. They weren't stumbling, but they *were* conspicuously clutching the handrail. Avery took his plate to the far counter and continued to eat standing up. Jack took Jill in his arms, and they waltzed around the kitchen. Jack was humming a tune, Jill was giggling, and they smelled strongly of gin, tonic, and lime. Always lime.

Jill kissed Avery on the cheek. "Honey, why don't you sit at the table? You'll get sick if you eat standing up. Here—take a napkin." She shoved it under Avery's arm.

---

[51] The character Tattoo, played by 3'11" French actor Herve Villechaize, was famous for his line, "The plane, the plane," when he spotted the airplane gliding into Fantasy Island with a new batch of guests.

"I'm fine, Mom. I was going in my room anyway—homework."

Sabrina appeared in the doorway behind them when Jack spotted the fryer on the counter. He huffed.

"Was Sabrina using that again?"

In the doorway behind them, Sabrina clasped her hands together and pleaded to Avery with her eyes.

"No, I did," Avery said.

Sabrina grinned and gave him a double thumbs-up.

"Hey," Avery said, "did you see that I shoveled?"

"Yeah," Jack said, "but you dumped the shovel in the friggin' snow. Why the hell'd you do that?"

Avery recalled the suffocating fog of lust he'd been dealing with, and then one of Bond's best lines from *Goldfinger* popped into his head. Bond is on the phone with Felix Leiter saying he'll meet him for breakfast when torridly sexy blonde Jill Masterson, wearing nothing but Bond's shirt, whispers seductively in his ear, "Not *too* early." Understandably, Bond puts Leiter off.

"Sorry, Dad," Avery said. "Something big came up."

Having delivered the perfect curtain line, Avery excused himself to his bedroom.

19

O N FRIDAY afternoon, because Penny was at her father's, Avery
decided to spend the weekend with his grandparents. A lot had
happened since he last saw them, and he was hoping that a weekend
with Pa and Gram, away from girls, would soothe the savage, horny
beast inside him. Between pining for Penny and craving Caitlyn, he
was a damn mess.

Avery was walking from the bus stop to his house when a U.S.
Mail Jeep drove past him on its way out of the cul-de-sac. The
postwoman, a shapely brunette in her early 30s, winked broadly and
gave him a finger-wave. Avery grinned and waved back. He got the
mail in the mailbox and saw his grandfather's Mercedes-Benz idling
in the driveway. Pa was behind the wheel reading a magazine while
cigarette smoke wafted out the car window. The driver's door opened,
and Pa got out.

He was wearing his usual casual clothes: a thin green quilted
jacket, red flannel shirt, paint-stained corduroy pants, white socks,
and slippers. When he spotted Avery, he broke into a shuffling run
up the walkway, and bounded up the front steps to the door. When
Avery reached him, Pa was panting.

"Beat ya, sonny," he said.

"Barely." Avery got out his key and unlocked the door. "And only
because you cheated. I didn't know we were racing."

"Avery Christy Craig, your grandfather is sixty years older than
you. He needs every advantage he can get."

"Fair enough," Avery said.

Inside, while Pa used the bathroom, Avery retrieved his pre-packed suitcase from his bedroom, fed the cat, and got two cans of Coke and a box of Cheez-Its from the kitchen. He was waiting by the front door when Pa came down the stairs. Avery opened the front door and waved Pa out with a flourish.

"Thank you, kind sir," Pa said.

Right on Time

When they were at the car, Avery nudged his grandfather.

"May I drive?" he said.

Pa fixed his twinkling blue eyes on him. "You legal yet?"

"Yup," Avery said. "Got my permit the other day."

Pa tossed Avery the keys and glanced at his watch. "Don't dawdle. Rockford's on in half an hour."

"You can count on me, Pa," Avery said.

Inside the car, Pa cracked the passenger window and lit a new cigarette. Avery handed him a Coke, opened one for himself, and started the engine. He ate some Cheez-Its, then Pa tried a few. Declaring them "not bad," he cautioned Avery about spoiling his supper; Pa had made one of Avery's favorite meals: homemade chicken pie. Pa tapped the dashboard clock.

"Hurry up, Jeeves. Time's a'wastin'.'"

Checking the rearview mirror, Avery put the car in reverse and backed down the driveway.

"Don't worry, Pa—we'll make it. I'll drive like Rockford to get us there, just watch."

At the corner of his street, Avery passed some of the younger kids. Hank, Dean, Bullfrog, Jen, and "Maizey" (Delilah) were making a snowman. Avery honked the horn, causing Hank to drop a clump of snow. Hank got the other kids' attention and pointed at the car.

"Friends of yours?" Pa asked.

"Yeah, the younger kids. They look up to me."

"Showin' off a little, eh?"

"Damn right. It's the older kid's prerogative, Pa—showing off for the younger ones."

Pa snorted and took a sip from his Coke. He held up the can and appraised it in the gray February light. It was good, but nothing like the Coca-Cola he'd had as a kid.

"Back then," he said, "a Coke had some real *kick*. I think they used to put a pinch of cocaine in it."

"*Cocaine*?!" Avery said. "No way, Pa! You're kidding."

"Nope. As I recall, the stuff had significant *zip*," he said.[52] "Drink a Coca-Cola, and ten minutes later you were ready to fight a lion."

"Hey, Pa—were there any Coca-Cola addicts when you were growing up? I bet there were."

Pa chuckled. "Not exactly, but one of your Uncle Cal's friends, Pete Godfrey, used to drink a couple of Cokes a day, and anytime you saw him around town, he was always walking briskly. Fastest walker I ever met."

"That's hilarious," Avery said.

Out on Woodside Creek Road, Avery got the car up to 60 mph. The posted speed limit was 45, but Pa didn't say anything. When Avery reached the T intersection at Merlinsville Road, he turned left, then made a right onto Saxon Road. They passed sprawling fields where corn stalk stubble peeked out of the snow, crossed two state roads, and headed up Chestnut Mountain.

"So, the prodigal grandson returns from our nation's capital," Pa said. "How was the trip?"

Avery said it was great, thanked his grandfather for paying for it, and described two of the highlights—Ford's Theatre and the Capitol. Regarding the White House visit, he first mentioned that because their congressman had screwed up the dates, when they arrived at 1600 Pennsylvania Avenue they were turned away. Pa interrupted him before he could finish the story.

---

[52] Actually, while the original Coca-Cola formula *did* have cocaine in it (it was a combination of cocaine and another stimulant, the African Kola nut), by 1903 (some six years before Avery's grandfather was born), the U.S. government forced the company to stop using cocaine in the recipe. The *zip* Avery's grandfather remembered was caused by a different ingredient. Because they'd had to remove cocaine from the formula, Coca-Cola *doubled* the amount of caffeine in the beverage. This high level of caffeine remained in the beverage until the 1920s.

"You're better off," Pa said. "No need to see the White House with that jackass in there."

"Pa, why don't you like President Reagan?"

"The man's an actor," Pa said, "and a mediocre one at that. He's not qualified to be President, and his economic policies are hogwash."

"I'm sorry, Pa, but I met with the enemy," Avery said.

He explained that when his schools were turned away at the gate, Avery called Senator Kennedy, whom he had met at the Capitol earlier that day, and the senator called the White House tours office and got them in. Avery added that his group met President Reagan face-to-face. However, he didn't tell Pa that he'd made President Reagan laugh, or that he'd had his picture taken next to him; there was only so much that his grandfather, an FDR appointee and lifelong Democrat, could take.

Pa shifted in his seat and looked at him askance. "How'd you meet Senator Kennedy?"

Avery told him that he was kissing a girl in the Senate Gallery when Senator Kennedy spotted them. The senator gently scolded Avery and summoned him to his office.

Pa squinted at Avery. "Are you sure it was Senator Kennedy and not one of his aides?"

Avery knew that when Pa asked if Avery was *sure*, he was really asking if Avery was telling the truth. A self-admitted shirker and exaggerator in his youth, Pa had a built-in, highly accurate bullcrap detector, and he also knew about Avery's burgeoning gift for storytelling. Not that Avery could blame his grandfather for being skeptical. Avery had exaggerated, embellished, and outright *lied* so often (and for no reason) that he hardly believed himself anymore.

"No, it was him, Pa, I swear," Avery said. "He was a great guy. He gave me a Coke from a bar in his office."

"Promise you're not pulling my leg?"

"No, I really met him."

Avery described how he'd told the senator that Pa had been in FDR's administration, and that the family had always voted Democratic. The senator, Avery added, had invited him to do an internship in his office, and he even called him by his nickname, Ace.

"Like," he said, "when I called about getting into the White House, the senator said, 'Don't worry, Ace. I'll take care of it.' He gave me his business card and said I could call anytime. Check it out." Avery flipped open his billfold and showed his grandfather the business card.

"That's something," Pa said. "You say he was a nice guy?"

"A great guy, super gracious," Avery said. "He said I reminded him of his older brother Joe when Joe was my age."

Pa chuckled, patted him on the shoulder. "Ace, you're a wonder."

Avery turned his attention back to driving. The Mercedes was a delight to drive—so smooth and effortless—but because it had an automatic transmission it was also a little boring. Avery preferred the standard shift on Jack's Toyota Camry.

On the other side of Chestnut Mountain, the road twisted and switchbacked, and Avery spotted a sleek red sports car in the rearview mirror. The car was two curves, or a quarter mile, behind him, but gaining fast. Avery sped up to lose the guy. With the snow on the mountainside, and the deep ravine just off the road shoulder, the scene made Avery think of Bond driving in the Alps in *On Her Majesty's Secret Service.* He sped up. At the end of the switchback, he coasted into the sharp turn and accelerated out of it.

"Take it easy," Pa said.

"Trying to get us there in time for *Rockford.*"

"Better we get there in one piece."

They plunged down the steep hill past Tyner Park. Avery braked and glanced in the rearview. The red sports car was nowhere to be seen. What if Avery's expert slaloming had caused the driver to crash through the guardrail, plummet into the ravine, and explode? But there were no signs of smoke; nothing but the white of the snow and the gray of the heavily salted road.

He was doing 60 mph down the long hill past the park's playing fields. The sun had come out and glared off the snow. Avery reached in his bomber jacket and slipped on his aviator sunglasses. Then, in his side-view mirror, there was a red flash. The Mercedes was jostled as the sports car, a red Corvette Stingray, streaked by like it was an F-16 fighter jet flying inches off the ground. The sudden kerfuffle startled his grandfather, who jumped in his seat, knocking some cigarette ash on his pant leg. He brushed it off.

"Jesus!" Pa shook his head. "That's too fast!"

"I know," Avery said, "it's like the jerk was racing me."

"Horse's ass."

When they reached the traffic circle, the speeding Corvette was long-gone, and the drama was over. Avery turned onto Pheasant Ridge Road, and they passed the new township firehouse. According to the clock on the dashboard, they only had nine minutes until *The Rockford Files*.

"How was the rest of your trip?" Pa asked.

Avery briefly mentioned some of the other places they'd gone—the Smithsonian; Arlington National Cemetery, with the Tomb of the Unknown Soldier and President Kennedy's gravesite and its Eternal Flame; Lincoln and Jefferson Memorials; the National Gallery, and the National Zoo. He also mentioned the tour of FBI Headquarters and told his grandfather that he'd decided he was going to work for the CIA, but Pa didn't seem to hear him.

"See that panda Ling-Ling?" Pa asked.

"Sort of, but the damn thing was hiding behind a rock." He thought of Caitlyn and smiled. "Talk about a bait and switch."

Pa snickered. Avery was about 100 yards from the driveway when Pa pointed and said, "The mail, Jeeves, if you please."

Avery pulled up beside the oversized mailbox and got the mail. He put the giant pile in the back seat, then turned into the driveway. He crept down the hill, crossed the brook at the bottom, and snaked carefully around the trout pond, but as soon as he reached the tennis court, he put the "pedal to the metal" to make it up the hill. Patches of ice caused the rear end of the car to fishtail. Just before he reached the crest, he let off the gas and the car's momentum carried them into the plateaued parking area. He pulled up next to the walkway and cut the engine. Pa patted Avery's shoulder.

"Good show, Jeeves," he said. "Jim Rockford couldn't've done better." He nodded at the dashboard clock. "And with time to spare."

"Go ahead in, Pa," Avery said. "I'll bring everything inside."

Pa got out, bounded up the steps, and shuffled into the house. Avery followed with his things and the pile of mail, which he placed on the sideboard near the back door. Gram tottered into the kitchen.

"There are my two men. Right on time."

"You can thank your grandson for that." Pa's voice faded into the bar. "Ace chauffeured me expertly…"

Avery put his bags in the living room, beneath the fold-down stairs to the loft. In the kitchen, Gram smothered him in wet kisses.

"My only grandson," she said. "Tell me about your trip."

"Can I tell you later, Gram? I'd like to watch *Rockford* with Pa."

"Okay, dear."

The Gracious Thing to Do

Avery went into the Bar.[53] A fire popped and crackled in the woodstove, and sun streamed through the windows that abutted the greenhouse. The door to Pa's office was closed. Pa stood at the sink behind the wet bar. The water was running. Avery knew what his grandfather was doing: urinating in the sink. Avery went down the steps to the TV, turned it to the correct channel, and adjusted the TV antenna rotator until the picture came into focus.

Gram walked in from the kitchen. The bar counter blocked Pa up to his neck, so she couldn't see what he was doing, but she'd caught him doing it before, so she knew. She sucked her cheek in disapproval.

"Oh, Henry, I wish you wouldn't do that."

He grinned. "No time, Tish." He zipped up, washed and dried his hands, and hustled down to his seat by the window. "Show's on."

"Would you like a cocktail?" she asked.

"Sure." Pa lit a cigarette. "A Perfect would be nice."

---

[53] A bit of *mise en scène*: In most homes, an extension off the kitchen would be known as the family room or TV room. In Pa and Gram's house, however, the quasi sunroom had been dubbed "The Bar" because it had a large wet bar, and since copious alcohol consumption was the top priority of visiting relatives and guests, the Bar was the most important landmark in the house. The sunroom half of the Bar had a heated tile floor and built-in sofas along the walls, and it held the only TV in the house. The number of south-facing windows in the room made it terrible for watching television, but it was a comfortable space for socializing.

"How about some cheese and crackers?" she asked.

"I'm fine, but if I know this fella"—he jutted his chin at Avery—"your grandson is hungry again."

"I'd love some, Gram," Avery said. "And a Coke."

She nodded and went into the kitchen. The theme from *The Rockford Files* began to play.

Pa was sitting on the built-in sofa in the sunroom area below, watching the TV. He held a cocktail in one hand and a cigarette in the other. A cloud of smoke hung in the air. Avery closed the curtains at their backs to stop the sun from glaring on the TV screen, then sat on the sofa next to Pa.

Gram brought in a cheeseboard with Muenster cheese and Keebler club crackers on it and placed it on a TV tray in front of them. Avery loved *Rockford*, but not as much as he loved watching his grandfather watch the show. Every time Jim Rockford made a wisecrack, Pa's mouth burst into a smile, showing his nicotine-stained teeth (which somehow on him was charming), and the smoke from his cigarette drifted around his face.

On the television, a tawny-haired woman with a great figure was talking to a guy in prison. Pa nudged Avery with his elbow.

"Good lookin' dame, eh?"

Avery scoffed. "You can say that again."

This was one of their favorite episodes: "Caledonia—It's Worth a Fortune!" In it, the girlfriend of a dying convict finds out where her boyfriend stashed the money from an old bank robbery, and she hires Jim to help her find it. In one scene, in order to shake some thugs trying to follow him and the girlfriend to the money, Jim drives his Firebird onto a car carrier until the thugs drive by.

"That is so cool," Avery said. "Someday *I* want to do that."

Pa took a drag from his cigarette and shook his head. "Foolishness."

After the show, Avery brought in several armloads of firewood. While he was building a fire in the living room fireplace, he told Gram about the D.C. trip, including meeting President Reagan, Senator Kennedy, and Special Agent Sloane at the FBI. He showed Gram the business cards from the senator and Agent Sloane, and she handed them back and said, "You should send them thank-you notes."

"They won't care if I send a thank-you or not," Avery said. "I doubt they'll even see it."

"You should do it," she said. "It sounds like all three of them took the time to meet with you, and everybody likes to feel appreciated—even Senator Kennedy and the President. It won't take much time, and it's the gracious thing to do. Trust your Gram on this."

Avery gave this some thought. It wouldn't hurt, and it'd be another way for him to stand out. He doubted any of his classmates would send thank-you cards.

"All right, Gram. I'll do it."

"I have the perfect cards," she said. "Back in a jif."

When she returned, Gram had already affixed stamps to the envelopes, so now Avery *had* to go through with it. Avery started by addressing all the envelopes using his new Mont Blanc fountain pen. He wrote the cards to President Reagan and Senator Kennedy first, thanking them for their time and for getting his school into the White House. Then, so they would remember who he was, he closed the cards with, "Sincerely, Avery 'Ace' Craig," and added a postscript: "If there is ever anything I can do to be of service to the country, or to you personally, please let me know." He wrote the same basic message to Agent Sloane, but after he'd written the postscript about "anything I can do to be of service," he realized there *was* something he could do: tell the FBI about Primo Pizza in Merlinsville, and how mob guys from the City met there regularly on Thursday nights.

He went up to the loft above the living room. It was a narrow space with a twin bed, bookcase, and a desk with a chair. The loft had a bathroom attached, though, which made Avery feel like he was an adult bachelor in his own apartment.

Last summer, Avery had brought Pa's old Royal Quiet Deluxe manual typewriter up to the desk in the loft. He imagined he was Ernest Hemingway, writing in a garret in Paris. He loved how, when he punched the keys on the typewriter, he became part of the machine itself—a machine cranking out words and sentences, with one sentence flowing into the next. Inspired, he started a letter to Agent Sloane to include with the card:

Dear Special Agent Sloane (Dan):

This is Avery "Ace" Craig. You might remember me as the student from Hancock High School who wants to work for the CIA after college.

Thank you so much for giving me and my classmates your excellent tour of FBI headquarters earlier this month. As a thank-you gesture, I'd like to give you a tip that I believe could lead to a major bust for the FBI.

Two years ago, during summer vacation, I worked for Primo Pizza, a pizzeria/Italian restaurant in Merlinsville, NY (only a few miles from my house; I would ride there on my bike). The restaurant is in the IGA Plaza, off the Empire State Parkway.

While I was working there, every Thursday afternoon the owner, Carmine, was a nervous wreck. He and his mother would cook up a storm, pull cash from the register, and stuff bundles of it in paper bags. At exactly four o'clock, three or four large sedans would park in front of the restaurant, and a dozen or so men entered.

On these evenings, Carmine and his mother closed the restaurant to the public, and any employees working that night were warned NEVER to enter the main dining room, where the men were gathered. The men would eat and talk in the dining room until well after midnight.

The reason I wanted to tell you about these meetings is that I think a lot of illegal activities were being discussed in that dining room. After a few weeks, I became curious about what they were discussing, and I went in a vestibule outside the dining room and eavesdropped. The men were talking about cement contracts and a union official, and one of them said, "Somebody should take care of that guy." One of them caught me, and he and the other men became irate. They didn't say anything specifically, but I could tell from Carmine's reaction (he kept saying, "Guys, guys, he's a kid, he's nobody, he doesn't know nothin'") that he thought I was in danger, and I—

"Aaaaa-vuh-ree!" Gram screeched from downstairs. "Dinner!"

Leaving the page in the typewriter, Avery washed his hands in the bathroom and went downstairs.

Halley's Return

Pa was at the head of the table, plating segments of chicken pie. With only Avery, Uncle Cal, Pa, and Gram tonight (there were seldom any guests during the winter), dinner was routine.

"Ah-hah!" Pa winked at Avery. "Glad you could join us, Mr. Hemingway!"

Gram and Cal chuckled. Pa had spoken loudly for the benefit of Charles ("Cal"), his 85-year-old brother. Cal was sitting at the far end of the table, squinting one eye, and aligning his placemat with something in the wood grain of the table that Avery could never see. He chuckled at Pa's comment.

"Hello, Avery!" Cal bellowed. "Sounds like you're hard at work on the next great American novel!"

"No, just a letter! It's nice to see you, Uncle Cal!"

Pa guided the dinner conversation toward Avery's D.C. trip, gesturing covertly with his thumb for Avery to speak up. Cal had been virtually deaf for as long as Avery could remember, but he refused to get a hearing aid. Initially, Avery wasn't thrilled to tell the story again, but once the storyteller in him got going, he talked nonstop about the highlights of the trip: meeting Senator Kennedy and President Reagan, visiting Ford's Theatre, and touring the FBI headquarters, where he got to see an agent fire a Thompson submachine gun. When Avery mentioned Senator Kennedy catching him kissing a girl in the Senate Gallery, Cal laughed and slapped the table.

Avery considered making his great-uncle laugh to be a major feat; most of the time Cal sat stoically in his chair, squinting down at the table, churning his jaw as if he were counting down his chews until he could swallow. Once Cal got a chewing rhythm going, his fleshy cheeks and jowls, and sometimes his ears, would jounce in time with his rigorous mastication.

When Avery finished his tale, he made up lost ground with the chicken pot pie by wolfing the rest on his plate and asking Pa for more. As if in payment for his storytelling, Pa gave him an extra-large scoop, dense with golden brown crust, big chunks of white meat chicken, two baby potatoes, several carrots and lots of gravy. Pa then steered the conversation toward Avery getting his driving learner's permit and the fact that he'd successfully driven Pa home in time to catch *The Rockford Files.*

When Pa finished, Cal cleared his throat and looked at Avery.

"Would you like to hear about some of your grandfather's misadventures with automobiles!?"

"Oh, dear," Gram said.

Avery smiled at his grandfather. "I'd *love* that, Cal."

Uncharacteristically garrulous that evening, Cal talked about the time that Pa started up the Model T and backed it right through the barn wall into the kitchen. The rest of the family had been eating breakfast at the time.

Pa chuckled and shook his head. "I never did learn how that shifter worked."

"How old were you, Pa?" Avery asked.

"Oh, I don't know … eight or nine."

Cal chewed his food metronomically while squinting one eye and adjusting his placemat. The table was quiet for a moment, and then Cal bellowed, "And then there was the day that father brought home the brand-new Hudson Super Six!" Cal peered down the table at his baby brother. "Henry decided to borrow it. He drove it sixty miles per hour, got two flat tires, and had to walk ten miles back to the farm to explain what happened. Father gave you the belt for that as I recall."

"He did. I couldn't sit for a week. Charles, do you remember what became of the Model T?"

Cal shook his head. Pa sat back in his chair and clasped his hands behind his head. His eyes twinkled. "*Well…,*" Pa drawled, glancing between Gram and Avery, "Cal came home from university one Christmas. A bunch of us were having a skating party on the river, above the mill dam. Somebody had brought a phonograph, and the group of us were skating to 'Toot Toot Tootsie Goodbye.'"

"Al Jolson," Gram said. "Must have been nineteen twenty-two."

"Sounds right, Tish." Pa continued with his story. He and his friends were skating on the river when Cal and his friend, Pete Godfrey, drove up with the Model T and went out on the ice with it. They spun the car in circles to the music."

"It's called 'doing donuts,' Pa," Avery said.

"Okay," Pa said. "Anyway, the song gets to the end and right when Jolson's sings, 'Goodbye, Tootsie … goodbye,' the Model T breaks through the ice."

Cal chuckled and slapped the table, then he and Pa sang together: "'Goodbye, Tootsie, goodbye … uh goodbye Tootsie … *goodbyyyye!*'"

Gram cackled, and Cal laughed so hard that tears came to his eyes. He dabbed his eyes with a handkerchief.

"To my knowledge, the Model T is still down there," Cal said. "We never could get it out."

"How deep was the water?" Avery asked.

"That's what made it so funny," Pa said. "When the ice broke, the water was only about five feet deep. The car disappeared, but their heads stayed above the surface."

"A remarkable automobile," Cal said. "Indestructible. I think the engine kept going underwater for a bit."

"Henry," Gram said, "you haven't mentioned your *accident*."

"Accident?" Avery said.

"It's how your grandfather and I met," she said. "He was fooling around in a car up near the university and had a major accident that nearly killed him. I was his nurse. Honestly, it's a miracle he's alive."

"You've never mentioned this, Pa," Avery said.

"Not one of my best moments," he said.

Gram patted Avery's arm. "That's how he got that bump above his eye. So, you take care not to drive like your grandfather."

Pa then shifted the conversation to current events, asking Cal when Halley's Comet would be most visible, to which Cal—a Cornell double-major in engineering and astronomy—replied with a frown, "Not until March or April—and poorly at that."

Cal said he'd seen Halley's Comet as a boy back in 1910, and he wanted to see it for a second time. He went into a dissertation about how the best views of the comet this time around were in the Southern Hemisphere. Pa joked that Cal should fly down to

Buenos Aires, which prompted another chuckle out of Cal. Gram chuckled as well.

"*Honestly*, Henry," she said. "Charles isn't flying to Argentina."

"He could." Pa leaned back in his chair with his hands behind his head and chewed a mouthful of pot pie. "Cal, Avery could join you!"

Avery perked up in his seat. Flying to South America with Cal to see Halley's Comet? What an adventure! What great material it'd be for a Jack London-esque novel!

"Sure," Avery said, "I'd be glad to. I speak a little Spanish—'*Yo hablo Español un poco*'—but I'll learn more before we go."

Pa looked at Avery and silently laughed.

"What I need is an observatory," Cal said. "Someplace high up so I can see the southern horizon. I contacted the alumni association to see if I could use the university's telescope, but apparently it's all booked up for Halley's return."

"That's too bad, Charles," Gram said.

A pall settled over the table, and then Avery asked Cal how high up he needed to be. Avery mentioned the fire tower on Chestnut Mountain—the tower visible from Cal's living room window. Avery had been up there many times, and it had a great southern view. Cal said he appreciated the offer, but the light pollution from the City (which was south of them) would obscure any view of the comet.

"But," Cal added, "now that you mention it, the university is allowing alumni to go to the summit if they bring their own telescopes. The trouble is, Ithaca is several hours away, and I'm not up to the drive."

Avery offered his and Mallory's services—for driving, carrying equipment, etc. Cal gazed at Avery.

"If you and Thomas were serious about this," he said, "I would pay you for your services."

According to Pa, Uncle Cal was quite wealthy, so for a split second a pleasant image played in Avery's head: Mallory and he smoking cigars, and each zipping his thumb across a stack of $100 bills. Pa spoke up from the head of the table.

"You wouldn't need to pay them, Charles." Pa narrowed his eyes at Avery. "*Would* he, Ace?"

Avery sighed. Pa had screwed him here a bit. Avery had seen Pa similarly seated at the head of boardroom tables during arbitration hearings in which he often ruled in favor of Labor over Management. Now he was selling Avery out, preventing him from being compensated for his labor.

"No, I guess not," Avery said.

"Let me think about it," Cal said. "If we do it, I'll pay the expenses."

"That sounds more than fair," Pa said.

Pa dished another scoop of pot pie on Gram's plate and tapped the spoon on the platter like a gavel. Having rendered his verdict, he returned to eating.

During dessert—Cal's classic apple pie, with homemade crust—Pa talked about an arbitration case for Eastern Airlines that he was traveling to next week. Cal, eating his pie and adjusting his placemat, apparently didn't hear him.

Out of nowhere, Cal boomed, "Sap buckets are full!" He fixed an eye on Avery. "I was hoping a certain muscular young man might help me for a few hours tomorrow! It's time to collect the buckets and boil the sap!"

Avery's mouth froze in mid-chew. For as long as Avery and his family had lived in New York, he'd always helped Cal with the sugaring, but he'd totally forgotten that it was late February already.

Avery had loved it when he was younger, but he'd gradually learned that the lugging of those heavy buckets, the thin wire handles biting into his hands, from the sugar maples behind Pa and Gram's house, across the driveway, the playing field, and the orchard, down to Cal's garage where the giant cauldron was set up over a propane burner, was beyond tedious. Last year, he'd been conveniently absent, on a winter camping trip with Scouts; this year, however, he was cornered. He was here for the weekend with nothing else to do, and there was no escape. Pa gave him a pleading glance.

"I think he'd enjoy that," Pa said. "Whaddaya say, Ace?"

Avery coughed. "Sure. What time?"

"We should let it warm up some," Cal said. "Let's say ten o'clock. Meet me at my garage, and we'll get started."

"Yes, sir."

Gram leaned into Avery's shoulder. "Wonderful of you to help your Uncle Charles."

"Yeah," Avery said.

Pa smiled. Avery knew the meanings of his grandfather's various smiles, and this one meant that Pa was laughing inside.

Away from Girls and Temptations

Hoping he could convince Mallory to join him tomorrow, after dinner Avery called his friend and talked up the syrup-making. One could say he *poured it on*, telling Mallory it was a lot of fun and promising he'd get to take some syrup home on Sunday.

"Lot of fun, my ass," Mallory said. In the background, the Mallorys' English Springer Spaniels, Pete and Riley, were barking up a storm. "Every year, you bitch and moan about how much you hate lugging those buckets."

"All right, you got me," Avery said. "I'll do it myself. Something else came up during dinner, though. This one I think you'll like."

Avery told Mallory about Cal's desire to see Halley's Comet again and his offer to pay all expenses for a road trip to the Cornell observatory, and for carrying his equipment and stuff. He said they'd take Cal's car, and he'd pay for the gas, food, hotel, everything.

"Sure, we can drive him," Mallory said.

The dogs' barking became obnoxiously loud. Mallory said he was stuck home alone with the dogs and needed to walk them.

"Call me tomorrow sometime," he said.

"I will. Later."

When he hung up the phone, Avery said goodnight to his grandparents, telling them he would be typing for an hour or so, and went back upstairs. He read over what he'd written to Agent Sloane so far, sketched a floor plan of the restaurant on a separate sheet of paper, and continued his letter.

> ... and I have to admit, from the way some of them were looking at me, I was afraid for my life. I quit the next day, but since then I've noticed that these mobsters continue to gather at Primo every Thursday.

If you decided to bug the restaurant (see enclosed sketch of the interior layout), there are four ideal locations for microphones:

1. The chandelier in the center of the main dining room (employees aren't allowed in here during their meetings). Indicated by "CH" on the sketch.

2. A small closet with louvered doors in the main dining room. Table linens and extra dishes and glassware are stored in here. Indicated by "SC" on the sketch.

3. Underneath the register counter in the front of the restaurant, or inside the electronic cash register itself. Many times, while assembling the bags of cash for the men, Carmine and his mother would speak in Italian. I think they did this so I and other employees wouldn't know what they were saying, and because they were talking about the mobsters visiting that night. I've noted the location of the register with an "R" on the sketch.

Finally, there are ceiling tiles throughout the entire restaurant (another great place for microphones and/or recording devices), and when I was working there, the restaurant didn't have an alarm system. The owner, Carmine, was a major tightwad, so I doubt he ever had one installed.

Agent Sloane, if you have some agents stake out the restaurant, the Bureau will see what I'm talking about. It's only about 2 hours north of New York City, making it an ideal, out-of-the-way mafia meeting place. If you end up using this tip, please keep my name out of it. I live only a few miles from Primo, and I don't want to put myself or my family in danger. Thank you for your time.

Sincerely,

Avery "Ace" Craig

P.S.: When you have a chance, could you contact the people you know at the CIA and tell them about me? If you need a character reference, you could talk to Senator Kennedy. We met when I was in D.C.

Finished with the letter, Avery signed his name, folded up all three pages (including his sketch of Primo's layout), and stuffed the letter inside the card. He sealed all three envelopes, took them downstairs, and left them on the counter with the other outgoing mail.

Avery got himself two more sumptuous slices of Cal's apple pie and ate them in the bar. At nine o'clock, he turned on the TV and rotated the antenna to the position for CBS.[54] The ♫"Theme from *Dallas*"♫ and credits sequence played. From its first season, the nighttime drama had been one of Avery's favorite shows. He loved how ruthless the J.R. Ewing character was, how the Texas oil baron was always three steps ahead of everybody else.

And then a scene came on with bosomy actress Victoria Principal in a low-cut blouse. Avery gasped, but not because of her cleavage; he'd seen a nude photo spread of her in one of Jack's old *Playboy*s, and to put it bluntly, her bare breasts were saggy and second-rate; they looked far better in a tantalizing tight sweater. It was the fact that tonight, between the way her hair was styled and her shimmering red lipstick, the woman looked exactly like Mrs. Jones.

Avery glanced at the box of Kleenex on the windowsill. He was considering rubbing one out when the picture became snowy and squiggly. He leapt over to the antenna rotator and adjusted it, but the picture stayed blurry. Damn it! He slapped the side of the TV set. If he were at home, where they had cable TV, he'd be watching the episode in perfect, static-free color.

The scene with Victoria Principal as Beverly Jones' lookalike ended. Avery eyed Pa's office door. Recalling Caitlyn's sexy talk the other day, Avery was tempted to call her and talk dirty with her. But he couldn't bring himself to do it. He'd shouted at her and hung up. Besides, he was stuck at his grandparents' for the weekend, so if Caitlyn got him revved up, they couldn't do anything anyway. It was too late to call her tonight, and tomorrow he'd be busy all day with the damn syrup. *Syrup.* That reminded him—he'd heard from some of the older guys at school about a scene in the movie *9½ Weeks* in

---

[54] In the days of analog televisions, when TV sets received their signals through the airwaves, it was common for a weak signal to manifest on a set as a "snowy," static-y picture with squiggles (wiggly lines) on the screen. Using an automatic TV antenna rotator, an antenna mounted on the house roof could be aimed in the optimal direction for that particular channel.

which a nude Kim Basinger had honey drizzled over her skin. Caitlyn, with her pillowy plump lips and bounteous breasts, looked a lot like Kim Basinger, albeit with shorter, differently styled hair. Avery imagined drizzling his homemade maple syrup over Caitlyn's naked body, then licking it off.

He thought of the nude Polaroids Caitlyn had sent him and regretted not bringing them along. But it was a good thing he hadn't; those things were so sexy, he'd masturbate until he died of dehydration. Besides, a couple of days away from girls and temptations would be good for him.

Groaning, Avery turned the rotator dial to the spot marked "NBC," tuned the TV to channel 4, and watched ♫*Knight Rider*♫ instead.

His Boyhood Days

Avery woke up the next morning in a nostalgic mood; somehow, he knew that weekends like this with his grandparents would soon be a rarity. Before breakfast, he went cross-country skiing around the property, then through the woods past the Crawfords' horse farm to the abandoned barn and back. He showered, dressed, and ate a big breakfast of blueberry pancakes, fried eggs, and bacon. Afterwards, he and Pa played chess, and then, at Pa's suggestion, they watched Bugs Bunny cartoons. At nine-thirty, Avery moaned that he was heading out to help Cal with the syrup. Pa, reading *The Atlantic Monthly*, said, "You're a better man than I, Gunga Din. Godspeed."

On his way across the playing field to meet Uncle Cal, Avery realized that this might be the last time he made syrup with him. He reflected on other fond memories of doing things with the old engineer: helping him install a Radio Shack alarm system in his house; sitting on the roller as Cal rolled the clay tennis court; and picking apples for him in the orchard and making cider with him. And there were all the generous things that Cal had done for him, his sisters, and the other kids that visited the property, like sharpening the kids' ice skates and testing the ice with an auger to certify its thickness; and when Uncle Cal said it was safe, it was safe. Avery was determined to do a good job with the sugaring today, and to help Cal see Halley's Comet again.

Cal was finishing up his second breakfast ("oatmeal, with salt") when Avery arrived. After Avery helped him set up the propane burner and cauldron, Cal described where the sap buckets were, and Avery trudged off to collect them. They were full to the brim and brutally heavy. The tapped trees were like three football fields from Cal's driveway, where they'd set up the cauldron, and because he had to walk slowly, it took Avery two solid hours to carry the buckets down, pour them through the strainer and into other buckets, rinse out the now-empty sap buckets, and return them to their tap hooks on the trees.

By the early afternoon, Cal, silently and patiently stirring, had boiled down the first batch of sap considerably. The sweet-smelling steam billowed around them in the cold air. Once again, Avery was reminded of how much work went into making a few quarts of syrup.[55] He agreed to meet his great-uncle again tomorrow morning to finish the job. He had a late lunch, then, with a few hours before supper, he went over to Harold Crawford's next door.

When Avery got there, Harold was in his basement playing with his model trains while Mr. Crawford tied flies at his workbench and smoked a pipe. Avery had always enjoyed running the locomotives around Harold's elaborate layout—loading logs onto the log cars; backing into sidings and hitching up boxcars and a caboose; whisking the long trains through tunnels and over bridges—and for an hour, he forgot that he wasn't a young boy anymore.

Then Avery's eyes landed on a plastic figurine of a blonde woman on a train platform, and for some bizarre reason, his mind was instantly hijacked by a vision of Caitlyn nude before him. He desperately wanted to have sex with her, and now that she was in his mind, he couldn't get her out.

Avery envied Harold's clear head. His 12-year-old friend wasn't plagued by thoughts of sex or girls; he was content to play with his trains forever. As for Avery, he knew that trains held no more interest for him, and that he'd never play with them again; his boyhood days

---

[55] The minimum sap/syrup ratio was 40:1, meaning that it took a minimum of 40 gallons of sap to produce 1 gallon of syrup, or 40 quarts of sap to produce 1 quart of syrup.

of carefree fun with other boys were over. He was on the verge of crying, so he wanted to get the hell out of there—fast. He patted Harold's shoulder.

"Sorry, buddy—I'm not feeling well. I've got to go home. It was nice seeing you."

Harold stared at the trains looping around the layout. "See you later, Ace. Thanks for coming by. Hope you feel better."

"Yeah," Avery said. "Later."

20

A VERY FOLLOWED Miss Shipley down a long concrete hallway dimly illuminated by sconces on the walls. She was wearing a pencil skirt so conspicuously thin, it was obvious she wasn't wearing panties underneath.

Enthralled by the sway and jiggle of Miss Shipley's impeccable backside, Avery followed her through a doorway, and the second he stepped over the threshold, four hulking men grabbed him. A tall woman with glossy black hair slinked toward him wearing nothing but a black brassiere, black panties, and knee-high boots. It was Irina Vacker. She tapped a riding crop against her bare thigh.

"Ah, if it is not the clever and handsome Ace Craig," she said. "I am Venus Mantrap. Thank you for joining us." She nodded at Miss Shipley. "Good job, Shapely Thinskirt."

"It was nothing, Number One," Thinskirt said. "Mr. Craig could not resist my callipygian *assets*."

In the far corner of the room, a spotlight switched on, lighting up an empty cane chair with a hole cut in the seat.

"Where have I seen this before?" Ace said. "Oh, crap! This is the torture scene from the Bond novel *Casino Royale*.'"

Next to the spotlighted chair, tied naked to an identical one, was Lee Skratt. Tied to two other chairs were Dina Tempestilli and Melody Bates, but sadly the girls were wearing bras and panties. Dina wore black underwear that looked great with her sable hair; Melody wore pale yellow underwear that matched her blonde hair. Venus Mantrap nodded at the henchmen holding Avery, and they stripped him, shoved him into a chair, and tied his wrists and ankles to it. His scrotum dangled through the hole in the seat.

"Hey, Ace," Lee said, "does this bite the big one or what? What do these chicks want? And why aren't they naked too?" He motioned with his head at Dina and Melody.

"Because Agent Thinskirt and I like nude *young men*," Mantrap said. "Girls do nothing for us."

"Yes, Number One." Thinskirt sat on Lee's lap and caressed his cheek. "And these two boys are like twin Adonises."

"Wait, I don't get it," Melody said. "Why are *we* here?"

"Yeah," Dina said. "I mean, it's awesome seeing Ace naked, but I'm not exactly stoked to be here."

"Silence, all of you!" Venus Mantrap slapped Ace hard on the chest with the riding crop.

"Ow!"

Lee leaned toward him and whispered, "Wait'll she gets you in the nuts. Lemme tell you, buddy—that shit stings."

Venus Mantrap sat on Avery's lap and rubbed his chest. She said Mr. Crain was on the verge of discovering his "little biology cheating scheme," and that if he was caught, the school, his Scout troop, his parents, the FBI, the CIA, Senator Kennedy, and President Reagan would all hear about it.

"It is clear, Mr. Craig," Mantrap said, "that you cannot continue to use the same cheating methods. If you do, you will be caught. You must change your system."

There was a loud rumbling noise, followed by the same rumbling noise, and then a bang. Avery was in his bed at home, lying on his back. The scantily clad girls in his dream had given him a preposterous boner, big-topping the covers around his groin.[56] Avery's cassette clock radio read, "6:02 A.M."—half an hour later than his usual wake-up time—and the first gray light of dawn seeped in his window. He heard the whine of the Toyota backing down the driveway, and he realized that the rumbling and banging that woke him had been his father opening and closing the garage door and leaving for work. It was a

---

[56] An obviously hyperbolic allusion to the main tent at a circus.

good thing his father had woken him, because Avery had been up late the night before making the mixtape for Irina, and he'd forgotten to set his alarm.

He had time for a short workout, a shower, and breakfast—boiled eggs on toast; he'd ask Jill and Sabrina if they wanted any—but ugh … he didn't want to get up. It would be cold and dark downstairs. He had to do it, though; he'd invested two years in building his body, and now that his efforts were paying off, turning the heads of several pretty girls, he had to maintain it. Speaking of turning heads, what about last week, in the school stairwell—Shannon O'Grady and Heather Doyle? Shannon had looked right at him, flipped her hair, and chirped, "Don't be a stranger … *Ace.*" Don't be a stranger? Was Shannon O'Grady, one of the hottest seniors at Hancock, encouraging him to ask her out? Unbelievable.

Another girl who liked his build—no, *loved* it—was Caitlyn. Why hadn't she been in his dream? Damn, he was dying to have sex with her! He wanted to be true to Penny, but Caitlyn was so hot, and she was throwing herself at him. He glanced at the bottom drawer of the filing cabinet, where he'd hidden her Polaroids and audio recording. He was dying to pull out the nude photos and relieve himself, but there was no time. And, if he masturbated now, he wouldn't have the strength to do the very thing that was garnering him so much attention from girls in the first place—work out.

Avery groaned and shook his fists. He'd have to swallow the discomfort and put his energy into the weights. He'd visualize Caitlyn and Irina together—like in his wet dream last week—and pound the weights as savagely as he wanted to pound the two of them. Given how horny he was, he could bench-press 250 pounds a hundred times. Now he couldn't wait to get down there.

Avery threw off the covers and swung his legs out of bed. He put on a T-shirt and a snug pair of briefs to compress and hopefully deflate his morning wood, then slipped on his Adidas track suit and sneakers. He grabbed his Walkman and the "SO SEXXXY BABYDOLL" mixtape, chugged a glass of water in the kitchen, and went downstairs, where he snapped on the light, switched on the space heater, and started his workout.

The Science of Kinesthesia

Avery finished his homework on the bus, and when he went to his locker before homeroom, Lee dropped by. Discreetly, because Dina's and Melody's lockers were nearby, Avery told him about last night's dream. Lee listened intently, like Avery was describing how to defuse a bomb, and when Avery finished, Lee commented on the dream.

"All right," he said, "so when Thinskirt sat on my lap, did she grind against me or anything? Like, I must of gotten *major* wood."

"I don't know," Avery said. "I wasn't checking out your *dong*."

Lee rolled his eyes back and to the side. "I must have got at *least* a semi. Make it a semi, Ace."

Avery tucked some books into his bag. "What do you mean 'make it a semi'? It was a dream, dude, not one of my stories."

"Oh, yeah."

"Besides," Avery said, "your balls were hanging through a hole in a chair. I doubt you were getting any kind of wood. You said Mantrap had whacked you in the nuts."

"What?! No way!"

Avery nodded. "You whispered to me, 'Wait'll she gets you in the nuts. Lemme tell you, buddy—that shit stings.'"

Lee cackled and shook Avery by the arm. Then, because Lee was holding an armload of books in one arm, the fingers of his other hand attempted a one-handed eyeball-boring. Somehow it wasn't as funny as a two-handed one.

"Oh, Acey-boy," Lee said. "See you at lunch?"

"Yeah. Later."

In English class, Avery got his latest test back (he'd received an "A"), and Ms. Wharton gave him an envelope with an 8″ x 10″ print of the White House photo inside. When class was over, he stayed behind to check it out. Like he remembered, he and Gemma stood on one side of President Reagan. Gemma had looked great that day: the sleek navy sheath dress, the string of pearls, the subtle makeup, the tortoiseshell glasses, and the gray cardigan sweater draped over her shoulders. Caitlyn was standing on the other side of the President, but what Avery hadn't seen when the picture was taken was the pose she had struck: standing saucily on one shoe with her other leopard print pump raised off the floor, and deftly touching President Reagan's shoulder to balance herself.

Later that morning, he got two more tests back, and neither grade was a surprise: a 73 in Latin, and a 68 in Geometry. For some reason, the poor grades in his two weakest subjects didn't depress him; today, as he headed to the cafeteria for lunch, he felt great.

Along the way, Avery passed the dark hallway where the burnouts and metal-heads hung out.[57] There was a ruckus at the far end. Avery strolled down to see what was happening. Quiet Riot's ♪"Cum On Feel the Noize"♪ blared from a boombox while a trio of girls on roller skates held hands and whipped around in a circle to the music. Not only was their skating technique awesome but their enthusiasm was infectious. Soon, a crowd, including Avery who had stopped to watch, was cheering and clapping to the beat.

Across from him, on the other side of the skaters, Dina was smiling, clapping, and bouncing on her toes in a flimsy Van Halen *1984* album T-shirt. The face of the pompadoured cherub was pleasingly distorted across her protuberant chest. Avery had been thinking about the biology quizzes since the bus ride into school that morning and hadn't thought of a single idea of what to do. Now, in one delightful slow-motion instant, Dina, his unwitting muse, gave him the solution. ♪"We're Not Gonna Take It"♪ began to play, and the rollergirls continued their routine to the new song. Avery smiled at Dina and gestured toward the cafeteria. She joined him inside.

"'Sssup, Ace?"

"Hey, beautiful—I've got a plan for the quizzes."

"Yeah, what is it?" Biting her lower lip, she made a fist and thumped Avery on the chest. "Tell me!"

"After lunch." He squeezed her slim upper arm. "Someone needs to put some meat on her bones."

---

[57] "Burnout" was a pejorative term for any teenager who did a lot of drugs and had potentially "burned out" his or her brain. Synonyms for "burnout" included "druggie," or "pothead" (or the abbreviated "head"). One had to be careful about using "head" to describe somebody, though, because there were also "metal-heads" (teens who loved "heavy metal" rock music) and "motor-heads" (guys into rebuilding cars).

"Nah." She stepped away then whipped around and thrust her chest in Avery's direction. "There's plenty of *meat* on me already."

She skipped away to the lunch line. When Avery turned around, Gemma Jones was staring at him from the cafeteria doorway. He waved. Gemma blushed, waved perfunctorily, and darted down the hall clutching a load of books to her chest.

The cafeteria cuisine *du jour* was the quintessence of inedible: pizza rolls (two hamburger bun halves topped with cold American cheese and watery, lukewarm tomato sauce), half-baked Tater-Tots, and soggy green beans. When they finished eating, the girls volunteered to take everyone's trays to the dishwashing conveyor belt. Avery got up and sat on the other side of the cafeteria table next to Lee, so when the girls returned, Avery would be across from Dina, and Lee across from Melody.

"What'cha doin', man?" Lee asked.

"You'll see." Avery nudged him. "You're going to like this, dude."

With their hands now free, Dina and Melody—the Double-D Wonder Duo—raced back to the table. Guys around the cafeteria gawked at them. Dina and her sublime endowments won the race. Melody, wearing a diaphanous pink blouse with the top two buttons undone, reached the table a second later, breathless. They slid onto the bench across from Avery and Lee. Dina stared at Avery with her thickly mascaraed eyes.

"'Kay, Ace," she said. "What's the plan, Stan?"

Avery tented his fingers. "Ladies, Lee … I read a great article in *Scientific American* last night. I think it's the solution to our problem."

This was an impromptu lie—another example of Avery's burgeoning abilities as a storyteller—but he kept a straight face. He said the article was about memorization techniques, and that psychologists at Harvard had given 100 students a list of multiple-choice answers to memorize. The students who memorized the lists by reciting the answers aloud *while bouncing* had the most accurate recall. Dina squinted at Avery with a whisper-thin smile on her lips.

"Bouncing, huh? Ace, it sure sounds like you're putting us on."

Avery decided to double-down. "Nope. It has to do with the science of *kinesthesia.*"

"Kin-ess-*what*?" Melody said.

"Bodily sensation," Avery said. "Like muscle memory."

"Oh yeah," Melody said. "I've heard of that thingy."

Avery cleared his throat. "Here, I'll demonstrate. Lee, today's quiz answers, please."

Lee tore a tiny scrap of paper out of his notebook and placed it in front of Avery, who skimmed the answers then recited them rhythmically while bouncing in his seat: "A-B, D-B, E-C-D"—Avery glanced at the paper—"A-A, C-C, B-A-D"—he took a breath and glanced at the paper—"B-D-A, A-B-E. See? Easy."

"Do it again." Dina covered the paper with her palms and gave him a waggish grin. "*Without* the paper this time."

"No problem." Grinning back at her, he started bouncing. "A-B, D-B, E-C-D. A-A, C-C, B-A-D. B-D-A, A-B-E."

"All right, I'll try," Dina said. "Gimme the list."

She recited and bounced like Avery had (although with infinitely more mammary allure), but only made it halfway through the list before cracking up, slapping the tabletop and convulsing with laughter. The cigarette-smoking cherub, stretched to the brink across her chest, seemed relieved. When Avery complimented her on a solid first attempt, Dina kicked him gently in the shin. By the knowing smirk she gave him, Avery could tell that Dina was on to him but would play along. He tapped his pencil on the edge of the table and raised his hands like an orchestra conductor.

"Okay, Dina, again—from the top. Sit up nice and straight."

She squared her shoulders and elongated her spine; she was an opera soprano about to launch into an aria. This had precisely the uplifting effect Avery had hoped it would. As she bounced and recited, guys at neighboring tables gawked and drooled.

She pumped her fist as she finished: "…A-B-E! Woo-hoo! Yeah!"

"Dina my dear," Avery said, "you're a natural."

"You bet I am. *All* natural." She gazed at Avery.

Melody leaned across the table and looked around wide-eyed at them. "Wow, it really works!"

"*Yeah* it does!" Lee nodded at Avery, then flicked his eyes back to Melody's cleavage.

Dina scoffed. "Yeah, it works all right." Under the table, she gave Avery a lingering nudge that was more footsie than kick.

Avery reminded them that everyone needed to change two or three answers to the wrong ones, because if they all got perfect scores every time, it would raise Mr. Crain's suspicions.

Lee folded his hands in front of him and leaned forward. "Okay, Melody, your turn."

Avery bristled when Melody opened her mouth. Sometimes her voice sounded like a dog's squeak toy.

"All right," Melody said. "Here goes … A-D, B-E, C—"

"No, no." Lee bounced in his seat. "A-B, D-B, E-C-D." Lee's pectorals, while impressively bouncy, paled in comparison to the girls'.

"Watch." Dina ribbed Melody and squared her shoulders again. "A-B, D-B, E-C-D!"

"Wow, Dina." Avery shook his head. "You have great … *memories*."

Dina threw her head back and laughed up at the fluorescent lights. Pot and perfume smells wafted across the table.

"Memories … mammaries?" Lee said. "Easy, Ace—*Penny* wouldn't like hearing you say that to Dina."

Damn you, Lee.

Dina stopped laughing. "Who's Penny?"

"Ace's girlfriend," Lee said. "Goes to Vanderbush."

"Ace, you've got a *girlfriend*?" Dina's eyes, normally hooded from a constant state of being baked, sprang open. For the first time since he met her, Avery saw them in all their hazel-green glory. Dina looked like she'd just heard that Avery was dying from a rare disease. "When did this happen?"

"We met about two weeks ago," Avery said. "On the Hancock-Vanderbush D.C. trip."

Dina gulped. "Oh. I'm really happy for you, Ace," and a crushing wave of regret slammed down on him.

Avery's shoulders slumped; his jaw slackened. Dina had liked him, possibly *loved* him, for years, and the agonizing fact was, he'd been too dense to notice, and he'd lacked the confidence to ask her out. As they stared at each other for a few seconds—seconds that felt like a complete reliving of the entire four years that Avery had known her—their chests heaved in unison. Avery's hands trembled from wanting to reach for her, but he couldn't move; regret over all those lost opportunities had frozen him in his seat.

All through junior high, Dina had given him so many signs, so many openings: smiling sleepily at him in class one rainy afternoon while the teacher blathered about *Silas Marner*; kicking his chair during the movie of *Romeo and Juliet* and gazing at him; laughing hysterically at his jokes; bumping into him "accidentally" as they passed in the Van Wilder stairwell; inviting him to drop by the deli where she worked after school, so they could "chat and stuff"; kissing a peanut butter cookie she'd made in Home Ec and handing it to him while it was still warm; and, during a field trip to the Museum of Natural History in Manhattan, yawning and resting her head on Avery's shoulder in the soothing shadow of the blue whale.

Oh, God, God, God, God—how could he be so stupid? He wanted to jump out of his seat and scream. He wanted to pound his head on the table, slap himself repeatedly in the face. He tried to tell her with his eyes that he'd always considered her a Roman goddess, and that he'd always loved her and always would. Behind her mascara, Dina's eyes glistened. Avery sensed that he and Dina were on the verge of diving across the table for each other, confessing their feelings, and making out right then and there, in the Hancock cafeteria.

And had there been a millisecond's more silence, they might have done just that. But then Melody's shrill voice startled Avery out of his daydream, and the moment was lost forever.

"Lee," she said, "I can't do this. Why can't we just do it the old way?"

"Because it's like Ace said—if we do, we're gonna get caught."

"We'll help you, Melody," Avery said. "Let's do it together. Ready?"

Dina subtly dabbed her eyes with a napkin. "Yeah, let's do this."

Huddling together over the table, bouncing in unison, they quietly recited the answers: "A-B, D-B, E-C-D..."

Operation Recompense

For Avery, Lee, Dina, and Melody, that afternoon's quiz went swimmingly, the four of them bouncing in their chairs as they wrote down their answers. Avery's bus ride home, however, was agony. He sat alone near the back and pretended to read but instead silently cried behind his book. The revelation about Dina at lunch had left him stunned, and now that school was over, he broke down.

A cauldron of conflicting questions bubbled inside him. Now that Avery knew how Dina felt about him, should he break up with Penny to be with her? Then again, what did Avery really know about Dina? They'd never had any deep conversations that he could remember. She might be his fantasy girl with a great sense of humor, and she might think Avery was smart and funny, but she was a serious pothead and Avery had never touched the stuff. She was also much more sexually experienced than Avery, having had older guys for boyfriends since junior high—a fact that made Avery uncomfortable.

After the bus dropped him off, Avery walked home and checked the mailbox. It was packed with mail, including a long box from the Columbia Record and Tape Club—his shipment of music on cassettes. This made him a little less depressed. Since he'd placed the order for his *other* shipment on the same day, that one might have arrived today as well. He needed to get to Brinkerhoff's house.

Holding the mail under his arm, Avery ran up to the house and dropped off the mail and his bag. He grabbed his pre-packed black covert mission knapsack out of his closet and stuffed a giant, empty nylon duffel bag inside it. Finally, he wheeled his mountain bike out of the garage and popped his "ACE'S COVERT MISSION" mixtape into his Walkman. With ♫"A View To A Kill"♫ playing in his earphones, Avery rode down the well-trammeled, snowy path behind his house to the Woodside development.

Operation Recompense was underway.

Originally a vacation community for city people built around a so-called lake (it was a glorified pond), Woodside was now a collection of aging bungalows with year-round residents. The streets around the lake were narrow, inconsistently one-way, and a goddamn maze. Brinkerhoff's house was actually in Avery's development, up the hill at the end of another cul-de-sac, but Avery needed to get there via Woodside in order to infiltrate Brinkerhoff's yard from behind. This way, if one of Brinkerhoff's neighbors spotted Avery, they'd think he lived in Woodside. He wended his way through the narrow streets, at one point riding along the lakeshore itself. This time of year, kids were often playing hockey out on the ice, but nobody was out there today; the lake ice was a mere skin.

Avery pedaled on, absently wondering if his elaborate scheme would be worth it, and whether it was fair to Brinkerhoff. Last summer, Avery had mowed the guy's lawn every week—twelve times total—but the man only paid him three times. At the end of the summer when Avery went to collect the balance, Brinkerhoff gave him a sob story about losing his job and agreed to pay Avery in a couple of months. At first, Avery believed him, but then he spotted the 30-something bachelor and IBM manager whisking in and out of the development in a brand-new yellow Corvette, the douche. When Avery went again to collect, Brinkerhoff outright refused to pay him, falsely claiming that Avery had done "a half-assed and sloppy job" and that he should be grateful he'd gotten anything.

All through the fall, Avery seethed over the insult, concocting elaborate plans for exacting revenge on Brinkerhoff. One such plan involved blowing up the Corvette. Since Avery's best friend E.B. ran a popular BBS that hosted hundreds of documents like "Phone Phreaking 101" and "Defeating Burglar Alarms," Avery had already read dozens of text files on illegal or borderline-illegal activities, including CIA covert operations and countersurveillance tactics, lockpicking, and making homemade explosives.[58] Avery had begun to make a list of the materials he would need when he had second thoughts. He realized that blowing up the man's car was way out of proportion to the offense, and so he tabled any plans for revenge.

But then, one day during Christmas Break while flipping through an issue of the Scouting magazine *Boys' Life*, Avery stumbled upon an ad for the Columbia Record and Tape Club: "THE BIG 1¢ STEAL! TAKE ANY 11 ALBUMS FOR A PENNY, THEN GET A 12th ONE FREE!" At that moment, Avery decided to recoup the money

---

[58] BBSes (Bulletin Board Systems) were the forerunner of internet websites, whereby two computers with modems (modulator-demodulators) could "talk" to each other over a telephone line. BBSes enabled computer users to send each other private messages; to read or contribute to public message "threads"; and to upload or download text files and computer programs.

Brinkerhoff owed him—and then some—by signing up the man and his fictitious wife and four daughters for a total of six club memberships. To make sure his handwriting and fingerprints didn't appear on the application cards, Avery had handled them with gloves and used the typewriter at his grandparents' to fill them out for the Brinkerhoff family. If the six memberships had been processed without a hitch, there should be 72 LP record albums (an $800 value!) waiting for Avery on the man's stoop.

Avery grinned. It would be "The Big Steal" all right.[59]

When he reached the end of the street in Woodside, Avery hid his bike in the bushes, tramped into the woods, and climbed a knoll that overlooked Brinkerhoff's backyard. The opening of ♫"The James Bond Theme"♫ with all its brassy swagger blared in his headphones. The birches and maples on the knoll were leafless this time of year; thankfully, the hillside was partially screened by scrubby evergreens. Halfway up the hillside was a phone company junction box that serviced the houses in his development and this part of Woodside. Avery knelt in front of it, threw off his knapsack, and shut off his Walkman. Then he pulled out his binoculars and testing phone.

The testing phone, a telephone company lineman's tool, was highly illegal. Two summers ago, E.B. had pinched a few of them out of an unlocked NY Bell Telephone van and gave Avery one. By clamping the testing phone's alligator clips to a pair of contacts in a junction box, Avery could use a stranger's telephone line to make calls anywhere in the world, or to listen in on conversations on that line. In this case, Avery wanted to be sure Brinkerhoff wasn't home before he swooped in.

Using the B-clip (or can wrench), a key-like tool attached to the testing phone, he got the junction box open. He connected the alligator clips to a pair of contacts, got a dial tone, and dialed Brinkerhoff's phone number on the rotary dial built into the one-piece handset. While listening through the earpiece, he trained the binoculars on Brinkerhoff's back windows, scanning for movement

---

[59] The fine print on the ad read as follows: a) "Plus shipping and handling." b) "If you join Columbia Record and Tape Club now and agree to buy 8 more selections [at regular club prices] over the next 3 years."

inside. The phone rang and rang. Apparently, the man wasn't just a skinflint about yard work; he was also too cheap to have an answering machine. When the phone had rung ten times with no answer, Avery put away the testing phone, closed the junction box, and scanned the property with the binoculars one last time. There were no cars in the driveway, no signs of activity whatsoever. From his vantage point on the hillside, Avery couldn't see the front yard, so there was a remote possibility that Mr. Brinkerhoff was out there.

Shouldering the knapsack, he walked through the woods bordering the yard until he could see the front of the house. He trained the binoculars on the stoop: six cardboard boxes covered the top step and the welcome mat. Each box was about one foot square— the size of LPs. Avery pumped a fist, put the binoculars away, and devised a plan for retrieving the boxes.

The front stoop was only 100 feet from his new vantage point, but if he ran straight across the lawn, his footprints would be starkly obvious on the untouched snow. A suspicious Brinkerhoff could easily follow the trail back to the junction box and where Avery had hidden his bike. The walkway and driveway, however, were clear of snow, which meant no footprints. Walking in the open increased the chances of him being spotted, but it was a risk he needed to take.

Avery continued through the woods to the cul-de-sac in front of Brinkerhoff's house. There, he pulled the empty duffel bag out of the knapsack, checked to make sure the street was clear, then ran along the pavement, up the douche's blacktop driveway, and up the cement walkway to the stoop. Sure enough, the six boxes *were* from Columbia House. Avery stuffed them into the duffel bag and got out of there, remarking to himself as he ran just how damn *heavy* six dozen record albums were.

From the cul-de-sac, Avery backtracked to the junction box, stepping in the footprints he'd made walking in. He hustled down the hill, slung the unwieldy duffel bag over his shoulder and balanced it on the bike rack over the rear tire. He pedaled toward his house.

There was only one thing left to do: get rid of the evidence. While he was on the other side of the lake, far from his house, Avery found a perfect place for a fire: under a small bridge where there were no houses around. At the bottom of the embankment, he removed the shrink-wrapped record albums from their incriminating outer boxes and packed them tightly in the duffel bag. Then he put the cardboard outer boxes, the mailing labels, envelopes, and invoices in a pile, lit them with a lighter and watched them burn. When they were cinders, he kicked snow over them, made sure the ground was cold to the touch, and climbed up the embankment.

Back on the bike, Avery put his headphones on and played the rest of "The James Bond Theme." As he pedaled home, Avery's favorite part came on: the swinging refrain with blaring horns.

"Screw you, *Dinker*hoff. The name is Craig. Ace Craig."

Operation Recompense—a.k.a., "The Big 1¢ Steal"—was complete.

A Damn Relationship

Back at his house, Sabrina was out. The Post-It note she'd stuck to the answering machine said she was at her friend Lacy's. Avery washed his face and hands, then brought the LPs upstairs, opened the box of cassettes he'd ordered, and lovingly shelved the music with the rest of his collection. It was one hell of a haul. He'd even gotten a few albums by bands he didn't care for, so he could give them to people as gifts: Weird Al Yankovic for E.B., Alice Cooper for Lee, and The Grateful Dead for Mallory.

The answering machine had a cassette tape that recorded messages from callers. There were two: one from Penny, one from Inge. Inge was noticeably drunk, rambling about how Avery never hung out with her anymore. Nobody was home, she said; they could drink some beers, listen to music, and make out. Then she complained about something, and Avery couldn't understand her because she was slurring her words. He shut off the answering machine and started toward his room to call Penny, but he was hungry. Penny could wait; food came first.

He made himself three grilled cheese sandwiches and took them into the dining room. While he was eating, Mr. Smithers hopped onto the chair beside his and bunted his arm. Avery fed the cat small pieces while staring out at the white and barren backyard. Outside, in the meadow near the woods, a pair of crows foraged in the tall brown scrub grass that peeked out of the snow. They zigzagged across the meadow, pecking under the snow, then, finding nothing, flew away. Avery pitied them for a split second, hoped they'd find something to eat somewhere else, but then he remembered he had to call Penny. He didn't feel like talking to her today. The revelation about Dina had hit him like a two-by-four in the skull. Adding to his worries, he and Caitlyn were fatally attracted to each other, and Avery had no idea whether Penny knew about the two of them.

Avery groaned. He'd thought that having a girlfriend would be a lot more fun than this: spending time with a pretty, sweet-smelling girl; going to movies and taking long walks with her; teaching her tennis, pool, and cross-country skiing; holding hands, hugging, and kissing her; pleasuring her and being pleasured by her; and eventually having sex with her. But with Penny, Avery hadn't had any of that yet; they hadn't even gone out on a date. With the exception of a few nice kisses, all he'd gotten with Penny was the annoying relationship stuff, which, Avery was learning, was friggin' exhausting. During the D.C. trip, Avery had had a constant low-grade headache, and now that headache was back and worse than ever. He needed fresh air; he needed to think.

He bundled up and walked out back, through the meadow where he'd seen the crows. It was cold, and the setting sun threw long, bruise-tinted shadows across the snow. A crow cawed in the distance, and then a breeze came up, blowing snow off a tree limb and scattering it into spindrift. Right off the path was a giant beech tree, a century old if it was a day. Avery leaned against it and gazed into the winter twilight.

He and Dina had had a moment today. Dina might love him, but he couldn't dump Penny, a girl who definitely loved him, for a girl who'd been giving him mixed signals for years. Dina had great taste (she thought he was brilliant and hilarious) and looks that stopped his heart, but she'd never said anything even remotely serious, and her only interests seemed to be rock bands and pot.

And what should he do about Caitlyn? Caitlyn was sexy and shrewd, had a jaw-dropping body, and was as attracted to him as he was to her. She was a terrific dancer, but she was also devious and unpredictable. Like, what kind of girl sends nude pictures of herself to her best friend's boyfriend? Avery wanted her desperately, but he didn't want to hurt Penny; the problem was, if he didn't see Caitlyn, she might tell Penny about Avery and her out of spite.

Penny was petite, cuddlesome, and classically pretty. She didn't have a body like Caitlyn's or Dina's, and she probably wouldn't do anything sexual with him for months, but she loved him and would be faithful to him. And she was a virgin, which meant that Avery would be her first. With Caitlyn and Dina, he might be their *fifth*. But did he want to be going out with Penny? Aspects of her personality— her constant anxiety about what other people thought, and her daily worry that Avery would break up with her—drove him crazy.

What if finding out about Dina's feelings today was a sign? What if he was supposed to dump Penny right now, before they went on a date, and ask Dina out instead? No, he wasn't doing that. Nor would he push away Dina or Caitlyn. If something developed between him and Dina, or him and Caitlyn, then he'd let it happen. He wasn't *married* to Penny.

It was getting dark and starting to snow. Avery crunched down the path. The back windows of his house were brightly lit, giving him a beacon to walk toward. He breathed the crisp clean air, felt the snow melting on his cheeks, and reflected on how wonderful it was to be young and alive with several girls interested in him. Wonderful, but also worrisome and a little terrifying.

Thrilled and Petrified

Inside, Avery changed into workout clothes, got the speakerphone from his Q-Branch drawer, and went down to the basement. The cat followed him and assumed his usual perch on the desk.

Avery turned on the space heater and connected the speakerphone to the rotary phone. He dialed Penny's number, switched on the speakerphone, hung up the rotary phone handset, and put the speakerphone on a chair next to his weight bench. When Penny answered, Avery was doing concentration curls with a 40-pound dumbbell. He said hello, finished ten curls, and switched arms. Penny remarked that the connection sounded strange, "like, far away and echoey." Avery said he was on a speakerphone so he could work out while talking to her.

"I was starting to think you weren't going to call," she said.

"I'm sorry. I had some things to do right after school."

Avery finished a second set of curls and moved on to flys. He lay supine on the bench and lowered the dumbbells slowly with his arms outstretched, then, breathing out, raised them in unison until they clanked together at the top.

When Penny asked what movie he wanted to see on Friday, Avery said he'd go to whatever she chose. Penny checked the newspaper to see what was playing this weekend.

"We'll go to the Fox Hills theater, right?" she said.

"Sure."

"How about *Pretty in Pink*?"

"Who's in it?"

"Molly Ringwald. You know, the redhead from *Sixteen Candles*? In this one, she plays a high school girl from the poor side of town and falls in love with a rich boy."

"Sounds incredibly dull," he said. "It's perfect. We can kiss in the back row through most of it."

Penny made a hissing sound, like she'd grazed a hot stove.

"Avery, my whole body is, like, *tingling*."

"Yeah? A part of me is doing a lot more than tingling."

She giggled. "Friday night—think about it. Finally! I've got butterflies. Anytime I think about you, my heart pounds and I can't breathe. And now that I have the pictures of you from the trip, forget it—I can't even think."

"You got the pictures back?" Avery went over to the desk, pulled a hand grip-strengthener from a drawer, and squeezed it ten times. "Are there any of you in that skirt I like?"

"I've got them spread out on the coffee table," she said. "Lemme see. Yes, it looks like there *are* a few of me in the skirt."

"Dibs," he said.

"Okay, I'll bring them on Friday," she said. "So, while you've been getting buff, I've been a total couch potato—vegging-out in front of the TV and eating chocolate. Something you should know about me, Avery—when I get stressed, I turn into a total chocoholic."

"What's stressing you, honey?"

"Everything. School, missing you, worrying you'll meet someone else and dump me, worrying about whether or not your parents will like me and—"

"They're going to love you. Everything will be fine."

"Okay, but there's something else," she said.

Caitlyn wanted Penny and Avery to double-date with her and Shane the following night—Saturday night. The four of them would go bowling. Avery flushed. The prospect of seeing his sexy Babydoll again thrilled and petrified him. In his mind, he fast-forwarded to Saturday night, and he *knew* Caitlyn would wear an obscenely sexy outfit, so he couldn't resist her.

He was doing everything he could to avoid Caitlyn and stay true to Penny, but fate was pushing him and Caitlyn together. If he went on the double-date, Penny might figure out that he and Caitlyn were nuts for each other, and Avery could lose both girls.

"I don't know," he said. "I don't like bowling."

"Please?" she said. "I'm a great bowler. We'll totally kick their butts."

Avery sighed. Who was he kidding? He couldn't turn up a chance to see Caitlyn again. Those legs, those lips, that butt, those boobs! He had to go, if for no other reason than to see her luminous smile again. God, he missed her.

"All right," he said, "one double-date."

"Oh, Avery, thank you! It's gonna be so much fun. I have to go now. Can we talk tomorrow, same time?"

"Sure."

"Bye," she said.

Click.

WHILE DOING his homework, Avery removed an old photo of his Scout troop from a picture frame and replaced it with the one taken at the White House. Jack and Jill were home for a change, and after dinner, Avery showed them the photo.

Avery described how, a minute before the picture was taken, he had made the President laugh, but his parents didn't seem to believe him. Jill glanced at the picture, said, "That's nice, dear," and returned to the kitchen. Meanwhile, Jack was stretched out on the love seat watching *Cheers*. When the program was over, Avery showed him the photo. Jack appraised the picture while drinking his usual quart-sized gin and tonic. In the middle of a sip, Jack's eyes bulged.

He pointed at the photo. "Who the heck is *she*? The one next to the President?"

Avery replied nonchalantly that the girl Jack was pointing at was Penny's best friend, Caitlyn. Avery had danced with her a lot during the trip, he said.

"Danced, huh?" Jack snorted, sipped his drink. "She's got a helluva nice set on her, Avery. You oughta be more than the girl's dancing partner if you can."

"'A nice *set?*'"

Jack chuckled and lowered his voice. "A nice set of tits."

For a microsecond, Avery considered telling his father that he'd seen, caressed, kissed, and sucked Caitlyn's most magnificent "set," and that she'd given him a magnificent handjob to match. But he'd promised Caitlyn that he wouldn't brag to anybody about what they'd done, and to Avery that included his father. He doubted Jack would believe him anyway.

"Who's *this* girl, the one right next to you?" Jack pointed at the photo. "She's cute, Avery, and she's sweet on you."

Avery said that was Gemma, an honors student bound for MIT. "And the only person she's sweet on is Bill Gates."

Jack shook his head. "See her starin' at you? She's not even looking at the camera—she's *moonin'* over you, son." Jack sipped his drink. "Looks a little on the straitlaced side, but she's pretty, and lemme tell ya, sometimes the ones that look like librarians, the smart, kinda up-tight ones, you get 'em in the sack and they just go crazy. Nine times outta ten, they're your best lay."

Avery groaned under his breath. "I'll keep that in mind, Dad."

Jack took another sip of his drink and stared into the distance. He smiled wistfully and lowered his voice.

"I once knew a woman that dressed like this girl—skirt and jacket sets, pearls," Jack said. "Her husband was a golf buddy of mine. One time, I go over to pick up a couple boxes of balls. The wife knows I'm coming by, and she answers the door in nothing but Saran Wrap. She'd wrapped it around herself and was wearing it like a dress. She asked me to take it off her. I'll never forget poking my fingers into that plastic and tearing it off." He sighed and sipped his drink. "Anyway, play your cards right, and I bet you could get this Gemma girl to greet you at the door wearing Saran Wrap. The Caitlyn girl too, prob'ly."

Caitlyn *definitely*, he thought.

"Yeah," Avery said, "but *Saran Wrap*, Dad? That's weird. I'd prefer it if they were wearing lingerie or a Wonder Woman or Batgirl costume. Something like that."

Jack shrugged. "Don't knock it 'til you've seen it." He scanned the rest of the photo. "Which one's Penny? That's her name, right?"

Avery pointed her out. Jack frowned with his mouth tightly shut and handed back the picture frame.

"Avery," he said, "this might sound strange coming from your father, but I don't know if you realize this or not, so I'm gonna tell you. You're an incredibly good-lookin' kid. Your cousin Leo isn't half as good lookin' as you, and he's always got a slew of girls hanging around the house, calling him at all hours." Jack glanced at the kitchen and lowered his voice. "You've got your whole life to be married, son. Enjoy yourself now while you can."

He sipped his drink and nodded at the picture frame again. "If I was you, I'd start by calling up those two—Caitlyn and Gemma. But don't seem too eager. The secret to handling women is acting like you can take 'em or leave 'em. If you seem like you can do without them, it only makes them want you more. Oh, hey, by the way, whatever happened to that sly minx that used to call and talk dirty to you? Your mother might have a problem with her, but *I* don't. Isn't she in her twenties or something?"

"Nineteen," Avery said.

"Play your cards right, and I bet you could get your pipes cleaned."

"Pipes? What?"

He chuckled, sipped his drink. "Never mind. Why not go see *her*?"

Avery wanted to say, "Because she's an alcoholic, and I never know what she'll be like," but with his father giving him advice while quaffing a quart-sized libation, it seemed a tad insensitive.

Jack made a sound that was half groan, half wistful sigh. "If I was your age and some hot piece of tail wanted to get into my pants..." He sipped his drink and raised the TV remote. "Keep your options open, son. It's good to have choices. That's all I'm saying."

Avery nodded. "Okay, Dad. Thanks."

Spontaneous Combustion

After talking on the phone to Mallory and Lee, Avery was finishing his homework when the phone rang. Who could be calling? It was quarter to nine, so he knew it wasn't Penny. He snatched up the handset before Sabrina or his parents could answer the phone. It was a girl's voice: "Hi, Ace."

Caitlyn! Avery's heart leapt in his chest; he was overjoyed that she'd called him, but he remembered what Jack had just told him about not seeming too eager.

♫"Treat Me Right"♫

"Don't hang up, Ace," she said. "Please. I want to apologize. You know—for last week."

"All right," he said, "apology accepted. Was there something else?"

"Oh, Ace, please don't be like that."

Caitlyn sniffled over the phone line—a sniffle that quickly became a sob. At least it sounded like she was sobbing. When Caitlyn had cried in D.C., it sounded a lot like this; he wished his telephone privacy monitor could also detect fake crying.

"Don't cry, honey," he said. "Everything's okay."

"It's *not* okay. You hate me, and my life sucks."

"I don't hate you. I hate the back and forth and round and round with you, but I don't hate *you*."

"I'm sorry, I'll be better from now on, I promise." There was the hollow sound of tissues being plucked from a box, and then her blowing her nose. "Ace, I have to see you. I miss you, baby."

"We *are* seeing each other—bowling, on Saturday."

"Yeah, but I mean, like, us *alone*. Don't you miss me?"

"God, yes," he said.

"Me too. I haven't even *kissed* Shane since I got back. After kissing you, it's like, why bother?"

"Caitlyn, your kisses are like magic spells," he said. "If there were a hall of fame for kissers, you'd be in it."

She giggled. "I miss your body, your talent, your hair, but most of all I miss your eyes."

"I miss everything about you, Babydoll, but you know what I miss the most? Your smile. It's so beautiful. I love to see you happy."

"It's you, Ace. You make me happier than anyone."

"I'm dying to see you, Babydoll," he said. "Look, if I tell you something, do you promise not to tell anyone or use it against me?"

"I swear. You can tell me anything, and I'll take it to the grave."

"And you won't laugh or think less of me?"

"I won't," she said.

"All right, here it is."

Avery confessed that he had masturbated to her nude photos the night he'd received them.

"Good," she said. "Not to sound conceited, but I would've been surprised if you hadn't. They're pretty friggin' sexy, aren't they?"

"Damn right they are. I had to put them in my steel filing cabinet. You know—in case of spontaneous combustion."

She giggled.

"By the way," he added, "I haven't told anybody about us in D.C."

"Me either. Isn't it awesome? It's our secret and always will be." She sighed. "Now I want to confess something. When I woke up this morning, my first thought was of you. I put a pillow between my legs and masturbated, imagining you were making love to me."

♫"When Doves Cry"♫

Avery let out a rasping moan. "I love how slender you are, Babydoll. The only curves on you are your lips, your butt, and your boobs."

"I've never thought about it before, but I guess that's true. Am I your sexy little Babydoll?"

"Yes," he said. "You know what else I miss? That little upward tweak at the end of your nose."

"*Eww!* I hate that about my nose."

"I love it."

"I love *your* nose," she said. "It's so straight, the people that make rulers should use your nose to check how straight their rulers are. You turn me on so much, and it's not just your bod, your eyes, your hair, or your perfect nose. It's how smart and talented and charismatic you are. And God, I *love* dancing with you. When we're dancing, our bodies naturally know what to do, instinctive-like. Ace, if we dance that well together, imagine how great the sex will be!"

Avery grunted.

"Don't you *want* to do it with me?" she said.

He scoffed. "Are you kidding? I'm concerned that once I get inside you, I won't want to leave."

"Well, I might not let you leave."

Avery moaned; Caitlyn giggled.

"Are you hard right now?" she asked.

"What do you think, you randy little minx?"

"'Minx'?" she said. "What's that?"

He flipped open his *Webster's Collegiate* dictionary and read the entry aloud: "'Minx. Noun. A pert, impudent, or flirtatious girl.'"

"Yeah, that's me all right." She lowered her voice. "If you're hard, do you want me to talk dirty to you while you take care of it?"

"I can't."

"Oh, like you don't have privacy?"

"Yeah, that, and I can't do it too much. It saps my strength."

"Right … which you need for working out," she said. "That's okay. Save it for the real thing. With *me*."

Avery groaned. "Oh, Caitlyn, I want you so badly."

"Same here, Lover. I want you to do me for hours and hours."

"When I do," he said, "I'm gonna make you come so hard, your pretty head will pop off—like a Barbie Doll's."[60]

"Oooh, listen to you with the dirty talk! Keep going, baby—please?"

"No, I'll get too turned on. All I'll say is this. You know how last week you were describing us doing it in a chair?"

"Yeah?" she said.

"That's how I want us to do it the first time. I want you facing me with your gorgeous boobs rubbing against me."

"And my tight little pussy clenching your rod as you bounce me like a ragdoll."

"I'll bounce you all right," he said. "I'll bounce you to the songs on the 'SO SEXXXY Babydoll' mixtape I made."

"*Oh, Ace … you made a mixtape for me?*"

"Yeah. I'll bring you a copy on Saturday."

"As we're doing it," she said, "you'll be massaging and kissing my boobs, and I'll be kissing you and whispering dirty talk in your ear."

"God, yes. And when I'm about to come, will you smile for me?"

"Trust me, baby, when we do it, I'll be smiling the whole time."

Avery's breath rasped. He was lightheaded and trembling.

"We need to change the subject," he said. "All of this dirty talk is soaking my underwear."

"Oh, right … the pre-cum," she said. "Well, guess what? My panties are pretty steamy too."

---

[60] Avery was referring to a girl's toy, the Barbie Doll, and the fact that a child could remove the toy's head and replace it with a different one. Girls, including Avery's sisters Julia and Sabrina, had often put the head of their teenage Skipper Barbie Doll on the original Barbie's more womanly body.

They sighed simultaneously. When Caitlyn spoke next, her voice was stone sober: "You know what else I love about you? How everybody thinks you're, like, this clean-cut Boy Scout, but I know that you're actually a bad boy in disguise."

"You bring it out in me. In fact, I did do something bad today."

♫"Bad Boy"♫

Without mentioning Brinkerhoff by name, Avery told Caitlyn about Operation Recompense—omitting mention of the testing phone in case Ma Bell was listening.[61] When he finished, Caitlyn laughed out loud.

"Ohmigod, Ace, it's brilliant! Serves that fucker right."

"You don't think it was wrong of me?"

"Hell, no," she said. "The jerk took advantage, and you got him back. If he'd paid you and *then* you did the record thing—that would of been wrong. You were totally justified. What albums ya get anyway?"

Avery rolled his chair to the bookcase with the LPs. He rattled off ten or so titles. Caitlyn asked if he would share some of the booty with her, and when he said he would, she asked him for new copies of Van Halen's *1984* album and Def Leppard's *Pyromania*. Hers had gotten scratches on them, making annoying pops as the songs played.

"Sure," he said. "And I'll throw in a third one. For giving me my first handjob."

She giggled. "Let's get together soon, so I can give you another one. Oops … I meant so you can give me the albums."

"Ha, ha. Listen, I could use your advice on a different mission. More of a problem. It involves my older sister Julia."

"Go ahead," she said. "Hit me."

Avery described Irina's problem but substituted Julia's name for Irina's. Avery said Julia was stuck working the early shift at her job, that her manager didn't like her, and that a married male coworker kept hitting on her.

"Oh, yeah, that happens all the time," she said.

"How can I fix it?"

---

[61] "Ma Bell" was a sometimes affectionate, sometimes pejorative nickname for Bell Telephone—the predominant U.S. phone company in the 1980s.

"Hmm … lemme give it a think. Hold on a sec." For thirty seconds, the only sound on the line was Caitlyn's soft breathing, then she abruptly broke the silence: "All right, here's what you do. Attack the weakest link. In your sister's case, the weakest link is the married guy hitting on her. So, you call that guy at home and say you're Julia's boyfriend, and you tell him you know she's been hitting on Julia."

"Boyfriend? Why not fiancé? I think fiancé is stronger."

"No, it's gotta be the boyfriend. If you're the fiancé, she'd have an engagement ring."

"Right," he said.

"Okay, so you say you're the boyfriend, and that you know the guy's been cheating on his wife."

"But I don't know that."

"Of *course* you don't know that," she said. "But *he* doesn't know that you don't know that. Look, if the guy's hitting on your sister, he's *totally* cheating on his wife."

"All right."

"So, you tell *Señor* Dickweed that you know what he's been up to, and that you'll tell his wife about it unless he goes to your sister's manager and gets your sister on a better shift or gets her a promotion or a raise or something. *¿Comprende? Señor* Dickweed is gonna be super-motivated to fix your sister's other problem—her job situation— because he doesn't want *you*, the boyfriend, calling his wife."

Avery shook his head in awe. Until now, he'd had no idea how good Caitlyn was at this kind of scheming. It was impressive but also frightening; he was glad that in this case she was on his side.

"*So*, whaddaya think?" she asked.

"I think you're a sexy criminal mastermind, and I'm doing it. Thank you."

There was a click on the line; somebody picked up another extension. The little bulb on the privacy monitor glowed red. A throat-clearing noise rattled the line; it was his mother. She'd begun making this warning sound a year ago, after she picked up the phone unannounced in the middle of a racy conversation he was having with Inge. Jill announced that it was time for Avery to get ready for bed; Avery said he would. When Jill hung up, Caitlyn said she was home alone until 1:00 A.M., when her mother finished her shift at IBM. She asked Avery to call back in an hour.

"I should go to sleep," he said.

"Please, Ace? I'm having so much fun—aren't you?"

Avery had to admit, he was enjoying himself. He said he'd call her back, but that because his bedroom was right next to his parents', they'd have to whisper.

Caitlyn lowered her voice. "Okay, we will."

"One hour. Or a little sooner."

He was about to hang up when Caitlyn said, "I can't wait to hear your voice again. I'm taking a shower now and getting ready for bed. Does that make you horny, baby?"

"Insanely."

She giggled. "Call me back in an hour, Lover. Mmm … waaaah!" *Click.*

Avery stared at the handset for a moment before hanging it up. All of the sexy talk with Caitlyn made him realize something: things were lining up so that he'd soon be having sex for the first time, and he didn't have any condoms.

Kill the Lion

Since Jack had been so encouraging earlier while looking at the White House photo, Avery thought that he'd be supportive on the issue of condoms, but Avery had missed his window. He should have broached the subject earlier, during the Magic Hour—after dinner and a couple of drinks, when Jack was usually agreeable and relaxed without being drunk. The later the evening went on, however, the more ursine Jack became.[62]

Avery tried to talk to Jack when his father was in the bedroom, watching TV in bed. Jill was doing something with Sabrina, so Avery thought this would be an ideal time. Even though Jack was in a surly mood, Avery asked if his father would buy him some condoms. Jack smirked and snidely remarked, "That's *not* how it works, Avery."

---

[62] Another vocabulary word from his Daily Vocab calendar: **ursine**, *adj.* of or pertaining to a bear or bears; bearlike.

Avery couldn't remember the details of his father's brief rant because he tuned him out, but he got the gist: Jack believed that a guy losing his virginity was a heroic rite of passage tantamount to an African boy's killing of his first lion, and if Avery needed his father to obtain "Safes" for him, then he simply wasn't ready.[63] Avery nodded and left the room.

Seething, he stormed out to the kitchen, cracked open a Coke, and went out on the back deck. *Well, Ace, that's what you get for trying to talk to him, for making one lousy request for his help.* He shouldn't have bothered. He chugged his Coke, belched, and crushed the can in his hand. Resolved: that was the *last* time he would ask his father's advice about girls or try to get his help related to them in any way. Never again. Never. He considered asking Jill, but he already knew what she believed—that contraception was the *girl's* responsibility—which was just friggin' weird. He went back inside and trudged down the hall toward his bedroom.

Now that he'd cooled off a bit, it occurred to him that Jack might be right; maybe losing his virginity *was* like an African kid killing his first lion, and if so, Avery didn't want Jack's help or anybody else's. He'd kill that friggin' lion but good—by himself.

He sat down at his desk, closed his eyes, and for some reason thought of Mrs. Jones. He didn't know her, but something told him that if *she* were his mother, not only would she have graciously agreed to buy the condoms for him, but she also would have given him a sage talk about sex—something that neither Jack nor Jill had done for him yet, and likely never would.

Avery got ready for bed, then, exaggeratedly yawning and stretching in Jack and Jill's bedroom doorway, he said goodnight. In his room, he put his "So SEXXXY BABYDOLL MIXTAPE" and a blank cassette in his dual cassette deck, turned the speakers all the way

---

[63] "Safes" was a term used by men of Avery's father's generation (men who were teens in the mid-to-late 1950s) to refer to condoms. A popular brand name of condoms in Jack Craig's time, the "safe" in the brand name "Safes" was meant to suggest to the would-be wearer, "Don't worry, son, we've got you covered! If you wear one of these, you'll be safe—safe from venereal diseases and safe from getting a girl *in trouble* [pregnant]."

down, and made a copy of the mixtape for Caitlyn. While the tape was dubbing, he wrote the song titles on the cassette liner notes.

When an hour had passed, Avery brought his desk phone over to the bed. He pressed the buttons for her phone number in the dark, held the handset to his head, and spoke into the mouthpiece with a mushy pillow behind it to muffle the noise. Caitlyn answered on the first ring, and her voice was so soft and sweet that initially Avery thought he'd dialed the wrong number.

"I missed you," she said. "Are you in bed now?"

"Yes."

She breathed softly. "Have you been thinking about me, Ace? Like during the week at school?"

"Yeah, why?"

"Because I've been thinking about you all the time. And about more than sex. I've missed you, your personality. I've missed *being* with you. Have you missed me that way?"

"Some," he said.

"Oh." She sounded dejected.

Avery moved the pillow down so he could breathe fresh air. "I'll be honest with you, Caitlyn. You getting close then pulling away is driving me crazy. Penny doesn't do that to me. With her, I know where I stand. But with you, I have no idea where I stand." He sighed. "You're saying these sweet, sexy things to me now, but I feel like tomorrow morning you'll waltz into Vanderbush and flirt with a dozen other guys, calling them all 'Sexy' and 'Lover' too."

"But I won't, I swear," she said. "I've been totally good. I haven't flirted at all—honest. As soon as we see each other on Saturday, and I kiss you, you'll know exactly how I feel about you."

"All right, there's something else I'm dying to say, but you have to swear not to mention it to Penny."

"I swear. Besides, if I did say anything, you could use the nude photos I sent you against me."

"You're right," he said. "It's Mutual Assured Destruction."

"What?"

Avery told her that "Mutual Assured Destruction," or M-A-D, was a term he'd read about in *Time* magazine. It was a theory that explained why the U.S. and Soviet Union hadn't had a nuclear war, and likely never would: because both sides knew they'd be annihilated.

"That's you and me all right—*mad*," she said. "Now, what did you want to say?"

Penny was sweet, he said, but they'd been going out for like two weeks and so far, it'd been nothing but emotional relationship crap; they hadn't even been on a *date* yet. Avery said he agreed with Caitlyn when she'd said it would be a "long … long … long time" before he and Penny did anything sexual.

"At this rate, I'll graduate from college before she gives me a handjob."

Caitlyn laughed.

"It's not funny," he said.

"I know, baby. Sorry I laughed."

"I care about her, but I don't want to be locked into marriage with the girl—especially without the, uh, conjugal benefits."

"*Conjugal.*" Caitlyn snickered. "That's a riot. Look, tell her you want to slow things down and just date. Meanwhile, you and me can start seeing each other on the side, and in a month or two, when you figure out that you and Penny aren't a good couple, you can break up with her quietly, and *we* can be together."

"I don't know," he said, "it seems disingenuous."

"Dis-in-jen-*what*?"

"Disingenuous—like fake or insincere."

"Look," she said, "Penny's been my best friend since third grade, so I don't want to hurt her any more than you do. I want her to be happy, but I want to be happy too, and you make me happy. I love being with you, I care about you, and I know that Penny won't make you happy. She's sweet, but she can't keep up with you like I can. And when it comes to sex, you and me are a perfect match. I've never had that instant chemistry—that, like, magnetic attraction—with *anybody* before."

"You make some good points."

"I know I do. Come on, baby … it won't hurt for us to see each other alone. You promised me."

"I know," he said.

"See me alone a few times, and if you still want to be with Penny, or if you and me are no good together, then we'll leave each other alone. Whaddaya say? *Please?*"

Sweet Dreams, Baby

Avery considered this. Granted, it was late, and he was tired, but her proposal seemed reasonable. He wasn't married to Penny, so why shouldn't he see Caitlyn a little bit?

He wished he had a book on his shelf—like a section in *The Official Boy Scout Handbook*—that told him how to handle girls and relationships with the opposite sex. Specifically, he needed advice on handling situations where the guy was attracted to multiple girls and they to him. In his imagination, a nauseatingly earnest man read a fictional section of the *Handbook* aloud:

> ### A "Studmuffin" Scout's Guide to Juggling Girls
> So, you're a Boy Scout who's become extremely good-looking overnight, you're now attracting the attention of several girls, and you want to get in on all the good, wholesome fun and sexual adventure that teenage girls have to offer? Congratulations. You, Young Man, have what's known as a "quality problem."
>
> Having one girlfriend is challenge enough for a young man, but if you're finding yourself besieged with phone calls, letters, and risqué photos from several teenage girls, and you're not keen on committing to one of them right away, then you'll have to develop your juggling skills. You'll also need to "Be Prepared" (the Scout motto) with ample prophylactics (i.e., condoms, "Trojans," or "Safes"), because with so many nubile, sexually flowering teenage girls vying for your attention, the chances of your "getting lucky" with one, or several of them, is far greater.
>
> Now, while you might "get lucky" with these girls, always remember: a Boy Scout is first and foremost a gentleman with members of the opposite sex. This means you should never pressure a girl, you should

always respect her, and you should never discuss with your buddies the things that you and she do together.

For the rare Boy Scout who finds himself in this enviable situation, often the best strategy is for him to focus his romantic attention on one girl, and his sexual attention on another. Accomplishing this, however, is tricky and—

"Ace?" Caitlyn said. "Hello?"

"Sorry. Spaced out there. How would we work it? I don't have my driver's license yet."

"I do." Caitlyn said she would drive her mom to work and take the car for the evening. She'd pick up Avery, they'd drive to Caitlyn's place and do it, and then she'd take him home afterwards and pick up her mom after her shift.

"Would you still be going out with *Shane*?" he asked.

"Yeah, like you'd still be going out with *Penny*. Why?"

"Because I don't want you fooling around with him, that's why."

"I won't. And I won't be going out with him much longer either."

Avery gave it some thought. He could manage two girls. And since they both went to Vanderbush, he wouldn't see either of them very often anyway.

"All right," he said, "we'll do it. Why don't we get together on Sunday or early next week?"

"But that's so long from now," she said. "Why not tomorrow night? I want to see you, baby. I miss you."

"I miss you too, but I've got schoolwork and other stuff to do. We'll see each other Saturday night for bowling."

"But it's not the same," she moaned. "We won't be alone."

Avery yawned.

"Did you just *yawn*?"

"Sorry," he said. "I'm exhausted."

"Okay, Sunday or next week. *Early* next week."

"Agreed."

"I wish you were with me," she said. "We could make love and fall asleep in each other's arms."

"Yeah." Avery covered his mouth and yawned again.

Caitlyn sighed; it sounded like a kitten mewing.

"Ace?"

"Yeah?" he said.

"I love you."

Avery sat bolt upright and gasped.

"Sweet dreams, baby," she said.

Click.

22

A VERY SLEPT fitfully that night, and at school all the next day he was haunted by Caitlyn's words: *"I love you."* He'd been half asleep at the time, so he wasn't sure she'd said it. If she did say it, did she truly love him, or had she only said it to convince him to break up with Penny and go out with her? And if she did love him, how did Avery feel about her?

He knew he didn't love Caitlyn; heck, he hadn't even told Penny that he loved her yet. He craved Caitlyn, how natural it felt to hold her body in his arms, and he wanted to have sex with her—repeatedly and as soon as possible—but he didn't miss her in the same way that he missed Penny.

When he thought of Penny, his chest ached because he missed her pretty face and her sniggering, sweet laugh. He missed how tiny she was, how adoringly she gazed at him, how the top of her head only reached his chin. He missed her innocence—that when he talked to her, he never had to worry about her having ulterior motives.

During lunch with Dina, Lee, and Melody, Avery temporarily forgot about Caitlyn's declaration, but only because he was now confused and tortured by Dina. However, it wasn't her outfit that got him revved up: a Bon Jovi T-shirt under an unbuttoned red plaid flannel shirt, and a pair of faded Levi's with holes in the thighs and seat; it was her silky sable hair in Laura Ingalls-style braids; in all the years he'd known her, Dina had never styled her hair like this. She cozied next to him on the cafeteria bench while they ate and practiced their "bouncy memorization" for the bio quiz. At one point, Dina rested against Avery's shoulder with her breast pressing against his arm. Now, instead of worrying about Caitlyn's declaration last night, he was tortured by thoughts about Dina. Was she possibly in *love* with him? And if so, did he love her? When he looked at Dina, it was like he was gazing upon smoldering *Playboy* Centerfold Patty McGuire; Dina was so beautiful that she often didn't seem real. And now Dina's hanging on him, smiling, flapping her braids, laughing at his jokes, didn't seem real either. It didn't seem possible that Dina Tempestilli, Roman goddess, was in love with him.

On the bus ride home, seeking inspiration for how to deal with the guy Victor who was harassing Irina, Avery reread the Sherlock Holmes story "The Adventure of Charles Augustus Milverton." It was about Holmes and Watson foiling a notorious blackmailer. It bothered Avery that he would essentially be blackmailing this guy Victor—behaving like the rat-like Milverton in the story—but after carefully thinking over Caitlyn's plan, he knew it was solid. From the story and CIA text files he'd read a while back, he'd learned that to blackmail someone effectively, you needed incriminating physical evidence, like photos, letters, etc. Avery wondered if Irina had any notes, cards, or answering machine messages from the guy.

When he got home, Sabrina wasn't at the house, and there was a message from Penny on the answering machine. She'd forgotten that she couldn't talk today because she and her sister had dental checkups, and then her mom was taking them out to dinner. She was sorry, but she and Avery couldn't talk before their "big date" tomorrow night. She was "super excited" about it, remarking that she hoped he wouldn't be "grossed out" when he saw her again after two weeks apart. She'd see him tomorrow at her house, at 6 o'clock.

Avery was about to get a snack and watch MTV when the phone rang again. He reached for the handset but didn't pick it up. It might be Caitlyn. He was dying to talk to her, to get clarification about her declaration last night. On the other hand, he'd already had one girl (Penny) say she loved him, which was confusing and complicated enough. Avery had his first date with Penny tomorrow night, and if he talked to Caitlyn beforehand, she might cajole him into saying he loved her before he said those words to Penny.

The phone rang a third time, and the answering machine picked up. After it had played Jill's outgoing message—a message that made the Craig household seem calm and organized instead of the chaotic and dysfunctional battle royal that it usually was—a girl's voice came over the speaker.

"Hi, Avery. It's Inge. I've seen you out there skiing, but it's been a while since I saw you in person. Like last summer, I think." Inge sounded the most sober and lucid that she had in years. "By the way, I want to apologize. I can't tell you how sorry I am about what happened. Anyway, I need a *teensy* favor." She paused. "Come on, Hunky, I know you're there. Pick up. Please?" She sighed. "Fine. I guess you're screening your calls, so I'll explain to your machine…"

While she was jabbering, for the next minute Avery debated whether or not to pick up. Avery hadn't returned any of Inge's calls since July or August, when he'd ridden 30 miles on his bike in one-hundred-degree heat to lose his virginity to her, only to reach her grandparents' house (where she was staying), walk into a massive party, and have a sloppy drunk Inge say some incredibly cruel things to him. Then again, the Inge speaking on his answering machine right now sounded sober and apologetic. He decided to pick up.

Just a Trim

"So, that's the deal," Inge said on the answering machine. "It should only take like an hour or—"

Avery snatched up the phone handset and shut off the answering machine.

"Hi, Inge," he said. "Let me switch phones."

"'Kay."

Avery ran down the hall to his bedroom, took his phone off the hook, then ran back to the living room and hung up that extension, then ran back to his room, closed the door and picked up the handset.

"Sorry," he said. "What's going on?"

Inge huffed. "I just left you a super-long message about this. Didn't you hear it?"

"Not yet."

"I saw you get off your bus a while ago. What'cha up to?"

He was hungry, exhausted, had homework to do, needed to work out, and—

"Come on, Hunky," she said. "What are you doing?"

"Eating and watching MTV. What's up?"

With a radio playing in the background, Inge explained that between shifts of her job at the mall (which she didn't care to discuss), she'd been training for her cosmetology license. Her final exam was in a few weeks, and she needed more practice cutting guys' hair.

"I haven't seen you since the summer," she said. "Is your hair still sorta long and shaggy, like a surfer?"

"I prefer to think of it as 'boyishly tousled.'"

"You're so cute. So, it's still, like, wavy and a little wild?"

"I guess," he said. "Jill says it makes me look like Robert Redford."

"Who's Jill?"

"My mother. Remember—the woman who chewed you out for talking dirty to me on the phone?"

"Oh, yeah." She chuckled again. "She's not mad at me about that anymore, is she?"

Avery thought about this. Jill forgave, but she never forgot.

"No, she's forgiven you, I'm sure," he said.

"So, do you want a haircut or not?"

Avery glanced at himself in the full-length mirror on his closet door. His hair was a little scraggly, and it would be nice to get spruced up before his date with Penny tomorrow night. But he was reluctant to take Inge up on her offer. She might be sober *now*, but if she started drinking after they hung up, she'd be a whole other person by the time he got over there, and he hated drunk Inge. He especially didn't want to get his hair cut by drunk, peevish Inge—grumbling and handling scissors with impaired motor skills.

"Come on," Inge said, "it won't cost you anything—unless you decide to tip me."

"It depends. Have you been drinking?"

"Drinking? What difference does that make?"

"Well, my dear girl," he said, "alcohol and scissors don't mix."

Inge chuckled. "Nope. Stone-cold sober. I swear."

"The thing is, it's freezing outside, and I haven't eaten since lunch."

"I'll make you a sandwich. C'mon, get over here. I've got the chair, lights, and everything set up in the kitchen."

"Okay, but just a trim, all right?" he said.

"Sure, no prob." In the background were the sounds of a refrigerator opening and glass containers rattling. "Making your sandwich now, Hunky. Bye!"

Click.

Five Blissful Seconds

Avery pulled his mission knapsack out of the closet and packed a few additional items. Unsure what Inge would have for non-alcoholic beverages, he added two cans of Coke Classic and a few packets of Swiss Miss instant hot cocoa mix with marshmallows. He grabbed his Walkman, popped in fresh batteries and his "Inge Ibsen Mix" mixtape, got a ¼″ to ⅛″ headphone plug adapter out of his trusty Q-Branch drawer, and plugged his new full-size stereo headphones into the Walkman. Shouldering the knapsack, he went down to the garage and put on his boots and hat, ski goggles, the headphones, and gloves. Then he pressed play on the Walkman, opened the garage door, and wheeled his mountain bike outside. He shut the garage door and headed out.

In the center of the cul-de-sac, there was a *Pennysaver* on the ground, its pages of classified ads flapping madly in the wind. Ordinarily Avery would perform his Boy Scout good deed for the day by picking up the litter and throwing it away, but not today, in this damn cold.[64] The yards were windswept and empty. It was freezing with a 20-mph wind, and it was snowing now. The snow was sticking to the ground, which meant if there was any accumulation, it would be a royal pain in the ass getting home.

---

[64] According to Avery's edition (9th) of *The Official Boy Scout Handbook*, a "good deed" or "good turn" is "an extra act of kindness," and that the good Scout should be "looking for chances to help throughout each day, then helping quietly, without boasting." In the four years he'd been a Boy Scout, Avery had done a variety of good deeds, including finding an old woman's lost cat, giving first aid to a girl on the tennis court, and getting a boy's kite out of a tree. However, disgusted with New York City drivers' constant ingratitude, he refused to give lost motorists free directions ever again.

His music sounded amazing through the new headphones, which were so big that they fit over his ski cap and doubled as makeshift earmuffs. Although he could feel the wind and the fine snow biting into his cheeks, Avery couldn't hear anything going on outside. It was surreal to see the wintry scene playing out in front of him through his amber-tinted ski goggles when all he could hear was a song he associated with high summer: Boston's ♫"Foreplay/Long Time."♫

After two minutes of "Foreplay," as the song reached its crescendo of organ and electric guitar, Inge's house came into view, looming atop the hill across from the entrance to Birch Knolls. Then, as "Foreplay" transitioned into thrusting "Long Time" with its screeching opening guitar solo, the bare shaking trees on her front lawn became verdant in Avery's mind, and he remembered the sultry August afternoon three years ago, when he first met her...

Beneath the leafy maples and oaks that flutter in a dog's breath of a breeze, Inge and a dozen of her bikini-clad girlfriends are gathered on her plush front lawn, sipping beers, dancing, and wiggling their butts to "Long Time," which blasts from an oversized boombox on the stoop. A long yellow Slip 'N Slide stretches down the hill.[65] Thin streams of water spray out of tiny holes on the Slip 'N Slide, glistening, arcing over the plastic, producing miniature rainbows in the bright sun. The girls—laughing, shrieking, squirting each other with squirt guns, gleefully shaking their heads of wet hair—take turns getting a running start, diving headfirst onto the slick plastic sheet, and careening headlong down the hill.

At the bottom, the girls skid onto freshly mown grass and hose each other's bikini-clad bodies to wash off the clippings.

Fuhhhhhhhhhhhhhhhck.

Avery, riding by on his bike to go friggin' fishin', skids to a stop on the sandy shoulder. A pickup truck slows, its driver rubbernecking

---

[65] The Slip 'N Slide was a long sheet of plastic (30–50 feet) with a connection for a garden hose. Inflowing water filled conduits in the plastic and sprayed out of tiny holes, making the ultra-smooth plastic surface super slippery— especially against bare skin. For best results, the Slip 'N Slide would be unfurled down a hill. Youngsters would run toward the plastic sheet, dive head-first, and slide to the bottom, then run back up and repeat.

at the girls and honking his horn like he's a telegrapher high on cocaine. When the girls smile and shout to Avery and wave him up the hill, and he doesn't see a single guy around, a thought pops into his head—a thought at once devastating and euphoric: that he might have been hit by a car and gone to heaven.

He warily climbs the driveway, pushing his bike, and at the top lays his bike, fishing pole, and tackle box on the grass. While "Long Time" continues to play, an old sheep dog drowsily keeps one eye on the rambunctious girls from the shade of the front porch, and from somewhere in the backyard there is the greasy smoke smell of a charcoal BBQ grill.

Mincing across the lawn, her breasts jiggling with her footsteps, her skin sun-kissed and dappled with mist, Inge approaches Avery with an enormous smile on her face. She's chewing gum and holding a can of beer. At first, Avery is dumbstruck by the striking contrast of her wet and darkened red hair, her white bikini, and her glistening red lips; but then her breasts get his attention. Although they're spectacular, in the end her eyes win out; they are the bluest, most sparkly things he's ever seen, and seem to contain whole universes. He and the girl introduce themselves. Her name is Inge.

"You moved in recently, right?" she says.

"Yeah."

"Today's my seventeenth birthday. This is my party."

"Happy birthday. Nice party. Sorry I don't have a gift for you."

She chomps her gum and motions her head to the side. "Wanna do the Slip 'N Slide? It's a lotta fun."

"Well, I don't have a swimsuit," he says.

She shrugs. "So what? C'mon."

Before Avery realizes it, he's removed his T-shirt, sneakers, and socks, and Inge has tugged him over to the crest of the hill. Avery runs, jumps headfirst onto the Slip 'N Slide, and is sliding when he's bumped in the ribs; Inge is sliding beside him. For five blissful seconds that seem to last an eternity, as "Long Time" rings out across the yard, he and Inge slide downhill side-by-side, gazing at each other. Inge laughs and squeals, the water sprinkles on her sun-kissed skin, and her breasts brim from the bikini cups.

At the bottom, they tumble together onto the grass behind an evergreen, and Inge, as luck would have it, lands on top of him. Her breasts are resting on his chest and water drips from her hair, but it's her eyes—those sparkly sapphire eyes—that utterly mesmerize him. His chest and stomach are fluttery, and he's panting.

"You're so beautiful," he says.

She giggles and taps his nose with her finger. "And you're *super* cute!" She glances over her shoulder at the Slip 'N Slide, cups his cheeks and kisses him on the mouth. The kiss, which is yeasty and bubble gum-sweet, and includes some spine-tingling flicking of her tongue, lasts only five seconds, but it gives him an instant erection— an erection he's certain that Inge and her friends will tease him about.

Avery runs to his bike, jams his feet into his sneakers, gathers his things and pedals madly down the driveway. As soon as he's out of eyeshot of Inge's house, with the yeasty, sugary taste of Inge's wet lips clinging to his lips, the fiery guitar runs of "Long Time" echoing in his brain, and the pillowy warmth of her breasts lingering on his chest, Avery dumps his bike and fishing gear in the weeds and darts into the woods.

Inge's tasty, titillating kiss has aroused Avery to the point where the only thing he can think about is her. She was so beautiful, so friendly, so womanly, and she'd called him *"super* cute!" Avery doesn't understand what's happening, but before he knows it, consumed with this vision of her, he surrenders to instinct. He halts at the bank of a small brook, springs himself from his shorts, closes his eyes, and, for the first time in his life, masturbates.

Bathed in the serene sounds of birdsong and the babbling brook, Avery imagines Inge, smiling and mincing up to him with her breasts jiggling, but this time removing her bikini top before kissing him.[66] Moments later, with Inge's creamy bare breasts and her sparkling sapphire eyes radiant in his mind, he shoots off into the brook.

---

[66] Without question, Avery's first-ever autoerotic fantasy was subconsciously shaped by the swimming pool-masturbation scene in the seminal teen romp *Fast Times at Ridgemont High,* wherein Linda (Phoebe Cates) climbs out of a pool wearing a cherry-red bikini and bares her breasts to a fantasizing Brad (Judge Reinhold).

Pop-n-Fresh

But that was three years ago. As Avery pedaled, and the late February snow swirled around him, he realized that he hadn't seen her since last summer—like seven months; such a *long time*. She'd said some incredibly hurtful things to him, and he'd been so furious with her that he told her he never wanted to see her again. And at the time, he'd meant it.

But in a moment, he *would* see her again, and the thought made his heart pound. She'd sounded so sweet and friendly on the phone. Maybe she wasn't drinking as much as she used to. Would she be Sweet Inge or Drunk Inge? Dr. Jekyll or Ms. Hyde?

A notion popped into his head that caused him to spring up on the bike: what if Inge sensed his current state of sexual distress and offered to give him a handjob?! He'd do his best to be true to Penny, but if Inge offered to give him a handjob (or, even better, a blowjob), no way was he saying no. He pumped harder on the pedals.

Inge's house, an imposing Victorian with chipped paint and dangling shutters, stood on a hill overlooking the entrance to Avery's development. Once he'd crossed Woodside Creek Road, Avery hopped off his bike and hiked up the steep driveway. Painted a dull, dirty white and surrounded by aging maple trees, their bare branches clattering in the wind, the house looked haunted, and this afternoon especially so. High overhead, a massive dead tree limb wobbled. Mrs. Ibsen's car, a red BMW she'd bought after Mr. Ibsen died, was at the top of the driveway, parked in front of the garage. The garage roof was caved in from a pine tree that had fallen on it last winter, and the tree was still there. Inge's car, a silver Saab 900 SPG Turbo was also there. Snow covered the windshields.

Avery extended the wipers on the cars in case there was accumulation or ice (there … his Good Deed for the day), and put his bike on the wraparound porch, where it would be under cover. Although it wasn't dark yet, the porch light was on. Avery leaned the bike against the house and knocked on the kitchen door windowpane. ♫"Burnin' for You"♫ played over his headphones. The door flung open and Inge was there.

As "Burnin' for You" kicked into its otherworldly guitar and choral anthem, Avery stood dumbfounded by Inge's beauty—her sheeny flame-red hair, wavy and long, fluttering in the wind, and the crystalline snowflakes swirling around her like fairy dust. Lovely Inge Ibsen, with her creamy pink complexion; her womanly figure; her melancholy face; and her unforgettable blue eyes. He'd seen them up close dozens of times, yet they still took his breath away. The irises were conflagrations of tiny sapphires around the pupils, each little jewel catching the light at a different angle and emitting electric blue glints like sparks.

She was wearing a blue gingham apron over a T-shirt and jeans. The wind flapped the apron hem. Being welcomed by a creature of such exquisite beauty, particularly on a windy, wintry afternoon, was pleasantly startling, and Avery found himself having to take several quick gulps of cold air to calm himself. Inge said something, but he couldn't hear her over his Walkman. She rolled her eyes and plucked a headphone off his ear.

"Come on in, Hunky," she said. "It's freezing out there."

Avery wiped his feet on the welcome mat and followed her inside, shutting the door behind him. He shut off the Walkman and removed the headphones, ski goggles and hat. The kitchen was warm, and the '70s-style spring green and daisies wallpaper made it feel warmer. Inge spun around.

"With those headphones and yellow goggles," she said, "for a second I thought you were an alien."

Avery told her that when she'd opened the door, he'd been listening to "Burnin' for You," and as soon as he saw her gorgeous face, it was like he was in a music video.

Inge smiled and faintly shook her head. "Oh, Hunky … you silver-tongued devil." She took his coat, knapsack, and other things and placed them on a chair in the adjoining dining room. The steamy aroma of dough and cinnamon hung in the air, and the oven was on. Avery knew that smell: Pillsbury "Pop-n-Fresh" cinnamon rolls.

A dining room chair, with a thick phone book on the seat, sat in the middle of the kitchen. Three tall floor lamps without shades surrounded the chair, and in front of the chair, a full-length mirror leaned against the kitchen cabinets. Rick Springfield's ♫"Jessie's Girl"♫ played softly on a boombox on the counter. Inge wiggled her shoulders to the music, minced across the kitchen, and gave Avery a hug, shamelessly pressing her breasts against him.

"Thanks for coming, Hunky. I've missed you. It's been a while."

"Seven months."

"Yeah, I'm super sorry about what happened last summer." She caressed his cheek. "Can you forgive me?"

Ugh … great. Avery had been in Inge's presence for thirty seconds, and he already had a jack handle in his pants. He was regretting coming over here. He cleared his throat.

"Sure," he said. "Let's forget it."

"Thank you, Hunky." She stood on her tiptoes and kissed his cheek. She squeezed his shoulders and upper arms. "My God, you've filled out so much. I barely recognize you."

Avery frowned. "What do you mean, 'filled out'? That's *muscle*, Inge, not fat." He raised his arms and flexed his biceps. Inge squeezed one, then the other.

"Wow," she said. "I meant 'muscle.' That weightlifting is paying off, that's for sure. You've finally grown into my nickname for you." She primped his hair, which made the swelling in his pants more acute. "I'm crazy about your hair, Hunky—I always have been. I can't wait to cut and style it. But sit down first. Wait 'til you see the snack I've made for you."

Inge waved him over to the breakfast nook by the kitchen window, then scurried over to the refrigerator, treating Avery to a brief, delectable sight. Through the hole caused by her bloused apron bib, Avery spied her breasts in a snug T-shirt. He sucked a breath through his teeth and stared at the green rubber placemat on the table. Coming over here today was a mistake. He wanted to stay true to Penny, but he was lonely and horny. If Inge came on to him, he didn't have the strength to resist her.

She returned with a sandwich, a small pile of Fritos corn chips, and a glass of milk. Inge had wanted to make his favorite—grilled cheese—but didn't have enough slices, and then she remembered that his second favorite was salami, cheese, and mustard. She'd even cut the sandwich into triangle-shaped quarters. Avery thanked her and gave her the packets of Swiss Miss instant hot cocoa he'd brought. She filled the kettle with water and put it on the gas burner to boil.

"Hey," he said, "are those Pillsbury cinnamon rolls I smell?"

"Yup. Should be done by the time the water boils." She smiled in the golden light from the stove hood. Inge had never been prettier. She waved dismissively. "Stop looking at me and eat."

Avery devoured the sandwich while Inge watched the cinnamon rolls in the oven window. He asked if her mom was still doing real estate; Inge said she was but was taking a nap this afternoon.

The teakettle whistled, and an egg timer on the counter dinged. Inge poured water into the mugs, shut off the stove, removed the cinnamon rolls from the oven, and placed them on the stovetop. Steam rose into the light from the vent hood.

After they'd cooled for a minute, she plated them, spread the icing on them, and carried everything over to the table. She sat down across from him. Cradling her mug in her hands, Inge crossed her legs and gazed into his eyes.

"I was worried I'd never see you again," she said. "How's your snack?"

"Amazing. Nate's a lucky guy."

She shook her head. "Nate's ancient history. We broke up at Thanksgiving."

"I'm sorry," he said.

"I'm not." She sipped her cocoa. "Try a cinnamon roll."

He ate one. "Perfection … like the cook."

Inge untied her apron and plopped it on the table. Under the apron she was wearing a *Charlie's Angels* T-shirt. Well … it was more the faded memory of a T-shirt than an actual garment; only the ghostly silhouette of the Angels remained on her chest, and the fabric was as thin as cheesecloth. Her bra was faintly visible underneath. The shirt had shrunken too; when she raised her hands to sip her cocoa, the hem rode up and exposed her cushiony stomach. Inge had a bite of a cinnamon roll, leaving a splotch of icing on her lip.

"May I make an observation?" he said. "It's nice being here when you're not drinking."

She looked at the kitchen floor. "Yeah, I know. But I've been cutting down. A lot. It was getting a little out of hand, so I—"

"A little out of hand?" Avery chomped into another cinnamon roll and reminded Inge that the last time he saw her, a bunch of strangers nearly wrecked her grandparents' place, and a biker douche who'd cornered her on the couch was about to rape her.

Inge nodded. "Okay, a lot out of hand. But I'm getting better."

"I'm glad to hear it. I was deeply concerned about you."

"You were? Deeply concerned?"

"Mm-hm." He ate another cinnamon roll and gestured at her mouth. "You've got some icing on your upper lip, beautiful."

With a deft flick of her tongue, she licked it off. Across the kitchen, the music on the boombox, which had faded into the background, erupted into a screaming guitar riff that he recalled as the opening of ♫"No One Like You."♫

"Oooh, Scorpions!" Inge scurried across the room, turned up the volume and danced back to the table. She gazed at him for a second, her eyes catching the light and glittering in a starburst of blue. "Okay, Hunky, let's cut your hair." She put her apron back on. "Ready?"

Girl Scout's Honor

Avery's groin thrummed. Damn, was he going to have a crippling case of blue balls tonight! He peg-legged over to the chair. It creaked and swayed when he sat down.

"Is this thing broken?" he said. "It feels kind of rickety."

"It's fine."

"Remember, just a—"

"—trim," she said. "Got it. Relax, Hunky. I won't hurt this gorgeous head of hair."

Because of the ad hoc setup, Avery had his doubts about the haircut, but it was surprisingly professional. Inge snapped a "Before" picture of him with a Polaroid instant camera, and then she got down to business—affixing a paper collar around his neck, spraying his hair, combing it out, and cutting the ends. When she started on a new section, however, her hands shook. Inge backed away. She steadied herself on the chair and took a breath.

"There's no need to be nervous," he said with a smile. "You're doing a great job."

"I'm not nervous," she said. "It's the shakes. What a pain in the butt. I'm sorry, but a drink's the only thing that stops them. Hold on."

She went to the freezer, pulled out a bottle of vodka and a shot glass, and poured a shot. When she downed it, she closed her eyes and savored it for a moment, then put the bottle and shot glass back in the freezer. The process only took ten seconds, but the efficiency of it smacked of having been done a hundred times. No—a *thousand*.

On her way back to the chair, she snipped her scissors like they were castanets. There was more color in her cheeks now, and she was more relaxed. She held out her hands. The shaking had stopped.

"See? All better."

"Inge, that's not good. I'm pretty sure it means you have a physical dependency on the alcohol."

"I'm fine." She screwed her lips into his cheek and took her time removing them. "But thank you for looking out for me. You're so good to me, Avery."

As she resumed his haircut, Avery admired the steely look in her eyes while she snipped with the scissors or combed his hair into place. He liked how dexterously she handled the scissors and comb, turning them in her hands so they weren't near his head when she used her fingertips to primp his hair or to trace the contours of his scalp. Her tactile attentions occasionally lingered on his ears and neck, and because she often had to get in close, her breasts brushed against his neck and shoulders, keeping Avery's groin in constant discomfort.

"What's wrong?" she said. "You're so tense."

"Nothing."

"Oops!" She winced and backed away. "I snipped off a huge hunk in back. It was an accident. Sorry."

"What!?"

Inge laughed. "Relax, I'm joshin' you. Look."

She held up a hand mirror behind his head; in the full-length mirror in front of him, he saw that his hair was perfect.

"A little stylist humor for you, Hunky." She gave him another frisky kiss on the cheek. "You look kinda stressed. Why don't you tell me what's troubling you? A big part of my job as a stylist is listening to clients talk about their problems. Pretend you don't know me and tell me what's on your mind."

While Inge used electric clippers on his neck and sideburns, Avery described his romantic saga of the past couple weeks: becoming Penny's boyfriend; fooling around with Caitlyn; talking on the phone and making plans with Irina; and finding out that his fantasy girl from junior high might be in love with him. He also briefly described Caitlyn's proposal for them to see each other on the side.

Inge washed his hair in the kitchen sink using the spray nozzle, and because of the tight quarters, her breasts were squished against his neck and shoulders the entire time. She blow-dried and styled his hair, removed his cape, and dusted his neck with Clubman talc. When she was finished, she smiled in the full-length mirror and primped his hair, gliding her fingernails between the wavy tresses, and twisting and teasing some of them.

"All right, Hunky, I've listened to everything you've said, and I have some thoughts. "I'm sorry to have to tell you this, but you're cursed." She massaged his shoulders. "I hate to break it to you, but your troubles with girls are just beginning. As you get older and even better-looking, there are only gonna be more of them, and they'll make you crazy if you let them." She held up the hand mirror behind his head. "How's the haircut?"

"It's the best damn haircut I've ever had," he said.

Inge beamed. "Seriously, hunky?"

"I *love* it. You're an *artist*, Inge. You'll ace your final easily."

Her eyes got a little teary. She thanked him, grabbed the Polaroid camera off the counter again, and snapped an "After" photo.

"I'm gonna hang these at my station at school," she said, flapping the ejected photo. "Wait'll the other girls in my class get a look at you." She put the photo on the counter and removed her apron.

"Now, I heard everything you said about your girl situation"—she exhaled sharply, fluttering some hair by her mouth—"and I think we should talk." She walked over, straddled his lap, and put her arms around his neck. The chair creaked. "I know I haven't always been the nicest person, and you're right about my drinking—it was way out of control—but I care about you, Avery, and I always have. I'm so sorry about the things I said and did last summer. It took me a while, but I finally recognize that you're a wonderful guy. I want to start seeing you." She stared into his eyes; their hypnotic magic was wearing him down. "Listen, I know you've got a girlfriend, and I can respect that, but you're only sixteen and you shouldn't be tying yourself down to one girl yet. But as far as this girl Caitlyn and her proposal are concerned, here's what I think. No matter how careful you are, because she and your girlfriend go to 'Bush, eventually your girlfriend's gonna find out and it's gonna be a disaster. I think if you're gonna see another girl on the side, it should be *me*."

Grinning, she flipped her hair over her shoulders. "For one thing, we already know and like each other. Two, I live nearby, but because I've graduated, there's no chance of your girlfriend finding out about me. And three, I won't put demands on you. We'll only get together casually for, like, dinner, movies, and sex."

When Inge said "sex," Avery's throat dried up; he tried to swallow but couldn't. Was she for real? Was this actually happening? He'd fantasized about this for 2½ years.

"What do you say?" She licked her fingers and smoothed out some hair on his temple.

Avery was about to blurt out that he'd always dreamed of this when Jack's advice rang out in his head: "...*don't seem too eager.*"

"It sounds great," he said, "but what would you expect in return?"

"Not much. Some of your attention—talk to me on the phone, take me out on dates in my car, which *you* would get to drive," she said. "Sleep over once in a while. Treat me nice. You know—loving, sweet."

Inge said this while gazing at him, and Avery's heart pounded like a kettle drum. What had begun as a vague hypothetical was now basically a certainty.

"Promise me you'll think about it at least?" she said.

"I promise."

Avery glanced out the kitchen window. It was dark out, and the snow was swirling around in the porch lights. "I should get home. Oh … your tip." Avery pulled a $5 bill out of his front pocket and tucked it into the back pocket of her jeans. "There."

When he looked up at her, Inge's eyes were wide. She smiled, and the next thing Avery knew, they were kissing and Inge was grinding her groin against his bulge. She spoke softly, kissing his neck.

"Oh, my." She rubbed against his bulge. "Have you been hard this whole time?"

"Uh, *yeah*. You were constantly rubbing your breasts against me."

"I was *not*."

"You totally were."

Inge playfully bit her lip. "Okay, maybe I was … a little bit."

Avery let out a ragged moan. "Inge, I have a girlfriend."

Inge kissed his neck.

"Where is she tonight, huh?" She kissed his ear and cheek. "Serves her right—leaving a cute guy like you all alone. And the other girls you mentioned … where the heck are they?" She kissed his nose. "If they really cared about you, they'd be with you tonight." She kissed his mouth.

Inge's soft kisses engulfed his brain in an intoxicating haze. The sensation reminded him of a time when the dentist gave him nitrous oxide. Which reminded him… "Penny's at the dentist," he muttered absently. "Our first date is tomorrow."

"Forget Penny." She sucked his earlobe. "I'm here, Hunky. You said I did a great job on your hair. Lemme have one nice, long kiss."

"One kiss?" he said.

She held up two fingers of her right hand. "Girl Scout's honor."

Avery narrowed his eyes. "You were a Girl Scout?"

"Nope."

Avery tried to sit passively and let Inge kiss him, but as she worked her lips on his, he found himself trembling with excitement again. His fingers grazed some of her hot bare skin along her midriff, and his hands were drawn toward the warmth under her shirt. Inge accelerated her gyrations. She was a voluptuous girl, and the thin layer of cushiony baby fat she carried on her body was much different from slender Caitlyn and therefore highly arousing. Her skin was actually *hot* as though she had a fever, and the tops of her breasts were pillowy like risen bread dough. Without a conscious thought, he wedged his thumbnail firmly underneath her bra clasp and flicked upwards, effortlessly unhooking her bra one-handed. He'd finally gotten to use the "single thumb-flick bra removal technique" that his Scout patrol leader, Carlton Clutch, had taught him and the other guys, and cradling Inge's bare breasts was his reward.

They were the size of Caitlyn's, and dense and heavy in his hands. Inge continued to kiss him as she swiveled her groin in small circles against his bulge. The chair made little squeaks that coincided with her gyrations. While kissing him, she pulled away with a smack and stared at him through slitted eyes.

"You're wicked hard, Hunky." She rubbed against it. "It's like a knob of wood in there—one of those, you know … *knotholes*? I love rubbing against it."

"You rub against knotholes? Dirty girl."

She grinned and tapped his cheek. "Shut up." She kissed him some more and rubbed against his bulge. "God, why'd it take me so long to see what an amazing guy you are?"

As Inge put her mouth over his again and Avery caressed her breasts, he was transported back to that August afternoon at the foot of the Slip 'N Slide, when Inge had cupped his cheeks in her palms and kissed him. On her lawn that day, Avery would have given anything to be kissing and feeling her up like he was now; therefore, a part of him felt that he owed it to 13½-year-old Avery Craig to keep going, to finally give young Avery what he'd craved for years.

When Inge resumed her grinding, her breath became fast and shallow. Avery's brain was bombarded by sensations of pleasure from his entire body—his bulge, against which Inge rubbed vigorously; his hands, where her stiffened nipples poked into his palms; his lips, where her sugary lips and chocolatey tongue further eroded his resolve; his nose, where the lingering aroma of cinnamon mingled with the subtle scent of Inge's perfume; his ears, where Inge's warm breath and murmurs that he had "turned into such a hunky young man" tickled his ear canals; and finally his eyes, which, peeking open from time to time as Inge gyrated on his lap, glimpsed her jouncing fiery hair and her creamy skin turning pink on her neck and cheeks.

Every cell in his body screamed for Avery to go as far as he could here with Inge—if not "all the way." The boy in him that had dreamed of becoming an explorer suddenly saw the chance to reach the North Pole, the South Pole, the Mariana Trench, the headwaters of the Amazon, the summit of Everest, the Moon … even Mars! Now, with the prize in sight, closer than it had ever been before (and possibly never so close again), Avery ached to forge ahead to conquest.

Iago, that little devil that lived on Avery's shoulder, whispered that if he told Inge about his discomfort—explaining that he desperately wanted to have sex with her but couldn't because he needed to be true to his girlfriend—Inge might offer to give him a handjob or blowjob. *"Why should you be in discomfort, Avery?"* the evil peckerwood said. *"Inge will give you relief if you ask her nicely. She's been so pleasant today since she hasn't been drinking. The two of you deserve some pleasure."* Iago had him convinced—until he mentioned Penny: *"Go on, Avery … Penny will never know."*

All at once, Penny's sweet, adoring face appeared in his head. He hadn't even gone on a date with her yet and look at what he was doing. Penny was a sweet girl; she deserved better. Avery withdrew his hands from under Inge's shirt and planted them firmly on her waist. She stopped kissing and rubbing against him. When she asked what was wrong, Avery said he had to stop.

Inge's eyes got misty. "Don't you find me attractive?"

"Are you kidding? You're totally *smokin'*. But why couldn't you have done this with me last year—before I had a girlfriend? God, I would have given anything for this back then."

"Because I was going out with Nate, and…"

"And what?"

She shrugged. "You were kind of a skinny boy. Now you're a hunky young man."

Avery huffed and shoved her off his lap. "I have to go."

"Come on, Hunky, stay." She stamped a foot. "Please?"

She was close to tears. Avery wanted to get out of here before she started crying, which would invariably lead to more drinking. He went into the dining room, put on his coat, and shouldered his knapsack. When he returned to the kitchen, Inge was leaning against the countertop. Her head was bowed, and she was crying. Avery went to the door and grabbed the doorknob.

"Go on, get out of here, leave me!" Inge said. "Leave me like every other guy does!"

Now he was stuck; he couldn't leave her like this. His father's advice echoed in his head: *"Keep your options open, Avery. It's good to have choices."* Jack was right. Avery had invested too much time with Inge over the past couple of years—cuddling and comforting her, getting aroused and sexually frustrated by her, doing her schoolwork, and nursing her when she was drunk—to throw it away now.

He did an about-face, marched back up to her, and kissed her. Inge threw her arms around him and whimpered with pleasure. When he tasted her salty tears in his mouth, he eased away from her, reached in his pocket, and snapped out a handkerchief. He dabbed her cheeks and gave it to her.

"I'm not leaving you, Inge. I'll be back, I promise. But my first date with my girlfriend is tomorrow night."

She wiped her eyes and sniffled. "I wish *we* were going on a date."

"I'm not sure when," he said, "but we will."

"When will I see you again?" She gazed at him with the full, hypnotic force of her sapphire eyes. For a split second, Avery considered dumping Penny this instant, carrying Inge up to her bedroom, and nailing her all night long.

"Soon. I promise." He touched her cheek. "I had a great time today. You're wonderful when you're sober. I don't want to leave, but I have to try to be true to my girlfriend."

"I hope this girl knows how lucky she is."

Avery kissed her one more time and brushed some hair off her cheek. "I'll see you soon, gorgeous." He walked to the door. "Thank you for the sandwich, the cinnamon rolls, and the kissing, and for letting me feel your bare breasts, which are awesome by the way."

Inge chuckled and rolled her eyes. "You're pretty awesome yourself, Hunky. Now get out of here."

As he was closing the door behind him, he glimpsed Inge opening the freezer and pulling out the bottle of vodka.

Kill Birds?

Avery arrived home just in time for dinner. Jill was a decent cook, but a few of her dishes were amazing, and tonight she had prepared one of Avery's favorites: fried pork chops, applesauce, Rice-a-Roni, spinach, and carrots. Typically, when the family ate together, it was on tray tables in front of the TV, but Jill had decided to make it a "family dinner" night.

Once a month, Jill made the four of them sit at the cobwebbed dining table and manufacture the illusion that they were a close-knit family. During tonight's "dinner conversation," Sabrina chirped about a handsome new boy from California that was in her algebra class, and Jill mentioned that one of her suggestions at IBM was being considered for a monetary award. Meanwhile, Avery and Jack were silent, eyeballing the dwindling platter of pork chops and eating each one as quickly and genteelly as possible so they could take another. In the end, Avery consumed four to Jack's three. The secret, he'd learned, was taking larger bites and chewing less.

It was quarter to seven when Avery retired to his bedroom. This was his first and last chance today to breathe and be alone with his own thoughts. Irina would be calling him any minute.

Tonight, he pined for his life of a month ago, when he'd had zero girls in his life. Now he had *five*: Penny (who had said she loved him), Caitlyn (who had also said she loved him), Dina (whom he suspected loved him), Inge (who wanted to *make* love to him), and now beautiful, sad, lonely Irina. And if he counted Gemma, who, according to Mallory, had a crush on Avery, it was six girls. What the hell should he do? How could he possibly stay true to Penny when there were so many other girls interested in him?

It would be simpler if he didn't like or care about them, but he did. It was all jumbled up in his head, but this he knew: he loved aspects of each girl, but not the whole person. He loved how Penny adored him and how girlishly pretty and innocent she was. He loved Caitlyn's smile and her body and how well she danced with him and how she brought out the "bad boy" in him. He loved Dina's laugh and her nose and how smart and funny she thought he was. He loved Inge's eyes and hair and how sweet and affectionate she was toward him when she wasn't drinking. As for Irina, he knew nothing about her, but so far, he loved that she was tall and insanely hot, and he even loved (he was ashamed to admit) that she was sad and lonely and looked to Avery for comfort. He even loved aspects of Gemma Jones: she gave him great advice and seemed to care about his well-being.

At precisely seven o'clock, the phone rang. He let it ring twice (didn't want to seem too eager), and when he answered it and learned it was Irina, he gave her a bright hello. He told her how much he'd been looking forward to her call and let her talk for several minutes. After Irina gushed about how she couldn't wait for him to visit her in April ("Perhaps we will see the cherry blossoms together," she said), Avery described his plan (actually Caitlyn's plan) for dealing with Irina's coworker. When he finished, Irina was silent. Avery swore he could hear her trembling over the line.

"This plan of yours," she said. "They will not deport me for it, will they? I am here on work visa."

"*Deport* you?"

"Send back to Finland."

"Why would they do that?" he asked.

"Because I make trouble."

"*You're* not making trouble; this jerk Victor is. Listen, if you don't want to do it, we won't, but I think this is the perfect way to kill two birds with one stone."

"Kill birds?" she said. "I do not wish to kill birds."

Avery groaned; he glanced at Princess Leia. *I told you, Ace—she might be incredibly sexy, but she's not the sharpest tool in the shed.*

"Easy, Irina," he said. "It's a figure of speech. It means to solve two problems with one action."

"Ah, yes, I understand now. Will it work?"

Would it? He wasn't sure. A lot was riding on this plan of Caitlyn's. For one thing, he hadn't even considered the possibility of Irina being kicked out of the country. However, he had ironclad confidence in Caitlyn's experience in relationship chess, and her masterful skills in scheming and manipulation.. If Caitlyn thought this plan would work, so did Avery. No matter what, he told Irina, this plan would put a good scare into Victor, and he'd stop hitting on her.

"Okay, Ace, we do this," she said. "I trust you. You are brilliant young man."

She gave him Victor's full name, phone number, and home address. Avery wrote everything down in his IBM "THINK" notepad.

"Good," he said. "Now, did Victor ever send you any love letters—notes, cards, or presents? Maybe he left you an answering machine message?"

Irina said that on Valentine's Day this year, Victor had given her a pair of silver heart earrings and a card. In the card he wrote that he wanted to take her out some night for dinner and "each other for dessert." Irina had been so disgusted that she ripped up the card and threw it and the earrings away.

"Does Victor know you threw the card and gift away?"

"No," she said.

"That's good."

Finally, Avery said, if Victor or her manager ever asked who her boyfriend was, Irina was to tell them, "Craig Kennedy from Massachusetts." She repeated it back to him. Avery said he would be calling Victor soon, and that he would call her at home afterwards.

"I am nervous," she said.

"Don't worry, beautiful. I'll fix this."

"Be careful, Ace."

"I will."

Click.

Operation Blindside

To get into the right mindset for this operation, Avery played the ♫"Theme from *The A-Team*"♫ on his stereo. While he dressed in all black—fatigues, sneakers, socks, gloves, watch cap, and utility belt with all its pouches and tools attached[67]—Avery recalled how Colonel "Hannibal" Smith handled situations similar to this one on *The A-Team*. Whether Hannibal called or spoke to the bad guys in person, he was always clear, direct, assertive, and brief, giving them

---

[67] Avery had bought this specialized paramilitary gear at a local Army-Navy store owned by a Vietnam vet named Sergeant Pete. Avery and Mallory were regulars at the store.

a stern warning about the consequences of their actions. Likewise, Avery needed to put a scare into this Victor douche.

He was more than a little nervous about doing this—calling an adult man and posing as Irina's boyfriend—but this guy Victor had never met him and had no way of knowing he was only 16 years old. If Avery ambushed the guy, deepened his voice, and controlled the conversation from the beginning, it would work.

Avery shut off the stereo, got his microcassette recorder, a new cassette, and his suction cup microphone out of his filing cabinet Q-Branch drawer, and stuffed everything, including his notebook with Victor's info, into his mission knapsack. He lowered the knapsack out the window by a rope, closed the window, and cracked the bedroom door.

He had planned to worm on his belly down the hallway and down the stairs to the basement, but it was quiet in the living room. The door to Jack and Jill's room was closed and the TV was playing. Sabrina was talking on the phone in her room, so the coast was clear. Avery hustled downstairs to the basement. He shut the downstairs bedroom door behind him, preventing the cat from following, and climbed out the ground level window on his stomach. He slid the window shut behind him, but left it unlatched.

In front, he retrieved his knapsack in the snow beneath his bedroom window and stole across the back lawn toward the Woodside development. It had stopped snowing, and the clouds had broken up. The snow on the ground was a ghostly blue in the moonlight. Having been down this path countless times, Avery jogged it easily, even hurdling a couple of blowdowns.

When he reached the labyrinthine streets of Woodside, Avery decided the junction box behind Brinkerhoff's was too far away and he needed to use the phone line contacts on somebody's house instead. And he knew exactly whose house: Terrence Watley's.

Terrence was a 21-year-old jackass who rode his motorcycle into Birch Knolls every so often and raced around doing wheelies. The idiot never wore a helmet, making Avery wish he'd tip over during a wheelie and crack his skull open. Back in the fall, while Avery and some of the neighborhood kids were playing touch football in the street, Terrence sped in, popped a wheelie, and almost hit his sister Sabrina; he then tore out of the development as fast as he'd driven in—without apologizing. Avery would use one douche's phone line to call another douche.

Avery jogged down the dark, narrow streets, staying out of the pools of light from streetlights, and when he reached Terrence's house, he hopped the chain-link fence and hustled to the basement entrance. Terrence lived in a converted apartment in his mother's basement. A light was on in a second-floor window, but the first-floor and basement-level windows were dark. A TV was playing loudly in the upstairs bedroom. Avery's watch read, "20:37."

Avery pulled his headlamp out of his utility belt, slipped it on, and switched on the red bulb. The faint red light it emitted enabled him to see the telephone connection on the side of the house, but it wasn't bright enough to be seen at a distance.

Following the basement telephone line back to the junction box, he lifted the rain cover and attached the alligator clips to the contacts. When he got a dial tone, he affixed the suction cup microphone to the testing phone, connected the plug to the microcassette recorder, and pressed Record. Next, he glanced at the paper with Victor's phone number on it, dialed the number on the testing phone, and shut off the headlamp.

The phone rang twice, then a third time. Avery took a few deep breaths to calm himself and get into character.

Remember, Ace … you're Craig Kennedy, Irina's boyfriend, and you're pissed that this guy has been hitting on her.

After five rings, a woman answered the phone. It was Mrs. Theodoros. Avery deepened his voice, making it more authoritative. He said his name was Craig Kennedy and that he worked in the corporate office for the Bethesda Colonnade. He was sorry to be calling so late, but he needed to speak to her husband Victor about a work-related matter. She said she would get him. Avery's heart pounded.

Ace, be like Hannibal Smith—clear, direct, assertive, and brief. Don't give Victor a chance to talk or think.

Blindside the guy and hang up.

A man got on the line. His voice was high-pitched, and he sounded confused.

"Mr. Kennedy, this is Victor Theodoros. How may I help you, sir?"

Avery had been slumped against the house; he stood up tall and snapped into the phone: "Is this the Victor Theodoros that works at the Bethesda Colonnade?"

"Yes, sir."

"Are you the same Victor Theodoros who lives at Eighty Glen Place and has been hitting on my girlfriend, Irina Vacker?"

"Well, I, um…"

"Look, Victor," Avery said, "I don't work for the Bethesda Colonnade. I'm Irina's boyfriend, and I'm calling to give you a warning. You are to stop harassing Irina at once, is that clear?"

"Listen, Mr. Kennedy, I don't know what she told you, but—"

"Shut up, Vic," Avery said. "Shut up and listen."

Avery said that he had the Valentine's Day card and earrings Victor had given her, and that if Victor so much as spoke rudely to Irina one more time, he would call Victor's wife and tell her everything, and he'd contact the hotel manager and have Victor fired.

"Please don't, Mr. Kennedy," Victor said. "I won't bother Irina anymore, I swear."

"That's good," Avery said, "but not good enough. Listen carefully."

Because Victor had caused his girlfriend a lot of grief, Victor needed to convince the hotel manager to promote Irina to assistant manager on the day shift.

"Mr. Kennedy, I don't think I—"

"Look, Vic, here's the bottom line," Avery said. "Tomorrow, you go in and sing Irina's praises to the hotel manager. Say whatever you have to say but *get her that job.* If Irina doesn't have that promotion by next month, I'll be calling your wife and the manager, and Irina will get *your* job. And I'd better not hear about you hitting on her again. I have extremely powerful relatives in Washington."

"I understand, Mr. Kennedy."

"Good," Avery said. "Now get it done, Vic. Goodbye."

Avery's stomach lurched. He yanked the alligator clips off the contacts, doubled over with his hands on his knees, and retched in the snow. Once he'd caught his breath and had a sip of water from his canteen, he stuffed the recorder and microphone in his knapsack. Then he reconnected the testing phone and called Irina.

The worry in her voice was palpable. Avery said he'd spoken to Victor and scared the hell out of him. He briefed her on the two-minute conversation but didn't mention the possibility of a promotion. If that happened, he wanted it to be a surprise.

"Trust me, beautiful—he won't bother you anymore."

Irina was quiet, then, like he'd heard while on the phone with Caitlyn, she sniffled. It was clear that Irina was crying.

"You are wonderful, Ace," she said. "I wish you could be here. I am in bed, under covers."

Avery moaned softly. Irina asked him if he was a virgin, and when Avery said he was, Irina said this excited her, that she wanted to be Avery's first. She had mailed him some sexy photos of herself yesterday.

"I hope you will be liking them," she said.

Avery said he was sure he'd love the photos, adding that he'd mailed her a letter, a mixtape, and a photo of himself.

In the distance, but getting closer and louder, was the sound of a motorcycle.

"Look, I have to go," he said. "Call me sometime next week? Say seven o'clock?"

"Yes, I do this."

"Goodnight, Irina. Sweet dreams."

"Goodnight, Ace."

He yanked off the alligator clips, jammed the testing phone in his knapsack and shouldered it, and sprinted across the driveway to the chain-link fence.

Sure enough, the motorcycle was Terrence's. The headlight raked across the front yard just as Avery vaulted the fence and disappeared into the woods.

Cutting through the neighbor's yard, Avery backtracked to his house. He tied the knapsack onto the rope beneath his window, went inside via the basement window, and padded upstairs. The TV was still on in his parents' room, and Sabrina was still talking on the telephone in her room. It was as if he hadn't left.

In his bedroom, Avery hoisted up the knapsack, repacked the black fatigues in it, and stowed it deep in his closet. He washed up, brushed his teeth, put on clean underwear for sleeping, and got into bed.

Operation Blindside was a success. It had been a long, long day, and he fell asleep the moment his head hit the pillow.

23

⤳

FOR AVERY'S first date with Penny, the plan was for his mother to drive him to Penny's house, where Mrs. Aston, once she'd met him, would drive Penny and him to the movies. Penny's house was hard to find, however, and Jill, as usual, got lost.

Penny's aging one-street development was besieged on all sides by more modern developments, by the Queenstown IBM plant, and by the busiest road in the county—a ten-mile stretch of malls and shopping plazas known as the Strip. As always, Jill got lost, and when they finally reached Penny's street, the houses looked like they'd been built in the 1920s or '30s. Penny's was a two-story brick one with white trim and a porch on the front. They were late, but fortunately Jill was driving Jack's smart Toyota Camry tonight instead of her flatulent Impala oil tanker, sparing Avery mortal embarrassment when she pulled into Penny's driveway.

"You look nice, dear," she said. "Don't forget your flowers."

She reached in the back seat and gave him the two bouquets—pink roses for Penny, mixed flowers for Mrs. Aston. Avery had bought them after school with Mallory.

"Have a good time," she said. "I'll be back at ten-thirty to get you."

"Okay, thanks."

"And don't forget—you, Sabrina, and I have a big group lesson in the morning. We'll be going 'til noon. I need your help."

"Yeah, I know," he said. "I'll be ready."

"Good. Now, about tonight—don't be nervous." She kissed his cheek. "You'll do fine."

"I'm not nervous. Thanks for the ride." He got out of the car. "Later."

Avery was brimming over with excitement at the prospect of finally seeing Penny after a two-week separation. He was a little concerned about what Mrs. Aston would think of him, but he was confident the flowers would help his cause.

Check Out My Moves

The walkway was raggedly shoveled. Avery made a note of it and bounded up the steps to the front door. The doorbell was an old-fashioned one: when you turned the crank, it rang a bell built into the door. Avery had never used one before and was dying to try it, but decided not to; after all, this was his first time at Penny's house. He clutched the bouquets behind his back and rapped on the door.

After enduring an intolerably long wait and torment from other girls, the moment was finally here. The front door swung open so fast and with such force that the cold outside air rushed over his neck on its way into the house.

There she was, petite Penelope Jane, the blossoming sweet sixteen girl with the fawn-brown hair and the lilac eyes. She bounced on her toes and beamed. Avery beamed back at her and shook his head in a trance.

Penny's eyes, dusted with pastel pink eyeshadow, glinted in the porch lights. She was wearing that super-cute outfit he liked so much, the same one she wore when she stepped off the elevator at the hotel and skipped over to him in the lobby: penny loafers, pink-and-gray argyle knee socks, the gray pleated skirt; and the snug, short-sleeved pink sweater. Between the tops of her socks and the skirt hem were eight sexy inches of bare knee and thigh. Avery shivered at the thought that he soon might touch that smooth skin in the darkness of the movie theater. The crowning glory of her outfit, however, was a matching pink argyle headband, looped under her hair at the nape of her neck and tied on top of her head, as one would adorn an expensive present—in a full, sumptuous bow.

Damn was she pretty, and what made her even prettier was knowing that she had made herself pretty for him and only him. He told her that she looked amazing, and it was so great to finally see her.

"I can't believe you're here," she said. "It feels like a dream."

"These are for you." Avery handed her the bouquet of pink roses.

"Oh, Avery, they're beautiful!"

Leaning over the threshold, she hugged him and kissed his cheek. She asked what was behind his back, and he said he'd brought flowers for her mom.

"Gosh, Avery, that was so thoughtful. She'll love them." She whispered in his ear. "I want to kiss you on the lips—so bad."

"Me too," he said. "Soon."

A woman's voice carried down the stairs in the foyer: "Penny, why don't you invite him in, instead of making him stand out in the cold?"

"Yes, I'm sorry," Penny said. "Come in."

She shut the door behind them. Avery was in a small foyer beneath an overhead light fixture, on a faux Oriental rug. Three pairs of women's snow boots were lined up tidily by the door. Across the foyer, a staircase rose to the second floor. Upstairs, doors were being opened and shut.

"Mom," Penny called out, "come see what Avery brought me!"

"Down in a minute."

Penny held Avery's free hand. Through an archway at his shoulder was a small living room. There was a sofa, a beanbag, a coffee table with magazines, shelves of knickknacks, and a TV and VCR. Another doorway across the living room led to a kitchen.

A skinny girl, 12 years old with a curly blonde bob, ran out of the kitchen eating an ice cream sandwich. Her curls wriggled like baby snakes. She halted at the foyer doorway, but her limbs kept moving as she regarded Avery with quick, mischievous eyes. This had to be Dora. Avery pegged her as a spaz.

"You're the boyfriend, huh?" she said. "I saw the pictures. Gotta say, you're cuter in person."

"You're pretty cute yourself, Dora," Avery said. "I see you're a fan of the ice cream sandwich."

"Got that right, dude. My favorite." She held it up, and an assortment of friendship bracelets and multicolored Swatch watches slid down her skinny forearm.

"Mine too," he said. "Know why?"

"Why?"

"'Cause it's an ice cream *and* a sandwich."

Dora giggled and squirmed around. When her laughter subsided, she offered Avery one, but he said that he and Penny were leaving soon.

"You could take it to go," she said, biting into hers. "Sneak it into the theater."

"Way ahead of you." Avery opened his leather jacket with one arm, revealing to her the packages of Twizzlers in his inside pocket.

"Oooh, *slick*," she said. "Hey, what'cha got behind your back?"

"Nothing. I've only got one arm. Thanks for bringing it up."

She and Penny laughed.

"Good one," Dora said.

"Flowers for your mom," he said. "But don't say anything. It's a surprise."

"Yeah, sure." She glanced at Penny's bouquet, craned out her nose and sniffed. "Roses *and* Twizzlers, huh? You're a class act, dude. But, young man"—Dora affected an English accent and gestured with the ice cream sandwich—"simply because you brought Penny roses, I hope you don't expect her to engage in *intercourse*."

Avery's eyes sprang open; he coughed. It was like Dora and he had been playing tennis, enjoying a rally of playful volleys, and she'd just slammed down an overhead smash. He glanced at Penny in disbelief. Penny's eyes flashed, affording him a fresh glimpse of the 800-pound Sasquatch that lurked inside her.

"Dora, oh my *God!* Shut up!" She glowered at her sister and shouted up the stairs: "*Mom* … Dora's being obnoxious!"

"Sorry," Dora said, "yeesh."

"Apologize, Dora!" Penny said.

"Sorry, Avery."

"It's okay."

"Here." Dora gave him the rest of her ice cream sandwich.

Avery gulped it down and smacked his lips fast. "*Deeeeee*-licious!"

Dora giggled and tapped his shin with her foot.

"Hey, Penny says you're, like, this totally awesome dancer. I've been practicing Madonna's ♫'Dress You Up'♫ video. Check out my moves!"

She sang and danced around the living room, wagging her arms over her head, snapping her fingers, doing knee kicks, twirling, making pistols with her hands, aiming at Avery and firing. Her gangly awkwardness was gone; the girl was highly coordinated and she had a melodious voice.

Avery complimented her on her dancing, but said she was missing a few moves. He put down the bouquet and had her sing the song. While Dora sang and hummed the song, Avery showed her how to do the spins that Madonna does in the music video, and then Madonna's signature "Dress You Up" dance move: a backwards, undulating shimmy. When he finished, he told Dora to practice it, and met Penny in the foyer.

The upstairs landing creaked, and then Mrs. Aston—house slippers, jeans, smoldering cigarette pinched between two fingers, silver wristwatch, gray sweater, stoic mouth, puffy cheeks, weary hazel eyes, short dishwater blonde hair, in that order—came down the stairs.

"Dora," she sighed, "stop fooling around, please."

All right, Ace—showtime. Avery picked up the flowers and held them behind his back. He and Mrs. Aston said hello and shook hands, and as soon as Penny showed her mother the roses Avery had given her, Avery held out the bouquet of mixed flowers.

"These are for you, Mrs. Aston."

"Oh, my," she said, and for an instant the weariness in her face vanished, and she looked ten years younger. "They're beautiful. You didn't have to do this."

"It's my pleasure, ma'am," he said.

Mrs. Aston took a drag from her cigarette and regarded Avery with an amused squint. "Thank you, Avery." She glanced at her watch. "What time is the movie again, Penny?"

"Seven-fifteen, Mom."

"We need to get moving." She glanced at Penny's outfit, zooming in on her skirt. "But before we go anywhere, you need to change into pants. It's bitter cold out there."

It was hardly *bitter* cold outside, but Avery didn't want to contradict Mrs. Aston the moment he met her.

"But Mom!"

"*Now*, Penelope Jane—if you want to go to the movies at all." Mrs. Aston took Penny's bouquet. "While you do that, Avery and I will put these in water."

Penny's face was flushed. Avery could have sworn he felt a blast of heat from her cheeks as she abruptly let go of his hand and stomped upstairs.

"Give me a hand, would you, Avery?" Mrs. Aston said.

Avery followed her into the kitchen, where Dora was eating another ice cream sandwich and dancing in the corner. Mrs. Aston told her to put on her coat and shoes. Dancing out of the kitchen, Dora bumped Avery's shoulder and did the backwards shimmy Avery had taught her. Avery gave her a thumbs-up.

There were several hanging plants, baskets and bric-a-brac in the kitchen, probably meant to give it a warm and homey feel, but they only underscored how outdated and run-down the room was: curling wallpaper in two mismatched floral patterns, linoleum flooring, stained ceramic sink, old-fashioned refrigerator with a giant door handle, and a Philco electric stove from the 1950s that looked like it weighed half a ton.

Mrs. Aston pointed with her cigarette hand.

"Avery, the vases are on the top shelf of this cabinet. Get them down for me, please?"

Avery reached up with ease and pulled down the vases.

With her cigarette firmly pinched between her lips, Mrs. Aston spread out the two bouquets on the Formica countertop and cut off the ends of the flower stems with a pair of heavy shears. She put each bouquet in a vase and added water from the faucet.

There was a nudge against his back. Penny, now wearing jeans and her winter coat, was behind him. She lifted Avery's jacket and shoved a clump of fabric into the hollow between his jeans and his back.

With Mrs. Aston distracted, Avery reached behind himself, tucked it in further, and draped his jacket over it.

"Can we go, Mom?" Penny said.

Mrs. Aston glanced at the wall clock. "Yes, it's time."

By the smile Penny gave him—a naughty Sylvester the Cat smile that hinted she could hiccup out a canary feather at any moment—Avery knew that the fabric they'd concealed together was her skirt.[68]

To Explore Strange New Worlds ...

Mrs. Aston dropped Penny and Avery at the Fox Hills Mall movie theater. Some high school age kids were standing outside the entrance, smoking cigarettes; Avery didn't recognize any of them. When Mrs. Aston's car was gone, he tugged Penny into an empty loading dock area around the corner from the theater entrance and kissed her.

His heart raced; his body buzzed. How was it that merely hugging and kissing petite Penny turned him on more than making out with womanly Inge yesterday? Maybe it was because Penny meant more to him than mere sex. She was so pretty, smelled so good. He couldn't look into her eyes long enough or intensely enough. Penny's hair was shiny and faintly redolent of artificial strawberry. They opened their coats, crushed their bodies together, and kissed, and then Avery cupped her cheeks.

"God, I've missed you," he said. "You're so beautiful, Penny."

She tilted her head back and beamed. "You make me so happy, Avery."

They kissed passionately for another minute or two, until Avery's concentration was broken by voices around the corner. People were heading into the theater.

"We'd better get in there." He pulled out the skirt and planted it in her hands. "You need to change."

Despite it being a Friday night, the theater was practically empty. While Penny went to the bathroom to change into the skirt, Avery bought them popcorn and sodas and secured them two seats in the darkest corner of the back row. The closest people, another couple about their age, were three rows ahead of them. Penny came in and shuffled sideways down the row toward Avery, her skirt waggling on her bare thighs. He couldn't wait to hold her again. Avery had saved

---

[68] Sylvester the Cat, a cartoon character in Warner Brothers' *Merrie Melodies* cartoons, was the mortal enemy of Tweety Bird.

her the seat against the wall. When she sat down, he put his arm around her. When the lights dimmed and the previews came on, they took their kissing up a notch. And when the movie started, they stopped long enough to eat some Twizzlers and popcorn and catch the movie's plot: a poor redheaded girl (Molly Ringwald) who lives on the wrong side of the tracks (literally) falls in love with a rich boy (Andrew McCarthy) at her high school.

The light from the movie screen flickered on Penny's smiling face and in her eyes. She curled up on her side facing him, and as they kissed, Avery ran his hand along the back of her skirt, reveling once again in the delicious contrast between the sharpness of the pleats and the firm curve of her butt. A part of him was content to keep doing this, but the explorer in him wanted to go farther, to embark into new territory.

Avery stroked Penny's bare knee and thigh with his fingertips—a sexy circuit from the top of her knee sock to a tantalizing inch under the hot hem of her skirt. With each pass of his hand, Penny whimpered into his mouth and wriggled her legs together. Thus encouraged, Avery glided his fingers a quarter inch, half an inch, then a couple inches farther up her skirt into the unknown. He slipped his tongue into her mouth and simultaneously made a 6-inch thrust up the back of her baby-smooth thigh. When his fingers touched the elastic of her panties, the motto from the TV series *Star Trek* flashed through his mind: "*...to explore strange new worlds ... to boldly go where no man has gone before.*"

Avery slid his fingers under the elastic, like he had under Caitlyn's bikini bottoms in the elevator, and caressed Penny's bare butt. She moaned breathily against his cheek, and Avery's groin turned to stone. It was a good thing they were in the darkest, most remote corner of the theater because Avery now had his entire hand, wrist, and part of his forearm up Penny's skirt.

They made out like this for a bit, during which his intrepid alter-ego wanted to radically change course toward the *front* of her panties, but which his rational brain told him was a foolish foray to attempt in a movie theater. He withdrew his arm and caressed her sweater between her collarbone and her breast. Avery stopped kissing her and whispered into her ear.

"Penny, may I hold them? On top of your blouse?"

"Gosh, I don't know. In the theater? We shouldn't."

"Just for a minute."

She gulped in the darkness. "Okay."

As he kissed her, Avery cupped her right breast in his hand, gently massaged it, and moved to the other one. They were larger than he remembered, and they had a pleasant soft heaviness. He could feel the textured fabric of her bra underneath the sweater, and as he continued to caress each breast, her nipples stiffened and poked into his palms. The hardness in his jeans bordered on painful; his johnson strained with surprising force against the rigid denim. It was also damp down there; Old Seminal Springs was bubbling up again. Penny put her lips to his ear and breathed.

"Do you like them?" she asked.

"I love them."

"They're not too small, are they?"

"No, honey," he said. "They're perfect."

"We should stop," she said.

"Yeah, you're right."

They watched the rest of the movie, fed each other Twizzlers, and kissed lightly through the end credits. Afterwards, they each went to the bathroom to deal with their jeans—Penny, to change back into hers; Avery, to clean up in his. As it turned out, his briefs were more aqueous than he'd thought; the wetness was on the verge of soaking through his jeans, so Avery was forced to pitch the briefs in the trash and suffer the secret shame of going commando. Back in the lobby, Penny gave Avery her skirt to smuggle home, and they kissed one last time outside in the loading dock area.

When Mrs. Aston picked them up, Dora was in the front seat, so Avery and Penny sat together in the back. The car's interior smelled vaguely like menthol and tobacco from Mrs. Aston's Salem cigarettes. Penny rested her head on Avery's shoulder, and they held hands and stared out at the traffic and lights on the Strip. Dora poked her head between the seats and asked how the movie was. When Avery replied that it was fantastic, with "lots of delightful curves," Penny sniggered against his shoulder; meanwhile, Dora gave him a confused look.

"You know, Dora," he said, "plot twists. Mrs. Aston, my mother isn't picking me up until ten-thirty. Would you like me to shovel the front walk for you?"

"That would be wonderful, Avery," she said.

"Can I do it with him, Mom?" Penny asked.

"Yes, if you bundle up. I don't want you getting sick."

The Porch Swing

At the house, as her mother went into the kitchen, Penny surreptitiously removed her skirt from beneath Avery's jacket and spirited it away upstairs. Mrs. Aston brought Avery the snow shovel and switched on the front porch lights.

"Would you two like some hot cocoa?" she asked.

"That would be great, Mrs. Aston, thanks," he said.

As Avery shoveled, Penny sat on the stoop watching him, her smiling, adoring face cupped in her mittens. The walkway wasn't more than twenty feet long, and, determined to maximize his time with Penny, Avery shoveled fiercely and fast, throwing the snow far into the street to show off. He shoveled from the driveway toward the house, and when he neared the stoop, Penny jumped down.

"Can I try?"

"Sure."

Avery gave her the shovel and showed her how to hold it, then got behind her and manipulated the shovel with her, as he'd done with her on the pull-up bar in the hotel gym. Penny kept laughing, which made for inefficient shoveling, but which enabled Avery to have his arms wrapped around her longer and to steal kisses on her chilled and rosy cheeks.

Together they cleared the rest of the walkway, and when they finished, Mrs. Aston brought out mugs of hot cocoa and a heavy wool blanket for them. They sat on the porch swing and sipped their cocoa, then sat back and stared out at the dark street. It was well below freezing, and their breath hung in the air around them. Penny sighed and snuggled against him.

"Avery? Please tell me we'll always be together and that you'll never leave me."

"We'll always be together, and I'll never leave you."

She kissed him and pressed an envelope into his hand. "Seven pictures from the D.C. trip. Four are of me in the skirt."

"Thanks."

Avery slipped the envelope in his pocket and sipped his cocoa. The front door opened, and Mrs. Aston peeked out.

"Aren't you two getting cold?" she said.

"No, we're fine, Mom," Penny said.

"My mother will be here any minute," Avery said.

"Okay," she said, "I'll say goodnight now. Thank you for shoveling, Avery."

"Happy to help. Goodnight."

She nodded and went inside. Headlights approached from far down the street. Avery put down his mug, kissed Penny one last time, and got to his feet.

"See you tomorrow night, honey."

Penny jumped off the porch swing and threw her arms around him. "I'm so happy, Avery, I feel like I'm going to explode! I had so much fun tonight, and I can't wait for you to see me bowl."

"I can't wait either." He hugged her and went down the steps to the car.

24

THE NEXT evening at seven o'clock, Penny and Avery got to Ten-Pin Alley and discovered that Caitlyn and Shane weren't there yet. Avery secured a lane for the four of them, bought Penny and himself sodas, and got himself shoes and a ball.

♫"Pretty in Pink"♫

Penny was fully outfitted: a pink bowling shirt, which she had made herself; a pair of gray trousers; a pink bowling bag holding a pink ball; and pink bowling shoes.

"I'm detecting a theme here." Avery hugged her. "I didn't know you'd be all decked out like this. You look like me when I get on the tennis court. You're about to kick my butt, aren't you?"

She turned around brandishing her ball and pecked him on the cheek. "Don't worry. I'll still love you, even if you turn out to be a rotten bowler."

Avery entered their initials into the scoring computer. The second he said, "Okay, we're ready," Penny stepped up to the line.

She stood up straight cradling the ball in front of her, stared down the lane, and began the most graceful bowling throw Avery had ever seen, a study of unified motion—the precise approach steps, the smooth windup with the ball, the long extension with her arm, the gentle skid to the forward line, and the sweeping follow-through with her throwing arm and back leg. The ball landed softly on the flooring with a moderate spin on it, and, rolling fast, curved in toward the center of the alley, striking the first pin at an angle. There was a tremendous clunking, woody crash; a strike resounding through a bowling alley is a sound like no other. Penny had thrown a strike on her first throw. Two lanes over, a group of male retirees wearing military baseball caps stopped and applauded.

"Nice strike, young lady!" the tallest one said.

"Wonderful form!" said another.

"Thank you." She must have spotted their military caps because she bounced on her toes and gave them a sassy salute. They laughed and saluted back.

"Amazing, sweetheart." Avery opened his arms. "Come here. You deserve a kiss."

She minced over to him and plopped onto his lap. They kissed, then leaned their heads together until their foreheads touched.

"I love watching you bowl," Avery said. "You're so graceful. Know what else I like about bowling?" He grabbed the bottom hem of her bowling shirt and flapped it around. "The loose, untucked shirts. Nice, easy access."

He tickled her tummy. Penny giggled and slapped his hand away.

"Not while I'm bowling. I can't have *any* distractions. Your turn."

She stood and handed him his ball. Avery's footwork on the approach was good, but his throw was much too hard. It lurched into the gutter, then ricocheted out, clipping the back two pins. On his second throw, he got one more pin. Avery shambled back to the scoring computer. Penny was standing by the ball return, cooling her hand on the blower fan.

"What am I doing wrong?" he asked.

"I have no idea. I wasn't watching your form."

"What were you watching?"

"Your buns." She grinned and picked up her ball. "Love those tight Lee jeans! Mmm!"

Penny returned to the back line, went through her windup, and threw another strike. Avery threw a six in the next frame; Penny, another strike. Avery threw an eight and got the spare, and then Penny threw *another* strike—her fourth in a row.

Behind them, a group of 20-somethings standing outside the lounge cheered and stamped their feet. As Penny walked back to her seat, a sheen of perspiration covered her face and neck. Her cheeks glowed. She sat on Avery's lap, took her soda off the break table, and sipped it while fanning herself with her shirt like a bellows. She glanced at her pink Swatch and frowned.

"It's seven-thirty," she said. "Where *are* they?"

Avery shrugged. A part of him hoped they didn't show. Yes, he was dying to see Caitlyn again, but he worried that their attraction would be obvious to Penny and Shane, and he'd end up hurting Penny. Avery got up to take his turn. He held his hand over the blower and stared down the lane, trying to visualize a strike. When it was clear in his mind, he went to the ball return.

Like the Scene in Jaws

He was about to pick up his ball when, in his periphery five lanes away, the entrance door flew open. The moment Avery glimpsed the girl's blonde, wavy-haired mullet, he knew it was Caitlyn.

♫"I Love Rock 'N Roll"♫

She swaggers inside, locks her eyes onto Avery's, and smirks. She sheds her Navy peacoat by letting it slide off her arms, and, without looking, tosses it to a doofus behind her. The guy looks a couple inches taller than Avery but is flabby with a nut-brown mullet. This, Avery surmises, must be Shane.

Caitlyn is wearing a ruby turtleneck sweater, ribbed and snug, with a short hem that shows off her bare midriff. On bottom she wears a black miniskirt, black stockings, ruby legwarmers, and black high-heel ankle boots. The guys nearest the entrance rubberneck as she passes. A couple of them hoot and whistle, but Caitlyn doesn't acknowledge them; her eyes stay locked onto Avery's. Her walk is the same exaggerated catwalk strut she did in her bikini outside the hotel pool two weeks ago.

Once again, time slows for Avery. Caitlyn struts in slow-motion, crossing the bowling alley to Avery's lane.

She draws closer. There's a bulge in her cheek and a white stick protruding from her lips; she has a lollipop in her mouth. She's wearing bold red eyeshadow and dark eyeliner that accentuates the predatory quality of her eyes; spangly ruby-red earrings that dangle below her jaw; and a pair of fingerless, ruby-red lace gloves, revealing sparkly, ruby-red nail polish. Avery, who has been holding his breath since Caitlyn walked in, gulps down some air.

The girl is satanically scrumptious.

Avery has been dreading and longing for this moment. After more than two weeks, he's finally seeing "SO SEXXXY" Caitlyn Cray in the flesh again. He flushes. For a moment, Avery is slammed out of his body; it's like the scene in *Jaws* when the police chief, sitting on the beach, sees the little boy being devoured by the shark. Paralyzed by the sight of Caitlyn, Avery wants to move but can't. While Penny springs up the steps and hugs her friend, Avery takes a deep breath and follows her.

Caitlyn lets go of Penny and gives Avery a lingering once-over—his face, his chest, and finally his arms, which strain against the cuffs of his Izod. Caitlyn's gray eyes dilate, her chest heaves. While staring at him, she drags the lollipop out of her mouth, stretching her pillowy lips over the hard candy shell of a red Blow Pop. She removes it with a smack, waves it in a circle, and tips it toward Avery, as if casting a spell over him.

"*Hell-lo*, Ace … how's tricks?"

ACE WILL RETURN

IN

EPISODE II: TRUE BLUE

OF

BODACIOUSLY TRUE & TOTALLY AWESOME

Acknowledgments

Twelve years ago, during a vacation to Great Britain, my wife and I drove from Dover, England to my ancestors' castle on the Black Isle in Highland Scotland. One of our stops on the trip was Winchester Cathedral, where the author Jane Austen is buried. There, I learned that Ms. Austen had published her works by a "subscription model," where, in exchange for acknowledgment, generous benefactors provided financial support for the publication of her novels. After my third or fourth year of writing *Bodaciously True & Totally Awesome*, the book became so big that I knew I would need financial support when I was ready to promote and publish it.

While I am grateful to everyone who has supported the promotion and publication of *Bodaciously*, certain supporters deserve special acknowledgment. The following "A-Team" supporters made substantial financial commitments to this series a year before it was published. The following patrons of the arts are, in my opinion, paragons of generosity:

Jeff Atwood, a Silicon Valley tech legend and philanthropist who, once he heard that I'd been working for a decade on an epic novel about the 1980s, sent me a gasp-worthy check and a note that simply reads, "Keep going!" The world needs more guys like Jeff: a smart, wealthy, and visionary person who is trying to make the world a better place by rebuilding the American Dream. His support is a godsend.

Maia Heymann, a steadfast friend from my college days, a graduate of Wellesley College, and an incredibly accomplished woman whom I've always admired for her intelligence, kindness, work ethic, and generosity. Beyond contributing financially to the promotion and publication of this book, Maia gave me unfettered access to her vacation house in the Green Mountains of Vermont during the critical first two drafts of *Bodaciously*. I enjoyed weeks of solitude at her mountain retreat, writing in a screened-in gazebo, and, in the winter, in a rocking chair in front of a blazing woodstove. For over 30 years, Maia has been there for me as a supporter, fan, and friend, and she gave me frequent pep talks while I was writing this novel—particularly during the dark days of COVID: 2020–2021.

Joseph Kubancik, my late father-in-law (and one of the only honest lawyers since Abraham Lincoln), who kept all my books at his bedside, and whose legacy to my wife provided a bedrock of financial support during the writing of this 9-book novel. Joe believed in me from the beginning—before he'd read a single word I'd written. Beyond his support of my work, he was also a great guy who, more than once, played tour guide for me when I visited him in California. Even though he passed away seven years ago, I still think about him often and am deeply grateful for the contribution he made to my life.

Alfred Clyde Lawrence Orcutt and Susan Rebecca Orcutt (Al and Susie), my parents, who inadvertently gave me the ideal upbringing for a novelist, which is one of instability, requiring me to develop self-direction, self-discipline, and self-reliance. They nurtured my love of reading, which began at age three; they pushed me to master touch-typing (essential for writing this 1.2-million-word novel); and they gave me one of my most beloved gifts as a child, a gift that sealed my fate in becoming a novelist: *The Macmillan Children's Dictionary*. From my mother I received my work ethic, sensitivity, and wicked-awesome skin; from my father I received childhood bedtime stories that stirred my imagination, the grit to keep going and finish what I started, and ample encouragement when I most needed it— during the decade that I was writing *Bodaciously*.

Jason Scott Sadofsky, a computer/internet historian, free-range archivist, documentary filmmaker, podcaster, and my best friend for 45 years (since fifth grade!), a guy who is that rarest of geniuses— brilliant but also compassionate and generous. As he has ascended the peaks of internet celebrity and success, he has shared his financial windfalls with me, other friends, and colleagues, and he has availed me of his considerable expertise on a variety of subjects including social media, crowdfunding, public speaking, and 1980s history. He provided me with copious research materials on the 1980s, ensuring the factual accuracy and verisimilitude of this 9-episode novel. He also has the virtue of being one of three people on the planet capable of making me laugh out loud. My friendship with this man is among the five best things in my life. I love him like a brother.

I am equally grateful to the following other supporters, and I'm deeply touched by their financial backing and their faith in me personally. These backers include **John and Diane Filiberti**, a marvelous former manager of mine and his lovely wife, reader extraordinaire; **Dennis and Mandy Mahoney**, my terrific brother-in-law and my younger sister (who has long been my most ardent cheerleader); and **Melissa Susan Routson**, my older sister and one of the warmest, kindest people I have ever known.

Over the years, a few people have encouraged me and/or honed my writing skills: **Dr. William DeAngelis**, my philosophy professor, who taught me the importance of clarity and precision in writing; **Thomas Gallagher**, an author, family friend, and my writing mentor through high school and college; **Dr. Thomas Knowlton**, my grandfather, who modeled reading and an appreciation for language, and taught me good English grammar by example; **Perrin Lovett**, a fellow novelist who showed up at Mile 20 in my literary marathon, cheering me on and shouting praise about *Episode I*; **Brian Maloney**, a great friend during and after college, who encouraged me in my writing from the day we met; **Stu Shinske**, a newspaper editor who taught me that mulling is not writing, and that you need a rough draft to have something to revise; and **David Tutein**, my Freshman English professor, who told me I was a born writer with a gift for fiction.

I would be remiss if I didn't also acknowledge the exceptionally talented and professional graphic designer who created the covers for all nine episodes of *Bodaciously*—**Victoria Heath Silk**. I told her I wanted a bold cover that would get a reader's attention and evoke the 1980s spirit, and she delivered. I am grateful for her creativity and artistry, but also for her advice on typesetting matters.

For the first five years of writing *Bodaciously*, I worked every day in **Vassar College's Thompson Memorial Library**. I thank the College and the library staff for affording me quiet spaces in which to work, for allowing me to check out dozens of '80s reference materials, and for providing research assistance when I needed it.

Most of all, I give everlasting thanks and homage to the brilliant and beautiful woman who has been my Muse for nearly 30 years—my wife, **Alexas Martine Orcutt**. Not only has she handled most of our day-to-day "life stuff," enabling me to focus on my writing but she has also been the first reader of my books and has always given me invaluable encouragement and articulate constructive criticism, making the final drafts incalculably better. Drawing from her experience—first as a trained actress and later as a nonprofit fundraiser—she has guided me on everything from character motivations and dialogue to spreadsheets and appeal letters. She has gracefully handled all of the business aspects of *Bodaciously* as well. As the years go by, her brilliance and her ability to multitask never cease to astound me—and she's done all this while maintaining a successful career and a clean, organized, and harmonious household. She has also tirelessly supported a temperamental maverick artist who is prone to emotional extremes. Were she not as patient, generous, level-headed, and forgiving as she is, this 9-episode novel never would have been finished. Alexas is unequivocally my Wonder Woman. Her faith in me and her unshakable optimism have kept me buoyed through the long, arduous years of writing.

Finally, thank you, **Dear Reader**. I'm honored that you chose to spend your valuable time and money on my work. I hope you enjoy the nine books of *Bodaciously*, and if you do, please spread the word by posting short reviews and telling your friends about them. I have labored over these books for more than a decade to give you an immersive time machine back to the mid-1980s. It's been an awesome ride, but I'm ready to give you the keys. Buckle up and rock on.

Chris Orcutt
Pleasant Valley, New York
November 9, 2025

Appendix: Mixtape List for Episode I

Following are the songs mentioned in the text of Episode I, listed in the order in which they appear in the novel. This list also appears on Orcutt.net, on the page for *Bodaciously, Episode I: Bad Boy*.

"Eruption," Van Halen.

"Bond 77," *The Spy Who Loved Me* movie soundtrack, Marvin Hamlisch.

"Theme from *The A-Team*," Mike Post & Pete Carpenter; The Daniel Caine Orchestra.

"(Keep Feeling) Fascination," The Human League.

"Raspberry Beret," Prince.

"Love Theme From St. Elmo's Fire (Instrumental)," David Foster.

"Rock You Like a Hurricane," *Comeblack* (2011), Scorpions.

"Dancing in the Street," Van Halen cover, The Kinks.

"Dirty Laundry," Don Henley.

"Panama," Van Halen.

"Got Me Under Pressure," ZZ Top.

"Immigrant Song," Led Zeppelin.

"Eye of the Tiger," Survivor.

"Overture," *Rocky II* soundtrack, Bill Conti.

"Rock Me Amadeus," Falco.

"Legs," ZZ Top.

"Into the Groove," Madonna.

"One Way or Another," Blondie.

"Easy Lover," Phil Collins and Philip Bailey.

"Beat It," Michael Jackson.

"How Will I Know," Whitney Houston.

"Physical," Olivia Newton-John.

"March from *Superman*," performed by The Boston Pops Orchestra; written by John Williams.

"The Way It Is," Bruce Hornsby and The Range.

"Crazy For You," Madonna.

"Rio," Duran Duran.

"Flash," "Another One Bites the Dust," and "We Will Rock You," Queen.

"Her Strut," *Nine Tonight* (live version), Bob Seger & The Silver Bullet Band.

"Let's Go All The Way," Sly Fox.

"Oh Yeah," Yello.

"Moving in Stereo," The Cars.

"The Reflex," Duran Duran.

"Someone For Me," Whitney Houston.

"I Feel for You," Chaka Khan.

"Let The Music Play," Shannon.

"The Safety Dance," Men Without Hats.

"Burning Up," Madonna.

"P.Y.T.," Michael Jackson.

"For Your Eyes Only," Sheena Easton.

"I Didn't Mean To Turn You On," Robert Palmer.

"Wake Me Up Before You Go Go," Wham.

"Footloose," Kenny Loggins.

"Thriller," Michael Jackson.

"Sussudio," Phil Collins.

"Stand Back," Stevie Nicks and Prince.

"Relax," Frankie Goes to Hollywood.

"Make The Move," Kenny Loggins.

"Physical Attraction," Madonna.

"Burning Heart," Survivor.

"Woke Up With Wood," ZZ Top.

"She Blinded Me With Science," Thomas Dolby.

"Take Good Care of My Heart," Whitney Houston (with Jermaine Jackson).

"Crimson and Clover," Joan Jett and The Blackhearts.

"Just The Two Of Us," Grover Washington

"Any Way You Want It," Journey.

"Hot for Teacher," Van Halen.

"March from *Raiders of the Lost Ark*," John Williams and the London Symphony Orchestra.

"Uptown Girl," Billy Joel.

"Twentieth Century Fox," The Doors.

"West End Girls," Pet Shop Boys.

"Sleeping Bag," ZZ Top.

"Our House," Madness.

"Rapper's Delight," The Sugarhill Gang.

"Heart And Soul," Huey Lewis & The News.

"She Bop," Cyndi Lauper.

"Back in Black," AC/DC.

"Theme from *Dallas*," Jerrold Immel.

"Theme from *Knight Rider*," Stu Phillips and Glen A. Larson.

"Cum On Feel the Noize," Quiet Riot.

"We're Not Gonna Take It," Twisted Sister.

"A View To A Kill," Duran Duran.

"The James Bond Theme," John Barry and Monty Norman.

"Treat Me Right," Pat Benatar.

"When Doves Cry," Prince and the Revolution.

"Bad Boy," Gloria Estefan and Miami Sound Machine.

"Foreplay/Long Time," Boston.

"Burnin' for You," Blue Oyster Cult.

"Jessie's Girl," Rick Springfield.

"No One Like You," Scorpions.

"Dress You Up," Madonna.

"Pretty in Pink," Psychedelic Furs.

"I Love Rock 'N Roll," Joan Jett and The Blackhearts.

Select Works Referenced

The following is a selection of the books, films, and TV shows referenced, alluded to, or quoted in the novel.

Books

Birnbach, Lisa, et al. *The Preppy Handbook.* Workman Publishing, 1980.

Comfort, Alex (Editor). *The Joy of Sex: A Cordon Bleu Guide to Lovemaking,* Simon & Schuster, Pocket Books, 1972.

Flexner, Stuart Berg, ed. *The Random House Dictionary of the English Language: Unabridged Edition.* 2nd ed. New York: Random House, 1982.

Gardner, John. *Icebreaker,* Berkeley Books, G.P. Putnam's, 1984.

Grimes, William (Editor). *The Times of the Eighties.* Black Dog and Leventhal, 2013.

Hillcourt, William "Green Bar Bill." *The Official Boy Scout Handbook.* Ninth Edition, Boy Scouts of America, 1979.

Homer. *The Odyssey.* Translated by T.E. Lawrence, Oxford University Press, 1935.

The University of Chicago Press. *The Chicago Manual of Style.* 13th ed. Chicago: University of Chicago Press, 1982.

World Book Encyclopedia. World Book, Inc., 1984.

Films

BBS: The Documentary. Directed by Jason Scott Sadofsky. Bovine Ignition Systems. 2005.

Caddyshack. Directed by Harold Ramis. Screenplay by Brian Doyle-Murray, Harold Ramis, and Douglas Kenney. Warner Brothers, 1980.

Dr. No. Directed by Terence Young. Screenplay by Richard Maibaum, Johanna Harwood, and Berkley Mather. United Artists, 1962.

Goldfinger. Directed by Guy Hamilton. Screenplay by Richard Maibaum and Paul Dehn. United Artists, 1964.

Raiders of the Lost Ark. Directed by Stephen Spielberg. Screenplay by Lawrence Kasdan. Paramount Pictures, 1981.

Spies Like Us. Directed by John Landis. Warner Brothers, 1985.

Star Wars (A New Hope). Directed by George Lucas. Screenplay by George Lucas. 20th Century Fox, 1977.

The Empire Strikes Back. Directed by Irvin Kershner. Screenplay by Leigh Brackett and Lawrence Kasdan. 20th Century Fox, 1980.

The Terminator. Directed by James Cameron. Screenplay by James Cameron and Gale Anne Hurd. Orion Pictures, 1984.

Trading Places. Directed by John Landis. Screenplay by Timothy Harris and Herschel Weingrod. Paramount Pictures, 1983.

Weird Science. Directed and written by John Hughes. Universal Pictures, 1985.

Television Series

MacGyver. Created by Lee David Zlotoff. Paramount Network Television, 1985.

The A-Team. Created by Frank Lupo and Stephen J. Cannell. Universal Television, 1983.

The Rockford Files. Created by Roy Huggins and Stephen J. Cannell. Universal Television, 1974.

Books by the Author

Bodaciously True & Totally Awesome, Episode I: Bad Boy
A Study in Crimson
Perpetuating Trouble: A Memoir
The Ronald and Other Plays
The Perfect Triple Threat
A Truth Stranger Than Fiction
One Hundred Miles from Manhattan
The Man, The Myth, The Legend
The Rich Are Different
A Real Piece of Work
I Hope You Boys Know What You're Doing!
Nick Chase's Great Escape

About the Author

CHRIS ORCUTT is a professional writer with over thirty years of experience and more than a dozen meticulously crafted novels to his name.

Born in Maine, he has spent most of his life in New York. He attended college in Boston, graduating *summa cum laude* with a degree in philosophy. His professional writing career began at the Taconic Newspapers (where he was honored by the New York Press Association), followed by freelance reporting for the *Poughkeepsie Journal*, New York's oldest newspaper.

In his 20s and early 30s, while honing his craft as a fiction writer, Orcutt earned a living as a high school American Studies teacher, college writing instructor, and speechwriter. His earlier fiction—including the Dakota Stevens Mystery Series and *One Hundred Miles from Manhattan*—has earned praise from *Publishers Weekly* and *Kirkus Reviews*.

For over a decade, Orcutt immersed himself in '80s teen culture and shunned the internet in monastic devotion to his magnum opus. Writing drafts on typewriters and vintage computers, blasting everything from A-Ha to ZZ Top, and drinking enough coffee to fill a swimming pool (seriously), he set out to craft an authentic and fearless exploration of the suburban teenage experience in 1980s America. The result prompted one cultural historian to dub him "Lord of the '80s" and another "The American Tolstoy."

He loathes bad writing, stoplights, Grammarly, and pretentious people—but loves old movies, *Peanuts* comics, Jamaican Blue Mountain coffee, and cross-country skiing. Orcutt lives quietly in New York's Hudson Valley with his wife and Muse, Alexas, and their dog Dashiell Hammett. For more about Chris, visit Orcutt.net.

* 9 7 8 1 9 6 5 9 9 9 0 1 1 *